IDOLS &
ENEMIES

IDOLS AND ENEMIES (Amplifier 4)
THE MUSIC BOX (Amplifier 4.5)
Copyright © 2020 Meghan Ciana Doidge
Published by Old Man in the CrossWalk Productions 2020
Salt Spring Island, BC, Canada
www.oldmaninthecrosswalk.com

This is a work of fiction. All names, characters,
places, objects, and incidents herein are the products
of the author's imagination or are used fictitiously.
Any resemblance to actual things, events, locales, or
persons living or dead is entirely coincidental.

Library and Archives Canada
Doidge, Meghan Ciana, 1973—
Idols and Enemies/Meghan Ciana Doidge—
PAPERBACK

Cover design by Gene Mollica Studios
Models: Devon Ericksen & Jonathan Cannaux
Oracle Cards designed by Elizabeth Mackey Graphic Design

ISBN 978-1-989571-20-0

THE AMPLIFIER SERIES: BOOK 4

IDOLS&
ENEMIES

MEGHAN CIANA DOIDGE

Published by Old Man in the CrossWalk Productions
Salt Spring Island, BC, Canada

www.madebymeghan.ca

Idols and Enemies is the fourth book in the Amplifier series, which is set in the same universe as the Dowser, Oracle, Reconstructionist, and Misfits of the Adept Universe series. While it is not necessary to read all four series, **in order to avoid spoilers** the ideal reading order of the Adept Universe is as follows::

Other books in the Amplifier and Misfits series to follow.

More information can be found at
www.madebymeghan.ca/novels

For Michael
Twenty-plus years.
And I still love you so much it hurts.

Author's Note

Idols and Enemies is the fourth book in the Amplifier series, which is set in the same universe as the Dowser, Oracle, Reconstructionist, and Misfits of the Adept Universe series.

Apple Blossom

REBIRTH

I KNEW THAT OPENING THE LETTER FROM THE sorcerer Azar would have deadly consequences.

So we had prepared.

We'd planned.

We knew we might have to defend ourselves, our freedom. And that I might finally get a chance to exact the revenge I kept telling myself I wasn't interested in exacting.

What we didn't know was that we'd find ourselves hosting a dysfunctional family reunion—the kind where everyone tries to kill someone at least once over dinner.

Sorcerers and witches.

With me in the middle.

Mediating.

I could wipe a small city from the face of the earth. I could vanquish a horde of demons with only two shortswords. I could infiltrate a magically fortified compound without detection, stand against black witches, and defy even those capable of manipulating minds.

What I couldn't do was mediate a family squabble that stretched back decades, replete with kidnapping, magical coercion, and rape.

Or I couldn't mediate with words, at least. Thankfully, though, draining everyone of their magic was always an option.

ONE

A DARK-HAIRED, DREADFULLY SEXY SORCERER SAT IN the copper-edged pentagram inset into the white-painted wood-slat flooring of the barn loft. Aiden had been fortifying the rune-etched, five-pointed star for the last three months, starting by adding smaller pentagrams at each point. At the beginning of May, he had embedded a black gemstone—obsidian—in the heart of each smaller star, then conducted tests for two more weeks. It had taken most of those first months to source the volcanic rock in a size and quality that satisfied the sorcerer. More glyphs had been carved into the stones themselves.

Dark-blue magic gleamed from the runes inked across Aiden's bare chest, shoulders, back, arms, and legs. I'd been exceedingly helpful with the hard-to-reach areas. Then—again, terribly helpfully—I had powered up the sorcerer until he'd groaned and panted under the onslaught of my touch. My magic.

Crouched an arm's length away with my blades at the ready, I grinned at the remembrance. The lingering pleasure still warmed my own limbs.

Aiden laughed at me huskily, flashing a toothy grin. His bright-blue eyes blazed with power. He was holding an envelope sealed with dark-blue wax in both hands. His long, dexterous fingers were each tipped in sparkly pink nail polish.

The manicure was a remnant of our most recent visit from Opal. The young witch had insisted she needed to practice casting during a break from the Academy, and Aiden was perpetually obliging when it came to the dream walker's wants and needs. My own fingers and toes were currently bright green. And I'd been completely—irrationally—upset when I noted upon waking that morning that two of my fingernails had been chipped.

No matter how much I adored my life in general, Opal's absence always left me feeling a little hollow.

Drawing my attention back to the present, Aiden muttered an arcane word in that unique language he used. Magic snapped into place, sealing him within the main copper pentagram. The sorcerer quietly voiced another command, and the black stones in the five outer pentagrams flared with power.

Opal was safely at the Academy. Christopher and Paisley had left two days previously to join Samantha in Budapest. The telekinetic had been tracking Bee—aka Amanda Smith, aka one of the Five—across Eastern Europe for weeks now, but the path was cold, and the telepath was still missing. Daniel had surfaced long enough to check in, confirm that he didn't know where Bee was either, and then go dark again. He was on his own separate mission.

In the end, Christopher had wanted to help make certain that Bee was okay, and I wasn't his keeper. Paisley seemed amenable to doing some tracking, and I trusted that she would listen to the clairvoyant. So other than the chickens and the cows, the sorcerer and I were the only ones remaining on the property.

Which was good. Because it was time to deal with Kader Azar.

Aiden's father, and a key member of the former Collective—aka one of my creators.

Aiden had invested three months into fortifying the pentagram just so he could open the letter that his brother, Isa Azar, had hand delivered last February.

"Ready or not," the sorcerer said. Then he winked at me.

A flicker of warmth—desire mixing with a gleeful anticipation—flitted through my stomach. My magically sharpened, black-coated steel blades sat by my knees on the wood-slat flooring. The open loft was at my back, with the barn doors thrown wide open below. Aiden's SUV was still parked beside the barn, but I'd moved the Mustang out, parking it by the house. It was likely that a ton of magic was about to be tossed around, and Lani Zachery would not be pleased if we ruined the car's paint, which was still the original clearwater aqua. Or the aqua vinyl seating, for that matter.

Each time Lani caught me driving around with Paisley, I could tell that the full-time mechanic, part-time intuitive had a difficult time not losing her mind. Lani's latent witch magic manifested in an innate sense of when something needed to be fixed and how to fix it. More so since I'd amplified her.

Aiden held the envelope forward, his attention riveted to the rune-embossed wax seal. He murmured quietly under his breath, repeating a short phrase that stirred the magic within the pentagram. Power I could see but not feel.

I had another chance to wish that Aiden had agreed to have me in the pentagram with him, amplifying him at the same time as he opened the missive from his father.

We had fought over it.

Concern had sharpened my words, but experience tempered Aiden's response. In the end, experience won, and I'd agreed to the sequence of events we were about to execute.

Aiden snapped the wax seal. It sounded like the explosive concussion of a high-caliber gun, discharging close enough that I expected to be winged by a bullet.

Nothing else happened.

Aiden laughed, quietly relieved.

Then a dark, shadowy pulse of power reached out from the broken seal, striking Aiden's chest.

He grunted, pained. Magic flared through the runes inked across every bare section of his body.

My blades suddenly appeared in my hands. I wrapped my fingers around the hilts on instinct, though I hadn't consciously reached for them. Damn it. I must have inadvertently triggered the intricate retrieval spell that Aiden had fixed in one of the three raw-diamond gemstones embedded in each of the hilts, wasting the energy it had taken him to cast it in my momentary rush of panic.

The shadowed spell expanded across Aiden's chest. He snarled, dropping the envelope to reach for the magic. The malicious shadow stretched, expanding until it looked suspiciously like a hand with five digits. A hand trying to grab the sorcerer?

All at once, the obsidian stones in the outer, smaller pentagrams flared, becoming brighter and brighter until I had to narrow my eyes against their intense blue glow.

The black stone nearest Aiden's right knee cracked.

Then another stone. And another.

Five loud, sharp pops.

The magic died within each obsidian gem.

"Fuck!" Aiden snarled. Shuddering with the effort, he cupped his hands before him, fingers spread wide as he began muttering a melodic phrase over and over. The ink-etched runes on his upper chest and shoulders shifted, as if they were being pulled into or siphoned by the shadow hand.

No.

Not siphoned.

Aiden was somehow using the inked runes to feed the spell trying to grab hold of him. More symbols slid up and over the sorcerer's shoulders and arms, leaving the deeply tanned skin of first his wrists, then his forearms bare.

Sweat broke out on his forehead.

I shifted, bringing my blades forward.

"No, Emma," Aiden grunted. "I'm handling it."

I stilled, trusting his expertise. Trusting him.

Even I could learn. It was just that the lessons involving Aiden, involving any of those I cared about, took longer to absorb.

My heart hammered annoyingly in my chest. But as I watched, the shadow hand was drawn from Aiden's chest. It coalesced into a dark, seething ball of power suspended between the sorcerer's outstretched fingers. More runes were quickly stripped from Aiden's legs, abdomen, and lower rib cage, running up to his shoulders and then down his arms as he continued to feed the spell. The sphere darkened, simmering between Aiden's hands but no longer touching his skin. I could see lightning strikes of power coursing within it, emanating from Aiden's fingertips.

With his body now completely stripped of the magical protections we'd spent hours putting in place and powering up, Aiden began condensing the spell he now held firmly, compressing it between his palms. Then, his chest heaving with the effort, he folded the spell in on itself.

The now-tiny black sphere dissolved with an audible snap.

I waited, blades still poised to slash and rend. All my senses were on alert, reaching through the stillness of the loft, of the upper suite behind Aiden, and of the barn around us. Waiting for the next assault.

Nothing else happened.

Aiden raised his head, grimacing. Power brought forth by his anger blazed in his eyes. Tension was etched through his stubbled jaw. He locked me in place with a soul-searing gaze.

Sometimes he was so breathtakingly beautiful that my heart actually stuttered at the sight of him. Not that I would ever voice such an outrageously idiotic thought out loud.

"Well …" Aiden's voice was husky, as if he had torn his throat raw while dealing with the magic, even though he'd barely spoken. "He knows where I am."

I couldn't help the smile that etched itself across my face. Anticipating facing Kader Azar shouldn't have filled me with such deadly glee. I didn't bother tamping down on my reaction, though. That wasn't how Aiden and I were together. We kept nothing hidden between us. Nothing important in the here and now, at least.

"We knew that was a possibility," I said.

Aiden bared his teeth, snarling through whatever residual pain he was still fighting. "Powerful bastard."

"We knew that too, Aiden."

He huffed, shaking his head. "Powerful enough to embed a forced-recall teleportation spell in a fucking wax seal?"

I shrugged. "Probably took him months to cast. And you thwarted it in less than a minute."

Aiden laughed darkly, wiping his brow with a shaky hand. "Months? I would have thought a spell of that magnitude was impossible."

I didn't answer. I didn't like dealing in impossibilities—because I often proved certain impossible things wholly possible just by existing.

"Sorry. Forgot." Aiden's words were blunt, but he wasn't angry at me. He shook his head as if clearing it. "And that felt like a lifetime, not just a minute or two."

I set one of my blades down, shifting forward until I could tease my fingers against the barrier of magic that still simmered between us, still sealing Aiden within the main pentagram. "Look how powerful you are, sorcerer," I purred. "How magnificent."

A lazy smile overtook the sharpness that had been etched into Aiden's features by pain and anger. His shoulders relaxed slightly. "Oh, yes, amplifier?" he murmured. "Liked that, did you?"

I just grinned back at him. I wasn't a skilled flirt, but I could try. For Aiden.

Laughing, he retrieved the envelope from the floor, opening it and extracting a folded single-page note from within.

The smile slipped from his face as he read the letter.

Magic flared through the rune-etched copper pentagram again. Magic involuntarily triggered by the sorcerer's reaction to whatever his father had written, I guessed.

The obsidian stones continued to smolder at the five points of the pentagram. The inlaid copper surrounding those stones had also darkened, as if tarnished or discolored by heat.

Aiden finally looked up. His expression was hard. Unreadable. Not the usual carefully blank countenance that meant he was working through a problem in his head. It looked now as if something was hidden under his skin, ready to seethe, to roil.

He read the missive a second time, then crumpled it. Then he just stared at it clenched in his fist. Seemingly lost in his thoughts.

The sorcerer stood. Still not looking at me, or filling me in. And suddenly, the feeling in my stomach wasn't at all gleeful. The emotion that had collected there felt much, much closer to a churning maw of…something. Concern, maybe. But more as though I was already somehow on the losing side of this pending conflict, without even having gotten a chance to fight.

I straightened as well, still playing my fingers across the barrier of power that stood between us. I kept the blade clenched in my other hand lowered.

Aiden stepped from the pentagram, effortlessly extinguishing the magic that sealed it. My hand fell without the barrier to support it, hanging uselessly in the narrow space that stood between us, our shoulders almost brushing but not quite.

I tilted my head, trying to read Aiden's expression, but his gaze was fixed somewhere ahead of him. Or perhaps he wasn't looking at anything at all. Then he inhaled deeply. Exhaling harshly, he pressed the envelope and the crumpled letter into my hand and turned away from me.

I closed my fingers around the envelope and the letter, not picking up any of the magic the wax seal had so obviously contained. That spell had been wholly extinguished by Aiden.

The dark-haired sorcerer hesitated just before loosening his grip on the envelope we now both held, as if remembering something. He angled his shoulders toward me just enough to brush a light kiss across my lips. His magic was dim, but not completely drained. Fighting off his father's attempted teleportation had cost him. The obsidian stones and all the magic he'd invested in the extra fortifications would have to be replaced and duplicated as well. Three months of work. Three months of living with me, amplified passively while we slept together or had sex, and of being actively amplified when casting together.

Kader Azar was far too powerful.

Aiden walked away wordlessly, crossing around the dormant pentagram through the open door that led to the studio suite.

I held onto the envelope and the crumpled letter, unsure if I should follow him or not. When I walked away from someone, it was generally because I wanted to be left alone. And I was at the point now where I tried to not leave a room unless I meant it. That was another learning curve when dealing with anyone who wasn't blood bound to me—specifically, Aiden and Opal. I couldn't get away from the other four that made us the Five even if I tried. But walking away from Aiden in the middle of an argument hurt the sorcerer. If I was overwhelmed, I now told him so. And I never wanted to act like I was abandoning Opal, even when I needed space to think.

All the way through the suite now, Aiden opened the door that led to the small landing at the top of the exterior stairs. He stepped out, standing in the sunlight and drawing in long, steadying breaths.

I understood that impulse, and the relief achieved by standing with the property spread before me, knowing I was home. A spark of satisfaction drove away my trepidation. Aiden felt that now too. That grounding.

I glanced down at the note crumpled in my hand. The dark-blue wax seal had snapped cleanly in half. The rune that had been pressed into the wax had disappeared, and the magic once embedded in it had been expelled. At least as far as my senses could tell. I picked up power easier from people than I did with magical spells or objects.

I smoothed the thick, slightly rough paper open, reading.

Aiden. My son.
I'm dying.
I desire to see you before I leave this too-mortal coil.
Forever your father.

The signature—a stylized K and A—was so elaborate that I didn't doubt it also functioned as some sort of magical rune when inked by Kader Azar. Presumably a spell that informed the sorcerer when and where his letters were opened.

Well. That was unexpected.

And damn it.

Aiden's father was dying.

Unless it was a trick of some sort? But I had no idea what benefit there would have been in lying. If Kader wanted to speak to his son, I was certain he could find another way. And based on Isa's overt desire to usurp his father as the head of the Azar cabal, admitting that he was dying placed the sorcerer Azar in an unstable position—though Isa had claimed to not know the contents of the letter when he'd handed it to Aiden.

I was waffling, standing in the loft, watching the obsidian stones smolder, while pretending I could sort things out in my head that I had no actual context for. I should have been engaging with Aiden, including him in the conversation, the decision-making process. More so than normal even, since the situation involved his actual blood relationships.

And if Aiden had needed to be alone to sort out things, he would have actually left the building.

Still holding the letter, I skirted the pentagram, following the sorcerer through the loft suite. The day was warm, but the painted wood-slat flooring was cool under my bare feet. The double bed situated to my right had been made up. A diamond-and-pink-dogwood-patterned quilt that I'd recently purchased from Hannah Stewart's thrift shop was tightly tucked in on three sides. Two pillows in plain white cotton cases lay flat against the brass headboard, not propped up.

Christopher must have made the bed before he left. Because not including the quilt, it had been made with the precision that had been drilled into us as children by the Collective.

The Collective.

Of which Kader Azar was one of the main members. One of the inner circle that had spent over a hundred years entwining magic and genetics to create me, create us. The Five.

Christopher more often opted for throwing an overly large down duvet across his own bed. If he slept with covers at all. His mind must have been elsewhere when he made up the bed in the loft.

I hesitated.

Why was I obsessing about the bed? Aiden hadn't slept in the loft since the first night I'd asked him to join me in my own bed.

No. That wasn't what was bothering me.

Why would Christopher have felt the need to make the bed at all before he left?

Damn it.

Again.

Apparently, we were expecting a guest. And the clairvoyant hadn't bothered to mention it. Either that, or the branch of the immediate future he'd seen before he left wasn't solidified. He might have picked up only a glimmer of the possibility, but nothing substantial. He could also be planning on returning with Fish or Bee in tow, with the bed made up for one of them. Even though I'd made it clear that I wasn't interested in any sort of reunion for the Five.

Shoving thoughts of close-mouthed clairvoyants away, I swiftly crossed through the suite, stepping up beside Aiden on the upper landing of the exterior stairs. Any serious conversation I'd had with Christopher lately was still muddied by the memory of the clairvoyant throwing me in front of a death curse in February, three months ago. No matter how rational I strived to be, I apparently couldn't force myself to so easily forgive that incident. That choice on his part. So I hadn't been surprised when Christopher announced he was joining Samantha on her next mission in her hunt for Bee, even though it was planting season.

Brushing my shoulder against Aiden's arm, I folded and tucked the missive from his father into the pocket of my light-blue linen sundress. Together, the sorcerer and I gazed out at the back half of the property.

The main garden spread out immediately below us, only a third of its raised beds planted. Beyond the fenced field that was currently seeded as hay for the cows, a forested area bordered Cowichan Lake. The large, white-sided, red-metal-roofed house sprawled to our immediate right. New vintage lace-edged curtains framed the windows of my bedroom on the upper corner. A breeze stirred the wind chimes I'd hung on the lower back porch a week before.

I was actually surprised the wind chimes were still in one piece. Paisley had been eyeing them darkly for days, presumably for disturbing her afternoon sun naps.

From my vantage point, the seedlings in the nearest beds were points of green within lush, dark-brown soil. The peas weren't bearing yet, but we'd been picking at the lettuce and other greens already.

"At least Christopher got the tomatoes planted before he left," I said.

Aiden grunted quietly. "I told him I'd finish digging the compost into the empty beds and keep an eye on the temperature at night for the peppers and cucumbers."

Christopher had an elaborate self-watering system of grow lights and heating mats set up on the workbench in the barn. The chicks that had hatched in the midst of the chaos in February were now in a temporary grow-out coop in the orchard, only a few weeks away from being transitioned into the main coop.

"He won't be gone that long," I murmured.

Aiden glanced my way. "You know? Or you're guessing?"

"He made the bed in the loft."

Aiden flinched, whirling to look behind us as if he expected to be attacked. Then he muttered to himself darkly. A curse, I thought, based on the magic that shifted through his words. Or perhaps a protection spell.

"Warding off evil?" I asked playfully.

Aiden grimaced, wrapping his hands over the top railing so tightly that his knuckles whitened. I knew I wasn't going to be able to cajole him through whatever he needed to work out. A decision based on his father's request, I presumed. A reaction to Kader Azar's attempt to take that decision away from him with a ridiculously powerful teleportation spell.

"Christopher had me help him set up a bed in the empty bedroom as well." Aiden's tone was calmer than his body language. He shifted his gaze back out to the expanse of the property. "I assumed it was for Samantha."

"Might be," I said. "Long term. But my point is, if Christopher's expecting visitors, he won't be gone long enough for us to worry about needing to plant the peppers."

Aiden nodded, only half listening to me. I brushed my fingers against his forearm. He had waxed almost all of his body hair in order to apply the runes. And now, stripped of their magic-imbued ink, he looked naked. Exposed. His muscles shifted under my touch, but Aiden kept staring outward, breathing in the warm spring air steadily, efficiently.

My latent empathy triggered with our skin-to-skin contact, but it didn't tell me anything I didn't already know. Aiden was frustrated. Pained, though not physically hurt. A hint of doubt and trepidation underlaid those main emotions.

"He must have known you'd be able to counter the teleportation spell," I said, trying to address the whisper of doubt I felt from him. "Given the wording of the letter itself."

" 'Forever your father,' " he muttered darkly.

Ah, that was what was bothering him. The claiming. "The Collective is big on ownership."

"Unfortunately, I share enough of his blood that he can actually claim me. Bend me to his will."

"No," I said. "Not anymore. You're too powerful for him now. The spell you just thwarted tells you that."

Aiden sighed, shaking his head and dropping it forward. He laughed shakily. Then he sobered, still looking away from me. "No. You're too powerful for him."

A tiny fissure cracked open in my chest, right under the spot that still occasionally ached from the death curse. A completely psychosomatic pain that felt utterly real.

Aiden snarled quietly, then reached for me, tugging me against his chest. He pressed a harsh kiss to my temple. "I'm acting like an idiot. I'm sorry."

I spread my hand across his bare, smooth chest, over his heart. "We're a 'we' now," I whispered.

"Yes. Goddamn it." He squeezed me tightly, then even tighter. "We…we are too strong for him.

Together. I agree. I just …" He glanced out at the garden again. "I feel like…like I'm about to lose…all of this …"

His declaration—echoing my own trepidation from a few moments before—made me feel raw. Aiden was usually so steadfast. "Including me?"

He shook his head, seemingly incapable of expressing himself. Empathically, I could feel the jumble of his emotions, with a layer of frustration that was no doubt all about himself and his father over top of it all.

Aiden sighed, easing his hold on me to run his fingers through my hair, then down my spine to rest at the small of my back. I leaned into him, not certain if I was trying to comfort him or myself. Both, perhaps.

And I decided that was okay.

Silence fell between us, comfortable and warm. I could hear the chickens cackling away. They had spent the winter and early spring foraging in the garden, fertilizing it, but we'd moved their coop into the orchard at the beginning of the month so they wouldn't tear up the young seedlings. The plum trees were already setting fruit. The apple and pear trees were in full bloom.

I enjoyed lingering in the orchard after letting the chickens out of the coop every morning, watching the mason bees coming and going from their 'condo' as they industriously filled in its channels with mud and pollen, collected from the fruit blossoms and the orchard grass that Christopher had planted so he didn't need to mow around the trees.

"I idolized him." Aiden's raw voice cut through the pleasantly warm air.

My heart pinched with what felt like shared grief, though I wasn't certain I'd ever experienced such a thing. Loving someone—multiple someones—had hurt me in so many different ways, more than any knife or magical wound ever had. I healed quickly, far quicker than most Adepts. Definitely far more quickly than other amplifiers. Stolen juice, Samantha would have called it. Stolen power. But my robust magical healing didn't work on emotional wounds.

"I idolized him for years …" Aiden trailed off, continuing to gaze over the gardens.

"Until you discovered what he did to your mother," I said softly. Not wanting to interject, but wanting to participate in the conversation. Neither of us talked about the past much. Only when we were pushed to do so by external circumstances.

And Kader Azar had just given us a hard shove.

Aiden laughed ruefully, scrubbing his hand over his face. "Honestly? Not even then. Because she stayed."

"After the enchantment wore off?" Kader Azar had entranced Aiden's mother, Cerise Myers, because he coveted her particular brand of witch magic. He'd entrapped her into a coerced, long-term sexual liaison that had resulted in Aiden. That much I knew.

"She was seventeen when he saw her. Took her. Wooed her on the streets of Paris, according to him.

Deep layers of beguilement take time to anchor. Weeks, months. Even for a sorcerer as powerful as Kader Azar was, even thirty-three years ago." The rawness was easing from Aiden's tone, as if he was working through it with each word he spoke. "Cerise was nineteen when she had me. He removed the last of the beguilement spells a few months after I was born. She could have left."

"But he used you as leverage."

"Of course he did," Aiden snarled darkly. "Maintaining the spells took too much energy."

"And the experiment had been completed."

Aiden looked at me sharply. But his expression softened as he absorbed my implication. "Yes. I suppose. Though he wouldn't know whether it worked until my magic matured."

"All experiments run their course," I said ruefully.

Aiden caressed a fingertip lightly across my cheekbone, pinning me in place with his sharp, bright-blue gaze. "Some more successfully than others."

I grinned. A fierce flush of my earlier anticipation returned. "And sometimes, those same experiments blow up, taking their creators with them."

"No, Emma." Aiden gently placed the heel of his hand over my heart, fingers spreading along my collarbone. "No blowing yourself up. Surviving him is the best way forward."

"Then that applies to you as well."

"Of course." He smiled, though the expression didn't reach his eyes or mitigate the frustrated anger I was still picking up empathically.

"What do you want to do?"

"Absolutely nothing. He can rot for all I care."

I felt the lie the moment he uttered it.

I had never felt a falsehood from Aiden before. Not ever. We didn't lie to each other. Not directly. I started to call him on it.

But then I realized he was lying to himself more than to me.

"You were telling me something? About your childhood?" I asked instead. Because even as emotionally stunted as I was, I knew he wasn't going to figure out what he wanted to do about Kader Azar without taking some time. Given the content of his father's letter, though, we didn't have much time. So talking was the next-best strategy. We had already fortified the house and property, built up Aiden's weapons cache, and powered up my blades.

And I had just wasted the retrieval spell that had taken Aiden over a week to tie to me, slowly coaxing my magic into accepting it. I'd had to absorb the spell, cast by the sorcerer, over and over—once again stealing the magic for myself—before it could become something I could personally wield.

Aiden pressed another kiss to my forehead, murmuring, "Can we continue this conversation over iced tea? And ginger snaps?"

"It's a little early for tea," I groused.

He laughed. And that genuine joy swamped the anger he'd been struggling to hold at bay. I could actually feel his ire ebb away from our empathic connection. A connection that was only ever a brush of fingertips away for us. Or even better, a touch of lips to lips…or other intimate places.

"All right," I said huffily, covering my own rising desire because the timing seemed inappropriate. "Just this once."

He wrapped his arm around my waist, turning us toward the stairs. The embrace made traversing those stairs awkward, but I didn't complain.

I adored my home and my partner. And it seemed very likely that I was about to kick some serious ass. Ass that—if I was being completely honest with myself—I'd been eager to kick for many, many years.

Kader Azar knew where Aiden was. And if and when he came to collect his son, he would find me waiting.

A pleased grin spread over my face. Apparently, it wasn't just the little things that made me happy.

AIDEN PLACED HIS IPAD ON THE SMALL ROUND TABLE set before the cushioned patio chairs as I poured the iced tea. I added a couple of teaspoons of sugar to both glasses. The Ceylon black tea was more traditionally flavored and slightly too bitter for me without sugar. Plus, I'd oversteeped it. I had rectified the error by cold-brewing a second pitcher of my favorite fruit tea, but it wasn't ready yet.

I curled my legs underneath me, nibbling on a ginger snap and watching Aiden out of the corner of my eye as he opened an app on the iPad, signed into it, then checked to see if Opal was online yet. Her profile picture—a recent shot that Aiden had taken of the young witch with her arms wrapped around Paisley's neck—wasn't accompanied by a green dot. Our daily chat was earlier on Fridays because Opal had a break in her schedule before an early dinner. Plus, oddly, the Academy's time zone was three hours ahead of us, even though the campus Christopher and I had taken Opal to was just outside Seattle.

The Wi-Fi was strong enough to pick up a call on the patio, but Aiden had upgraded and started paying for a data package when Opal went back to school. So we'd never miss a call from the young witch. Just one more reason I was utterly enamored with the sorcerer—our priorities aligned.

"Friday night is movie and sushi night," I murmured, licking the ginger snap's brown sugar from my lips. "She won't want to talk for long."

Aiden's gaze snagged on my mouth. He didn't answer me.

I took another small bite of the cookie. But before I could do anything more to tease him, Aiden leaned over. Practically knocking the cookie and my hand aside, he laid a blistering kiss on me.

I abandoned the cookie, shifting halfway out of my chair to meet his sudden intensity with my own.

He'd been quiet and withdrawn as we'd put together the tea and headed out onto the back patio. But now his fierce desire overwhelmed the lingering anger and uncertainty that I'd felt empathically when I touched him. Though as usual, his expression revealed none of that inner turmoil.

His tongue teasing mine, Aiden hauled me into his lap. I settled awkwardly with my legs hanging over the arm of his chair. But when I tried to shift, he pinned me in place by slipping a hand up my leg—and without any preamble, he pushed my panties to the side.

I gasped into his mouth.

He grinned wickedly, transferring his lips and tongue to my neck, only to dart back quickly to plunder my mouth. As if he needed me, needed this connection, in order to survive the next few moments.

I spread my legs for him—somehow having the wherewithal amid the mounting desire and heat building at the apex of my thighs to lean over and place the iPad flat on the table.

I was fairly certain we had to accept the call from Opal before the camera triggered, but I wasn't taking any chances.

Aiden's grip across my back tightened—I had one of his arms still pinned under me—and he groaned into my mouth, dipping his fingers into my heat, then slipping up to tease exactly where I wanted him. I pressed against his fingers, trying to shift so that I could free my own hands and reciprocate.

"Breasts," Aiden snarled.

I blinked, not quite certain what he meant, not by tone at least.

He flashed me an almost-feral grin. "I've only got the one free hand, and I don't want to move it. Not in any way that it isn't already being moved."

"Okay," I panted.

He increased the pace and pressure of his fingers between my legs. "You have perfectly useable hands—"

"The position is awkward for—"

"Not for what I want."

The deep heat in my core was spreading, radiating across my belly and down my thighs. I was having a difficult time concentrating on anything other than the pleasure Aiden was effortlessly coaxing from me. "Which is?"

"Lean back," he demanded quietly.

A slow smile spread over my face as I followed his direction. One of my arms was twisted behind me, hand braced on the arm of Aiden's chair, holding me upright.

Aiden grunted, satisfied. "Now open your dress."

With my free hand, I loosened the wide belt of my wrap dress. Then I tugged the front-wrapped fabric slightly open, widening the vee of the neckline. The linen dress softened every time I washed it, but was still thick enough that I didn't bother wearing a bra underneath.

I managed to get one breast partly exposed before Aiden leaned over and took the already-taut nipple in his mouth. Pleasure exploded, deepening the build I was already trying to keep under control. I gasped.

"Yes," Aiden murmured, transferring his attention to kissing the flesh of my breast. Then, tugging the other side of the dress open with his teeth, he focused on my other breast. "Yes, my Emma."

I was panting, moaning quietly, shifting my free hand to press just above my mound through my dress. Aiden had shown me that pressing like that, even rubbing in time with his ministrations, intensified my orgasms.

"Yes, Emma," Aiden repeated between sucks and gentle nips. "Come for me, my Emma."

My head fell back. I forgot about feeling awkward, about not contributing. A wave of fierce satisfaction filtered empathically through from everywhere Aiden touched me. I wasn't certain why pleasuring me was grounding him, settling him, but it obviously was.

The bottom of my feet started to tingle. I stretched into the pleasure, tensing all the muscles in my legs and abdomen, riding an almost-painful wave of pleasure as it arced up through me, then exploded.

I cried out. Loudly. Bucking under Aiden's hand as he continued to caress me through the crest of my orgasm. "Aiden, I—"

He sucked my nipple into his mouth.

I moaned, panting, as residual spasms of pleasure racked me.

Aiden slowed the pace of his fingers between my legs, but didn't stop.

I grasped his wrist. "I don't think I can make it a second time without—"

He kissed me tenderly, slowing his ministrations further until he was just teasing me, slipping to and fro in my heat.

I kissed him back, groaning into his mouth as a second wave of pleasure built between my legs, then crested so quickly that it seemed to come out of nowhere. I cried out, again bucking under his fingers.

He cupped his hand over my mound, just holding me as the spike of pleasure settled into a satiated warmth between my legs. A slight breeze prickled across my nipples.

I opened my eyes to meet Aiden's soul-searing gaze. "Well, you seem pleased with yourself, sorcerer."

He grinned. His smile was softer, less feral.

I shifted into a more comfortable position in his lap, brushing the hair that had fallen over his brow to the side. He reached up, capturing my hand and kissing the palm. I curled my fingers into his cheek, enjoying the rasp of his stubble on my skin while I tried to sort out the emotions I could feel coming from the sorcerer. He did seem satisfied, more settled. But there was something else still lurking behind it all.

Apparently, I was going to have to use words to figure it out. "I'm not going anywhere," I said.

"Of course not," he said lazily. As if he'd just been the one to orgasm rather abruptly. Twice.

Okay, I'd guessed wrong. "You're not going anywhere."

His shoulders stiffened, just for a moment. Then he smoothed his fingers down my arm, enjoying the skin contact. "I might need to—"

"No."

"No?"

"Yes, no. You're not going anywhere."

He blinked at me, then smiled and frowned at the same time. A sense of being pleased but concerned filtered through to me.

"We're a we," I reiterated.

"Yes."

"I'm just going to repeat that. A lot."

He nodded. "I seem to need it repeated."

A little pinpoint of pain opened up in my chest. Damn it. I hated that. I was a rational being. "Because you doubt me? My commitment?"

"No." His tone was rough, blunt. "No, Emma. I just…completely irrationally…I just don't want to expose you."

"To who?" I asked, genuinely confused. "The other members of the Collective?"

He ran a hand through his hair. "I'm not being …" He cleared his throat, then shook his head, changing his mind about what he wanted to say. "This is what I want. Here with you, and Opal and Paisley."

"And possibly the other four," I murmured.

He smirked in agreement. "I'm not interested in getting pulled into whatever game my father has going on. I won't be his pawn, and I won't allow him access to you. Not if I can help it."

I just looked at him, listening. The chances of Kader Azar not at least sending an emissary to follow up on his letter to his son were exceedingly slim.

Aiden growled quietly, then hissed as if displeased at himself. At his reaction. "I know...I know, we talked about it ..."

"We didn't discuss the possibility that he might be reaching out for non-nefarious reasons."

"Everything he does is nefarious!"

"Okay."

"Emma...I...I know you know ..." Aiden clenched his hands to fists, getting a handful of my dress in each, then immediately relaxed his grip.

I trailed my fingers up his forearm, and he sighed, relaxing his head back against the chair. I shifted in his lap, wiggling my ass just a little. Playfully.

A slow grin replaced the anger that had been edging his expression. His eyelids became heavy. He reached into the loose front of my dress to caress my breast, slipping his fingers underneath, taking the weight in his palm as he lightly flicked the nipple until it tightened and rose under his thumb.

"Bedroom," I murmured.

"I'm not going to get any farther than the kitchen table."

"That works." I straightened, capturing his mouth in mine as I shifted to straddle him.

He grabbed my ass, tucking me as close as the chair would allow. It wasn't close enough, so he shifted out from the chair, perching nearer the edge so I could rub myself against his hardening length.

I had no issue with Aiden working out what he was feeling, and what he wanted to do about it, while having sex. Or rather, after having sex.

A trill sounded behind us.

Too mechanical for a bird ...

"Opal!" I gasped into Aiden's mouth.

He laughed, far too pleased by his ability to distract me.

I jumped off him, tugging down my dress and cinching the belt. Aiden, still smirking, simply crossed his legs and reached for the iPad.

I sat down, picked up my iced tea, and pressed it against my neck, alternating sides. "I'll be paying you back, sorcerer."

He raised an eyebrow. "Twice?"

I growled playfully. "The once will sideline you so badly you won't have the use of your legs for hours afterward."

He laughed huskily. "Threats, amplifier. I like it."

"I don't threaten." I grinned at him, then met him halfway as he leaned over to brush his lips against mine.

Then he flipped the iPad over, propped it up, and accepted the call from Opal.

The young witch appeared on the screen, chin propped on her hands, earbuds in her ears, and a wild halo of sun-streaked dark-brown curls all around her head. She grinned, flicking her brown-flecked blue eyes between the two of us, taking in the iced tea in my hand and the ginger snaps Aiden had grabbed from the plate next to the iPad.

"Hey," she cried. "It's too early for tea!"

My chest warmed, as it always did whenever I caught sight of her crooked eyeteeth. Soon, she was going to ask permission to get her teeth fixed. And I was going to have to say yes.

"Aiden begged," I said.

Opal nodded. "There should be two tea times anyway. One before lunch, and then the regular one before dinner."

"Only logical," Aiden said agreeably.

The thirteen-year-old pouted playfully. "But now I want ginger snaps."

"Tell us about your day," I said, leaning back in my chair, curling my legs underneath me.

Opal huffed, playfully indignant that I wasn't going to indulge her about the lack of ginger snaps. But then she glanced around as if to make sure she was alone. Technology only worked in the designated media rooms of the Academy. Not in the dorms. At least not reliably.

A wide grin spread across the witch's face as she whispered, "Emily totally snuck an artifact in…from home, you know. We're researching it."

"Emily?" I murmured quietly to Aiden. Opal hadn't made many friends at the Academy, at least not initially. But in the past two months, she'd started to mention more names. Work and study partners mostly, but a few burgeoning friendships as well.

"Necromancer," Aiden murmured back. "Powerful family from the east coast of Canada. The Hawes. Old bloodline. Emily is the youngest by over a decade. The last generation was plagued with males."

Opal pointed her finger at Aiden. "You'd better not be checking up on me, sorcerer."

"Did you expect anything else?" I asked lightly, incredibly grateful for the sorcerer at my side. For so many reasons that I was losing count.

Opal huffed, crossing her arms. "No."

"The artifact?" Aiden prompted.

The witch's grin returned in an instant. Opal shifted forward, her animated face completely filling the screen, eyes flashing—with mischief. "It contains a spirit."

"Of course it does," I murmured.

"A trapped spirit?" Aiden said, sounding completely intrigued. "In an amulet?"

"A tiny music box. At least we think it's a music box, because it's got little gold feet …" Opal raised three fingers. "It's oval, and this wide, and, like, no longer than my forefinger. Gold with some sort of blue stone with gold dust in it. It's runed and everything. Emily thinks it's a great-grandmother who, like, went crazy and then had to be trapped in it."

That didn't sound right. "After she died?" I asked.

Opal shrugged.

"The stone is probably lapis lazuli." Aiden tilted his head thoughtfully. "So the gold flecks are actually pyrite. Fool's gold. Perhaps crafted so a necromancer could draw from the death magic contained in the artifact...to augment their own casting? Is that ability specially tied to the Hawes bloodline?"

Opal tugged a notebook in front of her, picking up the silver-etched fountain pen that Aiden had given her for passing her term exams, and rapidly jotting down some notes. "Don't know. I'll add that to our list of things to figure out. We're working on the inscription on the bottom first. It isn't English."

"Makes sense," Aiden said, ginger snaps and tea forgotten. "The inscription might let you know what, or who, you're dealing with. I would then suggest researching the great-grandmother and understanding her power set before moving forward with tapping into the power of the artifact."

Tapping into the power of the artifact sounded like a terrible idea, even if Opal—as a witch—wouldn't be the one to wield whatever magic was housed in the music box. I leaned forward, physically inserting myself into the conversation. "Is this something your principal should know about?" I asked. "Should she be overseeing your research? Or one of the professors of necromancy?"

Aiden, in person, and Opal, on the iPad, looked at me with mirrored looks of horror.

"No way!" the witch declared.

"Absolutely not," the sorcerer said, seemingly aghast.

I sighed, giving Aiden a look.

He winked at me, then turned back to Opal. "Just don't try to open it. Not unwarded."

Opal snorted. "What am I, an idiot?" Then she spun around in her seat, responding to something off-screen. She nodded and waved in apparent agreement, then turned back to us. "Got to go! Sushi! We're watching *Captain Marvel*! And it's still in the theaters!"

I had no idea what that was, other than an apparently military-themed movie. I had even less idea why the Academy would choose something like that for their magically inclined students to watch. "Okay. But listen to—"

Opal disconnected the call.

I blinked at the blank screen, then gave Aiden a look.

He laughed. "You know it's a dud."

"What?"

"The artifact. The music box. You think the Hawes family just left an heirloom of power out for the youngest necromancer in a generation to purloin?"

"So it's a…test?"

Aiden shrugged. "A harmless game. But yes, a bit of intrigue. A focus for Emily's power while she's learning."

I narrowed my eyes. I didn't like games.

Aiden laughed. Then he stretched out his legs and patted his lap. "I believe you were threatening me with a sexual act so intense that it would wear me out for days."

I grinned at him, unfolding my legs and setting my iced tea down on the table next to the iPad.

Aiden kept his gaze on me and a soft smile on his face as I crossed to climb back into his lap. He grabbed my ass with both hands as I captured his bottom lip between my teeth, playfully.

"I wouldn't mind being worn out," he whispered against my kisses. "Wrung out…just…without thought…for a little while."

"I'm happy to oblige," I murmured, wiggling off him and stepping back.

He groaned. But his feigned dissatisfaction was quickly quashed as I undid my dress, slipping it from my shoulders. Then, clad only in my lace thong, I crossed into the kitchen, teasing over my shoulder, "You said something about the kitchen table?"

Aiden was on his feet and after me without another breath. Without another word. And, hopefully, without another thought of his father's machinations.

TWO

A LIGHT, WARM BREEZE STIRRED THE LACE CURTAINS half drawn across the sunlit window, caressing the bare skin of my shoulder and back. The sheets crumpled underneath me were crisp, though my mind lingered in a hazy, delicious post-orgasm fog. My fourth of the day, and it technically wasn't even time for tea yet.

Sprawled on his back across three-quarters of the bed beside me, with every glorious bit of his tanned skin exposed, Aiden drew in a deep, fully relaxed breath, then slowly exhaled. I curled my toes under his foot, seeking some skin contact but not wanting to pull him from his light, obviously contented doze.

I wasn't certain yet if I'd followed through on the promise of physically draining him so much that he wouldn't be able to walk, because neither of us had left the bed in the last two hours. Or been fully upright.

I adored having sex in the afternoon. It was a luxury we were rarely able to indulge in—especially not with the bedroom windows and door wide open. Not without triggering the runes that Aiden had painted around the casings of those same windows and the doorframe to muddy Christopher's sight. Blocking the clairvoyant completely was near to impossible—at least not without working Christopher's blood into the runes. Even then, his magic would eventually break through.

So Aiden and I usually had sex late in the evening, keeping our endearments or demands to a whisper and our moans muffled. But there had been no need to stifle ourselves today, and Aiden had determinedly worked through the tension—and the draining of his magic—triggered by opening his father's letter.

The cellphone perpetually charging on top of my high bureau buzzed. The noise was almost too quiet to pick up under Aiden's steady breathing. Technically, it was my phone, set there by Christopher a couple of days before he'd left.

Except for the months I'd been hospitalized at the compound and kept mostly under sedation, the clairvoyant and I hadn't been parted for more than twenty-four hours in the entirety of our twenty-nine years. But now he was so far away that the magic of the tattoo that usually simmered on my spine—specifically, on my T3 vertebra—was completely dormant. It was a sensation I'd long gotten used to with my other three blood tattoos. But the feel of the clairvoyant's magic under my skin was something I missed.

Because it could only have been Christopher texting me, I climbed out of the comfortable cocoon of the bed—carefully, so I didn't disturb Aiden. My feet had barely touched the floor when a familiar magic welled behind me and the bed sagged. Deeply.

Already shaking my head, I looked over my shoulder to find a too-large, blue-nosed pit bull occupying the space I'd just vacated. The demon dog was sprawled next to the sorcerer, occupying the entire length of the bed, facing me, head on my pillow. She regarded me with red-slitted eyes.

"Paisley," I growled quietly. "You're supposed to be with Christopher and Samantha."

Evidently, the demon dog was capable of teleporting between continents. That was a surprise, though I had no idea whether she was doing so all in one jump. I was definitely going to have to reinforce some rules, though. The last thing I needed—especially while waiting for Opal's adoption to go through—was Paisley popping to and from wherever she pleased. Specifically, teleporting to the Academy to see the dream walker.

Paisley flicked her forked blue tongue at me, flashing the tips of her double row of sharp teeth. Then she pressed her back paw against my sacrum and tried to push me all the way off the bed.

I sighed, standing to retrieve the pink, green, and cream quilt that had pooled at the base of the bed. Crossing around, I covered Aiden's exposed midsection with the quilt, leaving his torso and limbs bare so he wouldn't overheat. Not that I was concerned about either of us being naked in front of the demon dog—she was the one who had invaded the bedroom, after all. I just didn't trust her not to test whether or not Aiden's 'tentacle' worked like one of her own tentacles, currently tucked away. Without a doubt, that was an experience I knew the sorcerer didn't need to endure.

Paisley chuffed, then made a show of getting comfortable on my pillow.

The phone buzzed with what I assumed was a second text message as I tugged on a delicate pink silk robe that Aiden had bought me. I'd never had the chance to wear it outside of my bedroom or bathroom, because it was thin enough to leave nothing to the imagination—a look the sorcerer apparently enjoyed immensely.

I swiped my finger up the screen, not otherwise touching the phone. That was more by instinct than necessity, as my magic didn't wear on tech—unlike Aiden, who had to recycle his electronic devices every three months or so. And that was despite the layer of protection spells he paid dearly for, as he also did for Opal's devices.

The phone recognized my face, unlocking to reveal a new text message from Christopher.

I tapped the messages icon, reading.

>*Socks. You're going to need your blades. We can be back in 24.*

>*And if you see Paisley, tell her I'm pissed she abandoned us.*

I gave Paisley a look. She ignored me, feigning sleep by mimicking Aiden's breathing pattern. I texted back.

Timeline?

>*Not clear yet. But the apples and pear trees haven't dropped the last of their blooms.*

Christopher usually saw most clearly within the next forty-eight hours. So whatever—or whoever—he had caught a glimpse of wasn't near enough for him to get a full picture, or the distance between us was dampening the clairvoyant's sight. But based on what he had observed of the fruit trees, whatever he thought I'd need my blades for would happen in the next week or so.

Do you actually see me decapitating someone?

>*What else would you be doing?*

So no?

>*No. But it's always just a matter of time.*

I ignored the tone of his last comment, which seemed nasty to me, because I wasn't about to start reading tone into text messages. It was also a statement, not a question. And an obvious one at that. So I didn't bother answering, setting the phone aside as I contemplated kicking Paisley out of the room, and all the ways I could wake Aiden. The nice thing to do would have been to let the sorcerer sleep. Thankfully, I didn't hold myself to being 'nice' terribly often.

The phone buzzed. I glanced at it in time to see the text message *Socks?* flash on the screen.

I might have just been missing the simmering magic of the blood tattoo that tied me to him, but I wasn't interested in being pissy with the clairvoyant. I'd had enough of that over the last three months. I picked the phone up just as another text appeared.

>*Do you want us to return or not?*
Not.

I thought about leaving the conversation at that. We had already discussed the plan to open Kader Azar's letter, and the fallout we'd expected, before Christopher left. But since my lovely postcoital buzz had already almost worn off, I decided I didn't want to be accused of being an asshole. So I added:

Not yet. And Paisley just showed up.
>*Send her back. Please.*
I'll ask.
>*Thank you.*

I set the phone down a second time, making sure it was still plugged in. But before I could turn back to the bed, another message came through.

>*I miss you. And our home.*

Before I could answer—or not answer, really—a shiver of power ran up my spine. I recognized the sensation. Someone had just touched the outer property wards, requesting entry. But the intensity, and the way it was lingering, was highly unusual.

The shiver of magic came again, warming the back of my neck in particular.

Aiden bolted upright in the bed, startling Paisley so thoroughly that she growled and snapped at him. The sorcerer flung himself away, magic flaring around him as he tumbled onto the floor.

Paisley stood in the center of the bed—larger than she'd been a moment before—and shook herself all over.

On the floor on the other side of the bed, Aiden sat up, peering at the demon dog, then through her legs at me. I tilted my head, noting the sheen of magic coating him. It winked out as the sorcerer raised an eyebrow at Paisley.

"Was that really necessary?" He gained his feet, grabbing the quilt before it could fully fall to the floor, and wrapping it around his waist.

Paisley stretched back, bowing before the sorcerer. Then, chuffing happily, she stretched forward, inviting affection. Aiden obliged, grinning as if she hadn't just tried to take a bite out of him.

"Hello," Aiden said, scratching Paisley behind the ears. "Have the others returned as well?"

"Just Paisley." I smiled. "I just got a text from Christopher."

"Oh yes? Are you going to need your blades?"

"It's unclear."

Power pinged up my spine again. But the tenor was quieter, softer, as if the Adept requesting passage through Aiden's outer wards had stepped back, patient to wait.

I really shouldn't have been picking up that much detail. Magic didn't work for me like that. I was more of a blunt instrument, really. Channeling or absorbing power. I could wield some spells, such as the spell Aiden had patiently fed to me for weeks so that I could call my blades to me. And when I absorbed enough power, I could wield it subconsciously. My strength, speed, invulnerability to magic, and healing ability came from the power the Collective had forced me to absorb over long years.

"An Azar sorcerer," Aiden said, his head slightly tilted.

"Just one?"

Aiden started sorting through the discarded clothing littering the fir flooring. He set my dress at the foot of the bed while donning his pants. The dress had made it up from the back patio, just not on me. "Only one has brushed against the wards so far."

"Isa?" Aiden's brother hadn't been in contact with him since he'd fled during a snowstorm in February.

"Could be. Though I'd be surprised if he'd face either of us willingly. Or alone."

A slow grin of vicious anticipation spread across my face. Aiden tugged a light-green T-shirt over his head, pinning his vibrant blue eyes on me with an answering smile.

Still centered on the bed, Paisley threw her head back and howled triumphantly. The undulating wail assaulted all my senses, physical and magical. Aiden clamped his hands over his ears.

The demon dog leaped off the bed, landing in the hall. She'd somehow cleared the doorway despite the sharp angle.

"Wait for us!" I called after her, shaking my head to brush off the effects of her howl.

She grunted, slowing her pace as she headed for the stairs but otherwise ignoring me.

"Isn't Paisley supposed to be helping Christopher and Samantha?" Aiden asked, crossing to me.

"I'm guessing they didn't cater to her every whim," I said.

Aiden threaded his fingers through my hair, cupping the back of my head and tugging me closer to brush his lips lightly across mine. "So she missed us," he whispered.

I darted my tongue past his lips playfully, and he pulled back, grinning slightly. "She's probably just here to check on the cows and chickens."

"And the sorcerer at the gate."

"Let's hope she hasn't developed second sight. One seer in the family is enough."

"Agreed. And I gather the clairvoyant is heading back?"

"Not yet."

Aiden arched an eyebrow at me.

"He'd take all the fun out of the upcoming fight," I said, still grinning.

Aiden chuckled, running his fingers down the front edge of my silk robe. "I love this on you," he murmured, cupping my breast through the fabric and flicking my nipple with his thumb.

I shuddered slightly, leaning into his touch. "I'm not going to meet an Azar sorcerer in a silk robe. I'd hate to ruin it."

Aiden brushed another kiss across my lips, then stepped away. "I'm grabbing a few things from the study, then I'll be ready." He glanced back at me from the doorway, eyes simmering with power. "Emma...thank you."

I wasn't certain what he was thanking me for, but he headed down the stairs before I could ask for clarification. I dressed, going so far as to pull my hair back in a ponytail, but not so far as to outfit myself with any weapons.

I didn't need anything more than my bare hands to bring down a sorcerer, after all. Even one powerful enough to convey intention—maybe even mood—through the outer wards.

PAISLEY PROWLED AHEAD OF US UP THE EDGE OF THE gravel driveway, her paws silent in the grass, right shoulder brushing the rose bushes. The demon dog had been waiting on the porch as we came down, front door open wide at her back, wearing her large pit bull aspect. The toothy grin of anticipation on her face reminded me to keep my own expression neutral.

Aiden and I walked side by side, not meandering but not rushing either. Fingers and shoulders occasionally touching. Our three cows were munching through the tall green grass to the far right. Christopher had been talking recently about breeding the eldest with one of the Wilsons' bulls, but had decided to help Samantha in her hunt for Bee instead.

A figure in a tan-colored suit and hat stood in the shade on the far side of the gate at the end of the driveway. Just beyond the property boundary wards that I could feel as we approached, though I couldn't see them. He was leaning back against the farm stand with his hat low enough to obscure his face. Feigning taking a standing nap, perhaps. Or he was just that sensitive to the sun. I had set eggs out on the stand that morning, but the lid of the cooler was raised, indicating that someone had purchased the last dozen already.

As we approached, our visitor raised his head. His eyes instantly locked on Aiden.

Not Isa.

Kader Azar.

And he looked old. Older than the eight years since the last time I'd seen him should have aged him. Sorcerers aged slowly. The gray that had speckled his temples on a rooftop in Los Angeles now feathered up under the edge of the hat. His darkly tanned skin was sallow, slackened in places as if he'd recently lost a lot of weight. The whites of his eyes were yellowed.

My stomach did an odd roll with a combination of emotions that I couldn't immediately place. It felt as though one of them might have been trepidation, but that would have been absurd.

Aiden's shoulders stiffened, tension edging his jaw. He stuffed his hands in his jeans pockets, presumably palming at least one of the premade runed spells he'd collected from the magical arsenal he kept locked in the safe in the study.

Kader didn't even glance my way. He smiled at Aiden. The expression softened the hard planes of his face.

I didn't like him smiling at Aiden. I didn't like having him near enough to speak with Aiden. I checked myself before I lost hold of my magic. I'd been clenching my hands. Any display of weakness was a weapon my adversary could use.

Paisley snorted dismissively in Kader's direction, then prowled to the right along the fence line, checking the perimeter. And the cows.

Interesting. I wasn't certain what the demon dog could sense through the boundary wards—or if she could even sense the wards at all. Even though she was blood tied to those protections, along with the secondary house wards, as were Opal, Christopher, Samantha, Jenni Raymond, and Lani Zachary.

But whatever Paisley sensed of Kader Azar didn't hold her attention.

Aiden and I paused a stride away from the gate.

Kader shifted his hat back on his head, stepping forward. He decided to actually glance my way for the first time.

His second step faltered.

A flash of recognition, then shock, flitted across his face. Then his smile widened. He was pleased to the point of…gloating?

"Your wards are impressive, my son," he said. His accent was smooth, cultured.

Not gloating.

Pride. Or at least Kader Azar's version of being proud of his son.

Aiden didn't respond.

Kader took another step forward, running his gaze over me, then meeting my eyes steadily. "What a pleasant surprise, amplifier."

I couldn't tell if he was feigning that surprise.

Aiden snorted, obviously doubting his father as well. "Don't tell me that Isa is actually capable of keeping secrets."

Kader frowned slightly, transferring his attention to his son. "I haven't seen him since he delivered my letter."

"Which you knew the instant I touched it," Aiden said, as if just putting that together himself. Unhappily.

Kader inclined his head.

Silence fell between the three of us, punctuated only by the quiet cackling of the distant chickens, and the sound of even-more-distant traffic. Kader smiled again, gently. Which was odd, given everything I knew him to be. He glanced between us, his gaze lingering on Aiden the longest. Seemingly content to just let us look at him.

I realized belatedly that the sorcerer Azar had arrived without a vehicle. A small satchel that presumably belonged to him was set on the farm stand, but he carried no other luggage. As if he'd teleported, perhaps with little preparation.

Risky.

I glanced at Aiden, suddenly finding my own anger, my own gleeful anticipation of confronting Kader, waning. Aiden's face was blank of all expression, gaze riveted to his father. But in response to my look, he pulled a hand from his pocket and threaded his fingers through mine. Giving me access to what he was feeling.

Confusion and frustration, with only a hint of anger simmering underneath, filtered through to me.

"He wants something," I said.

Aiden nodded, not taking his gaze off his father. "Of course he wants something."

I glanced at Kader, who appeared to have no issue with us not including him in the discussion. "Why shouldn't I just kill you where you stand, sorcerer?"

He blinked. "To what end? Exacting revenge? For what? Your existence?"

More games. "To protect Aiden," I said.

Kader smiled, allowing his lips to curl softly, to hint at a warmth of feeling. But this time, I could see the calculation behind the expression.

"I would never hurt my son."

Aiden snorted.

"Is that why Isa still lives?" I asked. "When it was he who betrayed you to Silver Pine and Chenda, allowing the rogue shifters to kidnap you in LA?" I had first met the elder sorcerer while rescuing him with the Five. That mission had led to Silver Pine trying to kill me, and the Five destroying the compound as we fled the Collective. But I hadn't known the reason for my death sentence until years later.

Kader's smile broadened. I could see the resemblance between father and son in the bone structure of his face, though the contours of his eyes were different. Aiden's nose was more refined. His chin more defined as well. But there was no doubt they were blood related.

"Did the witch and the mystic survive their contact with you, amplifier?" Kader asked. "Did the telepath tear the answers you seek out of their heads while you drained them of all resistance?"

I didn't answer. He hadn't answered my question either.

Kader glanced at Aiden, silent by my side, then down to our linked hands. "I'm eager to hear the tale of how you two met, and …" He waved his hand, trailing off.

It was a completely innocuous gesture, but Aiden steeled himself, gripping my hand as if expecting to be attacked.

Kader lowered his hand. "Fate moves in interesting ways …" he murmured.

"No," Aiden said bluntly.

His father lifted his chin. "No? To?"

"Everything. Anything." Aiden's tone was flat, uncompromising. But his emotions—picked up through my latent empathy—were tangled, roiling.

Paisley wandered along the edge of the fence to our left, presumably having done a fast circuit of the property. She paused beside Aiden. Then, when he didn't immediately acknowledge her presence, she leaned her shoulder into his knee. Heavily.

Aiden swore softly, benign magic shifting in the arcane words. Then he finally looked away from his father just long enough to scratch Paisley behind the ears.

I kept my gaze on Kader, watching the elder sorcerer's expression as he in turn watched his son. I wasn't particularly good at reading people, but I felt certain in that moment that Kader hadn't come to hurt Aiden. Not outright, at least.

So maybe it wasn't all a game.

Maybe he really was dying.

And if Kader died without having one last conversation with his youngest son, what might that come to mean to Aiden? The emotions that had been emanating from the dark-haired sorcerer since he'd opened his father's letter were clear in one way—they conflicted.

"It's almost time for tea," I said.

Aiden stiffened in surprise, looking at me.

I waited for him to counter my suggestion. Instead, he just glanced around the property, then nodded.

Kader Azar unlatched the gate, pushing it open just far enough to step onto the property and close it behind him. He had crossed through Aiden's wards without needing an invitation.

Aiden squeezed my hand in warning. I nodded, not taking my gaze from his father.

From the moment he latched the gate, I could feel the elder sorcerer's power. It was dimmer than I'd expected, though I had no doubt he could mask it by choice or design. Many powerful Adepts chose to do so, mostly so they could move through the world without drawing too much attention to themselves. I'd been able to do the same since before I'd understood the necessity. But by design more so than talent.

After draining my magic taking down the compound in Peru that had been home to the Five since we were born, I'd spent over a year hoping that magic wouldn't return. So when that power had come seeping back, I'd begun suppressing it in earnest, training that ability, keeping my power continually bottled up. It was second nature now.

Paisley shoved herself between Aiden and his father. A single tentacle sprang forth from her neck, wrapped around a large bovine bone. The demon dog flashed a double row of sharp teeth at Kader. Then she poked him in the thigh with the bone.

"Ah," Kader said. "Look at you, beautiful. I didn't know that any of you had survived." He glanced at me. "Did you get the entire litter out?"

I didn't answer. Only Paisley had survived the destruction we Five had wrought on the compound when we'd escaped the Collective.

Paisley poked Kader with the bone again.

"Yes, sorry," he said to her. Then he wrapped his hand around the end of the bone, gazing deliberately into Paisley's suddenly blood-red eyes.

Silence stretched. A distant rooster crowed, then the rooster overseeing our flock responded. The drone of a light plane rose as it passed overhead.

Aiden glanced my way questioningly.

I shrugged. Paisley had done something similar when Opal had first appeared on the property, making her hold the bone as well. I'd been too distracted at the time to mention it to anyone. But the demon dog seemed to be using the bone that Aiden had given her as some sort of way to vet intruders, separating friends from possible tasty treats.

Not that I would consciously allow the demon dog to eat someone. Though even I couldn't stop everything that might happen in the heat of battle.

Paisley flashed her teeth at Kader again, tugging the bone free from his hand. It promptly disappeared, folded back into her currently invisible mane.

"Magnificent," Kader cooed.

Paisley chuffed, pleased. Then she turned to wander back to the house.

Kader transferred his smile to me. "Just magnificent. Though I wouldn't expect anything less from you, amplifier."

"You don't know me well enough to make that assessment, sorcerer."

"No?" He arched an eyebrow.

The expression was disconcertingly reminiscent of Aiden's. I'd seen a disturbing echo of the sorcerer I loved in his brother's face as well. Thankfully, the feeling of familiarity quickly faded, because I was already feeling off. I wasn't remotely acting how I'd assumed I would react to meeting one of my makers—specifically, with my blades in hand and that maker's life blood marking their edges just moments afterward.

"I suppose not," Kader said despite my silence. "It has been over eight years."

He hadn't noticed that I'd just been trying to decide when I was going to murder him.

When.

Not if.

Of that, I had no doubt.

I had gotten accustomed to being able to scare people just by looking at them. It was possible I was losing too much of my edge. It was also possible that in dealing with the sorcerer Azar in any way that didn't involve following his orders or taking his head—as extreme as both of those options sounded—I was going to find myself outmatched.

Kader glanced between Aiden and me again. "You said something about tea? I'd be delighted to get out of the sun."

Aiden frowned, both of his hands shoved in his pockets again. Then he looked at me. "I'll trust your judgement."

"He's passed Paisley's test."

Aiden hummed softly, noncommittal. Then he looked at his father. "Safe passage to you. But the moment you move to bring harm to my family, I'll kill you. If Emma doesn't get there first."

A slow smile spread across Kader Azar's face. He deliberately turned to bestow it on me with a nod. "Emma. Pleased to finally meet you properly."

He hadn't known the name I'd taken on when we all fled the compound.

Of course he hadn't, and …

Tension etched through Aiden's jaw as he realized the same thing I just had. He'd unwittingly given a tiny piece of power to his father. My name.

I brushed my fingers against Aiden's forearm, but addressed Kader. "No. I'm no one but Amp5 to you, sorcerer. A weapon of mass destruction, not a person. Not to you."

Kader opened his mouth—presumably to protest, given his furrowed brow.

"Just remember what you made me," I said.

He curtailed whatever he was going to say, nodding stiffly. "Amp5 it is, then."

I pivoted away, feeling a bit hollow. As if I hadn't won back that private piece of myself at all. But since that was an idiotic notion, I brushed the feeling away, preparing for a different sort of warfare. A battle to be conducted over tea and cookies with words and innuendo.

Thankfully, no matter how silent Aiden had been so far, he was more skilled with those sorts of weapons than I was.

Behind me, I could feel Kader scanning the property as we walked back to the house. Aiden stayed a half step behind his father. Not in deference, but so that we flanked him.

I glanced back before climbing the stairs to the front patio. Aiden was casually flipping a runed stone in his left hand. Energy flashed around the stone as it spun in the air, then dropped back into the sorcerer's palm. He winked at me.

Kader had paused to admire the Mustang parked in front of the house. But the moment he turned to question Aiden about it, his son's expression blanked.

I didn't bother participating in the conversation that followed. As far as I could hear, other than the words 'no' and 'yes,' neither did Aiden.

Paisley was waiting by the front door, the bovine bone out again and tucked under a front paw. She smiled broadly as I approached, her mouth far too wide for her face. I ghosted my hand over her broad head as I passed. She picked up the bone in her mouth, then fell into step with me. I toed off my white sneakers just beyond the door, then scooped them up to carry them into the laundry room.

It was interesting that the demon dog had hidden the bone from Ember and Capri Pine when they visited in February. We had asked Paisley to make herself scarce around the witches, understanding that they might have been seriously disturbed by her demon genetics—but that hadn't lasted. Still, she hadn't brought out the bone.

Did that mean she accepted Kader's presence? Or was she just lining up her next meal? Consuming the elder sorcerer would be best accomplished away from the main road, after all.

That thought made me smile. And since being amused by the demon dog's possible motives was far more comfortable than feeling hollow, I would take it. Gladly.

MOVING AROUND THE KITCHEN ISLAND, I SET A chilled pitcher of iced tea, ginger snaps, plates, glasses, and napkins on a tray. And while doing so, I felt every step that Kader Azar took through my home.

Aiden remained a step behind his father as they crossed through the house. The younger sorcerer's magic was robust, even without his body runes. The depths of his own power were almost continually amplified by me now, simply in the course of living our lives together. Though every now and then, Aiden decided to test another variation of the refraction rune he was developing to see if he could resist being involuntarily amplified.

By contrast, the elder sorcerer's power was neatly tucked away. But I had no doubt that Kader Azar could have leveled the house with only a few well-chosen words. Or that he might not need to speak at all to wield his magic.

Father and son lingered near the partly open door to the study, murmuring. They were both speaking that other language that Aiden occasionally lapsed into, and which Isa and Ruwa had also spoken. Arabic of some kind, I had always thought. Though I wouldn't have put it past Kader Azar to have developed his own language, then forced generations of his cabal to learn it.

Why had I invited him into my home?

Right.

Aiden.

Plus, draining and killing Kader on the back patio would shield my activities from the sight of the road. And the Wilsons' property.

Leaving the laden tea tray on the island, I stepped around the kitchen table and through the open French-paned doors. I rearranged the table and chairs, situating one of the chairs in the shade—and making sure that doing so meant it was boxed in by the house, the porch railing, and me. Once I sat down, at least.

Kader knew as well as I did that he couldn't get away from me. He'd known that long before he'd chosen to set foot on the property.

He would have to hit me hard to overcome me, and with a curse I'd never taken before. Presumably, Kader Azar had a thorough knowledge of all the magic that had been tested against me for the first twenty-one years of my life. He would know what it had taken back then to put me in the med bay—a rare but still occasional occurrence. The Collective hadn't believed in controlled or regulated training sessions.

But I was feeling more certain that Kader had been genuinely surprised to see me at Aiden's side. And if he hadn't had time to access his records and plan for this meeting, then I had the advantage. I'd also had eight years to grow stronger, develop a higher resistance. Magic aged well.

Kader stepped up to the threshold, his gaze on the yard and the garden beyond. He'd removed his dress shoes, so his feet were clad only in thin brown socks. It didn't diminish him in the least.

It bothered me that I was so intimidated by the elder sorcerer. It made me ache to lash out, completely irrationally.

I adjusted the seat cushion on the third chair instead, centering it perfectly. Even though I knew doing so gave away what I was feeling.

"You have a lovely home," Kader murmured.

I didn't respond.

He angled his dark-eyed gaze at me. Then, noting the arrangement of the chairs, he smiled. The expression was once again edged with that fulfilled expectancy. The same pride. As if he was pleased that I'd set up a kill seat for him.

Aiden stepped up behind his father, carrying the tea tray. Kader obligingly stepped forward, removing his satchel from his shoulder as he crossed toward me. The sorcerer hadn't picked up the bag from the farm stand before he'd crossed through the gate, which likely meant he could call it to him. Another blatant display of power.

Or perhaps such things came so easily to the sorcerer that he did them without thought.

No.

Every single thing that Kader Azar did was calculated. Eight years ago, it had taken the betrayal of his eldest son, two other members of the Collective, and a pack of rogue shapeshifters to take him down.

And then the Five rescued him.

So no matter how rushed his sudden appearance now seemed, the Kader Azar I knew would have backup. And then more backup. Plans and protection.

The elder sorcerer stepped by me, near enough that I could have touched him without effort. But I kept my hands to myself, exceedingly aware of Aiden as he set the tray on the low table. The dark-haired sorcerer was tense, but if he was truly worried, I couldn't sense it.

Kader slung his satchel across the back of the chair situated in the shade, boxing himself in without hesitation.

Aiden sat down across from his father, placing the empty seat for me in the middle. His expression softened as he caught my gaze. Or perhaps picked up my concern. "May I pour?"

"Yes, please." I sat in the third chair, keeping both of my feet firmly planted on the patio.

Kader removed his hat, setting it on the wide end of the arm of the chair. He crossed his legs. His hair was almost completely threaded through with steel gray.

The skin around Aiden's eyes tightened. But he simply added a teaspoon of sugar to a tall crystal glass of rosy iced tea and stirred. I had cold-brewed my favorite fruit blend to replace the overbrewed Ceylon tea we'd shared earlier. Silence stretched, punctuated by the soft tinkling of the wind chimes.

I picked up the tenor of Paisley's magic in the barn, where she was most likely raiding her fridge. I hadn't defrosted anything for her, not knowing she'd return so soon. Or without Christopher.

I took the glass of iced tea that Aiden offered me, forcing myself to settle back in my seat with it and tucking my legs underneath me as I normally would.

I was deadly in any position. I might as well be comfortable.

I took a sip of the perfectly sweet and tangy tea. A smile flitted over Aiden's lips as he noted my movements, but he spoke gruffly to his father. "Sugar?"

"No. Thank you."

Aiden set a glass near Kader. Then he placed two ginger snaps on one of the stoneware plates and set it alongside the glass, with a napkin next to it. Kader pointedly waited until his son had shifted back in his seat before he leaned forward, lifting the iced tea and sipping.

Aiden put two more ginger snaps on a plate, balancing it on the wide end of the arm of my chair and tucking a napkin underneath the edge.

"Thank you," I murmured.

He then served himself tea. Grabbing a cookie in his other hand, he settled back in his chair, long legs stretched out, crossed at the ankles.

I nibbled on a cookie, occupying both of my hands as well.

We both looked at Kader Azar.

It would have been the perfect time for him to attack us.

The elder sorcerer grinned knowingly, taking another sip of his iced tea. He cast his gaze out over the railing toward the garden and spoke conversationally.

"Your mother is slowly killing me."

I looked at Aiden sharply, unable to hide my surprise.

The dark-haired sorcerer blinked, then frowned. "Excuse me?"

Kader waved a hand, indicating himself. "As you can see."

"You're claiming …" Aiden laughed, briefly but harshly. "A witch is slowly stealing your life force?"

Kader held his son's gaze steadily, but he didn't elaborate.

A nasty smile twisted Aiden's face. "And you aren't powerful enough to block a witch spell?"

Kader's tone was even, considered. "None of the cabal have been able to break the connection. Not me, or Khalid. Not even Grosvenor."

I glanced at Aiden again.

He kept his gaze pinned to his father, but answered my unvoiced questions. "Khalid is my next-oldest half-brother, and Grosvenor is a cousin. British."

"My eldest brother's son," Kader said. "A curse breaker."

"From a long line of curse breakers," Aiden added quietly. "All dead now. As far as I know."

"His mother, a paternal aunt I don't believe you've met, and his youngest sister survive," Kader said. "But yes. Curse breaking is a lucrative business, but deadly." His gaze settled on me, lips quirked in amusement. "Something all Azars are well acquainted with."

I didn't bother analyzing what he was suggesting—because it seemed as though he was comparing me to curse breaking. Partaking in a conversation about my relationship with any Azar was off limits. I wouldn't talk about Aiden. And Kader wouldn't survive a chat about my creation and childhood.

Because I had no moral issue with killing the architect of the Five. Kader Azar's crimes were numerous, and wiping him from the face of the earth would likely save many other lives. Though that was a little abstract.

Either way, though, I didn't need to justify the elder sorcerer's pending demise by my hand. I was just being cautious about doing anything I couldn't undo until I knew what Aiden wanted.

The conversation completely lapsed. I nibbled on a ginger snap, savoring the crunch of the brown-sugar topping, and sipped my tea. Kader shifted his gaze from me to Aiden and then back again.

Aiden was watching his father, frowning thoughtfully. His iced tea was forgotten in his hand, one ginger snap already consumed. "So you come to me," he finally said. "As a last resort."

"Cerise hasn't responded to my—"

Aiden snorted. "You expect her to chat with you willingly?"

"I expected her to want to avoid an incident." Kader's tone had become clipped. "The witches Convocation won't take an accusation of this level lightly."

"From you?" Aiden scoffed. "Against a Myers witch?"

Primarily situated in Paris, France, the Myers coven held one of the thirteen seats on the Convocation—the witches' governing body. According to the background check Ember Pine, my lawyer, had sent me when I'd first met Aiden, the Myers coven focused on delicate, precise magic and had a stellar reputation among the Adept. She had later mentioned that it had been centuries since a black witch had cropped up in the Myers bloodline. But I knew that a witch backed by a full coven didn't need to summon demons or sacrifice the innocent to wield immense power. And even a witch surrounded only by a like-minded portion of her coven could accomplish a great deal—as long as they were all focused on a single task.

So even without wielding blood magic or black magic, it was possible that a small group of the Myers coven could kill Kader Azar.

If they could get to him.

Or get a piece of him.

Still. Eight years ago, it had taken the combined efforts of Silver Pine, Chenda the so-called Mystic of the Golden Peninsula, and Isa to entrap Kader Azar. I had no doubt that since that incident, he would have made it nearly impossible to penetrate the protections that were sure to surround every estate he owned.

All of which would seem to make the sorcerer Azar's claim that Cerise was killing him absurd.

Kader hadn't answered Aiden's question. He sipped his iced tea with a relaxed watchfulness. Waiting.

"Or do you mean an accusation from me?" Aiden asked in disbelief, reinterpreting Kader's last statement differently than I had. "You think the Convocation would take a complaint from me seriously? And why would I even be inclined to speak on your behalf?"

"I'm not suggesting that you would inform on your own mother." Kader sipped his iced tea. He hadn't touched the cookies. "But I would think that after verifying that the spell is Cerise's work, you might perhaps want to clear her name. I assume you'd try to speak to her first, before ..." He waved his free hand. "Before consequences occur."

He didn't elaborate on what those consequences might be. But the sorcerer's tone made it clear that he wasn't speaking of his own death.

Aiden's voice was cold. "You want me to intervene? To try to prevent your self-proclaimed pending murder? Or else what?"

Kader speared his son with a sharp-eyed gaze. "Or else when I die, I will reach back through the binding Cerise has forced upon me. And with my last breath, I will wipe every last drop of Myers blood from the face of the earth."

Energy skittered down my spine at his utterly cold, completely dispassionate statement. It was an irrational reaction, and one that I—

Aiden shook his shoulders, as if feeling the same thing I was.

Magic.

Kader Azar had just unleashed a spell to prove he was telling the truth. It felt exceedingly similar to a binding spell. Now that I recognized it, the magic slowly dissipated across my skin.

Aiden snarled, power bright in his eyes. "Haven't you done enough?"

Kader arched an eyebrow. "In what sense?"

The dark-haired sorcerer stood abruptly, pivoting and walking away. He paused at the far end of the patio, looking toward the gardens. Still clutching his iced tea in one hand.

The elder sorcerer flinched, then quickly blanked his expression. Picking up a cookie, along with the napkin, he took a bite.

"It's more than that," I said. Not wanting to intervene, but knowing that Aiden was only a breath away from exploding.

"Yes." Kader settled back in his chair.

Aiden glanced over his shoulder. At me, not his father.

"We've already replaced the French-paned doors once," I said teasingly, though it came out stilted.

Aiden huffed, playing along. "You could drain him enough to incapacitate him. Without me having to break anything."

"True," I said, taking a sip of my iced tea as if talking about murdering Aiden's father was as normal as discussing what to eat for dinner—even with him sitting right beside me. "Then we could keep him unconscious until whatever is killing him finishes him off. Not allowing him to utter another word, let alone a death curse." I looked at Kader coolly. "A death curse isn't something you can send by proxy or attach to one of your letters, is it?"

Kader smiled smugly. "No. I can do a lot of damage by proxy, as you call it. But you are correct. I would need to utter the curse at the moment of my death."

I looked at Aiden, shrugging. "Your call."

Kader laughed, quietly delighted.

I ignored him, but he was becoming seriously irksome. I loathed it when Adepts weren't at least wary around me. It demanded so much extra effort on my part to keep them in line.

"You were saying, Emma?" Aiden leaned back against the railing, ceding the conversation to me. "There's more to it …?"

I glanced at Kader. "You think that Aiden can break the spell, if it's of Cerise's construction." Kader's hasty and demonstrably reckless use of a teleportation spell only hours after Aiden had opened the letter told me that the elder sorcerer was desperate. He'd had no idea what else he might find when he found Aiden. That was incredibly risky. "Because he and Cerise are blood tied."

Kader nodded. Looking at Aiden, not me. "To both of us."

I snorted. "It's always about blood ties with you."

The elder sorcerer flicked his dark-eyed gaze my way, amused. "You can thank me later."

Anger flushed through me, but it felt utterly cold. I leaned forward, abruptly dropping any attempt to mediate the situation. I might not want Aiden to have to live with killing his own father, but I wasn't going to play games or make nice.

"For the power that runs through my veins, you mean?" I asked darkly. "For the ties that bind me to the Five? For everything you did to me, to us, without our permission?" I was whispering now, watching a range of faint expressions flit across the elder sorcerer's face. "And how would you have me thank you, Kader Azar?"

My words fell heavily between us, dissipating into another lengthy silence as we sat there, staring at each other, poised on the edge of violence. Even Aiden was barely breathing, his magic held in a tight coil. My own power was leaking out, writhing around me, licking toward Kader as if it could grab him, drain him, without my even touching the sorcerer.

It couldn't, of course. Not even if I unleashed it fully. My abilities—innate and latent—required skin-to-skin contact.

Kader just looked at me, a glass of iced tea in one hand and a cookie in the other. The elder sorcerer didn't need his hands to attack me. He barely needed words or runes.

So I looked him straight in the eye, and I dared him. I silently urged him to make a move.

He didn't.

Instead, he cleared his throat, blinking three times. "I misspoke," he said simply.

My anger guttered, swallowed by disappointment.

"I would think," Kader continued, addressing Aiden, "that you'd prefer your mother to not be a murderer."

"My pentagram is in the loft of the barn," Aiden said, his tone clipped. "I'll need about thirty minutes to reverse some of the damage done to it by quelling the teleportation spell embedded into your letter."

Kader nodded. "Indeed. Masterfully done. As I'm sure you understand, it would have been far easier to have brought you to me."

Aiden ignored the change of subject. "After I verify that the spell you believe is slowly killing you is of Myers witch origin, I will then consider whether or not I'll attempt to thwart it."

"Completely understandable. And expected. I'm delighted to find you in the...possession of such resources and a newly honed ability to thwart a spell of your father's making." Kader side-eyed me. "Blood ties and all. That bodes well."

He was inferring that Aiden wouldn't have been powerful enough to negate the teleportation spell without being amplified by me.

The secondary inference was that I was valuable only for my magic.

That was an old wound. A recently buried concern that the elder sorcerer had no ability to reopen or dig up—at least for me. Aiden, however, clenched his hands into fists, readying some retort that I was fairly certain was going to contain more magic than words.

"I do really like these glasses," I said, setting down my iced tea.

Aiden's gaze flicked to me. Reluctantly. As if he was having trouble reining himself in. Then he nodded, just once. "Right. He's not worth breaking them."

"Or the stoneware," I added, keeping my tone light. So light that I felt almost out-of-body as I uttered the words. Again, I wasn't reacting in character.

As I would have reacted if Kader Azar had shown up at my gate before I'd met Aiden…before I'd loved Aiden …

I shoved the thought away, focusing on the present because that was where I'd chosen to be. Not fretting about the past.

The elder sorcerer glanced between me and Aiden, though we were just staring at each other, not speaking. He set down his glass and stood. "Perhaps I can be of some assistance with the pentagram."

Aiden nodded, still looking steadily at me. And I realized he was doing the same thing that I was. He was using me to anchor himself, moment by moment, just as I was using him.

Ignored by both of us, Kader stepped around me. He crossed into the house and toward the front door, and his shoes.

I smiled. A genuine, joyful smile.

An answering smile spread across Aiden's face. He swiftly closed the space between us, leaning over and whispering in my ear, "I love you."

"I know it." I brushed my lips against his cheek. "I love you."

He held his hand out. "Will you join us?"

"I will." I placed my hand in his, standing.

Aiden's eyes glimmered with power. His grin sharpened, edged in dark anticipation.

Something deep within me responded, recognizing exactly what the two of us could accomplish together. As long as we were willing to cross every line, destroy everyone and anyone in our path.

No one could stand against us, not even Kader Azar.

I brushed a kiss across Aiden's lips. Tender and full of promise. Not a promise of wanton destruction in the accumulation of power, but a promise of the life we'd chosen together.

Aiden sighed softly. "Yes," he murmured. Then he firmed his tone. "Yes."

He stepped away, quickly collecting the glasses and plates onto the tray, then carrying everything into the kitchen. I snagged a second cookie, following him into our home.

SETTING HIS SATCHEL JUST INSIDE THE DOOR TO THE loft suite, Kader slowly paced a circle around the tarnished copper pentagram set into the white-painted wood-slat floor.

"The obsidian was an excellent choice," he murmured to Aiden. "I'm surprised it didn't hold."

Aiden crouched by one of the five smaller pentagrams, prying the cracked obsidian gemstone from its center. He held it up to the weak sunlight filtering in through the upper windows of the barn.

Kader held his hand out to his son, silently requesting the stone. Magic flickered in Aiden's eyes as he quashed whatever violence that gesture triggered within himself. Then he dropped the chunk of obsidian into his father's open palm.

Peering at the stone, Kader rolled it between his fingers. "The rune?"

"Of my own construction," Aiden said gruffly, moving to and prying another cracked gemstone free from the next smaller pentagram. He glanced over at me, magic simmering in his eyes.

I met his gaze without reaction, holding myself in check. Steady. Despite his threat of wiping the entire Myers bloodline from the face of the earth with his dying breath, I understood that Kader saw Aiden as some sort of salvation, so keeping myself centered was coming more easily.

I didn't, however, underestimate the elder sorcerer's ability to shift his plans when something didn't go his way. I didn't underestimate what my presence—and therefore a possible reconnection to the Five—might mean to a dying sorcerer. One who had most likely already exhausted his considerable magical resources trying to undo the magic that was killing him.

I was exceedingly glad that Christopher wasn't even on the continent. I didn't want the clairvoyant anywhere near this situation. Chenda, aka the Mystic of the Golden Peninsula, had already done enough psychological damage. No matter how powerful the Collective made us, they hadn't made us impervious to nonmagical mental manipulation.

I also didn't want Kader anywhere near Daniel or Samantha—who would most likely try to kill him on sight. As I would have done, had I actually been the sociopath the Collective had tried to make me. I would have slaughtered Kader Azar by the roadside.

But instead, I'd invited him into my home. Because I cared for Aiden.

The fourth gemstone Aiden removed broke into three pieces in his hand. The fifth shattered to countless shards. He swore, resting back on his heels. "I was hoping to salvage them," he muttered, offering me a twisted smile.

"No matter," Kader said from the doorway. "Though it was a solid first choice, the obsidian isn't the right stone." He tucked the gemstone he held in the pocket of his suit pants. Even I knew he was more interested in the rune etched into it than the stone itself.

"It's attuned to me." Aiden leaned forward, brushing his fingers along the copper that outlined the main pentagram. Power swept along the star, removing the tarnish. The runes etched into the metal flared, then faded.

"The pentagram is impressive," Kader said, not stepping any closer. "An acknowledgement of your witch and sorcerer roots. A strong anchor for your unique power signature."

"Which only benefits you," Aiden snapped, straightening. He deliberately stepped between two of the pentagram's points.

Kader inclined his head. "Consider your birthstone next time."

Aiden frowned. "Carnelian? For what? Good luck?"

"A stabilizing agent. Controlling the flow of energy."

"The obsidian is more receptive to my magic."

Kader smiled. That thin, possessive, pride-filled twist of his lips. Then he settled his gaze on me. "I believe you will discover that you took too much power with you into the pentagram."

As he processed his father's implication, Aiden's jaw tensed, eyes narrowing. Then he carefully blanked his expression.

"Too much power for the obsidian," Kader said smoothly.

My power, the elder sorcerer meant.

My amplification of Aiden was what had blown the obsidian out. And now Aiden was clearly feeling like an undereducated idiot in front of his uber-powerful father. A father he loathed—but who somehow, somewhere deep inside, he still idolized.

I didn't know that feeling. I couldn't empathize. But I could see it etched in every tense muscle of Aiden's body, and in the spike of his magic.

"I'll run some tests," he said, his tone remarkably neutral.

"Of course." Kader waved a hand toward the newly shiny pentagram. "Shall I?"

"Please."

The elder sorcerer's gaze flicked to me.

A smile curled Aiden's lips. "If Emma was going to kill you outright, she would have done so already."

"Yes." Kader set his dark-eyed gaze on his son as he stepped into the center of the pentagram. "I know the amplifier far better than you."

Aiden laughed quietly. "No. You simply think you know what you had a hand in creating. You have no idea of the person she's become."

"That any of us became," I said quietly, pointedly speaking to Aiden.

He nodded, but I didn't think he caught my full implication—that he had been the product of his father's predilection for magical genetic experiments as surely as I was. I hated having to couch my words, to mitigate my reactions. I had grown accustomed to being who I wanted to be with Aiden in a very short period of time.

Kader didn't respond, settling down in the pentagram with his legs crossed and his hands set on either knee, palms facing up.

Paisley chose that moment to trundle up the interior stairs. About half of her mane of tentacles writhed around her neck, but she was otherwise in her larger blue-nosed pit bull aspect. She was holding her bovine bone, an egg she must have purloined from the chicken coop, and a book in three of the tentacles.

The book was smudged with dirt. As if she'd dug it up after having buried it somewhere in the yard or garden.

Paisley shouldered past me, leaning in the way she did when she wanted to be petted. I tried to oblige, but she moved steadily out of my reach, angling for Aiden.

Aiden sealed the pentagram around Kader with a whispered command. Blue-tinged power rippled across the inlaid copper bars, sparking each of the runes.

The demon dog paused, blinking at the elder sorcerer with red eyes that had been deep brown a moment before. Kader kept his gaze on his son.

"I've been looking for that," Aiden muttered, reaching for the dirt-smudged book as Paisley flicked it toward him. The demon dog yanked the book just out of Aiden's reach, demanding his full attention. She flipped through the pages, opening the book to what appeared to be the beginning of a spell.

She tapped the selected page with the bone, blinking up at Aiden.

The dark-haired sorcerer peered down at the book, reading. Then he flashed her a smile. "Is that what the egg is for?"

Paisley dropped her massive maw open, displaying a double row of sharp teeth and a lolling blue tongue.

"All right. Later?"

Paisley chortled darkly, apparently pleased. Then she settled down next to Aiden to watch him work.

Kader's gaze was now riveted to the demon dog. "Remarkable. It can read?"

No one answered him.

Aiden held his hands forward, palms facing out, gaze remote. The same pose as when he had tried to assess the block on Samantha's magic. "Yes, I see it."

"It's rather obvious," Kader said dryly. "I'm surprised you needed the pentagram."

Aiden ignored his father, but Paisley tapped the edge of the pentagram with her bone, narrowing her eyes at the elder sorcerer.

Kader smirked at her. "Included my son in your programming, have you?"

Something in me snapped. I assessed the space between me and the elder sorcerer. I visualized clearing the distance in a single stride, easily reaching through the magic that sealed him within the pentagram, and tearing his head off his shoulders.

It would be messy, bloody. But properly harnessed, the magic in his father's blood would feed Aiden's pentagram for decades.

"Emma …"

Aiden's gentle tone pulled my attention away from Kader. I realized I'd called my blade into my right hand, most likely draining the last of the retrieval spell.

The elder sorcerer had raised his hands, palms turned to me. Pulses of blue magic, so dark that they appeared almost black, simmered between his outstretched fingers.

I tightened my grip on my blade, recalculating how it extended my reach, and factoring in how big a hit I could take from the elder sorcerer and still meet my goal—

"Emma," Aiden whispered again. "Just…a few more minutes?"

I tore my gaze from Kader. Aiden had stepped to one side, as had Paisley. Clearing my path. The dark-haired sorcerer's hands were also raised. But in a plea, not preparing to cast.

"A few more minutes?" Aiden repeated. "To clear my mother of his accusation? Then you can kill him. I won't stand in your way. It's your choice. Your right."

Kader snorted. "It would be ill advised."

Right.

Kader would see me coming. And he'd already informed us of what exactly he intended to do with his dying breath. The death curse. A curse that—if the elder sorcerer could pull it off—might take Aiden with it as well. He was also of the Myers bloodline.

I pointed my blade at Kader. "You will watch your mouth in my home. I'm done with the insinuations, the nasty verbal jabs."

"I didn't realize you were so delicate, amplifier."

Aiden barked a laugh. "I'd never realized you were so unobservant, Father." He spat the title with derision and an inadvertent punch of power that rippled across the sealed pentagram. "Emma wouldn't kill you just for any slight, large or small, that you've inflicted upon her. No, when she takes your head, it will be to protect those she cares about."

"Perhaps you could give me a list," Kader said coolly, though he had dropped his hands back down onto his knees. "So I know who is off limits."

"I believe Emma has already outlined her parameters."

Kader smirked. "Of course. She always was exceedingly efficient. My apologies, amplifier. While in your home, I will attempt to keep my insinuations—regarding those you care about—to myself."

Aiden stepped back to the edge of the pentagram, carefully keeping out of my direct path to his father. "There is definitely a smudge, a wound, in your magic. Over your heart. Ironically."

"Yes." Kader's tone was icy, clipped.

It must have been painful to suddenly need to take orders from your creations. I smiled, loosening my grip on my blade.

Paisley paced the outer edge of the pentagram, occasionally flicking one or more of her tentacles against it. Each time, she would pause to peer at Kader, as if trying to see what Aiden saw.

The dark-haired sorcerer muttered a few more words, and the power in the pentagram shifted, coalescing in a light-blue cloud over Kader's chest. Aiden muttered another arcane word—a question this time, by its tenor. A thick rope of magic appeared, resolving into the links of a hazy chain. The chain cut off at the edge of the pentagram. To my sight, at least.

Aiden's expression was inscrutable. He uttered three more commands, power shifting and churning in the pentagram with each word.

Kader was smiling to himself. The expression was knowing, smug.

Aiden hissed quietly, then looked at me. He ran his hand through his hair.

Then I realized that the cloud of magic over Kader's chest was light blue, as was the hazy, thick-linked chain.

Not the deeper blue of Aiden's sorcerer power.

Not the dark, almost black hue of Kader's power.

The light blue of witch magic.

Aiden pulled a short steel blade from his back pocket—a blade I was certain hadn't been there a moment before. It was the same blade I'd seen him use when mentally trapped by the mystic, or very similar at least. Though the rune along the edge of the bolster was newly inscribed.

"Really?" Kader huffed disdainfully.

Ignoring his father, Aiden sliced the blade across his forearm, just enough to draw blood. He tucked the blade into his back pocket, where it somehow managed to not slice through his jeans. Like everything the sorcerer wielded or wrought, it had clearly been honed with magic.

Aiden pressed the forefinger and middle finger of his right hand in the wound, coating them lightly in blood. Then he leaned down and transferred the blood into the carved center of one of the small pentagrams, where the obsidian stone had been embedded.

He moved to the next outer pentagram, repeating the blood transfer. Adding the power residing in his blood to the power he could manipulate within the main pentagram. Then on to the next.

"A personalized rune would be cleaner," Kader said. "Blood is so…sloppy. Lazy."

"You're very chatty for a dead man," I said.

Kader raised his chin, smirking. Again. "I am dying. A dying father. Shouldn't I see that my wisdom is passed on to the next generation? To my most favored son?"

"Favored?" I scoffed. "Before you set him up to usurp Isa, you mean?"

Kader's smile sharpened. "Is that what Aiden told you?"

"No." It was my turn to be smug. "Isa."

His face blanked.

So that was an Azar trait.

"Didn't mention it, did he?" I said.

The elder sorcerer transferred his attention back to his son, not bothering to answer me.

Aiden straightened from the last of the outside pentagrams. Once again raising his palms toward the power simmering in the magically sealed, copper-inlaid main pentagram. Blood slowly dripped from the shallow cut on his forearm.

"Wasteful." Kader sniffed. "And risky. In the wrong hands." His gaze slid to me.

I smiled. "I don't need blood to bring you to your knees, Kader Azar."

Kader's tone warmed. "I'm already bowed at your feet, amplifier."

Aiden ignored us, muttering commands that sent waves of churning magic throughout the large and the smaller pentagrams alike. Their copper edges glowed with power.

Kader flexed his fingers, then rolled his shoulders and neck. Not in pain, but as if he was actively trying to accept the touch of his son's magic. To not fight or negate it.

Aiden stepped back, arms falling loose at his sides and his gaze on the ground. His voice was thick with emotion. "I can't break it. Not without...some more time." He lifted his gaze to me, his expression unreadable.

So I closed the space between us, touching his arm to trigger my empathy. "Heal this, please."

He shook his head as if just realizing that he was still bleeding. An arcane word closed the wound. Another word scoured the blood from his arm and from where it had dripped on his jeans and the white slat floor.

Under my light touch, his emotions were tangled and confused.

"I'll take Kader," he said quietly, though his voice was still rough, "back to his compound. I'll deal with...this ..." He shrugged one shoulder toward his father, blazing blue eyes locked to mine. "I'll take care of it there. Away from you, from the...property."

From Christopher and Opal, he meant.

"No," I said. "You'll deal with it here. You can get any books or tools you need sent to you."

Relief flooded through our empathic connection, and Aiden nodded.

"Delightful," Kader said, straightening to stand. He stepped from the pentagram, again easily passing through Aiden's magic. The boundary didn't dissipate. It didn't even flicker. "If you don't mind, I'd like to nap before dinner."

"The sheets on the bed in the loft suite were just changed," I said. It was definitely clear now that Christopher had glimpsed someone staying in the loft, hence his making the bed before he'd left. But I had no idea if Kader was also the threat the clairvoyant had seen when he'd texted earlier about me needing my blades. "There are fresh towels in the bathroom. Dinner will be at seven."

"Your hospitality is most appreciated." Kader stepped toward the door to the suite, retrieving the satchel he'd already set there. As if he'd known he'd be staying.

He stepped inside. The door shut behind him, and magic flared behind it. Wards, I presumed. Erected without any preparation or runes to anchor them.

Aiden's shoulders slumped. He snapped his fingers and the magic of the pentagram dissolved. "I'm sorry," he whispered. "I'm so, so sorry."

"No," I said fiercely. "You don't say that to me. You think that I wouldn't agree to help protect your family?"

"Of course not." He scrubbed his hand across his face, then said it again. "Of course not, but—"

"There is no 'but' between us, Aiden Myers." Myers. Not Azar. Reminding him who he was, who he had chosen to be.

A slow smile curled across his face. It didn't quite meet his eyes, but it was almost there. "Well," he drawled, "there could be a butt between us. I'm always open to suggestions. Though I do adore looking you in the eyes."

I laughed huskily, surprising myself.

Aiden leaned in to kiss me.

I tilted my head back in anticipation, then paused.

Paisley was sitting practically between our feet, gazing up at us. She dropped her mouth open in a sharp-toothed smile when I noticed her.

I sighed. "Isn't it time for you to get back to helping Christopher and Samantha?"

Paisley poked Aiden in the thigh with her bovine bone, waving the dirt-smudged book over her head again.

Aiden chuckled. "Next time, you could just leave the book in the study."

Paisley shifted her gaze to me and huffed.

"I'm not stopping you from reading," I said neutrally—even though the idea of the demon dog actually trying to manipulate magic beyond her own inherent powers was disconcerting.

I really adored my home. I really didn't want to see it destroyed.

Paisley shouldered her way between us, heading down the interior steps and clearly expecting us to follow her.

"The spell she wants?" I asked Aiden quietly.

"Tracking," he said. "I'm guessing she wants to test it with the egg."

"She's having trouble homing in on Bee," I whispered.

"Seems so. Though I didn't pick up even a moment of hesitation in all the tests we ran with you, Christopher, and Samantha."

"She's only met Bee once. As a puppy ..." I trailed off, recalling Kader's loaded comment regarding Paisley including Aiden in her programming.

Aiden brushed his fingers against the back of my hand, questioningly.

I shook my head. "We don't actually know how Paisley is tied to the Five. Samantha still hasn't found a powerful enough tech to unscramble all the data she collected when we took down the compound."

"The Collective," Aiden spat, glaring at the loft door.

"Yes, one part of the Collective. But it wasn't Silver or Chenda or even your father who oversaw the division that bred Paisley. We know that much."

Aiden grimaced. Then he looked thoughtful, lowering his voice as if he was worried about being overheard. "The Five ..." he said. "Do you think Daniel ...?"

He let the question trail off, but I understood what he was asking. I knew someone—intimately—who could nullify just about any sort of magic. Perhaps even the spell that was killing Kader Azar. There weren't many spells that Fish couldn't nullify, especially when amplified by me. But I shook my head.

"I had the same thought when I first saw your father," I said. "But Daniel would try to kill Kader the moment he saw him." As well, I wasn't putting Aiden's fate in anyone else's hands. I didn't add that out loud, though. I just sighed as I said, "I'd better text an update to Christopher."

Aiden snorted, quietly amused.

"What?"

He shook his head. "Just that you're more dismayed by the idea of communicating with your blood-bound brother via text than you are by having your sworn enemy sleeping in your loft."

"I have no sworn enemies," I said archly. "The very idea is beneath me. But if I did, keeping them near would just make them easier to deal with."

Aiden's expression sobered. "And easier to protect me."

I didn't answer. He was right, of course. I didn't want him to have to spend a moment alone with his father.

The dark-haired sorcerer brushed a kiss against my cheek. "What did I ever do to deserve you?"

I twined my fingers through his. "You found me. Me, Emma." My throat closed up so much that I couldn't finish the thought, couldn't fully express the idea that I'd only truly started figuring out who Emma Johnson was after making the choice to let Aiden, and then Opal, into my life.

"Yes," Aiden breathed, as if he perfectly understood me.

A terrible howl rose from below, prickling up my spine and undulating through the open rafters of the barn.

"Really?" I cried down the stairs. "We're not at your beck and call, Paisley!"

Aiden moved toward the stairs, tugging me with him. Together, we descended to collect the mouthy demon dog.

"Two days of freedom. That's all we get."

Aiden chuckled. "Would you really have it any other way?"

I grinned at him. "I do get a bit stabby when bored."

"You're always stabby, Emma. Delightfully so."

I snorted.

THREE

AIDEN WAS BURIED IN BOOKS IN THE STUDY. LIT-
erally. The pile on the side of the desk nearly blocked
my view of him from the hallway door. I could see his
fingers, though, covered in the same ink soaking into
the pages of his notebook in tiny puddles.

Paisley was situated in a chalked circle in the
center of the wood-paneled room. Opal often practiced spell work in the same position, with Aiden
close enough to rescue her but not focused solely,
intimidatingly, on her.

The tracking spell the demon dog had found in
her spellbook required a personal item of the person
she wished to track—namely Bee. But since we didn't
have anything for her to use, Aiden had persuaded
her to try a sense-enhancement spell instead. Paisley
had been practicing for the last hour.

After texting an update to Christopher with no
immediate response, I had come down to water the
lemon, lime, and avocado plants that resided in the

window seat. But there really wasn't much room for me in the small study. Nor could I contribute much to the spell work or research being conducted. So I wandered into the kitchen to mix up a new batch of ginger snap dough, to freeze and slice as needed.

A casserole that I'd put into the fridge to defrost earlier that morning would do for dinner. Aiden could steam some asparagus or make a salad to go alongside it. Christopher had prepped a half-dozen meals before he left, each enough to last us for a couple of days. Apparently, the clairvoyant thought we were incapable of feeding ourselves. Or, as with the made-up bed in the loft, he'd seen the need for us to have extra food on hand—though clearly without actually seeing that our guest was going to be one of our makers. If he had seen that, Christopher never would have agreed to meet with Samantha in Europe.

I was rolling the last log of cookie dough when magic shivered up my spine, dissipating as swiftly as it hit. Then a second and third shiver followed.

Aiden swore robustly from the study.

It wasn't just a single impatient Adept waiting at the driveway gate, but three separate points of power. Sorcerer magic, as far as I could assess. And my heightened sensitivity to the outer property wards was a little disconcerting.

For the first time, I wondered if it was possible I was absorbing power from Aiden without realizing it. I had never had a long-term partner other than Daniel, and we hadn't had sex as regularly as Aiden and I did. Samantha and Daniel had always sneered at my 'stolen juice,' but the other powers I'd absorbed while under the control of the Collective had all been deliberately and aggressively taken. If I was stealing magic from Aiden, it was a much subtler process—and was likely offset by the fact that I perpetually amplified him in turn.

The dark-haired sorcerer appeared at the arched doorway to the hall. His eyes were a little wide. Stressed. I shoved away the thoughts of what I might be slowly stealing from him, and finished sealing two of the rolls of dough in plastic wrap. I left the third roll on the cutting board to slice and bake.

Apparently, we were about to have additional visitors.

Aiden grimaced, scrubbing his hand across his face. "More Azars," he said.

"Isa?"

He nodded.

"And the other two?"

He tilted his head. "You felt that?"

"I did." I washed my hands, drying them as Aiden calmly watched me. I adored it when he homed in on me. His shoulders relaxed, hands now loose at his sides instead of curled into fists.

"Best guess, another brother…or two. Plus someone I don't know well."

I crossed toward him. "Shall I bring my blades?"

"The second retrieval spell should still be active, so one of them is only a thought away."

I nodded, then moved for the front door.

"Unless you…want to kill Isa? Right off, I mean."

I paused in the hall, gazing back at Aiden and taking a moment to consider his question seriously. Did Isa Azar deserve to die? Was I the person to judge him?

No. Though I had plenty of reasons to kill Isa after what he'd done to Jenny, Opal, and Paisley, I wasn't the law. "If he attacks me. Or you," I said.

"He's more likely here to kill our father."

"Really?"

Aiden nodded stiffly, frowning as he stepped close to me. "Why else would he risk coming back? And in force?"

"Isa knows that it would take more than three sorcerers to overpower me and you. And he has no idea that Christopher isn't here."

"We hope," Aiden muttered.

"You think he's compromised someone in town? To keep watch on us?"

"I wouldn't put it past him. And whoever he hired wouldn't necessarily think there was anything nefarious about him keeping tabs on his wayward brother."

I grinned. "Because that's what you would do, my dark and deadly sorcerer?"

Aiden laughed. "I currently have a network of thirteen…no, fifteen operatives sending info my way every week regarding various people. Including one at the Academy with Opal."

I blinked, then laughed.

"I just wish I had eyes on the main Azar compound," he said ruefully. "I never managed to find anyone willing to risk it."

"Your father is formidable."

Aiden raised both eyebrows suggestively. "I've met more powerful individuals."

I leaned into him. "Really? We have three sorcerers at the gate, and one in the barn loft, and you think this is an appropriate moment for flirting?"

Aiden stepped into me, hands slipping into my hair. The next moment, my back was against the wall and his lips were crashing over mine. All the frustration and confusion he'd been battling since he'd opened his father's letter was superseded by a hungry welling of desire. I parted my lips, flicking my tongue against his, melting into his tight hold.

Yes, for Aiden I could soften, yield. Eagerly.

He broke the kiss, pressing his forehead to mine and breathing heavily.

I mewed in disappointment, drawing a half-smile, half-growl from him.

"Later," he said.

"Promise?"

"Everything that comes out of my mouth is a promise to you, Emma."

I cupped his face with one hand, running my other fingers through his hair. "I was teasing, Aiden. I know. Having your father here doesn't change anything."

He grimaced.

My chest tightened for a moment. I released it by pushing forward. "Am I wrong?"

"No. Never. It doesn't change anything between us." He pulled away, just a step, but was already looking toward the front door and beyond, where a trio of sorcerers awaited us.

"But you think it changes you?"

He cleared his throat, then shook his head at whatever he was going to say. "No, just…I'm off balance. And I'd gotten used to …" He gestured with both hands, indicating the house and everything it encompassed—or so I presumed. "I had begun to believe …"

"Believe what?"

He shrugged, shoving his hands in his pockets. "Just…that I…that I could have this …" He lifted his bright-blue eyes to meet my gaze. "That I could have you."

I pressed my hands back against the wall, wishing that Aiden was still pinning me against it, wishing that we were still in that moment. Words, expressions of self, were just so difficult. Both to articulate and to comprehend.

So instead of addressing the doubt and confusion that I thought might underpin Aiden's confession, I went on the attack. I was always better on the offensive, more confident.

"I'm not letting you go, sorcerer."

Aiden blinked.

I barreled forward. "You think you have a choice, but you already made your decision. I'm keeping you. You belong to me now. To Opal. And Paisley. We're the ones who love you. Whether or not I deserve you, deserve this life. I …" My voice cracked. "I…I'm taking it, making it. And you…I won't let you go. I'd hunt you to the ends of the earth if you tried."

Aiden cleared his throat. His eyes were wet. He inhaled, then exhaled. "Okay. Okay. Yes."

"Okay. Good." Shoving down the emotion threatening to suffocate me, I turned away abruptly, prowling down the hall toward the front door. "Let's go deal with your brother, then. I have cookies to bake."

Paisley joined us in the hall from the study, falling in at my side. Her spellbook, bone, and mane were tucked away under her regular pit bull aspect. I opened the door without pausing, but Aiden caught my wrist as I stepped out onto the front patio.

He stepped around me, forcing me to meet his fierce gaze. Then he deliberately reached up and wrapped his hand around my throat, holding me gently—and mimicking the first time he'd ever touched me.

The moment stretched between us, a myriad of emotions flickering through the empathic connection I made by skin-to-skin contact. A connection Aiden didn't share. The only way he ever knew what I was truly thinking, or feeling, was when I told him. That was entirely unfair.

Playing along, I reached up and brushed my fingers across his lips, giving him a kiss of magic with the touch. Just as I'd done at the diner. Then, it had overloaded his senses. Now…now it was…love.

"Feeling possessive, sorcerer?" I asked playfully.

"You'd better fucking believe it," he growled, tightening his grip, then lightly brushing his thumb against the sensitive skin of my neck. "I battled through hell to find you, Emma. And I didn't even know…I never even believed that I could find you. That you and…this…were even possible. For me. I'm not going anywhere. Throw me out, toss me away, and I'll keep coming back."

I swallowed a sharp spike of emotion in my throat—an odd manifestation of extreme happiness, I thought. "That's settled, then. We're both completely trapped."

He grinned. The expression was edged with that same fierce possession that still fired his magic. "And utterly free to be who we want to be. With each other." He loosened his hold on my neck, stepping back as if giving me a moment to reconsider, to think.

But I just held his gaze. Agreeably—and utterly truthfully—I said, "Yes."

Aiden held out his hand.

I took it.

And together, for the second time that day, we crossed toward the front gate. We kept to the grass in deference to our bare feet, our pace unhurried. Paisley prowled along on my left.

Three figures stood beyond the gate at the top of the drive, near the farm stand, but not tucked into the shade as Kader had been. All three were wearing dark suits. Two of the sorcerers were dark haired with deeply tanned skin. The other was broad shouldered and dark-skinned, with short-clipped hair. All looked shorter than Aiden.

Isa Azar, standing at the far left, waved off a taxi that he must have kept waiting in case there was no one home. But unless they'd been on their way or already nearby, it seemed unlikely that they'd travelled to Lake Cowichan by conventional means. I already knew that Isa was capable of teleporting.

"There are a lot of declarations going on today," I said conversationally. "Between us."

Aiden nodded. "Circumstances, perhaps. Our first time really being alone with each other, plus the need to confirm things."

"Because everything else feels a bit shaky?"

"For you as well?"

I nodded. "I'm … navigating my impulses around your father, factoring in your needs …" I shrugged. "I rarely take other people's feelings into account."

"That's not true at all, Emma." Aiden tightened his hold on my hand.

"I'm not saying I'm a sociopath. Well…I'm unlearning my training, just not particularly quickly …"

"Emma."

"No, Aiden. I'm not being down on myself. I'm just trying to say that I'm a little off kilter with your father. Not because of me. Or him. But because I love you." I glanced at him.

He kept his attention on the trio waiting for us at the gate. "I loathe him. I would never question your judgement."

"Because normally I'm rational."

He nodded.

"I'm not feeling so rational right now."

"Okay." He looked at me. "Okay."

"And, Aiden…you don't hate him as much as you wish you did."

The sorcerer's jaw clenched. "Yeah. I know. But I'm just going to keep denying that. Because the person I want to be, for you, and Opal, and Paisley, and all the other people who belong to us, should hate him. Okay?"

I wasn't sure what that said about me. I also didn't hate Kader Azar. But for a long time, I hadn't thought myself capable of loving anyone who hadn't been forced upon me with a blood bond, so maybe hate was an emotion born from a similar place. "Okay."

Isa Azar and the two other sorcerers watched us as we approached. Aiden's eldest brother was frowning slightly, his gaze flicking between Paisley, Aiden, me—and our entwined hands.

The taller, dark-haired male in the center of the trio stood with his hands shoved in the pockets of his pants, rucking up his navy suit jacket at the sides. His expression was carefully blank, his hair long enough to fall over his brow and curl slightly at his collar. He was in his mid-thirties.

"Khalid," Aiden said quietly, pronouncing it KHA-leed. "Younger to Isa, elder to me. His mother was a sorcerer as well, but she let Kader raise him and set up his training. They had some arrangement."

The third male was grinning at Aiden. He was shorter but broader through the shoulders than Isa and Khalid. His hair and skin were almost as dark as Samantha's. Light-brown eyes. Dark-gray suit. No tie. In his early twenties.

"Grosvenor," Aiden murmured. "Cousin to all of us."

"The curse breaker?" Kader had mentioned him already. So presumably whatever reason the trio had for showing up here, it wasn't to kill the patriarch of the Azar cabal. "What kind of name is 'Grove-ner' anyway?" I asked, pronouncing it as Aiden had.

"Very English. Spelled 'Gros-ven-or,' " Aiden articulated, clarifying. "We call him 'Grover.' "

We paused at the fence, still on the grass, forcing the three to step over to us. Paisley placed her paws on the top rail, surveyed the sorcerers, then huffed dismissively.

Aiden laughed.

Paisley looked over at the dark-haired sorcerer, chuffing. He reached behind me, patting her soundly on the shoulder. She grunted appreciatively, then wandered off to the west, patrolling the fence line.

"Is he still alive?" Isa asked, practically biting off each word. He clearly wasn't going to bother with the stilted, formal introductions he'd insisted on the first time we met.

Aiden tilted his head, as if deciding whether or not he was actually going to acknowledge his elder brother. Then he bared his teeth in a nasty smile. "You think I'm capable of killing him?"

Isa's dark-eyed gaze shifted, eyeing me through the simmering barrier of magic that I could feel cutting between us.

The other two sorcerers followed Isa's gaze, frowning, confused. At a guess, Isa hadn't explained where he was bringing them. Or who I was.

I let them look.

Isa shook his head, grimacing ruefully.

Aiden laughed joylessly. "Emma hasn't murdered our father, Isa."

I bared my teeth, smiling. "Yet."

Khalid's frown deepened, glancing between Isa and Aiden as if he could uncover the truth of the assertion—of what I was capable of doing—from them, rather than me.

Inexplicably, a wide smile spread across Grosvenor's face. "Really? Excellent." Unlike Isa's cultured, smooth tone, his accent was so specifically British that even I recognized it. But then, I did watch a lot of *Downton Abbey.*

Isa shot him a look. "Don't be an idiot, Grover."

"No," Khalid said, his tone clipped but overlaid with a French blur. Just like the late Ruwa. "We'll leave that to you, Isa."

The Azar cabal schooled their children differently, presumably according to skill set. Aiden and Isa were proficient in runes, like Kader. And as far as I could tell, they'd been trained by their father. But perhaps Khalid's skills were less prized by the sorcerer Azar? I found myself wondering if he'd been sent away to be raised with whoever had trained Ruwa.

Isa clenched his teeth. "I'm not the one who cursed him! And I'm not the one who then misplaced him!"

Khalid sneered at Isa, just tall enough that he could look down on his elder brother. Then he turned his attention to Aiden. "Grant us safe passage. If Father is going to die, he'll do it on his own land and buried with full rites."

"No matter where he dies," Isa spat, "his power isn't going to transfer to you."

A muscle in Khalid's jaw twitched.

I glanced at Aiden. He looked utterly bored.

"The power of an elder sorcerer transfers to a successor when they die?" I asked.

"It does when you're Kader Azar," Aiden said drily. "And you want your children fighting among themselves, rather than trying to usurp you." He glanced at me. "It's bunk. Propaganda."

"But it will still be one hell of a party," Grosvenor said, still grinning.

Isa closed his eyes, muttering, "If I have to spend one more moment with Grover...I'm going to kill him."

"Get in line," Khalid said.

Grosvenor leaned forward onto his toes, grinning at me. "Don't worry. I'm hard to kill." Then he winked.

"So am I," I said.

Isa muttered something under his breath—what sounded like a curse in that arcane language of the Azar sorcerers. Whatever he said wiped the smile from Grosvenor's face. The young sorcerer frowned, glancing disconcertedly between Aiden and me.

"Is that a curse or a benediction, Isa?" Aiden asked, his tone neutral. Though his hand had tightened on mine.

Isa eyed me, then shook his head, speaking to me. "Why stand between us? Falling back on your programming?"

Before I could remind the pretentious sorcerer exactly what my programming had entailed, Aiden's magic shifted. He released my hands, clenching both fists. The other sorcerers each took two deliberate steps away from Isa, clearly indicating that although they'd followed him here, they didn't stand with him.

I always appreciated it when battle lines were clearly drawn. I gifted the two with a smile. They didn't reciprocate.

Isa stuffed his hands in his pockets, tilting his head. "Do you think if you amplify him, he'll be able to break the curse?"

Grosvenor sighed heavily. "I've told you over and over, it's not a curse. I break curses. I've broken every curse I've ever—"

Isa held up his hand, cutting the curse breaker off. "Emma?" he prompted. "What is your assessment?"

He was truly interested. Weighing his options, I presumed. Trying to figure out if I was loyal to his father, and whether or not he'd have to go through me to get to Kader. If he did, it would be the second attempt he'd made on his father's life. I could understand him wanting to survive it.

A power grab. Assuming that Aiden was wrong, and that Kader's assertion that his power would transfer to a successor upon his death wasn't a lie.

The situation was about to get even more messy, more convoluted than it already was. The anticipation that had waned as I watched Aiden interact with his father started bubbling in my stomach again. I really was a creature born and bred to fight, and few opportunities presented themselves as nicely as the sorcerers were currently doing.

I glanced at Aiden.

He tilted his head toward me, not taking his gaze off Isa.

"Do I have your go-ahead to kill them?" I said. "All of them?"

Aiden cast a dispassionate gaze across the three sorcerers on the other side of the property ward. "Yes."

Khalid flinched, but quickly covered his reaction. Grosvenor's jaw dropped.

I looked at Isa.

He smiled at me grimly.

"It's almost time for dinner," I said, already knowing that I was traversing some version of the future Christopher had gotten a glimpse of—as evidenced by the prepared meals and the extra beds.

Isa nodded, once. "So it is."

"Christopher made a Dungeness crab casserole. You can make the salad."

"I make a great dressing. Do you have a lime?"

"Usually."

"I'd be delighted."

The wards opened around the front gate. Isa stepped off the grass onto the gravel drive, reaching for the latch. Khalid trailed behind his elder brother, looking confused.

"What the fuck?" Grosvenor exclaimed. "She just asked for permission to kill us!"

Aiden laughed darkly. "That wasn't permission, Grover. Just clarification."

Paisley appeared at the gate, blocking Isa's forward progress. Khalid flinched. Grosvenor scrambled to catch up to the other two, latching the gate behind him.

Isa looked Paisley in the eye. "It was just business, you understand. A difficult partnership. I never meant to hurt...anyone ..." He cleared his throat, glancing at me, then back at Paisley. "Not here, anyway."

The demon dog huffed.

"Those under your protection have nothing to fear from me." Isa held his hands out, palms forward.

Paisley opened her mouth. It was suddenly far too wide for her pit bull face, flashing spiked teeth at the sorcerer. Then she chomped the air only a couple of centimeters away from Isa's hand. He would have felt her hot breath. Even some spittle.

Khalid muttered in that language the Azars used, and magic shifted around him. I assumed he was only calling forth a shield, by the way Aiden remained impassive at my side.

Isa, to his credit, barely flinched.

Paisley chuckled darkly. Then, swishing her suddenly long tail like a cat, she turned her back on the sorcerers, dismissing them completely as she wandered back to the house.

"What the bloody hell?" Grosvenor muttered.

I followed Paisley. But as the demon dog veered off toward the barn, I continued on to the main house. Aiden was at my side, our shoulders and fingers brushing as we walked. The sorcerers kept a few steps behind us.

"I thought you said she was an amplifier," Khalid whispered to Isa.

"I did. I just didn't elaborate on what that meant."

I glanced at Aiden.

He was smirking.

"Sorcerers and their secrets," I said.

"Indeed," Aiden said agreeably. "Always playing the advantage, hedging their bets."

I didn't play games. I just didn't enjoy doing so. Perhaps I was afraid of losing.

Aiden chuckled as if reading my mind. "I look forward to you utterly destroying their plots and machinations, my darling, just by refusing to play."

I traversed the steps to the front patio, my thoughts turning toward the sorcerer napping in the barn. And for the first time ever, I worried that Aiden might have been overestimating my abilities. I might already have been caught up in some plot of the elder Azar sorcerer. Just another player to be moved and used as he accumulated power.

What if Isa was right? What if there was something embedded deep inside me, by training or by conditioning? Did I have an instinctual need to protect the sorcerer Azar?

No.

The other members of the Collective would never have agreed to any such programming, not if it didn't also include them. And I had killed Silver Pine—twice—without a second thought. I could have killed Chenda the same way, if not for Christopher.

No. I was behaving like a normal person who cared for her lover, her friend. And that was good. That made me happy. Because that was the person I wanted to be—not what the Collective had bred me to be.

Turning slightly as I stepped over the threshold into the house, I brushed my fingers against the back of Aiden's hand. He met my gaze and smiled. Truly, joyfully.

"Yes," he murmured. "Completely. Utterly."

My chest warmed at his understanding. Perhaps the empathic connection didn't need to go both ways. Maybe I didn't even need to know the right words to say.

I crossed through to the kitchen, leaving Aiden waiting on his brothers and cousin.

"If it's that same old dressing you'll be making," Aiden drawled behind me, "it needs way more pepper, Isa."

Isa snorted in response. "Add pepper yourself, Aiden."

"I always do."

Leaving their barbed conversation behind, I crossed into the kitchen. The white tile was cool under my feet as I pulled the casserole out of the fridge and set it on the counter to warm while the oven came up to temperature. Then I went back to slicing cookie dough for baking a new batch of ginger snaps.

KHALID AND GROSVENOR QUICKLY HOLED UP IN THE study, undoubtedly pawing through Aiden's books and looking over the research he'd done after trying to break the spell on his father.

Isa made a salad with lettuce Aiden harvested from the garden, along with other ingredients excavated from the fridge—including apple, cucumber, and green onion. He then dug through the pantry, finding pistachios, which he shelled and chopped.

I worked alongside him, adding a leaf to the kitchen table, scouring the house for extra chairs, then setting the table. During the time that Opal had been with us, I'd added to my collection of stoneware, finding the same local potter who had crafted the first pieces and building a set of eight.

Isa and I didn't exchange a single word, though I felt the sorcerer's gaze on me multiple times.

Just before seven o'clock, I made a last-minute decision to try to make some garlic bread. Isa winced as I sliced the loaf unevenly, but I ignored him as I pulled garlic powder out of the cupboard and butter from the fridge. He then grimaced, pretty much shouldering me away from the cutting board to start mincing raw garlic himself. Then he whipped the butter by hand.

I ceded to the bossy sorcerer without comment, pulling the foil-wrapped casserole from the oven so we could broil the garlic bread.

Aiden, Khalid, and Grosvenor wandered into the kitchen. All three were reading from thick books as they walked, though the curse breaker tried to steal a ginger snap as he passed by the corner of the island. Isa viciously lashed out with the chef's knife. The young sorcerer dodged the blade, abandoning his attempted thievery.

Khalid settled in the chair at the foot of the table without ever looking up from the red-fabric-bound book he held. His hands were scarred. He'd kept them in his pockets before, so I hadn't seen the old wounds crisscrossing his fingers, puckering his darkly tanned skin all the way past his wrists.

I found myself wondering what the scars meant. There wasn't much that magic couldn't heal. Eventually. Though even I still bore the scars from being disemboweled by Silver Pine's greater demon.

Aiden set his book on the opposite corner of the island, pressing a kiss to my temple as he took the water pitcher from me and began filling up the glasses already set on the table.

I pulled the foil off the casserole. Grosvenor skirted the island, leaning over my shoulder and inhaling deeply.

"Wow! That smells amazing." He grabbed a potholder, lifting and carrying the steaming dish to the table and setting it at the center, on top of the two other potholders I'd placed there. Aiden stepped around me, refilling the water pitcher. The curse breaker stepped back for the salad bowl, set it on the table, then sat at Khalid's right, facing the open doors to the patio.

With nothing left to do, I followed Aiden to the table, taking the seat at the opposite end from Khalid. Isa grabbed the garlic bread from the oven and dumped it into a stoneware bowl. I'd commissioned three of different sizes, with the largest currently holding the salad. Then he joined us.

I found it odd that the previously squabbling sorcerers could settle in for a meal with each other so easily, so effortlessly. As if doing so was just an ordinary, everyday occurrence. Even though I now referred to Christopher as my brother, the Collective had made it very clear we weren't family while growing up, so I really didn't have any comparative experience.

Khalid put down his book. Aiden glanced at the clock over the oven. It read 7:02. He reached for my plate, serving me a generous scoop of the casserole—large shell pasta stuffed with a mixture of Dungeness crab, peas, and leeks in a creamy sauce, topped with a layer of breadcrumbs and garlic.

Two seats remained open.

Aiden set the plate in front of me, then served himself. Isa did the same from Khalid's left. Grosvenor grabbed a piece of garlic bread, quickly dropping it on his plate and shaking his singed fingers.

Isa snorted.

"Is Paisley joining us?" Aiden asked.

"I'm not sure." I glanced at the other three sorcerers, all of whom were filling their plates and pointedly ignoring us. "She's wandered off again." Gone to check in with Christopher and Samantha, I presumed, since I couldn't feel her magic on the property.

Kader Azar stepped up on the back patio. I hadn't felt him approach. I still couldn't pick up the full tenor of his magic.

Every sorcerer in the room went on alert. Shoulders stiffening, backs straightening. But no one stood, no one greeted the head of the Azar cabal. Kader crossed into the kitchen through the open

French-paned doors. He smiled at me, then Aiden, pulling out a chair to my right and sitting down.

Without speaking, Isa took his father's plate, serving him a scoop of casserole and a piece of garlic bread.

"Thank you," Kader murmured without otherwise acknowledging his eldest son. "The sun sets late in this part of the world."

No one answered him.

Inwardly cringing at the prospect that I was going to have to endure small talk, I simply said, "Yes. Sunset is still a couple of hours away."

Kader took a small bite of the casserole, chewed, swallowed, and smiled at me. "Delightful. Thank you for inviting me to your table, amplifier."

Isa frowned slightly.

All the other sorcerers started eating, as if Kader's approval of the food had given them leave to do so. Even Aiden. I wondered if the dark-haired sorcerer would even recognize the deference he was showing his father.

"I didn't make it," I said stiffly.

"No?" Kader glanced around, but no one else owned up to cooking dinner. "The crab is local, though. Yes?"

I nodded. "A friend of ours bought a small boat this spring. She sets traps." Lani Zachary had taken up crabbing and fishing, and supplied a bunch of us with her fresh catch since she lived alone.

The younger sorcerers cleared their plates, taking seconds, and then digging into the salad while Kader was still nibbling on his first small serving. Though they had been chatting fairly easily, mostly about Aiden's books and collected spells, prior to Kader entering the house, no one made any further attempt at conversation. That was fine by me.

Eventually, Kader pushed his still half-full plate slightly away from himself, and Grosvenor stood to begin clearing the table. When he'd worked his way around to Kader, he took hold of the elder sorcerer's wrist and paused.

Kader sighed heavily. "Nothing's changed."

"You didn't sleep enough," the curse breaker said mildly.

"I'm in a completely different time zone."

"We all are."

Kader twisted his wrist, and Grosvenor let go of him. The younger sorcerer crossed to rinse the plates in the sink, then began to load the dishwasher.

Khalid picked up the book he'd been reading.

The sorcerer Azar finally deigned to look at everyone, twisting slightly to level a glance at Isa on his far right. "Why are you here?"

"You dying isn't a strong enough motivation?"

"No matter what Grosvenor told you, I'm not in immediate peril."

"It was serious enough for you to pull him from school," Isa snapped. "And to come to Aiden, of all your sons, for help."

"Perhaps I'm simply visiting my youngest child and his lovely...partner."

Isa bared his teeth. "I'm surprised Emma even let you onto the property." He stood abruptly, stalking over to grab the kettle and fill it with water.

Kader swiveled to look at me, eyebrow raised. "And why is Isa allowed to refer to you by name?"

Paisley appeared beside the open dishwasher.

"Jesus bloody Christ!" Grosvenor shouted, jumping back and losing hold of a stoneware plate.

Paisley lunged, snapping at the sorcerer playfully while catching the plate in one of her tentacles, right before it hit the tiled floor.

"Holy mother of God," Grosvenor breathed, hands raised, fingers flexed as he readied some curse.

Paisley gave the plate a long lick, then set it within the dishwasher.

Inexplicably, Kader threw his head back and laughed—a full-bellied, deeply amused chuckle.

Mouths agape, we all stared at him.

Paisley chortled as she lumbered over to the table, situating herself between the elder sorcerer and me. Tentacles tucked away, no hint of red in her eyes. She looked at Kader, then looked pointedly at the almost-empty casserole dish at the center of the table.

She tilted her head, blinked slowly, and displayed her teeth.

Kader, still chuckling, reached over, retrieved the dish, and held it out for the demon dog. Two tentacles flicked out from her otherwise invisible mane, one taking the casserole, and the other caressing the exposed skin of Kader's wrist.

The elder sorcerer, still grinning, murmured something that sounded like an endearment in that arcane language the Azars used.

Paisley took the casserole and headed back into the kitchen.

Isa, Khalid, and Grosvenor were staring at Kader as if they'd never seen him before. Aiden's expression was purposefully blank.

"Delightful creature," Kader said, smiling at me.

"All the better to eat you," I murmured, reflecting on Paisley caressing Kader as if tasting his magic. As if acting endearing was a new hunting technique she was trying out.

"That's a wolf," Kader corrected, his tone stiff.

"What's a wolf?" I asked.

"The fairy tale you were quoting."

"What fairy tale?" My tone was suddenly smooth, like velvet darkness. "And when do you imagine I had the opportunity to read a fairy tale while growing up under your care?"

Tension ran through Kader's jaw, but was gone as quickly as I'd spotted it. "I made you powerful. A tsunami—"

Isa stepped away from where he'd been preparing the tea tray, the kettle still coming to a boil on the stove. Khalid set his book aside. Grosvenor slowly closed the dishwasher with his foot, keeping his hands free.

Aiden just regarded his father steadily.

"A force of utter destruction," I said coolly. "Of utter annihilation."

"Peace can be achieved only after the chaos ensues, amplifier." The elder sorcerer matched my cool tone. "Change is the only constant."

My magic was leaking, loosened in anger and quickly fed with a sharp need for vengeance. A need that had been present, just under the surface, ever since Kader arrived.

No.

Ever since Isa had delivered the letter to Aiden.

I didn't bother trying to pack my power away. I would let Kader Azar see what he'd created.

The elder sorcerer didn't drop my gaze. Not even a hint of fear flickered in his almost-black eyes.

"I could change your circumstances, sorcerer," I said in that same velvet tone. "Ease the magic consuming you from the inside, slowly, painfully killing you…with a brush of my fingers."

"As I well know. You forget, I've felt your gentle touch before." He paused, then smiled. "Both ways."

I had amplified Kader to get him up to the roof on his own feet in LA over eight years ago. I'd also absorbed a spell from him, amplified it and cast it, to clear our path to the helicopter, carrying him across my shoulders at the same time.

I slid my hand across the table. Deliberately. Slowly.

Kader's smile widened.

I wrapped my fingers around his wrist. His skin was warm and dry.

Khalid darted wary, questioning glances at Isa and then Aiden. But no one else moved.

"I don't think you have felt my touch," I purred. "Really, truly felt me. Not outside the context of being a mission, a package I was tasked to retrieve. You have no idea what it's like to face me. To fall before me. To be consumed by me." I leaned a bit closer, relishing every word dripping from my mouth. "And not one of your sons will step forward to save you, Kader Azar. You're gazing at your legacy right now. Shall I put you out of your misery?"

His smile widened, delighted. Intrigued. As if I hadn't just threatened him. As if I wasn't capable of murdering him with a mere touch. But before I let him goad me into proving him wrong, his gaze shifted to my left—from me to Aiden.

Right.

Aiden.

"Don't let me interrupt," the dark-haired sorcerer said with a flash of white teeth. He was leaning back in his chair, tone low and unaffected. But I knew that if I touched him, I would feel all the same frustrated and confused emotions churning under that facade. A facade he hadn't needed to erect in months, brought forth by his father's appearance.

I loosened my grip on Kader. "Killing you would be too easy."

The elder sorcerer nodded. "For both of us." Then he glanced around. "Dessert?"

No one responded, each of us watching Kader silently. Then Paisley jabbed Grosvenor in the back of the knee with the now-licked-cleaned casserole dish. The kettle began to whistle. Isa turned off the burner, then poured to fill the teapot.

Only Khalid kept his attention on his father, his scarred hands pressed flat on the table. I saw some sort of calculation behind that look as he glanced at me, then back to Kader.

Aiden shifted forward so he could rest his hand on my knee under the table. I pressed into the touch. Then the dark-haired sorcerer cleared his throat and spoke. "No matter what Kader has done to her, to all of us, I don't want my mother to be a murderer. I don't want her soul sullied."

Kader smirked.

Khalid shifted back in his chair. "Cerise Myers? A witch laid this curse?"

Grosvenor grumbled under his breath. "How many times do I have to say it?"

"This spell, then," Khalid snapped. "What the hell does what word I use matter?" He looked at his father. "Why haven't you just killed her? That would dispel any sort of ongoing working."

Aiden's grip on my knee tightened. "Try it, asshole."

Khalid waved a hand at his younger brother. "I'm asking why Father hasn't. I'm certainly not going to kill a coven witch myself."

"The fact that you have no idea why the proper word or term matters," Kader said smoothly, "is exactly why you won't progress any further in life, Khalid."

"You're a massive asshole," I said dispassionately. "For someone who needs his sons' help not to die."

"One son," Kader said smartly. "I requested help from one son."

"What the hell am I?" Grosvenor asked Kader, shutting the dishwasher again. He'd finished loading it, but had been forced to wait until Paisley inspected all the plates for remnants. "You snapped your fingers three weeks ago and I missed midterms. Then you just disappeared!"

"So you contact Isa and Khalid, crossing continents to chase after me?" Kader's tone was cool, dispassionate. But he curled his lip as he eyed Isa approaching the table with the tea tray. "You tagged the letter yourself. To let you know when Aiden opened it."

"Did you expect anything less?" Isa set the tray at the center of the table. The tea was steeping, mugs set around the teapot. A plate was piled high with ginger snaps. "Did you think I was just your dutiful messenger?"

Kader didn't answer.

"I couldn't figure out the why of it all. Until Grover told me that not only were you dying, you'd disappeared." Isa took his seat. "You thought Myers blood could break a Myers witch spell. And?" He looked at Aiden questioningly.

"Not on first attempt," the dark-haired sorcerer said.

Khalid grimaced, drawing his book closer but not opening it. Grosvenor leaned back against the island counter, head bowed thoughtfully.

Paisley trundled over to the table, butting my arm lightly with her head. I stood slightly, snagging two cookies from the plate. I passed one cookie to Aiden and the other to Paisley.

The demon dog took my offering gently—but managed to make a show of her double row of sharp teeth at the same time.

Aiden shifted in his seat, holding the cookie. "I hesitate to suggest it …"

Isa was already shaking his head. "Our power is too discordant."

"For a mutual casting?" Khalid asked.

"What if you were all amplified by me?" I asked. "Bound by my magic? Grounded by…by the copper of the pentagram?" I looked to Aiden for clarification. That level of spellcasting was way, way beyond my own expertise.

Khalid's mouth dropped open. "All of us…at the same time?" His voice was hushed.

Isa snorted. "And just like that, she's got a new devotee. It must be so difficult, amplifier, to keep them all from dragging you down. Draining you."

"Not at all, Isa," I said. "I take more than I give. As you well know."

Kader looked at Isa with interest—possibly for the first time since the conversation had begun. "Tangled with Amp5, have you? That must have been—"

MEGHAN CIANA DOIDGE

Aiden slammed his hand down on the table, causing the tea to slosh from the pot. "That's enough!"

Even I flinched.

"I won't have it," Aiden snarled, glancing between Kader and Isa. "Not in my home, Emma's home. You will be civil, or I'll drain you myself."

Isa raised his hands in a placating gesture. "My apologies. It's a difficult memory to shake."

Kader smirked. "I imagine."

Aiden thrust a finger at his father. "You will leave in the morning."

That wiped the smile from Kader's face.

"The four of us will spend the evening researching your...predicament," Aiden continued, heated. "But you will leave whether or not we've found a solution."

"And then what should I do?" Kader asked coolly. "Wait to die? Prepare my death curse?"

Aiden ignored the threat, but he moderated his tone. "We four will continue to research—"

"We need a Myers witch," Grosvenor interrupted.

"We have a Myers," Isa snapped.

The curse breaker shook his head. Then he looked at me as if trying to get me on his side. Or maybe he thought I could read his mind.

I couldn't. But I realized what he was asking.

"You need multiple Myers witches," I murmured. "Including Cerise."

"Yes," the young curse breaker said. "Sky Myers, Aiden's sister, attends school with me."

Feeling an unaccustomed level of trepidation, I reflected for a moment on the glimpse of the future Christopher had seen. A future that required extra beds and food and eventually me reaching for my blades. Did I want to invite that level of sure-to-be chaos into my life? Into Aiden's life? When we were both already feeling so off-balance?

Did I have another choice?

No.

Not if I wanted to thwart Kader Azar's death curse.

I glanced at the elder sorcerer. "You'd have to be willing to make concessions."

He waved his hand offishly. "Anything."

"Emma?" Aiden asked. Though we weren't touching, I could feel his uncertainty. I didn't, however, want to let him, or any of the sorcerers, see that I shared it.

I kept my gaze on Kader. "And to offer safe passage. In writing."

Kader shrugged, smiling. "Of course."

"This is exactly what you planned," I said. It wasn't a question.

"I had hoped that my son could take care of it."

"I can," Aiden snapped. Then he softened his tone. "Given time."

"Time I no longer have," Kader said. "As a result of how long it took for you to open my letter."

Aiden leaned across the table. "You're a fucking prick who deserves to die."

"That may well be," Kader said smoothly. "But I'll take all of you with me. Maybe even the amplifier. Depending on how much I contributed to her genetic mix."

And there it was.

"Excuse me?" Isa snarled.

Aiden's power unfurled, licking outward across the table.

It was my turn to try to balance us. I just wasn't completely certain I was up to the task.

"Really?" I asked mockingly. "That's all you're going to claim? You might have contributed some genetics? And you think that should hold sway over me? Over Aiden? Why?"

"Well, bloody hell," Grosvenor muttered. "You might be siblings. At least that's what the old man seems to be implying."

"Please," I scoffed. "Look at me."

They all did. Even freckled from spending so much time in the sun, I was so much paler than the four of them that my skin appeared practically white. Green eyes. Dark-red hair. The shape of my face and nose was rounder, softer than the carved features of the Azars.

Aiden settled back in his seat, once again contained. Unruffled.

"Plus," I said, settling my gaze on Kader—completely unable to keep my mouth shut now that I'd opened it. Again. "You made certain none of us could breed. So what does it matter who we sleep with?"

"What?" Isa asked, outraged.

"Oh, that's the line for you, Isa?" Aiden smirked. "A step too far?"

"No," Isa snapped. "The messing with DNA was already too far. But depriving a sentient being of—"

"We're off topic," Kader said, his tone commanding and backed by a slight push of power. He cast his gaze over all of us, lingering on Aiden, then settling on me.

"I don't take orders from you, sorcerer," I said quietly.

He grimaced. "The boys don't play well together."

"When did you ever give us the chance?" Khalid snapped.

Kader sighed, ignoring his middle child and looking at me expectantly. I could feel Aiden's gaze on me as well.

If the situation was already this out of control, with all of us only moments away from attacking each other, then the decision I was making—the course of action I was about to suggest—was ridiculously idiotic.

I turned to Aiden.

He raked his gaze over my face. "You...think I should go to Paris? Appeal to my mother? Intervene?"

"Do you think he can follow through with his promise?" I asked for the second time. "The death curse?"

Aiden grimaced, looking to Isa.

His elder brother frowned deeply, thoughtfully. Then he shook his head slightly. "Not including Emma." He glanced at his father.

Kader was leaning back, head slightly bowed, smiling quietly. As if he was simply enjoying the moment.

Isa snorted. "The amplifier is too powerful, and…unless there is another bond I'm unaware of?"

He was alluding to the blood tattoos. Bindings embedded in my spine, in my nerves, and anchored in my magic. Bonds whose existence I'd alluded to in front of Isa before breaking out of the cage he'd held me in. Bonds that he might well have felt himself when Christopher arrived with Aiden in the demon dimension to rescue Opal, Jenni, Paisley, and me.

"There is no other bond." I glanced at Kader. "There's no other programming, magical or otherwise. It must have been a terrible concession, sorcerer, allowing us to think for ourselves."

"Yes," he drawled flatly. "A shame, but the fourth generation failed. You understand how they could be easily defeated if faced with any sort of situation that required problem solving. Or if they were suddenly cut off from the handler running the mission."

Aiden hissed.

Isa grimaced, but he spoke. "Then I doubt any death curse could touch Emma, not unless it was tied to her directly. But doing so wouldn't be dramatic enough for Kader Azar."

"Not enough of a threat," Khalid said. "To hold over us."

Isa settled back in his seat, fingers tapping on the table. Thoughtful, once again in control. "Grosvenor and that side of the family should be fine. But …"

"Aiden?" I prompted. "And he threatened the entire Myers coven earlier."

A muscle in Kader's jaw twitched. He didn't like being talked about as though he weren't in the room. Good to know.

Isa's eyes narrowed, like a predator seeing a weakness in its prey. I wondered if his expression was echoed on my own face. "He'd have to have access to Myers blood …" He looked at his younger brother.

I went cold. Completely and utterly cold. "And if I kill him now?"

"I'm already dead," Aiden said tonelessly. "He would have prepared the death curse, refined it, before he set foot on the property."

Everyone but me looked at Kader. All their expressions were hard, edged with disbelief.

I looked at Aiden. "I … I invited him in."

He shook his head. "The wards wouldn't have stopped him or a death curse." He looked at Isa for confirmation.

His elder brother's attention was riveted to his father, as if he was possibly contemplating killing him. And maybe murdering Aiden at the same time.

"Isa?" Aiden repeated. "He walked through the property boundary unhindered."

Isa flicked his gaze from his father to his young-est brother. "Agreed. Any ward constructed by you, he'd be able to pass through. He doesn't even need your blood. He can just use what runs in his own veins. Harness the energy released by his death."

"What if I kill him from far away with no no-tice?" I asked.

Isa shook his head. "Too risky."

"While this is a riveting conversation," Kader said, "you certainly don't need me here for it."

"I can't believe you'd kill your own flesh and blood," I said, not caring what weakness I was pot-entially revealing. "After everything you did to Cerise Myers to get Aiden."

"Everything I did," Kader scoffed.

"It's still rape, asshole," I said. "Even if you co-erced consent. Just ask Isa."

Isa blinked at me, surprised.

"Did you give me permission?" I asked.

Isa's jaw dropped—then he figured out what I was referring to. Our conversation about forced amplification in the diner months ago. He laughed darkly. "Well, I didn't know what you were capable of, did I?"

"Exactly." I glared at Kader. "But you need me to invite Cerise Myers here. You need me to guarantee her safety."

"You are a somewhat neutral party," he said smugly.

I felt the overwhelming urge to wring that smugness from every cell of Kader Azar's body. I would drain him until he wept for forgiveness, slowly, painfully. Until he was simply frozen in terror.

Grosvenor cursed under his breath, breaking into the moment. "So just to be clear, I never want Emma to look at me like that, right? Is that the look you see right before she murders you?" He looked at Aiden pointedly. "With permission from your cousin?"

"Yes," Aiden growled.

"Oh, yes," Isa said.

"You're still alive, sorcerer," I said evenly to Isa.

"You weren't actually trying to kill me."

"No, I wasn't."

Aiden touched my arm lightly. "I don't want your…our home involved any more than it is already."

"I know," I said. "But I won't have you in Paris, traveling with him. Without me." Because I knew I couldn't accompany Aiden. I had other responsibilities. To Opal. To Paisley.

Something I should have given a little more thought to before inviting Kader into our home. Though I was starting to think that the sorcerer would have figured out some way to force the issue, to push me to this decision, even though my presence had initially been a surprise.

"No one need die," Kader said. "Reach out to your mother, Aiden. I'm willing to negotiate. To make concessions. But she needs to be here. She needs to agree to meet, and to lift the spell before I sign anything. She can have anything in my power to give her."

"Even ten years of her life back?" Aiden asked caustically.

Kader beamed as though he'd been waiting for the chance to address exactly that point—the years he'd stolen from Cerise Myers. "I just happen to know someone who knows the most powerful telepath in the world." Slowly, deliberately, he shifted his gaze to me. "You'll want to negotiate with me as well, amplifier."

"You didn't know I was here. You didn't know I was with Aiden."

He shrugged. "I didn't. And I'll be taking that up with my eldest son after we get this little mess sorted. But that doesn't mean that I don't have people everywhere, and those people tell me that you've lost a teammate."

"I could torture her location out of you," I said casually. "You can't fling a death curse at anyone if I don't actually kill you."

"Of course you could. At least if I had the information you seek. But all I have are…whispers."

"This is ridiculous," Aiden muttered.

"Indeed. I am weary." Kader rose from the table, carefully setting his chair back in place. "Thank you for the lovely dinner, Emma."

His use of my name was deliberate.

I didn't react. At least not outwardly. But in my mind's eye, I grabbed the sorcerer Azar by the neck, slammed him to the table, and sucked every last drop of power from him.

And that gave me a thought.

I looked at Aiden. "What if I gave you all your father's power? Could we kill him then?"

Kader sighed heavily. Again. Then he turned and crossed out onto the patio and down the stairs, heading for the barn. Paisley slid past me, and I ran my fingers along her side and flank. Squeezing the end of her tail, now short again. "Caution, please."

She looked over her shoulder at me, huffed indignantly, then continued to prowl after Kader.

Grosvenor was glancing between us all. Khalid was outright staring at me. I was so going to start chafing at that weird reaction if he didn't knock it off. Or maybe I would just shock him out of it.

Aiden started laughing. His head fell back, shoulders slumping.

Isa chuckled darkly. "Draining him is too risky."

Aiden shook his head, but not in disagreement. "It would also ruin all your plans, Isa. Eight years in the making. The first attempt was thwarted by Emma as well, wasn't it?"

"Ten years," Isa spat ruefully. "It took two years to manipulate the rogue shifters into place."

Aiden snorted. Then he stood with a sigh, leaning over to press a kiss to my forehead. "Apparently I have a letter to write?"

I looked up at him, nodding. "We can always kill him afterward."

"We'll never know," Aiden said quietly. "If he's modified his death curse."

I smiled smugly. "Given enough time and the right people, we'll get around that. For example, if he doesn't know he's dying, there would be no reason to curse anyone."

Aiden grinned, understanding that I was alluding to using Bee to get to his father. "Diabolical, amplifier."

Then he straightened, heading toward the hall and the study beyond.

Isa poured the tea, dropping a teaspoon of sugar in a mug then sliding it across the table to me with a flick of his fingers and a flicker of magic.

I took the warm mug, inhaling the steam deeply. Chocolate mint. Lovely. And hopefully not too bitter, given how long it had oversteeped.

Isa poured himself a mug of tea as well. Grosvenor started tidying the kitchen.

"What the hell?" Khalid finally asked. "Is no one going to address her claim that she can give Father's power to Aiden?"

Isa ignored his middle brother, looking at me over the rim of his mug. "We've checked into the lodge. I assumed you wouldn't want us here. But you have open rooms? I suspect the witches will refuse to be housed anywhere you can't guarantee their safety."

"If they come," I said, ignoring a flicker of un-certainty about hosting the witches, day and night. I would do what I needed to do. As always.

"They'll come," Grosvenor said.

Isa smirked. "Been informing on Sky Myers, have you, Grover?"

"We all do things we find distasteful," the curse breaker said. "For family."

"Yes," Isa mused. "Family."

"You said she was an amplifier!" Khalid snarled.

Isa smiled nastily. "I did. And you refused to stay behind. Where I could protect you."

Khalid snarled again, lapsing into the sorcerers' shared language.

"English," Isa said snottily. "Anything else is just rude."

Bored by all the mind games seemingly being played around me, I stood. Taking a cookie, I wandered toward the study, seeking Aiden. Sipping my chocolate-mint tea, I ran over the dinner conversation in my head, hoping to find a loophole. Something that would let us work around Kader's death curse—and the need to involve the Myers witches.

Unfortunately, I wasn't that sort of clever.

THE FINAL WASH OF THE SUNSET WAS STILL LIN-gering in the sky as I left Aiden crafting the letter to his mother, and went to secure the chickens in the coop for the evening. Isa and Grosvenor were in the front sitting room. Isa sat staring broodingly out the front window, a thick leather-bound book open on his lap, and swirling a couple of fingers' worth of a dark amber liquid in a glass. Scotch, I presumed.

His gaze flicked to me as I paused briefly in the open doorway to the front hall. He raised the glass slightly with a twist of a smile, then stuck his nose in it, inhaled deeply, and took a tiny sip. The sorcerer must have brought the alcohol and the glass with him—or summoned both from some cache he maintained—because as far as I was aware, we didn't have either in the house.

The curse breaker was seated on the floor in front of the coffee table, leaning back against the love seat that backed the front window. At first glance, he appeared to be playing some sort of game that involved intricately etched wooden rectangular tiles, each about ten centimeters long. I didn't recognize the symbols set into the wood—some appeared to have been seared, others painted in primary colors. His scotch was set to one side on the table, poured over half-melted ice.

Grosvenor shifted a series of five tiles into a line, then swapped the first two for each other. He tilted his head, as if seeing something within or above the tiles.

"Grover is still building up his repertoire," Isa said, noting the direction of my gaze. "Manipulating the flow of his power. Thankfully, he's unlikely to kill us—or blow up the house—should he make a mistake."

The curse breaker snorted. "I don't blow things up. I simply unlock them."

"And the tiles?" I asked. Despite not wanting to get involved any deeper in their family dynamic, it made tactical sense to understand any magic being wielded in my home. "They're like the notches on a key?"

"The pattern of the bit?" Isa mused. "An apt analogy. I would expect nothing less from you, Emma."

Grosvenor took a small sip of his drink, then made another adjustment to the tiles arrayed on the coffee table in front of him. He slotted a sixth tile—what appeared to be a sun symbol, topped by a blue wave—into the center. "Are you working at being an asshole, Isa?" he asked without looking up. "Or does it just come naturally to you these days?"

"Wait until the amplifier tries to kill you. Then see if you get a little testy around her." Isa took another sip of his drink.

I smiled. "Again, I never actually tried to kill you, Isa."

The curse breaker glanced between us, then shook his head. He gestured toward the tiles. "The best analogy I can come up with is, it's like a mathematical calculation. When I'm presented with the sum—a curse or a spell that has already been triggered—I have to try to come up with the equation that produced it."

"Because you can't just break it?"

"Right. Breaking a set spell or curse often has deadly repercussions."

"So you reproduce the curse with the tiles?"

Grosvenor shrugged. "As best I can explain it. It's how my magic works, other than the basic sorcerer stuff we can all do."

"Are you working on Kader's spell?"

The curse breaker laughed joylessly. "Hell no." He reached for the notebook that sat open before him, flipping through pages and pages of neatly handwritten symbols. "I ran out of tiles trying to replicate its flow. I'm actually not certain it is a single spell. More like multiple insidious layers, all carefully anchored at a single point."

"Except Cerise Myers isn't that powerful," Isa said.

Grosvenor shrugged. "I'm just explaining it as I see it, cousin. Maybe the entire coven is in on it."

Isa glanced at me, grimacing.

I had no trouble picking up the meaning behind his look. Taking on an entire witch coven would be suicide—no matter how united the Azar sorcerers were, and even given the Myers coven's reportedly lackluster power set. Although each individual witch might have been weaker than Isa or even the curse breaker alone, they would be formidable united. That was the fundamental reason why witches formed covens, and why it was so important for Opal to eventually be accepted into one.

It was also yet another reason that Kader Azar had reached out to his youngest son instead of appealing to whoever headed the Myers witches, or even to the Convocation itself.

"Did Isa really put you in a nullifying cage?" Grosvenor asked, leaning back against the couch and taking a sip of his drink. He grimaced, disgusted, then inexplicably took another sip.

"Ruwa," Isa said. "Ruwa kidnapped and put Emma in a cage."

"But you didn't let her out."

"I didn't have a chance," Isa snapped. "Because Emma rescued herself."

The curse breaker hummed thoughtfully, took another sip of his drink—sucking in his breath as if it burned—then turned his attention back to his tiles.

I started to turn away. Then I looked back at Isa—the heir apparent to the Azar cabal. "What did it look like to you, then? When you assessed the spell on your father?"

Isa kept his gaze on the front windows, taking another sip of his drink.

Thinking he wasn't going to answer, which was certainly his right, I started to turn away again. But then he spoke quietly.

"He won't let me near him."

"Well, colluding to have him kidnapped—and, I assume, murdered—eight years ago might make him a little wary."

"Please," Isa sneered. "He's staying under your roof, isn't he? He isn't scared of you, and he certainly isn't scared of me."

"It's the transference," Grosvenor said helpfully.

"What transference?" I asked.

"If Kader dies without formally choosing a successor, his power will—"

"Might," Isa interrupted.

"His power might transfer as it wills," the curse breaker amended. "Usually to the next most powerful in the bloodline." He tilted his chin at his cousin. "Which would be Isa. But occasionally, such power goes to a favored child, or someone the sorcerer has spent a lot of time with. Enough time that their power, their magic, has created a bridge of sorts."

I blinked. "And when you tried to kill Kader eight years ago, you were his chosen successor?"

Isa saluted me with his drink.

"And when Aiden tried to kill you?"

"That was my father's way of amending his will, yes."

"But Aiden ..." I trailed off, realizing that I shouldn't have been having this conversation with Isa and Grosvenor. If I had questions, I should have been taking them to Aiden.

"Aiden doesn't want it," the curse breaker said without glancing up. He shoved all the tiles into a messy pile, pulling a second set out of thin air with a flick of his fingers. Magic simmered through the room, gone moments after the curse breaker had called it forth. "You know, the cabal. The responsibility of keeping the Azars in check."

I smirked at Isa. "Like you kept Ruwa in check?"

"You're alive, aren't you? Along with the little witch and the shifter?" He meant Opal and Jenni.

"Right," I said mockingly. "All due to your kind-hearted intervention."

Isa's expression tightened. "Being kind is not a trait that keeps you alive in the Azar cabal."

Grosvenor snorted agreeably. "He's got that right."

I almost retorted, almost brought up my own so-called childhood. But I wasn't interested in sharing terrible tales with Isa Azar. Or anyone, for that matter. In fact, I was surprised that I'd lingered to converse at all. Having Kader, one of the Collective, so near was obviously having a psychological effect on me. I was acting out of character. Questioning, watching, instead of taking decisive action.

And sure, I had solid, rational reasons for doing so. But Amp5 would have taken Kader out at the gate and then dealt with the consequences.

I walked away from the conversation, opening the front door and crossing onto the patio as I heard Grosvenor speak again. It was doubtful that either he or Isa knew I could still hear them. I was, after all, just an amplifier.

"For a person worried about his future," Grosvenor murmured, "you sure are mouthy with someone who, in her own words, could 'drain you dry.'"

"Emma isn't going to kill me. Drain me, maybe. Kick me off the property, for certain. But she won't kill any of us."

"You think Aiden will stop her?"

Isa laughed coldly. "Not a chance. Love. Stupid, moronic love will stop her. Has stopped her. One of the people responsible for her existence, for her shitty childhood, is sleeping in her fucking barn."

"Because she loves Aiden."

"Yes."

I shut the door, not interested in listening to any further analysis of my behavior. As Christopher often said, I'd endured too much of that for the first twenty-one years of my life.

Khalid was standing at the base of the front patio stairs, staring to the west at the setting sun. He was smoking something that smelled sweet. Cannabis, maybe. But more likely something magical in nature. Whether it was meant to relax him or heighten him, though, I didn't know.

I stepped past him, crossing through the grass in my bare feet, heading toward the orchard. Khalid moved to follow me at a sedate pace. Keeping his distance, but drifting as if inadvertently drawn into my wake.

I refrained from snapping at him in response to so much seeming familiarity. Doing so would likely be taken as a weakness, and I wasn't interested in having the sorcerer thinking about whether it was a weakness he might subsequently exploit.

The Wilsons' property sat to my far left. The cows had been moved out of their front fields in the spring to allow the grass to grow. The orchard that had come with our property hadn't needed as much revitalization as the gardens and the house. The trees had been mature enough that they'd withstood a few years of neglect. Christopher had pruned heavily the first year, but then applied a lighter hand this spring, in the hopes of getting more fruit.

I stepped among the plum trees, set far enough apart that I would have had to stretch my arms to touch the branches of two trees at the same time. They were fully leafed, with tiny fruits already forming. As far as Christopher had figured out, there were five varieties, though two hadn't set fruit the previous year. He also hadn't identified the yellow-skinned plum with the rosy blush yet.

The chicken coop was tucked in between the pears and the apples. The pears had mostly lost their white blossoms. I had never tasted a pear quite as good as the few Bartletts that Christopher had ripened on the counter last year. My mouth watered just thinking about them.

The chicken run was empty, as expected. I paused by the meshed gate, listening to the soft, sleepy chatter emanating from the coop—the rooster talking to his hens, and them cooing back contentedly. The chickens quieted as I unlatched the gate and stepped into the run. Christopher had built the coop in sections, so we could disassemble it when we needed to move it. He'd used reclaimed white-painted siding from some repairs we'd had done to the exterior of the house, along with scraps of red metal left over from when I'd had the house and the barn reroofed.

Annoyingly aware of Khalid now watching me from among the pear trees, I closed the smaller door to the coop, whispering good night to the chickens as I did every evening. Unwilling—even unable—to ignore the ritual involved in doing so, even as I felt like an idiot chatting to chickens in front of a sorcerer. Still pissed at the imposition of him being there, I collected the chickens' food and water, crossing out of the run.

Hands full, I gave Khalid a look, jutting my chin toward the gate. Still a silent specter, the sorcerer shut and latched it behind me. He'd either finished whatever he'd been smoking, or had tucked it away.

"You don't collect the eggs?" he asked. His accent once again reminded me of Ruwa's.

"Not at night," I said. "I don't like to disturb them after they've cooped themselves."

"For breakfast, then," he said, flashing a white-toothed smile at me, though his other features were shadowed as the last of the sunset faded from the sky.

Not bothering to answer—I'd frankly had enough small talk to last me the remainder of the year—I headed to the barn. The sorcerer fell into step beside me, hands clasped behind his back, gaze on the house as we crossed the yard toward the rose bushes that edged the gravel drive.

I set the chicken feeder down, dumping the remaining water at the base of two of the rose bushes. I'd watered the two closer to the house the night before. Then I crossed the driveway, the gravel rough under my feet but not unpleasant.

Aiden had parked the Mustang back in the barn, but left one of the wide doors partially open. I stepped through, noting the way Khalid's step hitched and his gaze shot overhead to the loft.

I crossed between the workbench and the car into the back of the barn, going to the sink. Setting the food down, I washed the water container. I would fill both in the morning, then open the coop. I enjoyed the ritual, the rhythm it brought to my day.

Khalid was surveying the plants starting under the grow lights. Christopher's self-watering indoor greenhouse stretched the length of the workbench that ran underneath the stairs to the loft. The middle Azar brother appeared to be reading the labels of the cucumbers, melons, peppers, and basil that were still too tender to be planted out.

"Are you the gardener?" Khalid asked doubt-fully, as if he already knew the answer.

"Why wouldn't I be?" I dried my hands, folding the towel over the edge of the sink.

Khalid brushed his fingers over the basil, then raised his hand, smelling it and smiling. "Residual witch magic."

That was a surprise. Not only because Christopher, a clairvoyant, was the gardener—but also that Khalid was sensitive enough to pick up residual magic. Though the former probably shouldn't have been surprising. As Kader had so clumsily claimed earlier, the Five had been created with a mixture of DNA and magic. Christopher had always been the most proficient at witch spells. And since Kader had also been deliberate with his own reproductive choices when it came to Aiden, it was likely that he'd done the same when selecting Isa's and Khalid's mothers.

"Of course, you could have purchased the seedlings from a witch." Khalid rocked back on his heels, hands once again clasped behind his back. "I didn't have time to research the area as thoroughly as I would have liked. Isa was most impatient. But I understand that the main coven is in the major city on the mainland? Vancouver?"

He'd formed the last sentence as a question. But since it didn't actually need answering, I didn't bother.

The grow lights winked out, throwing us into darkness.

Khalid flinched. A sharp pulse of power formed behind him, presumably in his clasped hands.

"The lights are on a timer." Blinking to adapt my eyesight, I stepped to the side as silently as possible. The timer emanated a blue glow, and the light was still on in the overhead loft. Even if I was capable of taking the spell Khalid had instinctively called forth, I really liked the linen dress I was wearing, so I had no intention of getting into a fight while wearing it. Plus, based on the way all the hair stood up on my arms at the power the sorcerer held, what he'd amassed without a single word or rune was combat-grade magic. It was exceedingly likely to damage the interior of the barn.

Christopher would never forgive me.

Khalid sighed quietly, loosening his hands until they swung free at his sides. Magic I could feel but not see crackled between his fingers, then faded.

I crossed back through the barn. Khalid followed, pausing at the base of the stairs to look up.

"Close the door behind you, please," I said.

He shook his head. "I'm coming with you."

We stepped out into the deepening night. Khalid shut the door, then caught up with me as I crossed around the house.

"I can see why Aiden stayed," Khalid murmured. "Wants to stay."

"The fresh eggs and basil?" I asked mockingly.

Khalid snorted. "All of it is beguiling."

Light streamed from all the windows on the bottom level of the house. If I reached for it, I knew I would feel the magic of its occupants. Aiden still in the den, Isa and Grosvenor in the front sitting room. Paisley had returned to wherever Christopher and Samantha were spending the day, though I didn't think Aiden had had another chance to help the demon dog with the spell she'd wanted.

I ran my fingers up the top rail of the stairs as I stepped up to the back patio. Then, unable to quash my curiosity, I spoke. "A sensitive who instinctively wields combat magic is an unusual combination."

Khalid went still. Then he deliberately leaned back against the patio rail, looking through the French-paned doors into the empty eating area and the kitchen. He fished whatever he'd been smoking out of his pocket, placing it between his lips and lighting the tip with a snap of his fingers. He inhaled deeply, held his breath, then exhaled slowly.

"It's not instinctual," he finally said.

"It is now," I said, understanding him immediately.

He blew out another breath. "Yes."

"Because Kader Azar had no need of a son who was sensitive to magic."

Khalid settled his dark gaze on me, smiling wryly. "Overly sensitive. But such things can be …" He waved the hand holding the joint. "Mitigated." He leaned his head back. "There is a lot of magic in your land. Layers upon layers of power." He looked at me, lips twisted again. "As if a goddess has walked here… more than one."

Aiden stepped into the open doorway. His expression was tight, gazing at his middle brother. I'd felt him approach behind me, so Khalid must have seen him and not reacted.

"I've finished the letter," Aiden said. "Isa is reading it over."

"How easily you fall into old patterns, my brother," Khalid said, quietly mocking. "And when the mantle of the cabal falls to him, will you kneel along with the rest of us?" He glanced at me pointedly. "What a prize you'd bring with you."

"Having Isa read a contract that binds all of us if it's accepted is only prudent." Aiden stepped forward, teeth bared. "And Emma isn't some prize to be collected or traded. The fact that I have to tell you that makes it clear you've been imbibing far too much."

Khalid huffed out a laugh, snuffing the ash-hot end of his joint between his fingers. "How can you stand to be this close to him and not wring his neck?"

"Who?" Aiden asked. "Isa or Father?"

Khalid glanced toward the barn. "You'd think his power would feel weakened, given that he's dying. Instead, it feels even more deadly. Like a wounded animal. If Grover hadn't confirmed the presence of a spell that he couldn't break, I would have thought it some kind of ploy."

"To what end?"

Khalid shook his head. "What is his reason for doing anything? Power." He slid his gaze to me again. "Something he can't get through brute force or manipulation …"

"He didn't know that I was with Emma."

Khalid stepped closer to Aiden, lowering his voice. "You could kill him. You could take the cabal."

"Kill who?" Aiden repeated mockingly. "Isa or our father?"

"The power here," Khalid hissed. "The power that your mating bond with Emma brings you—"

Aiden raised his hand, silencing his brother. "You see ties between Emma and me?"

Khalid shook his head as if it wasn't important. "Multiple thin strands. Listen—"

"Composed of power from both of us?" Aiden interrupted. "Flowing both ways?"

"Yes," Khalid hissed again, annoyed.

Aiden stepped back, looking at me with his head tilted. A soft smile appeared on his face. "We haven't formalized anything. Yet."

A contented warmth flushed across my chest, and I smiled back at him just as softly.

Khalid blinked, glancing back and forth between us. Then he shook his head. "Play with powerful people, brother, and it doesn't necessarily take a formal ceremony or a bonding spell."

Aiden reached for me. I loosely twined my fingers through his. Then together, we stepped into the house.

Khalid swore behind us. "That's a 'no,' then?"

"It's always been a no, Khalid," Aiden said, though not unkindly. "I have no interest in heading the cabal. And, whether I'm bonded to Emma or not, Kader Azar could kill me with a single word." He glanced back at his brother. "He could kill any of us."

"Maybe," Khalid said. Then he looked at me. "But maybe not anymore."

Aiden squeezed my hand. "Will you read the letter as well?"

"If you'd like me to," I said.

"I would." He grinned at me, as if we were suddenly talking about something else altogether. Then he leaned closer and whispered, "Later."

I huffed a laugh. He already looked exhausted. And by the way his brothers and cousin were camped out in the front sitting room, I was fairly certain they were planning on being up all night. "Don't promise what you can't deliver, sorcerer."

He chuckled as we crossed through the hall toward the front sitting room. Khalid closed the French-paned doors and followed behind us.

A SOFT BUZZ DREW ME FROM MY SLEEP. AIDEN WAS tucked in beside me, covers half thrown off because he was always warm. I'd been asleep when he finally climbed into bed, murmuring about kicking his brothers and cousin out as he'd quietly paced the bedroom, adding protections to the runes that normally sealed sound within.

Another soft buzz. From the top of the bureau.

I slipped out of bed, noting the light beginning to seep in around the edges of the curtains. It was near dawn, which was early this time of year. The number of strangers in the house when I went to bed meant that I was wearing a silk nightie, though I'd gotten into the habit of sleeping naked, as Aiden currently was.

I touched my thumb to the screen of the phone still connected to its charging cable, revealing a text message from Christopher.

>*What the hell are you doing over there, Socks?*

I laughed quietly.

"Christopher?" Aiden asked, voice heavy with sleep.

"Yes."

"Are we all going to die at my father's hands?"

The question was presumably meant to be playful, but it didn't come out that way. "Shall I ask?"

"God, no. I don't want to see it coming." He turned to me, eyes bright with his vibrant blue magic. "As long as I'm with you. As long as you are the last thing I get to see, to touch, then I'll be okay."

"But I won't be okay," I said gruffly.

Aiden closed his eyes, sighing. "Sorry. I need more sleep."

The phone buzzed with another text.

> *More apple blossoms...I keep getting the rebirth card with a mess of other combinations.*

Christopher had been casting cards. I tried to remember what the apple blossom represented.

Immortality, healing, good fortune?

>*Yes. Death, transition, inevitability.*

I waited for the clairvoyant to elaborate, as I would if I were standing within the comforting weight of his magic. And as I hung in that space, feeling Aiden's exhausted gaze on me, I realized that I missed Christopher, my Knox, acutely.

>*If it is possible to be consumed by...peace, benevolence...then that is what appears to be coming your way.*

Why is me being consumed always a thing with you?

A laughing-face emoticon appeared on the screen.

>*Might not be you. It's not clear. At all. Might be the distance. Might not be set in stone. A pending proposal?*

Pending. "Did you get the letter sent off to your mother?" I asked Aiden. The brothers had still been going over it word by word when I'd wandered upstairs to bed.

Aiden grunted. "Yes. Though Isa was even more anal with the wording than normal. On edge."

"Wouldn't you be?"

"Yes. Are you coming back to bed?" Tucking one arm behind his head, he grinned all sorts of promises at me while his other hand travelled across his chest, down his flat stomach, and beneath the sheets.

"I thought you were tired."

"There's more than one way to catch up on sleep."

The phone buzzed again, pulling my attention away from the sorcerer's hand underneath the now-tented sheets.

>*Paisley's back.*

Bee?

>*Samantha's lead was old. If Bee was here, she's been gone for at least three months. We tracked down the hotel where we thought she might have been staying, but I didn't pick up anything from the residual in the room. Between you and me, we might even be on the trail of a different telepath. The power signature feels too dim for Bee. But Paisley seems eager to keep moving.*

I hesitated, fingers hovering over the onscreen keyboard. Then I typed, *The sorcerer Azar offered to help find her.*

There was a long pause on Christopher's end. So long that the screen winked out, leaving me in sudden darkness. A chill ran down my spine.

"Emma?" Aiden asked, sounding much more alert. "Everything all right?"

"I'm not sure. Christopher dropped the—"

A single word appeared on my phone.

>*Fuck.*

>*Does he have her?*

I don't think so. A negotiating tactic.

>*We're coming back. Today.*

I glanced over at Aiden. His hand was resting on his chest again, not playing under the sheets. His expression was serious. "Christopher wants to come back."

Aiden nodded, acknowledging but not necessarily agreeing. "Having Christopher and Samantha here would be …"

"Dangerous?"

He laughed. "Most assuredly. But beneficial. For us."

"Too much firepower."

"And possibly too much of a temptation."

Faced with three of us, three of his creations in one place, what would the sorcerer Azar do? Could he stand against us alone? He who knew us so well?

Eight years ago, Silver Pine had almost managed to take all Five of us at once. She'd had access to our DNA, though, and the hardest hits we'd taken that day had all been from blood-fueled spells.

I turned my attention back to the phone.

Wait a little longer. See where Paisley leads you? Finding Bee might be just as important now.

>*The second I see you in danger, I'm coming.*
Okay.

I started to head back to bed, but then hesitated and picked up the phone again. I wasn't completely sure what I needed to say, or how to say it. But I was more than just myself now, more than just one of the Five. The Five who each were so powerful alone that they really didn't need anyone else.

Knox. If anything should happen to me, I need you, and Samantha, and Bee, and Daniel to look after Opal. And Aiden. And everything, everyone else.

>*It bothers me immensely that you think you even have to ask.*

I'm not asking. I'm telling you.

>*Right. Don't worry. I'm on mission. As always.*

Don't let Fish and Samantha just burn it all down.

>*I'm coming home. Now. I never should have left.*

I sighed, glancing up at Aiden. "I'm triggering him."

Aiden arched an eyebrow. "Over text? You're very skilled, amplifier."

I laughed.

157

Give it 24 hours. Find Bee.

I waited for a moment, but Christopher didn't text back. I wasn't certain how ingrained following orders from me was for the clairvoyant anymore, meaning he might ignore me and return with Samantha. Once I decided I didn't want the responsibility for the Five, I'd actively tried to not just issue demands. But if Christopher was keeping Samantha informed, the telekinetic would jump at any opportunity to tear Kader Azar limb from limb.

"It's a good thing Samantha's power doesn't work on flesh and bone," I muttered, setting down the phone.

"No?"

I crossed to the bed. "She can toss people around and do terrible things to internal organs, but that's why she constantly carries small projectiles."

"Come closer," Aiden murmured. "I want you on top of me. I want to be buried deep within you, at your mercy."

"That was an abrupt change of subject."

"Was it?" He grinned, clasping both hands behind his head and lounging back.

Avoiding his reach—I knew when a predator was setting up to strike—I snagged the edge of the covers, tugging the fabric away to reveal every last bit of his tanned skin. Thankfully, the room was lightening as dawn approached, so I could see every centimeter. Deliberately eyeing his groin, I smiled He growled, stirring under my gaze.

"And shall I be merciful?" I asked teasingly.

"God, I hope not."

I pushed the thin straps of my silk nightie from my shoulders. It fell, catching around my hips.

"Emma," Aiden growled.

"So impatient, sorcerer." I shimmied my hips until the nightie fell to pool around my feet.

"Yes," Aiden stretched out on the bed, shoving all the blankets onto the floor. "Exactly like that, but right here." He pointed to his groin.

"So demanding." I paced toward the bed, climbing over him, deliberately slowly, until I hovered above him.

His heated gaze raked over me, magic leaking from his eyes. I leaned over, not breaking his gaze as I dragged my nipples up his chest.

He groaned.

I paused, my lips barely brushing his. "Tell me about these bonds we share. That Khalid sees between us."

He lifted his head, capturing my lips in a kiss. "How about I show you instead?" His hands slid to my hips, gripping gently.

And instead of responding verbally, I settled onto him. Still undecided as to whether I was going to be merciful or not.

FOUR

AFTER OPENING THE CHICKEN COOP AND COL-
lecting eggs, I spooned generous amounts of
homemade granola into small stoneware bowls while
Aiden brewed his first mug of coffee. Christopher
had made the granola with honey, almonds, and
cranberries, but he wanted to dry our own fruit this
fall so he had more options.

Aiden leaned back against the counter with
his arms crossed and head thoughtfully bowed. The
sleeves of his navy henley were pushed up, exposing rune-free tanned skin. He hadn't bothered with
socks, though neither had I. We'd slept for about an
hour after sex, then showered.

I splashed some coconut-and-almond milk
into the granola and offered Aiden one of the bowls.
He took it, along with a spoon, grunting quietly in
thanks. Though he'd been playful only a couple of
hours earlier in bed, Aiden had been withdrawn
from the moment we'd stepped from the bedroom.

His head snapped up, cranked in the direction of the study. "And so it begins," he muttered, setting the granola aside without even taking a bite, then striding down the hall. He'd abandoned his coffee as well.

I followed behind him, savoring spoonfuls of my own granola and totally checking out Aiden's backside. The henley tightened across his shoulders and biceps, loosening around his tapered waist, and—

"Emma," Aiden growled playfully, not turning around.

"What?" I asked, all innocence. I shoved another spoonful of granola into my mouth.

"I can feel your magic," he said, laughing. "Beckoning."

"What?" I squeaked, nearly choking on the granola. No one had ever mentioned my magic beckoning them before. But then, I had never looked at anyone like I looked at Aiden.

He flashed me a grin as he entered the study, but didn't elaborate.

I followed to lean in the doorway of the dark, wood-paneled room, mining my bowl for the dregs of my breakfast as Aiden crossed to the desk.

A thick parchment envelope sealed with light-blue wax was placed in the center of an elaborate cluster of runes—which the sorcerer appeared to have carved into the desktop. Aiden pressed his fingers over the runes in a sequence. "Sorry about the desk. But I had to anchor it to get the magic to open up through the house and property wards."

I shrugged. "It's your desk."

Aiden paused. Just paused. Then he turned and looked at me. His hand hovered over the envelope, and his eyes…his expression was so tender. Hopeful.

"Am I beckoning you again?" I asked, trying to be playful. Otherwise, I was going to have to grab him and take him right there on the fir floor. And we'd just managed to get out of bed. His father was probably going to wander over for breakfast. Plus, the other sorcerers would be showing up at any moment.

Not to mention that the witches had presumably responded.

Aiden's laugh turned into a sigh. "It was a mistake to open my father's letter."

"No."

"No?"

"No."

He nodded, then he picked up the new envelope and broke the seal. Opening it, he scanned the contents. "It's from Sky."

The eldest of his half-sisters on his mother's side. In her early twenties, Sky was pursuing a specialization in charms at the Academy, the UK campus. Specifically, useful spells for household chores, health and wellness, and beauty.

Aiden looked up, surprised. "They've agreed to come." He paged quickly through the letter. "And Sky has sent preliminary terms."

I'd been the one to suggest it. But now that the witches had agreed to that seemingly crazy plan, opening my home—my safe haven—to greater numbers of powerful Adepts who hated each other seemed idiotic.

That was an emotional reaction, though. So I ignored it. "You're surprised?"

"If I were them, I'd let him rot."

"That's not true," I said quietly. "Otherwise, you never would have opened his letter."

Aiden laughed ruefully. "We'll have to house them here."

"How many?"

He scanned the letter again. "She doesn't say specifically. Just that they're on their way. Likely just Sky and Cerise…plus maybe another aunt? Pulling Ocean from school and exposing her to …" Aiden shook his head ruefully. "Exposing her to all of this would be ridiculous."

Ocean was Aiden's youngest half-sister. The eighteen-year-old was also attending the UK Academy, focused on potions—specifically, cosmetic magic. Aiden had mentioned the importance of not getting on her bad side, given that her idea of retribution usually came in the form of sneak attacks that tied her victims to a toilet for hours.

"And what if it's the whole coven?"

"It won't be." He grimaced. "All the Myers line are witches of the light. And whatever curse…whatever spell Cerise is using…the strength of it…I don't even know how she managed to anchor it, to get it past his wards and personal protections."

I did. Because I knew how all spells of that magnitude were anchored. In DNA—hair, skin, nails, blood, or bodily fluids. I had four explicit examples of blood binding tattooed on my own spine. But I really didn't want to mention that if Aiden hadn't figured it out already.

Except…that wasn't who I was with Aiden. We were partners.

"When was the last time you visited your mother?" I asked quietly.

He shook his head, reading the letter for a third time. "About a month before I returned here. So five months ago."

Kader had been trying to get the letter to Aiden for longer than that. "And before Silver Pine? You were living in Paris?"

"Yes, temporarily …" He trailed off, slowly raising his head and looking at me, putting the pieces together.

"Did Cerise seem…normal?" I asked.

Aiden grimaced, hands falling to his sides, clenching the thick parchment pages of the letter. "Goddamn it." He took a harsh breath, then exhaled. "I don't know her well enough to make that sort of assessment, do I?" He started pacing. "She invited me to visit over a year ago. To reconnect. Fuck me."

Cerise Myers had used Aiden to get to his father. Though why she would have done so after waiting so many years was still a mystery. Aiden was an Azar, though. A direct descendent of Kader. Properly handled, his DNA could possibly be used to get to his father. Though I wouldn't have normally thought that a witch from a coven known for delicate, precise magic would be casting a spell of that magnitude. At least not successfully.

"You would have noticed if it was blood," I said.

Aiden rolled his shoulders and neck, trying to rein himself in. But magic poured from him, inadvertently unleashed in anger and frustration, thrumming across the floor. "I was in Paris for months. She could have collected hair and fingernail clippings. Months and months' worth." He laughed, pained. "And I was with family, wasn't I? No need to take extra precautions—"

He cut off abruptly and strode toward the door, passing me and getting all the way out into the hall before I figured out where he was going—to the bathroom, to clean up any possible DNA.

"I've done it already."

My whisper stopped him. His shoulders were rigid, hands fisted at his sides.

"When?" he asked without looking at me.

"After our shower this morning, when you came down to start the coffee. I burned it all," I said, keeping my tone steady. "If Paisley were here full time, we wouldn't have to worry about it. I can never convince her to stop eating our hair and fingernail clippings. It's the used Kleenex she likes the best."

Aiden bowed his head, shoulders shaking slightly. I wasn't sure if he was laughing or losing his mind.

"This family stuff is seriously complicated," I said.

Aiden turned to face me. "I do it by rote when cleaning, but …"

Christopher did most of the cleaning when he was home. Or me, if I was bored or feeling useless. Aiden most often cleaned up after meals, but he always left the bathrooms and other rooms to the two of us.

"I'm such an idiot. I've been here for months. I knew what inviting my father through the wards meant, and I …" He clenched his teeth, shaking his head.

I closed the space between us, placing my hand on the center of his chest. His emotions welled under my touch, battering my senses. I blinked, steadying myself. "You're in your own home."

"And I'm letting it be invaded."

I bared my teeth. "Luring enemies into your lair is not the same thing, sorcerer."

He barked out a laugh, then pressed his forehead to mine. "Yes. Yes."

We stood like that in the hall, energy and magic shifting between us until the soft sound of the exterior laundry room door shutting drew us apart.

Kader Azar had just entered the house. His power was as muffled, as tightly contained, as ever.

Aiden sighed. "You know the bastard has already figured it out. That Cerise used me to get to him."

"Well, he used Cerise to get you. So it's already in his nature to expect that level of betrayal."

Aiden snorted. Then, sighing begrudgingly, he strode toward the kitchen, smoothing the crumpled letter in his hand. Apparently, it was time to speak with his father—and that wasn't a conversation I needed to participate in. In fact, given that I was still feeling the residual of Aiden's torrent of emotions, it was probably best if I kept my distance from the elder sorcerer as much as possible.

Plus, if I was going to have guests, I needed to make up more beds. And order some more groceries. I would have preferred brunch at the Home Cafe with Aiden, but unfortunately, I wasn't currently following my own schedule.

That was a new and uncomfortable realization, which I instantly shoved into the background. It wasn't the time for personal revelations.

AIDEN STEPPED INTO THE HALL FROM OUR BEDROOM, wearing one of his suits. A perfectly pressed dark-gray number that hugged his shoulders and tapered slightly at the hips. A crisp white dress shirt, polished black shoes, no tie. And all of it layered with powerful protection spells. I hadn't seen him wear a suit since we'd had dinner with Isa and Ruwa.

My chest tightened, anger flushing through my limbs. He didn't feel safe. In our own home.

I should have kicked Kader Azar to the curb.

No.

I should have brought my blades out to play before the architect of my birth had a chance to open his mouth.

The handle of the cleaning bucket I was holding snapped in my hand. The bucket listed sideways, spilling dirty, soapy water down my bare leg. I had just finished cleaning the upstairs, making up the beds with fresh sheets and scouring the main bathroom. All of that even though Christopher had done so before he'd left.

Aiden swiftly closed the space between us, sliding his hand into my hair to cradle my head as I shoved my anger aside—to simmer, not to abate. I raised my chin to welcome a warm, lingering kiss.

"I love it when you let your magic out to play," he murmured against my lips.

I hadn't realized I'd done anything of the sort. But I could feel that magic raging around me now, my hold on it loosened by my emotions. I had learned how to keep my power in check at a young age. But apparently, Aiden and I were both clothing ourselves in power in anticipation of dealing with another influx of his relatives.

Not bothering to rein my magic in, I sucked lightly on his bottom lip. "When I let it come out to play with you, you mean. But I should tuck it away so I don't scare everyone else."

A darkly tinted laugh rumbled in his chest. "Scare the shit out of them all, Emma."

I pulled back slightly. "Even your mother? Your sisters?"

He sighed, running his hand through his hair. "I don't know. I…the whole situation is …" He dropped his hand, not finishing his thought.

"We should go to the diner for a late lunch. Just us."

"And leave the house unprotected?"

I smirked. "Well, only after I scare the shit out of everyone, of course."

Aiden grinned with a joy so genuine and fierce that I could read it even though I wasn't touching him skin to skin. I rectified that oversight, lifting up on my toes to brush my lips against his, playfully.

Magic danced up my spine. Someone had just brushed against the property wards. The gentle, playful caress of a request for entry was completely different from the tenor of the sorcerers. All four of them.

The witches had arrived.

"That was fast," I murmured against Aiden's lips when he didn't seem inclined to break our embrace. "They must have teleported at least part of the way. That's risky, isn't it?"

Aiden only grunted, tightening his grip on me.

Magic tingled across my spine again, this time raising all the hair on the back of my neck. "Impatient."

Aiden sighed, withdrawing reluctantly. He waved his fingers at the spilled water and muttered a word. The dirty water disappeared. Witch magic. Power that he'd inherited from the parent waiting at the front gate.

"See?" he said tightly. "I'm capable of doing some cleaning."

I frowned, not quite certain what to say to that.

He grimaced. "I'm sorry. I'm not dealing with all of this very well. I have this feeling that I've invited something that I'm not sure I can handle." He shook his head, squaring his shoulders, then offered me his hand.

"We invited it. And we can handle it. Just let me put on a dress and put the bucket in the laundry."

Aiden took the bucket from me, holding it by the lip. The two halves of the handle dangled uselessly. "I'll meet you on the front porch."

I headed for my bedroom, achingly aware that there was some emotional component to our current situation that I had no context for, and therefore no ability to help Aiden through.

His own magic coiled tightly around him as the dark-haired sorcerer headed downstairs, footsteps silenced by the spells on his dress shoes. And as idiotic as the thought was, that made my chest ache.

It hurt to see Aiden wearing that damn suit.

ALL FIVE OF THE AZAR SORCERERS WERE ARRAYED on the front patio by the time I stepped out from the house. Aiden on the top step. Isa immediately to his right, standing at the railing. Kader to my left, standing at center, and alone. Grosvenor stood in the far right-front corner, while Khalid lounged back against the wall next to the front door. He was the only one to look at me, scanning me head to toe.

I'd selected an azure linen dress that Aiden had bought for me. It had a scooped neck and was belted at the waist, flaring just below my knee. The fabric was sturdy but soft. I hadn't missed noticing the runes that had been marked along the inner hems. And though I couldn't feel the magic, I presumed the dress was coated in protection spells similar to those of Aiden's suits. Similar to those of the suits all the sorcerers currently wore.

The tableau made me uncomfortable. The show of force. The four outsider sorcerers versus the three indistinct figures I could see beyond the front gate. The witches. And since it was far too early in the day to just start stabbing any of the figures occupying my front patio, I opted for belligerent taunting.

"Scared of three witches, are you?"

"You haven't met the witches in question," Grosvenor muttered.

Kader chuckled quietly. His tan suit jacket was open, hands stuffed in his pants pockets.

Aiden reached back for me. I stepped forward to take his hand obligingly, traversing the steps to the front path with him.

"Try not to kill anyone, Emma," Isa said. "I'd like to get a better look at the working before going that route."

I chafed at the inference that I was under orders from any of the sorcerers, but Aiden squeezed my hand and I kept my mouth shut. For now. I wasn't particularly effective with words anyway.

"So, Isa," the curse breaker drawled behind us, "you're a complete prat around Emma because she scares the shit out of you, right?"

Khalid chuckled darkly.

Isa didn't answer.

I stepped off the path into the grass, crossing alongside the rose bushes that edged the gravel drive. Aiden was silent at my side.

The figures at the gate came into better view as we neared them. Three women, ages ranging from late teens to early thirties, all with various shades of brown hair.

The eldest wore a cream-colored wrapped dress with a wide-belted sash, shorter than both of the younger witches standing on either side of her. The youngest witch, still in her teens, was clad in jeans with a single ripped knee, along with a navy tank top. The second youngest, in her early twenties, also wore jeans, paired with a yellow silk peasant top.

I frowned. "Your mother? She decided not to come?"

"She's the one in the middle." Aiden's tone was low and tense, his gaze fixed on the witches.

Aiden's mother should have been in her early fifties. All of the Adept tended to age well if they didn't die young—as was the case for some. Shapeshifters and clairvoyants, specifically, though for exceedingly different reasons. But if the cream-clad witch was Aiden's mother, there was nothing natural about her youth. By her appearance, she was more likely to have been his sister than his parent.

"I thought your great-aunt was the head of the Myers coven?" I asked, slowing my pace slightly.

Aiden matched my stride. "She is. It will pass to her daughter."

So Cerise Myers wasn't even in line to head the coven. Therefore, she shouldn't have been able to pull power from that connection—specifically, the power behind whatever she was doing to appear so young. And even if she was, she shouldn't have been able to do so from Lake Cowichan.

No. I was overreacting.

Not that I'd admit it out loud.

Perhaps Cerise's appearance was simply an aspect of the subtle magic that the Myers coven was known for. The more powerful covens would certainly consider such a heavy-handed spell to be a waste of magic. Age was revered among witches, because with age came power.

Aiden brushed his thumb against the back of my hand, leaving a warm tingle of magic behind. "We can kick them all out. Then we focus on finding Amanda."

I shook my head. "Don't worry. We'll be pulled into the hunt for Bee when we're needed."

Aiden slanted his eyes at me in a warm, genuine smile. One I really hadn't seen from him since he'd opened the letter from Kader. "I like that we are a 'we.'"

"So do I." I met his gaze steadily. "Very much."

"Just say the word, Emma. And they can just kill each other and get it over with." His smile disappeared as quickly as it had appeared.

I missed it. Which was ridiculously sappy of me.

I shook my head, traversing the final steps to the gates with the sorcerer. The risk of Aiden getting caught up in Kader's curse was too great to change my mind now.

Cerise Myers was beautiful—as least as far as I understood that sort of thing. Her features were delicate but well defined. Dark, straight hair brushing her shoulders. Pert nose, high cheekbones. Her bright-blue eyes were fixed on her son through the magic that defined the property boundary.

"Introduce us, please," she directed Aiden, smiling pleasantly. Her accent was French, as expected. Refined, smooth.

Aiden nodded, turning his shoulder to me. "Emma Johnson, amplifier." He gestured toward his mother. "Cerise Myers, witch. Mother to Sky."

He nodded at the witch in the yellow silk blouse. Sky's hair was the lightest of the three—a medium brown threaded through with shots of copper and blond. She was wearing brown sandals and had a gold ring on each of her second toes.

"And Ocean."

Aiden grinned at the third witch, the youngest. Ocean grinned back at him. Her dark-brown hair was bleached almost white at the tips. Her eyes were lighter blue than her mother's. She was the tallest of the witches.

"All of the Myers coven," Cerise added gently.

Aiden nodded slightly at his mother. The smile he'd offered Ocean had disappeared.

Cerise raked her gaze across his face, looked at me, then looked back at her son. Sadly, I thought. "Will you invite us in?" she finally asked.

"I'm just trying to figure out how deeply your betrayal goes first." His tone was quiet but dark. Venomous. "And whether or not I should expose my family to it."

Cerise Myers flinched.

I felt an echo of her obvious shock and pain cross my own heart. I never, ever wanted to elicit that tone from Aiden. Never.

"How can you say that?" Sky demanded, thrusting her chin toward the house. "And you call them your family? Over us?"

Aiden looked at his sister steadily, not speaking for long enough that she shifted on her feet, then stopped herself. She clenched her fists instead.

"Is someone going to explain?" Ocean asked softly, glancing between her mother and her brother.

The bleached tips of her hair slipped up and over her shoulders with the movement.

Aiden arched an eyebrow at his mother. "Cerise?"

The elder witch raised her chin. "I'm not going to apologize to him."

"And to me?" Aiden asked darkly. "If I'm to stand between him and the entire Myers coven? If I'm to protect and shelter you? And Sky? And Ocean?"

"I'm not the one who asked you to get involved," Cerise said stiffly.

Aiden laughed darkly. "No, you simply involved me without permission."

"What?" Sky asked, quieter now, trying to piece things together. "How?"

Ocean had gone pale. She touched her mother's arm questioningly, but then immediately withdrew her hand, rubbing her fingertips together. As if Cerise Myers was emanating a magical field that I couldn't feel through the property wards.

Confusion flickered across Cerise's upturned face. Then she frowned. "He deserves everything coming to him."

Apparently, she wasn't even going to acknowledge Aiden's other accusations.

"You honestly think he can hurt all of us?" Sky asked. "Through the leeching spell Mom set on him?"

"Leeching spell?" Aiden repeated mockingly, not taking his gaze off his mother. "Is that what you're calling it?"

Cerise didn't answer.

"Well, that's what I'm calling it," Sky said. "Answer my question, Aiden."

"Yes," her brother bit off the words. "I believe he can access the entire Myers coven through the ongoing working that Cerise has tied to him, through me."

"Through you?" Ocean echoed, blinking at her mother.

"Through me."

Both of Cerise Myers's daughters just looked at her then. Silence fell. A red pickup truck drove by on the road behind them. I waved, assuming it was a neighbor, though I didn't look closely enough to tell.

"You …" Sky cleared her throat. She was looking at her mother. "You need vengeance so badly after all these years that you would risk Aiden? Risk us?"

Cerise still didn't answer her daughter. Her gaze was remote, her expression stiff.

"Why not just kill him?" Sky cried. "If you had to do something?"

Again, confusion flickered over Cerise's face, but it was instantly quashed as she settled her gaze on her son. "You invited me. I'm here."

"To negotiate," Aiden said.

"I will consider it." She smiled suddenly, a full, sweet smile. "For your sake."

I didn't like that smile.

Not at all.

But Aiden's shoulders softened, and he reached for the latch on the gate.

"Wait," I murmured.

Aiden paused, head tilted toward me.

All three witches also tilted their heads toward me. Myers witches. These three were not even remotely a match for me, even if Ocean wielded deadly potions. I was likely at least partially immune to just about anything she might try to dose me with, thanks to the tender training provided by the Collective.

"No harm will come from mine to yours," Cerise said quietly. "Not while we bide by your rules on your property."

If magic underlaid her words, none filtered through to me, due to the property wards.

I smiled at her blithe attempt at deception. I didn't like being bound by anyone else's word anyway.

The skin around Aiden's eyes tightened. "That oath means nothing, Mother."

"What the hell, Aiden?" Sky blurted. "Since when did you become such an asshole?"

"I've always been an asshole," Aiden said mildly. "But I'm not an idiot. Words offered on the far side of a boundary line are worthless."

Sky blinked rapidly.

Ocean frowned.

"Give me the opportunity to repeat them, son." Cerise laid her hand on the top rail of the gate, fingers caressing the magic simmering between us.

The seemingly casual touch triggered the property wards, setting power tingling up and down my spine. Continually.

Games.

Actually, more games. Since the sorcerers were already playing by their own rules as well.

Aiden glanced at me.

I nodded.

He opened the gate, inviting the witches through. Cerise stepped forward, instantly cupping Aiden's face—first gazing at him, then kissing each of his cheeks. Then she stepped around her son, already reaching for me.

Ocean flung her arms around her brother's neck, and Aiden opened his free arm toward Sky.

Cerise stepped toward me, her smile as wide as her open arms. Her bright-blue eyes were almost a perfect match for Aiden's.

Every cell in my body clenched.

All the hair stood up on the back of my neck.

My chest constricted, my throat tightening.

And some instinct—previously unheard, unneeded, because I was always the biggest threat in the room—screamed in the back of my brain.

Cerise closed the space between us, clasping the hands I'd thrown in front of me without realizing it.

"Oh," she cried quietly, delighted. "Emma. You are so, so lovely." Then she leaned into my space and pressed her cheek to mine, first one side, then the other.

An answering smile bloomed across my face. "Cerise. Welcome to my home. Our home."

"Yes," she gushed, tucking her hand around my elbow and turning back to gesture to her daughters. "Sky. Ocean."

I looked over at Aiden.

He was smiling at me. At us.

Happily, I thought.

So I ignored the tiny voice clamoring in the back of my mind, and smiled back at him.

Everything was going to be fine.

Everything was perfect, actually.

I couldn't be happier.

EASILY SLIPPING PAST HER GUARD, I SLAMMED MY palm against the shapeshifter's chest. She flew back, landing on the grass without any attempt to break her fall, gasping for air.

Laughter filtered across the yard from the back patio, where two of the five sorcerers currently in residence lounged. Khalid and Grosvenor. The witches were in the kitchen, baking bread and prepping dinner even though it wasn't even time for tea yet. Aiden was in the study with Isa, rewriting the contract they'd prepared based on Sky's additions and corrections. Kader was in the pentagram in the loft—I could feel the power of it rising and falling. He and Cerise hadn't come face to face yet.

I placed my hands on my hips, glowering at the downed shifter wheezing for breath.

Dark hair tumbling around her face, Jenni Raymond snarled, "I'm going to tear their faces off!" Her magic welled, glinting green in her light-brown eyes.

Finally.

"Not if you keep dropping your left elbow," I said dispassionately. Then I leaned in, making a show of eyeing her right ankle.

She tore her gaze away from the chuckling sorcerers on the back patio, frowning and looking at her foot. "What?"

"I'm just wondering when you injured your ankle."

She hauled herself up onto her feet. "It's fine. I'm fine."

"Really? Because you keep tripping yourself."

She stalked toward me, hands clenched at her sides. "If you weren't so freakishly strong," she snarled quietly, flicking her gaze over my shoulder.

Constable Jenni Raymond hadn't been pleased to find the house filled with sorcerers and witches when she'd shown up for her afternoon training session on her day off. I couldn't quite tell if she was happy Christopher wasn't around or not. Though Jenni was usually fairly easy to read, she was completely oblique when it came to the clairvoyant. Perhaps she simply wasn't interested anymore.

"I barely touched you," I murmured back, pleased that Jenni was being guarded about my own abilities.

She rubbed her chest, grimacing. "I know."

"I've had my ass kicked numerous times by a shapeshifter."

"So you've said. Over and over."

I gave her a look. Once. I'd mentioned it once before. As encouragement.

She grinned unrepentantly, then sobered. "There's no way I'm trying to take warrior form in front of them." She nodded in the direction of the sorcerers.

I didn't blame her. Jenni's warrior form was definitely a work in progress, and something I wasn't at all capable of helping her with. Transforming was still a struggle for the shifter, only becoming easier for her around the full moon. I'd informed her that was just a mental block, and that her magic was strong enough now—having been amplified by me twice—that the transition between forms should have been coming easily at any time.

She accepted and practiced the meditation and strength-training exercises I gave her—even as she steadfastly ignored the psychological component.

Jenni set herself into a ready stance, but her gaze flicked to the patio again. She was completely distracted. I'd already thrown her five times, and I knew that doing so a sixth time wouldn't help.

I turned, pointing at Grosvenor. "You. Make yourself useful."

The curse breaker blinked at me, startled but half rising from his chair at my command. Khalid laughed, shoving his cousin in the direction of the stairs.

"Emma," Jenni growled quietly, "I'm not interested in testing any 'natural resistance' to magic with asshole evil sorcerers."

"Dark," I corrected. "Dark sorcerers. Except for the one in the loft, I'm not certain they've been established as evil. Yet."

She jabbed her finger toward the house, her magic flaring around her. "Isa Azar put me in a cage!"

Grosvenor strolled toward us over the grass. He had abandoned his suit jacket and rolled up the sleeves of his dress shirt, exposing his dark-skinned, muscled forearms.

"I'm pretty sure that was Ruwa," I said to Jenni, noting Sky as she paused in the open doorway to the kitchen. Her gaze was on the curse breaker.

Jenni huffed, peeved.

Isa had made himself scarce since the moment the RCMP officer pulled into the driveway. Smart sorcerer.

Grosvenor grinned at me, and then turned the expression on Jenni. I gathered it was charming, since the shifter tilted her head slightly and offered him a curl of her lips in response.

"I've been enjoying the show," he drawled, still smiling at Jenni.

"Yeah," Jenni drawled back. "Because seeing a woman getting beaten is such a turn-on."

The curse breaker lost the smile. "That's…not …" He glanced at me, as if he thought I was going to help him.

I kept my expression blank. The shifter could fight her own battles, and I needed to let her.

Grosvenor cleared his throat. "How may I be of assistance? I would prefer to not be…beaten either."

Jenni looked at me, hands on her hips. Completely belligerent. Yet she showed up to train, week after week. She was already stronger and faster than she had been three months ago. And she hadn't asked me to amplify her again. No shortcuts for Jenni Raymond.

I was oddly impressed.

My standards had obviously been lowered.

"I'd like you to set spells around the property," I said. "Curses and such, nothing lethal. For Jenni to sniff out."

The shifter's expression soured, but she didn't protest.

Grosvenor's eyes narrowed thoughtfully as he nodded. "In human form?"

"Yes."

He tilted his head, assessing Jenni. All business now. "That's more difficult."

"And therefore a more superior skill set to try to build."

"True. Give me a few minutes." He glanced back at the house. Sky was no longer hovering in the doorway. "I'll start in the front yard. And Khalid can work through the garden. Actually, one of the witches should help as well, to change it up." He started toward the house.

"I have dinner plans," Jenni grumbled.

"Khalid," Grosvenor said, jogging up the patio steps. "Do you have any charges on you?"

"Charges?" Jenni squeaked. "What the hell?"

"Hey, Sky!" The curse breaker bellowed into the house. "Come make yourself useful."

Jenni raised an eyebrow. "Charming."

"He seems to think so," I said.

She barked out a laugh. "I'm surprised you noticed."

I lunged for her, moving deliberately leisurely.

Her eyes widened, arms flailing—but she at least attempted to lean out of my way. Way, way too slowly.

I grabbed her wrist, feigning snapping it while still holding onto it. "This arm is now useless." Still moving at quarter speed, I slammed my hand into her chest—again. She stumbled but didn't fall, but only because I was still hanging on to her wrist. "And that would have fractured a few ribs."

"Damn you," she wheezed. And then—finally—she twisted, freeing her wrist from my loose grasp and managing to get her leg up to kick out at me.

I snapped a front kick to the thigh of her standing leg—deliberately avoiding her knee. Shifters healed quickly, but if I mangled Jenni's knee, she'd be off work for at least a week, then limping and useless for weeks after.

She fell. Then she just lay there on the grass, panting up at me angrily. "One of these days," she snarled. "I'm going to hit you. And it's going to hurt."

I grinned at her. "I look forward to it."

"Insane," she muttered, making it upright into a crouch. Her gaze settled on the two sorcerers and the witch taking off in different directions from the house. Grosvenor and Sky crossed around to the front while Khalid strolled toward the fenced garden.

Familiar magic bloomed in the kitchen.

Then the screaming started.

I ran, instantly leaving Jenni behind me as I leaped the patio stairs.

More magic exploded. Witch magic by its tenor, though I wasn't sensitive enough to know who was casting or what spells they were wielding.

A terrible roar rattled the windows.

Paisley.

In pain.

I cleared the doorway, feeling the magic of the witches to my immediate right. The kitchen table and chairs had disappeared.

The demon dog, all wild mane, blazing red eyes, and flashing jagged teeth, occupied the entire surface of the kitchen island. Sickle claws curled around the edge of the speckled quartz counter, digging into the side gable. Magic not her own writhed around her, as if attempting to grab hold. She gnashed and roared again, bellowing her rage at the two witches cowering in the corner.

I pivoted, getting myself between them and Paisley.

I'd been wrong about the cowering. Cerise was standing with her hands thrust forward. Ocean was tucked behind her.

Magic boiled from the dark-haired witch, blue strands of power twisting down her arms. And in the center of her forehead, set between her eyes, a deep point of power glowed. Like a third eye, so bright that I couldn't look directly at it.

I'd never seen anything like it.

I threw up my own hands in a protective gesture, warning Cerise off. Clearly demonstrating that Paisley wasn't to be harmed.

The dark-haired witch looked me dead in the eye, a slight smirk curling one side of her mouth. Then she released the spell she'd been building.

I knew the moment before it hit me that it was going to hurt.

I didn't recognize the tenor of the magic—which meant it was a spell I hadn't encountered yet.

I let my own magic loose, flaring it around me in the hopes that somehow the raw power would mitigate the hit.

Cerise's spell seared across my hands, wrists, and forearms, slamming into and across my chest. It actually picked me up off my feet, flinging me back into the kitchen island, into Paisley.

Despite the protections Aiden had adhered to my dress, it shredded. My skin seared, pain streaking through every nerve, every bone.

Paisley caught me in her tentacles, holding me aloft. She slowly lowered me to the tile floor, scouring me with her magic, easing the bite of the witch's spell as I found my footing.

No.

That wasn't witch magic.

At least no witch magic I'd ever been exposed to.

The entire time, I'd kept my gaze on the witches. I saw horror bloom in Ocean's eyes. I saw her grab her mother's shoulder—before Cerise cast the spell.

I knew that Cerise had seen me standing between her and her target, Paisley. I knew because a look of smug satisfaction had bloomed on her face as the spell hit me. Then that strange reaction only deepened, her expression becoming knowing and pleased as I regained my footing.

"Stop!" Jenni roared, thrusting herself between me and the witches, arms flung to the sides.

Only seconds had passed.

I finally stopped twitching long enough to step forward and pull the shifter behind me. Paisley jumped off the counter, shrinking to her regular pit bull size and standing at my side.

Magic shifted behind us, emanating from the door to the dining room. Deep, dark sorcerer power, sleepily unleashed—Isa.

"First blood," Isa drawled darkly from behind us. "To the good witches."

Cerise just stared at me with that smug smile on her face. The third eye was still blazing on her forehead, her hands surrounded by magic.

I raised my own hands, calling forth the blade still imbued with Aiden's retrieval spell. I wrapped my stiff, burned fingers around the hilt.

Jenni shifted around me, covering my right side.

"Next time," I growled to the shifter, "just cold-cock her. She was idiotically fixated on me."

Jenni nodded, looking disconcerted. "Next time."

I tilted my head at Cerise, anger dampening the pain as my stolen healing ability struggled to deal with the damage. "Care to try that again, witch?"

"Mom," Ocean hissed, panicked. "Mom. It's just the dog. I told you it was just the dog! Playing! Mom! You've hurt Emma!"

Cerise blinked. Then frowned. The third eye on her forehead winked out.

Aiden leaped the back patio steps, barreling into the house. He was quickly followed by Khalid. Grosvenor and Sky paused on the patio, facing the yard. Just in case the threat was coming from without.

It wasn't. But it was still a smart protocol.

Aiden hesitated, his gaze raking over me, including the blade in my hands. He darted an incredulous glance at his mother. Then all emotion blanked from his face. He lowered his hands and deliberately relaxed. But his tone was cold when he spoke.

"What the fuck is going on?"

"Nothing," Cerise whispered, her voice high and almost childlike. "Nothing."

"Emma is a moment away from taking your fucking head, Mother," Aiden said, still cold. "And by the state of her dress, of her skin, I'd say it's going to be a justified kill."

Cerise blinked, raising her hands to her face. "The demon is your...pet?"

"Her name is Paisley," I said stiffly.

"Neither a demon nor a pet," Isa said from the dining room doorway. His magic was still primed.

I ignored him, not interested in having him speak for me.

"A misunderstanding, then," Cerise said, smiling at Aiden brightly.

"But Aiden sent that picture of Paisley last month," Ocean interjected. "With his foster daughter, Opal—"

"A misunderstanding," Cerise repeated, still looking at Aiden. "The demon—"

"Paisley," he corrected.

"Yes, Paisley just appeared on the kitchen island. Snarling and snapping—"

"Playfully," Ocean muttered, peering around her mother.

Cerise continued ignoring her daughter. "So you can see how I might misunderstand."

Aiden blinked. Then he turned to me, eyeing my still-raised blade. "Emma? A misunderstanding?"

I frowned. Aiden's mother had clearly had more than enough time to quash the spell. A spell that still felt as though it was eating through my right shoulder. That didn't seem like a mistake to me. But I lowered my blade.

"Yes," Cerise sighed, still using that almost singsong tone. "A mistake."

For some reason, I turned and looked over my shoulder at Isa. The sorcerer was still leaning in the doorway to the dining room. I could see the purloined table and chairs behind him, magically expanded to accommodate more guests.

Isa narrowed his eyes at me, nodding. Just once.

"Emma?" Cerise turned her bright-blue eyes on me. "Please let me help heal you ..." She stepped forward, but I flicked the blade up in my right hand again, raising my left to ward her off.

"I'm fine."

She touched her fingertips to my outstretched palm, raking her gaze across me, along my arm and chest. A hint of the earlier pleased smirk crossed her face. "Yes, you are. You heal ... remarkably quickly."

I frowned—and realized even as I did that I was doing a lot of frowning. I didn't like the implication that lay beneath her words, nor what I could feel creeping through the involuntary empathic bond made by her touching me skin to skin. Something almost…greedy.

"Cerise," Aiden said, a warning in his tone. "Emma doesn't like to be touched. I believe you've shit on her hospitality enough already."

"Oh," Cerise cried prettily. "Forgive me, Emma."

But instead of dropping her hand, she wrapped her fingers around my wrist.

My skin crawled, but I didn't look away from the witch.

"Forgive me, Emma," she repeated.

I glanced over at Aiden. He looked pained. And we'd been so happy just a moment before.

I looked back at Cerise. "It's fine. I'm fine."

She leaned into me. "Give me the dress after you change. I'll have it repaired before dinner."

I nodded, but there was something continuing to creep up, to slip through the empathic bond, that I didn't like. I twisted my wrist against Cerise's hold.

"Oh," she cried again, as if not realizing she'd still been holding on to me.

The timer on the oven went off.

The dark-haired witch stepped around me, brushing her hands together. "Excuse me. I have to take the lid off the sourdough."

"You ready for me?" Jenni asked Khalid, far too brightly.

The silent sorcerer nodded, stepping back out onto the patio, though his gaze remained on Cerise. Ocean continued to stare at her mother, as did Aiden.

Then Aiden shook his head, and nodded toward the hall.

I nodded back, and he stepped away.

Paisley trundled over to Ocean, and the younger witch hunched down to greet her, grinning. "Ha ha," she cried. "You thought you were being funny!"

Paisley chortled agreeably.

I turned to follow Aiden, my gaze lingering on Cerise as she moved around the kitchen. Isa stepped up beside me, and we entered the hall together. Ahead of us, Aiden was nearing the base of the stairs.

"Before attacking a demon," Isa mused, his tone pointed, "one might have wondered how a demon would have managed to get through the wards."

"Summoned by one of the sorcerers tied to that boundary," I said, before fully thinking through the point he was trying to make.

Isa snorted. "Who? Aiden? Because the rest of us can't cast through it." He paused in the doorway to the study.

I glanced back toward the kitchen, feeling only witch magic and Paisley. Aiden had headed upstairs. "Kader walked through the property wards easily enough."

"Kader Azar doesn't traffic in demons," Isa said. "Because Kader Azar doesn't share power."

I looked at Isa. "Cerise is a 'good' witch, as you said. She might not understand that Aiden's wards are powerful enough to thwart a demon summoning."

Isa flicked his fingers toward me, no magic in the gesture. "A good witch?"

I looked down, taking in the shredded dress hanging off me. The crisscross red pattern was still fading from my exposed skin.

He leaned slightly closer. "Can you tell me what spell she hit you with?"

I shook my head. "Some sort of pure energy."

"But masterfully channeled. Not just wild magic flung in a panic."

I nodded.

"Wouldn't you know?" he asked intently. "With all your training, all your…conditioning? Wouldn't you know?"

"I know now," I said grimly, stepping away from him and the conversation. I was suddenly tired. Too much of my energy pumped into healing, perhaps. Aiden was waiting for me upstairs to assess the damage. And I needed to get the dress to Cerise so she could repair it before dinner.

Isa's energy was chaotic. His questions were intrusive. I just wanted to be peaceful again. At peace, happily.

OPAL'S SMILING FACE APPEARED ON THE SCREEN OF the iPad. "Hi!" Aiden and I had cloistered ourselves in the study for our late afternoon check-in with the young witch, having just woken from an unexpected nap.

A light-skinned teen was seated to Opal's left, holding a small blue and gold box aloft. Her dark-blond, short-cropped curls were clipped back from her face, bobbing around her head when she moved. She was slim and slightly taller than Opal. A darker-skinned teen towered over both girls on Opal's right. His dark hair was clipped close to his head. His dark-blue eyes were alert, intelligent.

"This is Emily," Opal said, nodding to her left. "And Jack."

"Hi." Emily smiled, reserved. Perhaps nervous.

"Jack Harris Fairchild," the other teen said formally. "Witch. Son of Wisteria, the head of the Fairchild coven."

Adopted by the head of the coven, if I remembered Aiden's primer on Opal's friends correctly.

"Oh, yeah," Opal said. "I keep forgetting the etiquette classes."

"You do," Jack grumbled. "You know there's a reason for it."

Opal waved her hand. "Yeah, yeah, so we don't go around attacking people who we might get into trouble for attacking."

Jack frowned. "That's not it at all."

Emily hid a smile behind her hand, and I had to stop myself from doing the same. I could actually feel Aiden relaxing beside me, stretching his legs under the desk. He slung an arm behind me, leaning back. Grinning. Happy.

But hadn't we'd been happy a moment before?

And relaxed? Before?

We had. Hadn't we?

We had napped through tea. That was unusual.

Aiden gestured toward me. "Emma Johnson. Amplifier. Mother of Opal."

The young witch centered on the screen grinned at me, displaying her crooked eyeteeth. "Adopted, but yeah."

The adoption hadn't actually been formalized yet, but something sweet bloomed in my chest. I let it be, enjoying the warmth as I nodded toward Aiden. "Aiden Myers. Sorcerer. My…mine."

Aiden chuckled quietly. Then, covering my sudden inability to articulate myself, he said, "And what have you got there, Emily?"

I blinked, focusing on the screen.

Emily was still holding the small box aloft on her fingertips. She glanced nervously at Opal, then Jack.

Opal elbowed her. "You go."

Emily bobbed her head, setting her curls tumbling. "It's a soul vessel. Sealed."

"Hmm," Aiden mused thoughtfully. He was clearly planning on playing along even though he'd already decided that the purloined vessel was a project, not an actual artifact of power.

"We're researching the inscription," Opal interjected excitedly. "Like you said we should. So now we want to open it."

"I see." Aiden flashed a smile at me.

"Don't look at me," I said. "I'd just pry the lid off."

"You'd just leave it gathering dust on the shelf," Aiden retorted playfully.

I grinned. "Yeah, I would."

"Really?" Emily gasped. "You'd ignore it?!"

Jack also looked aghast at this prospect.

"Emma isn't into this sort of stuff," Opal said.

"Necromancy isn't really my thing," I said agreeably. "It wouldn't call to me."

"Not just necromancy," Opal crowed. "It's sealed with runes."

"And at least one witch spell," Jack said.

I glanced at Aiden, who smirked at me knowingly. A make-work project indeed. I settled my hand on his knee, and he covered it with his own. It was odd, I realized, how a conversation with Opal's friends that would likely amount to nothing but empty chatter didn't chafe me in the least—in contrast with how quickly my patience with the sorcerers and the witches was wearing out.

"The runes?" Aiden prompted. "Have you worked out the core alphabet?"

Opal pouted. "Not yet."

"You need a sorcerer," he said. "And most definitely before you try to open it."

Emily and Jack grimaced.

Opal sighed. "Really? They're all, like, snobby bores."

"Yes," Aiden said, completely serious. "A project like this takes time, patience, and the right players."

Opal huffed. Emily and Jack looked doubtful.

"But you'll look at what I have?" the young witch asked hopefully.

"We," Jack corrected. "What we have."

"We." Opal rolled her eyes, then she was back to grinning at Aiden excitedly. "I took a picture. I'm going to send it to you along with what we've worked out, as an attachment." She reached for the screen.

"Wait," I said, leaning forward. "What about your classes and—"

The call ended.

I slumped back in my chair.

"And?" Aiden prompted. "What were you about to ask, Momma Amplifier? How they've been feeding her?"

I glowered at him. I had been about to ask exactly that. Melissa at the Home Cafe had mentioned something about making sure Opal was getting enough protein and calcium just the other day, and ...

Aiden's eyes were twinkling.

"I'm allowed—"

He leaned over and kissed me. "Yes, yes, my love."

I curled my fingers through his hair. "I don't want to sit through dinner with your family. I know that's idiotic, but …"

He frowned, touching my bare collarbone. "It's not idiotic. I still can't wrap my head around that spell…or Cerise even being able to cast anything of that magnitude."

"You said you didn't know her well. And the spell she's got on Kader is really impressive."

He laughed. "Trust you to be impressed by a spell slowly draining the life from one of the most powerful sorcerers in existence—all the way from another continent."

"You're totally impressed as well."

"Well, yes. But I'm a dark sorcerer."

"Dark, dark, dastardly."

He grinned wickedly. "Most definitely."

"I wouldn't call him the most powerful sorcerer in existence to his face, though."

"Don't worry," Aiden said quietly, speaking mostly to himself. "He uses the title already." Then he sighed, sitting back in his chair, gaze settling on the blank screen of the iPad almost mournfully. As if Opal had taken all the light with her when she'd ended the call. As if we were both struggling to remain focused, on task.

That was an odd thought.

A soft knock sounded on the closed door. "Dinner," Ocean called through from the hall.

Aiden looked at me grimly. "I reiterate …"

"We can kick them out at any time."

He nodded stiffly, stood, and offered me his hand. "Let's go reintroduce my parents."

I took his hand. His skin was warm and lightly callused. I stood, smoothing my dress. When I'd woken, I realized I'd forgotten to give the damaged dress to Cerise, so I was wearing a green cotton-and-silk sundress for dinner. "Maybe we should have had dinner outside, picnic style. Mitigate any damage the house might take."

"It's too late now."

PAISLEY HAD DISAPPEARED AGAIN—POSSIBLY ANNOYED that there was no place set for her at the table. The table that had been purloined from the kitchen now occupied the dining room, and was twice as large as it should have been, even with the extra leaf.

I wasn't certain how I felt about my house being rearranged, or even about how the witches had commandeered the kitchen in the first place. But there were suddenly nine people to feed and I didn't cook, so I shoved my unease away. Holding Aiden's hand while wandering into the dining room helped.

The centerline of the table was laden with platters of food. I spotted a chicken dish featuring meat falling off the bone, mushrooms, and small onions, all drenched in a gravy that stank of pungent red wine. There were mashed potatoes and a large green salad slicked with a creamy dressing. Cerise's sourdough bread—clearly started and raised with a hefty dose of magic—rounded the meal out. Lots of herbs and butter in every dish. I glanced through to the kitchen as I moved toward an empty seat, spotting a series of cheeses on a cutting board and another platter filled with fruit.

I didn't recognize any of the larger serving dishes.

I paused before the empty seat that would put my back to the open doorway into the kitchen, realizing that the only other seat available was across the far side of the table.

Cerise was at the foot of the table to my left. Knowingly or not, she'd placed herself between or before all three exits to the dining room.

The china cabinet that the previous owners of the house had left behind had been moved into the back left corner of the room. Courtesy of Christopher and Aiden, it now contained three china teacups and saucers in the Royal Albert black rose pattern.

Kader Azar was sitting at the head of the table, at the farthest point away from any of the exits except for the window behind him. Isa sat to his left. An empty seat—obviously intended for Aiden—was on the elder sorcerer's right.

Ocean sat to the right of Cerise. Sky was on her mother's left, next to Grosvenor in the middle. I then noted that someone had actually assigned the seats. I leaned over, seeing my name written in a curly cursive script on a little card set on what appeared to be a china rose. Personalized place settings. And again, unless the attic had suddenly yielded up more than Christopher or I had excavated, they weren't ours.

My seat placed me between Khalid and Ocean.

Silence had taken over the dining room at my inspection of the seating arrangements. Still holding Aiden's hand—his grip on the edge of being too tight, even for me—I leaned across the table and picked up my placeholder card. Then, nearly dragging my hair through the chicken dish, which honestly smelled terrible, I grabbed Grosvenor's place tag, swapping it out for my own.

Cerise opened her mouth.

I looked at her.

Just looked.

And looked.

She shut her mouth, peeved but quiet about it.

Grosvenor stood up.

I crossed around the table, taking his seat. Aiden settled into the chair next to his father.

Wearing a dark tan suit, Kader was smiling, eyes downcast. He sat slightly away from the table, hands folded in his lap.

Isa reached to his right and swapped his card for Khalid's. His brother stood without comment, trading seats with Isa to sit across from Aiden.

Sky then swapped places with Ocean, placing herself beside Grosvenor, and leaving Ocean beside me. That was interesting.

And now no one was sitting where Cerise had placed them, excepting her and Kader. At least I assumed it had been her idea, based on her pinched expression.

"If you are all settled," she said haughtily. "We may begin."

Plates were passed around. Grosvenor served the chicken dish. But when Ocean reached to take my plate, I held it in place.

"I'm happy with the salad and the bread," I murmured, feeling Cerise's gaze on me.

When everyone was served, we started eating. I slathered what appeared to be whipped herb butter on a hunk of the sourdough, and tried to ignore that there was too much dressing on, and not enough variety of vegetables in, the salad. Too many herbs in the butter as well.

Aiden pressed his knee against mine, eating while alternating his gaze between his father and mother.

Kader nibbled on the chicken. "The coq au vin is delightful," he said to no one in particular.

That was the pungent chicken dish, I presumed.

"I worked with what I had," Cerise said stiffly.

"Aiden didn't mention that you were a vegetarian," Sky said apologetically, speaking to me.

"I'm not."

Grosvenor coughed, though he might have been stifling a laugh. This drew a sniff from Cerise. The curse breaker took a large bite of the mashed potatoes and made exaggerated pleased sounds.

Sky lowered her head, hiding her smile with a bite of chicken.

The curse breaker glanced around at all of us. Khalid had already cleared his plate. Like me, Ocean was just nibbling at a mound of salad. And Cerise wasn't eating at all. For that matter, neither was Kader, though he was making a show of it, pushing the food around on his plate.

Who ate what or when or how much really wasn't any of my business. But I actually had to quash the impulse to get up and make the elder sorcerer a peanut butter and strawberry jam sandwich. Why I thought he'd eat that, I didn't know.

I stuffed another butter-laden hunk of bread in my mouth.

"Jenni did well," Grosvenor said.

It took me a second to realize he was talking to me. I looked at him blankly.

"Your…trainee?" He raised an eyebrow. "She found all of Sky's planted magic, two spells of mine, and one of Khalid's presets."

I'd forgotten. What with all the magic being thrown around in the kitchen, and getting hit by Cerise's spell …

I had just wandered upstairs and taken a nap.

A nap.

Leaving Jenni alone with sorcerers and witches she didn't even know. Jenni, who was still really half in hiding.

Interrupting the confusion roiling around in my head, Aiden said, "You had Jenni sniff out magic foreign to her? That's a good idea. I'll contribute next time."

"I'm surprised her pack didn't train her," Sky said. "But I guess she doesn't come across many Adepts in a small town like this."

"She found your spells easily enough," Grosvenor said.

Sky shrugged one shoulder, not looking at the curse breaker. "I didn't try very hard to hide them. I didn't think that was the point of the exercise."

Sky was right. It hadn't been the point. I was just trying to help Jenni build a database in her head. But again, even knowing how trivial the assignment was, it was completely unlike me to walk away from a training session, leaving Jenni exposed and—

Aiden squeezed my knee. I had a feeling I'd missed some bit of conversation, or some question directed at me.

"It was interesting that Jenni had a harder time with Khalid's presets," Grosvenor said, as if he might have been repeating himself.

Kader was watching me with narrowed eyes. Then he turned that gaze on Cerise. I could feel the dark-haired witch stiffen under his regard.

"Combat spells?" I asked, forcing myself to focus.

Khalid nodded. "Just a basic charge, a disruptor, and—"

Cerise grabbed the napkin off her lap and tossed it on the table. "How can you all just sit here?" she cried in a high-pitched voice. "Talking about…nothing?!"

I frowned. Training Jenni wasn't—

"With him! Evil incarnate, just…just sitting there!" She jabbed a finger toward Kader.

Everyone moved.

Magic roiled.

Multiple shields snapped into place.

Grosvenor stood, grabbing Sky's chair and dragging it back a few steps, taking them both out of the line of fire as he shielded her. Khalid's chair actually slammed against the wall, leaving a dent in it. He stepped to his father's side, placing a hand on Kader's shoulder. A shield snapped up around them both.

Aiden, beside me, and Isa, across the table from me, both stood. Each sorcerer placed one hand flat on the table and flung the other hand outward. A wall of magic snapped between the hands they held on the table—a dual shield, encompassing about two-thirds of the room, ceiling to floor. The magic slid outward, coating the table and all the items on it. Presumably so the food and plates couldn't be used as projectiles.

Smart.

I wouldn't have thought of that.

But then, I'd never had a family dinner before.

Isa's outward-facing hand was stretched toward Cerise. A dark-blue spell of some sort glistened in his palm.

Aiden placed his free hand on my shoulder. I felt a cool shiver of power coating me.

Her reaction more delayed, Ocean jumped to her feet, chair falling back. She placed herself at the corner of the table, next to her mother. She was holding a small round bottle in each hand, pulling the cork stopper of one out with her teeth.

Whatever was in the bottle smelled foul.

Only Kader, Cerise, and I remained seated.

Magic slashed through the dining room, encasing us in a strained silence, on the edge of violence. Sorcerers versus witches. Sky had stepped away from Grosvenor, her eyes glowing light blue.

And I was in the middle.

A look of what I thought might be satisfaction flitted across Cerise's face as she stared across at Kader. A hint of that third eye—just a glimmer of light, really—winked open on the witch's forehead, then disappeared. The elder sorcerer's face was utterly blank. Bored, even.

Then he turned, looked pointedly at me, and smiled. As if he knew I was only a breath away from charging in and settling everyone down with a mere brush of my fingers.

I looked away, back at Cerise. She blinked. And then, as if the situation was just dawning on her, her eyes widened, hands coming up to cover her mouth. "Oh," she cried. "I'm…I was never …"

Isa snorted. "Tell that to Emma's dress."

Still blinking—to an extent that made me wonder whether the action was feigned—Cerise looked at me. Her big blue eyes slowly filled with tears. "That was unforgivable of me, Emma. I'm just so…I'm just so …"

She didn't finish the thought. Her words just hung there, as if she expected someone to step in and soothe her.

And Sky did just that, touching her mother's shoulder. Cerise sighed, hunching down. But none of the tears she'd called forth fell down her creamy cheeks.

"Ocean," I said.

The young witch flinched, her gaze snapping to me from her mother.

"Put the stopper back in that."

Her lip curled as if she was going to refuse. The cork stopper was still clenched in her teeth, and an identical bottle of what I knew to be a deadly poison—the scent was unmistakable—was still clenched in her other hand.

I stared her down. "You will stopper that. And then you will dispose of it. All of it. And not anywhere on my property."

Ocean raised her chin. "You haven't made the sorcerers dump their—"

I moved. Standing and lunging in the same motion, passing through the shield that Aiden still held over me, I wrapped my hand over the open bottle in

Ocean's hand. Then I wrenched the stopper from her teeth. She shrieked in pain. I had definitely hurt her jaw. I jammed the stopper back in the bottle, twisting her wrist until she let go.

She stumbled back, belatedly bringing the second bottle into play. I plucked that out of her grasp as well. None too gently. Then I forced myself to step back before I decided to punish her for not following my orders.

"Aiden!" Ocean howled, holding her jaw.

Sky and Cerise were looking at me, wide eyed and slack jawed. The faces of the sorcerers were inscrutable, excepting Grosvenor.

The curse breaker, grinning like an idiot, whistled. "Holy shit. Nice moves, amplifier."

I passed the bottles to Aiden. He took them, holding both up to the light. On the other side of the table, Isa leaned forward, eyeing the poison.

"Aiden!" Ocean howled again.

"Belladonna," Kader said coolly. "Mixed with witch hazel, which helps it break through the cell structure. And a touch of something else nasty."

"Death cap," I said, keeping an eye on the witches. "One drop in any of the food, and Ocean kills us all. Friend and foe."

"Well," Kader said blandly, "any of us who couldn't smell it, identify it before consuming it. So not you or me, amplifier."

"It would still hurt like hell, sorcerer," I snapped back, baring my teeth. "Ask me how I know."

He shut up.

"What the fuck?" Aiden roared.

Ocean's bottom lip and chin trembled as she made an effort not to crumple under her brother's rage. "Aiden…you know what he did to Mom—"

"And you thought killing all of us over dinner was equal revenge?"

"No, I…I…I thought …"

"That's enough, Aiden," Cerise snapped. "You and Emma are blowing this out of proportion."

Aiden went still. A terrible, blank stillness even while his magic snapped and roiled around him. "I'm blowing this out of proportion," he repeated quietly, locked into a staring contest with his mother. "In my own home. When you have now not only attacked and wounded Emma, but allowed your daughter, a witch still under your tutelage, to threaten all of our lives with a highly illegal poison."

All the hair stood up on the back of my neck.

Khalid and Isa took a step back from the table. Then another. Grosvenor, his gaze locked to Aiden, slowly reached for Sky's arm and tried to yank her behind him. She shrieked in protest, holding her ground.

Ocean glanced back and forth between her mother and her brother, tears slipping down her face. "I…I'm …"

Cerise stood. For a moment, it appeared as if she was going to press forward. Then her face crumpled. "You always take his side," she said to Aiden. "I keep hoping and hoping that if I just love you enough, that some goodness will …" Her voice broke. She covered her face with her hands, then turned and ran from the room.

I contemplated going after her. I thought about draining her dry even as I forced her back into the dining room, back into her seat, and made her apologize to Aiden.

"I'm…so sorry," Ocean mumbled, wiping the tears from her face. "Aiden?"

He nodded once, stiffly.

Looking utterly dejected, Ocean turned from the room and followed her mother. Their magic trailed behind them, all the way upstairs.

"Well," Grosvenor said, righting his and Sky's chairs, "that was exciting." He sat, pulling the platter of chicken toward him.

Sky looked torn between leaving and staying. Then leaving won out, and she wandered slowly after her sister.

"There is belladonna and death cap on the damn table," Isa said to Grosvenor. "And you're eating?"

"What?" The curse breaker shrugged, grabbing a piece of bread. "The vials are capped. Why should the food go to waste?"

"Food the damn witches prepared." Isa pushed his chair back to the table.

"I already checked it for poison," Khalid said quietly. "Though it's become rather obvious that

Emma would have known if we were about to be murdered."

The sorcerers were all staring at me. I was staring out of the open doorway, still contemplating going after Cerise. But to do what? Say what?

Aiden settled his hand on the back of my neck, then stepped closer to kiss my temple. "She's said worse about me," he murmured. "And she's not wrong."

"She is," I growled.

"Now," he said, his tone meant to be soothing though his own magic still raged around us unchecked. "You're right. She's wrong now."

I nodded, just once. Then I crossed into the kitchen, grabbing the cheese and fruit platters from the island and carrying both back into the dining room.

Aiden and Isa were staring down at the two bottles of poison. Khalid helpfully cleared a spot in the center of the table, pushing the food but not the bread in front of Grosvenor. Then he took the platter of fruit from me, setting it down.

I set the cheese board next to the sourdough, then started cutting thinner slices of bread. Sandwich thickness.

"I can't figure out how she got it through the wards," Aiden muttered, still staring at the bottles of poison.

"Maybe she mixed it here?" Isa rubbed his temples. "Though the death cap …"

"Exactly," Aiden muttered.

"Some of us need to be filled in," Grosvenor said around another mouthful of mashed potatoes. "We aren't all old."

" 'Wise' is the word you were looking for." Isa smirked.

The curse breaker laughed. "Nope."

Aiden's magic slowly settled as he explained. "Even after I opened the property boundary and let Ocean in, the death cap should have created a...ripple effect when the wards sealed behind her."

Khalid started slicing a block of the white cheddar cheese with the knife that had been set on the cutting board. For just that purpose, I presumed. "So she got the ingredients here?"

Aiden shook his head.

I stepped back into the kitchen, retrieving mayo and Dijon mustard from the fridge.

"Emma?" Aiden asked as I returned to the dining room. "Christopher wouldn't use belladonna or death cap in the garden, would he?"

Kader straightened slightly, his attention shifting from the stoppered poison to me—clearly interested in who 'Christopher' was. Based on the size of the house and the amount of work the extensive garden required, it was clearly obvious to the elder sorcerer that multiple people lived here. Had he already guessed that another member of the Five was among them?

"How many of the others are you in contact with?" he asked. "How many usually live here?"

So that was a yes.

Aiden grimaced, turning to his father. "Can you just stop? Stop with your obsession with Emma and the others? They're out of your reach. They're not players in this little drama of yours."

Kader's expression became hooded.

"I don't think he would," I said calmly, answering Aiden's question. I spread some mayo on two pieces of sourdough. "But you could text him. I have no use for either."

Aiden nodded. "Neither do I."

"Paisley," Grosvenor said, watching me closely as I added a touch of Dijon mustard on top of the mayo, then started layering the cheese that Khalid had thinly sliced.

"No," Aiden snapped. But then, apparently thinking about it, he looked at me. "No?"

I snorted a laugh, cutting the sandwich I'd made and placing it on the edge of the platter of fruit. I started making a second one. "Anything is possible with Paisley. But I don't see why she would have stored it any place that Ocean could find."

"The witch would be attuned to it," Khalid said quietly. "Her magic."

Right.

Silence fell for a moment as the sorcerers all watched me make a second and third cheese sandwich, placing them on the edge of the fruit platter.

Then all those eyes turned to Kader. The elder sorcerer pushed his still-full plate out of the way, reached across, and took one of the halves. The camembert, I thought. Though once it was sliced, I couldn't distinguish it from the brie.

The elder sorcerer leaned back in his seat and ate the sandwich, not bothering with a plate or napkin.

Aiden, Isa, and Khalid settled back into their seats, not as spread out along the length of the table as before. Aiden placed one half of a sandwich with white cheddar on my plate, along with a branch of red grapes, then served himself.

I made more sandwiches, eating my own, until I ran out of bread. Then I settled down.

"I don't know how to dispose of it safely," Aiden muttered.

"You don't," Isa said. "I'm surprised the fumes didn't knock out those closest to it."

"Ocean's likely immune," Grosvenor said, dipping the scraps of the sourdough loaf into the last of the whipped butter.

I remembered Fish and Knox eating like that in their late teens and early twenties, consuming everything and anything. For energy, though, not enjoyment.

"I don't see her much," he continued. "At school. But I've shared a couple of classes with Sky."

"Your aunt has you spying on the Myers witches?" Kader asked coolly.

The curse breaker shrugged. "It's their territory, so yeah. If there was anything to report, I assumed it would make its way back to you."

Kader just hummed thoughtfully.

"You know it goes both ways," Isa said. "Right? Sky is reporting on you as well."

"Sure." Grosvenor cut a huge hunk of cheddar from the remaining block and took a big bite out of it.

Unable to contain myself, I said, "There's more bread. And crackers."

"Cool, cool," he said, getting up and heading into the kitchen.

"I can't have it here," Aiden said, getting back to the subject at hand.

"Why?" Kader asked, nibbling on a piece of apple that Khalid had sliced.

Aiden just shot his father a look.

Kader smiled, amused. "You can't possibly think I don't know about the child. Her imprint is all over the loft in the barn."

Around the pentagram, he meant. Aiden often had Opal practice her spells within its boundary, where he could see what she was casting more clearly.

"Lock it up," the elder sorcerer said matter-of-factly when Aiden didn't reply. "It's a difficult brew. In fact, I doubt Ocean has refined her poison making to that level yet."

Grosvenor wandered back in from the kitchen with his hand buried deep in a box of crackers. "She likely bartered for it. Her cosmetics and creams are the best. They last the longest, keep their color, that sort of thing." He looked a little chagrined. "Not that I know from experience."

Khalid laughed. "Right."

Aiden glanced at me. "It's not Opal I'm concerned about. She knows not to touch the items in the study safe, if she could even get through the wards and the lock." He meant Paisley. The demon dog was big on eating magic. "Do you know if she's been exposed to belladonna or death cap?"

Isa leaned forward, intrigued. "The dog? Paisley?"

I ignored him, answering Aiden. "Not that I know of."

"Could Daniel neutralize it?" he asked quietly.

"No," Kader said before I could speak, his gaze on me. "The magical elements, yes. But the nullifier wields no power over the organic elements."

I bared my teeth in a sharp smile. "Not that you know, sorcerer."

Kader grinned at me widely. "True. It was always a thrill when one of the Five developed a new ability."

I just stared at him, not rising to the bait. Or not any farther than I already had, at least. Aiden settled his hand on my knee. Anchoring himself, I thought, not to hold me in place.

"And on that delightful note," Kader said as he slid his chair back, "I believe I shall retire for the evening. You will all be present for negotiations tomorrow? Isa has outlined an agenda."

Isa nodded, not looking at his father. He was holding a half-eaten sandwich, seemingly forgotten.

Kader touched Aiden on the shoulder as he crossed around the table, going the long way, then into the kitchen and out through the laundry room door.

"Am I the only one, like, completely in the dark around here?" Grosvenor asked.

"No," Khalid said.

"Well, that's good." The curse breaker smiled at me. "You got any more of those ginger snaps, Emma?"

I smiled back at him involuntarily. "In the freezer."

"Woot!" He jumped up from the table and took off for the kitchen.

Isa slumped back in his chair, eating the last bites of his sandwich. "Tomorrow is going to go really well."

"Completely smoothly," Aiden said agreeably.

Then the brothers all started laughing. The sound was full, warm, robust. But edged with tension. As if the three had spent many years navigating family dinners that inevitably imploded.

I hadn't come out of my childhood laughing. But we all bore our scars differently. And I felt quite certain that all of those scars would be reopened—emotionally speaking—during this parley.

LEAVING THE SORCERERS DEEP IN DISCUSSION IN THE front living room—and surrounded by what appeared to be at least half of Aiden's collection of magical texts—I headed to bed. Grosvenor had wandered off about an hour before, and I was too tired to bother tracking him. The simmering witch magic on the top floor was annoying—a product of the wards they'd placed on the other bedrooms—and I wasn't interested in playing babysitter to anyone who wanted to wander about the property.

The door to my upstairs sitting room was slightly open. A blue light that had nothing to do with magic emanated from within. I touched my fingertips to the door, pressing it open.

Ocean was seated, legs crossed, in the middle of the couch. Her face was puffy, eyes red. She appeared to be watching the TV on mute. But then, spotting me, she blinked, pulling a small earbud out of her left ear.

"Emma," she whispered, touching the remote control to pause whatever she was watching. "Is it okay that I'm in here?"

I nodded, starting to withdraw.

"Um, Emma? I am sorry."

I thought about what to say to that. My time with Opal—and with Aiden, for that matter—had informed me that taking a moment to be compassionate was often the best course. Rather than simply expecting those around me to understand what they'd done wrong and correct their behavior without a drawn-out discussion.

But the fact that Ocean had, at a minimum, threatened to murder the bulk of Aiden's family—whether or not she'd deemed them deserving—didn't make me inclined to be compassionate. Even if she'd been fighting for her life, that poison was overkill. She could have quashed an assault without resorting to belladonna and death cap.

"I'm sorry …" Ocean said again, whispering into the dark silence between us.

"You said. But you could have killed Aiden tonight, when there was no immediate threat—"

She opened her mouth to interrupt me.

I gave her a look.

She snapped her mouth closed. Then, eyes downcast, she nodded as if actually listening.

"You know that poison is illegal," I said, not quite ready to let it go, despite being weary. "By the rules of any of the governing bodies."

"I don't know why I even bought it," Ocean murmured. "Mom pulled us out of school in the middle of the night, getting Sky to answer Aiden's letter. And she was…off …" She shook her head, as if editing herself. "We only had a couple of hours to pack, and I…I…just felt like I needed something…I needed…something…to protect her."

Something in her words, in her delivery, caught me. That sounded a lot like magical coercion or mind control. Except I hadn't picked up anything like that from Cerise. Or from anyone else, for that matter. "To…protect your mother?"

"Yes. I …" Ocean's words, or whatever she was trying to express, got caught in her throat. "It was the same tonight. The same reaction. But a thousand times worse. I'd never felt anything like that before."

"Adrenaline."

"Yeah, I know. Just …" She shrugged. "I hadn't felt it that way before."

"You saw that spell your mom hit me with in the kitchen, right?"

Ocean grimaced. "I really don't think she meant to—"

I waved my hand, cutting her off. "My point is, Cerise Myers can take care of herself."

"Yeah." But Ocean didn't sound at all certain, even as she agreed. "I guess so."

"Enjoy your movie," I said, stepping back into the hall.

She grinned at me, though her eyes were still red. Still sad. "I'm rewatching *Brooklyn Nine-Nine* from the beginning. So funny."

I had no idea what she was talking about. "Great. Good night."

"Good night." She popped the earbud back into her ear, then slumped back on the couch, more relaxed than she had been at the beginning of our conversation.

Chatting about nothing apparently worked wonders for some people. And since it usually didn't kill me, I could suffer through it. I closed the sitting room door most of the way, then headed to bed myself.

I WASHED MY FACE AND GOT READY FOR BED AS I mulled over my conversation with Ocean—specifically, about what she'd said regarding feeling compelled to protect her mother. Twice. After applying cream to my hands, I climbed into bed. And as I did, I spotted a bouquet of apple flowers in a mason jar on my side table.

I blinked in disbelief. Someone had snapped three branches off my apple trees. That was ridiculously destructive.

I leaned closer. The center of each blossom was oddly dark. Almost resembling the third eye I'd seen on Cerise's forehead.

I frowned.

That was an odd thought.

So they weren't apple blossoms. I inhaled the sweet scent of the flowers. Perhaps Aiden had found some other fruit tree or bush growing wild on the property and thought I might like a sprig from it? That made more sense.

The sorcerer did love giving me little gifts.

I snuggled under the quilt and the top sheet, tucking my pillow under my head, facing the flowers. Even though this was our second spring on the property, random crocuses, daffodils, and now tulips were continuing to pop up all over the place. Christopher had actually gotten all excited about some crocuses he found in the garden, thinking they might be saffron. Apparently, one flower produced just a single strand of the spice, which didn't seem all that sustainable to me.

I drifted, feeling Aiden's magic as he climbed the stairs, slipped into the room, and stepped into the bathroom. A few minutes later, he climbed into the bed, tucking up behind me, but careful to not disturb me.

He murmured something quietly, and the wards that encased the bedroom shifted. Then he stilled.

I slipped deeper into sleep.

Aiden rose, lifting up on his elbow and looking around.

I rolled toward him, murmuring, "What is it?"

"What's that smell?"

"Umm…from the flowers?"

I could feel him frowning, more than I could see him in the dark. Then he was suddenly on the other side of the bed, picking up the pretty bouquet. Either he'd moved far too quickly, or I'd somehow drifted off again.

"Sorry, Emma," he murmured. "These stink."

It was my turn to frown. Why would he have picked the flowers in the first place if he didn't like them?

"Didn't you pick them?" I felt as if I was fighting to form the thought, to voice the question out loud.

"No. I assumed you did. Ocean or Sky, maybe? They're both completely enamored with the property." Aiden crossed to the bedroom door, opening it. Then he laughed quietly. "Did you want to come in?"

I rolled over.

Paisley was blocking Aiden's way into the hall. She huffed at him, presumably because the new wards he'd set were stopping her from teleporting into the bedroom.

Then she sneezed.

A loud, sharp, snot-filled explosion.

Aiden groaned. I couldn't see, but his bare legs were now undoubtedly covered in demon dog mucus.

Paisley sneezed again. Shaking her head indignantly, she glared at Aiden.

"Okay," he said. "I was just going to put the flowers in the—"

With a flick of her tongue, Paisley grabbed the flower bouquet, mason jar and all, and ate it.

"Not the jar ..." I whispered. I'd started a collection of antique mason jars, and I had only three so far.

Paisley blinked at me, then grinned.

Apparently, I had only two jars now.

I huffed, collapsing back on my pillow. I heard Aiden enter the bathroom, presumably to wipe his legs down.

"Sorry," he whispered as he climbed back into bed and tucked in beside me, cupping me.

I must have fallen asleep again for a moment, because I was suddenly aware that Aiden's wards were fully up, and I could feel Paisley stretched out beneath the south-facing windows.

I surfaced long enough to snuggle my ass into Aiden's groin. He murmured encouragingly, but then didn't take the suggestion any further. It was unusual for us to climb into any bed and not at least fool around.

I drifted off again. But just before I fell fully asleep, my thoughts turned to how I'd never seen Paisley eat flowers before. She wasn't a big fan of anything resembling leafy greens.

But there was one thing she always tried to consume. Magic.

And the sneeze beforehand—

My eyes snapped open. Blinking into the darkness, I felt my mind racing. Piecing together the events of the last few hours. The feeling of strained happiness with Aiden. The odd afternoon nap. The compulsion Ocean had reported feeling.

And now Paisley's reaction to the flowers.

There had been some sort of magic embedded into the blossoms. Or the flowers themselves were a magical construct—maybe even the source of the apple blossom oracle card that Christopher kept casting?

Anger flushed through me, chasing away any and all of the lingering sense of …

What? Beguilement? Enchantment?

I shifted, intending to wake Aiden and share my thoughts with him. He tightened his hold on me, but didn't wake. He was exhausted. And stressed. On edge.

I settled back onto my pillow, allowing my anger to resolve into a cool rationality.

Someone was screwing with me. Using magic I hadn't encountered before.

It might have been Cerise. The elder witch had plenty of reasons to want to keep me compliant and on her side. But it could just as easily have been any of the others. For multiple reasons.

I could confront the witches and sorcerers directly. I could force the reveal of who was using magic to mess with my head, and why. But doing so might absolutely derail the negotiations.

And then Aiden would suffer the consequences.

Somewhat ironically, though, I knew instinctively that I could exonerate Kader Azar from suspicion. The elder sorcerer knew that I had a robust magical immunity. He wouldn't dare try to use magic to mess with me.

The others didn't know that, though. Which meant whoever was doing this would try to compromise me again. And the more they did try, the faster I would learn to resist it. The faster I would figure out who was responsible.

So I would bide my time.

And then I'd show them what happened to those who tried to control me.

FIVE

KADER WAS LOUNGING ON THE COUCH NEAREST THE front windows of the sitting room, one leg crossed over the other, hands loose at his sides. His tan suit was pristinely pressed, collar open. He wore brown argyle socks. Three dark-suited sorcerers stood between the window and him—Isa, Khalid, and Grosvenor—blocking the bulk of the light coming in from that direction. Cerise, dressed in crisp white linen, sat stiffly, hands folded on her knees, in the center of the opposite couch, flanked on either side by Sky and Ocean.

The length of the coffee table was all that stood between the warring factions. The contract was sitting on it. Cerise hadn't yet picked it up.

I was situated near the door to the front hall, my gaze lingering more often on Aiden than anyone else. The dark-haired sorcerer was across from me, near the unlit fireplace.

One of the people in this room was trying to screw with me. Or perhaps more than one of them. And although I was choosing to stay my hand until Aiden was in the clear, I looked forward to exacting retribution.

No one came into my home, attacked me, and walked away unscathed.

We'd all been standing around, not talking, ever since Isa had placed a short stack of documents before Cerise. Apparently, the terms contained within that proposal had already been agreed to by Kader. The brothers had been working with Sky since the witches had agreed to the mediation, first by message and then late through the night.

Kader glanced at the clock on the mantel—11:13 A.M. Then he sighed heavily. "I understood that you had agreed to my terms, Cerise."

"She has," Sky said.

Cerise had been refusing to speak directly to Kader all morning, using Sky as her mouthpiece. Given how annoying I found that, I was surprised the sorcerers hadn't walked out yet. I just wanted the contract signed, the spell removed, and everyone gone. Preferably before lunch.

Aiden had shaved and put his suit back on that morning, with none of our usual light banter. No morning sex, even though Paisley had disappeared at dawn. And I was near done with the emotional toil being exacted on him.

I was a breath away from forcing the issue. All the issues.

"I was under the impression that I had already been generous," Kader said. "The house in Paris when you wished to return to your coven, the yearly allowance."

Sky furrowed her brow.

Cerise cast her gaze out the window overlooking the barn and gardens.

"The trust funds for each of your children."

"Mom?" Ocean whispered.

Cerise didn't answer her daughter.

"But it's all nothing," Kader said, his tone sharpening. "I'll give you whatever you want. The gold and platinum. The extensive list of artifacts. Some of which I was honestly unaware I possessed." He smiled. "You were thorough in your documentation before you left the compound."

"You stole ten years of her life," Sky snapped. "You forced her to…you raped her! And then you stole her child, her son."

Kader narrowed his eyes at Sky. Then he slowly transferred that gaze to Cerise.

The dark-haired witch's back stiffened.

"Is that how you recount it?" Kader's tone was smooth, even. "Rape?"

Sky clenched her hands, pressing her fists to the tops of her thighs. "Magical beguilement is still rape. You took away her ability to say no. That's rape!"

Behind Kader, Grosvenor flinched.

"Beguilement …" Kader murmured. "Why not report me, Cerise? To the Convocation?"

"What proof did she have?" Aiden asked, his tone cool. "You stopped enforcing the binding after I was born."

A quiet look of triumph filled Cerise's expression as she transferred her attention to her firstborn.

That was an odd reaction, wasn't it? And for some reason, I felt the need to counter it.

"How did you know you wouldn't hurt Aiden?" I asked before anyone else could speak. "When you stole his DNA to construct your strike against Kader. To drain his life, his power, through your son."

Aiden's face blanked, then he looked sharply at his mother. As if he'd forgotten what she'd done, even though we'd already discussed it. As if something was affecting his judgement.

Like the flowers had affected my judgement the previous night.

Today, though, I couldn't feel anything untoward in the sitting room. No unexplained magic. Nothing being currently cast. So had I built up a resistance already? Or was it just exhaustion and stress—and trying to not outright hate his mother—that was affecting Aiden?

Sky's mouth had fallen open, and she looked at her mother incredulously. Ocean placed her hand over her mouth, slumping against the arm of the couch.

Aiden's gaze flicked to his youngest sister, his expression becoming grim. "You used Ocean?" he said quietly. "The study sessions? I thought ..." He quashed the emotion threatening to break through his measured words.

Ocean's eyes filled with tears as she looked at her mother. "That was for this…spell?" she asked in a whisper. "You said you were strengthening the wards on Aiden's apartment."

"You didn't know," Kader said smoothly, watching Cerise like a raptor watches a mouse. "You had no idea whether or not the price of killing me would cost you Aiden. Because the only reason he is standing before you, hale and hearty, more powerful than ever, is because of Emma."

Magic started shifting around the room, emanating from multiple sources, including Aiden. The dark-haired sorcerer—my dark-haired sorcerer—stood stock still, his face completely blank. Thinking everything through, piecing together the timeline.

Specifically, the downhill spiral that he'd been on before being dumped in Lake Cowichan by Silver Pine.

"But, Mom," Ocean whispered. "What about my hair and nail clippings, and Sky's? They were for the house wards, right?"

"What?" Sky hissed.

Aiden's gaze locked to mine, a sudden desperation shining in his bright-blue eyes. "Emma …"

"I know."

"That is not why I'm here."

"I know."

He took a step, coming up against the coffee table hard. "That is not why I stayed."

"I know, Aiden. But let's move forward with getting the spell off you." I looked pointedly at Cerise.

Sky stood up. "No."

Aiden blinked at his sister, shocked. "No?"

She glanced at him, clearly fighting through her own confusion. "Not that. I just mean…our mother would never hurt you. Never. Or us." She glanced at her younger sister.

Khalid snorted. "All evidence stands to the contrary."

Sky pointed her finger across the room at him. "Don't you get involved, sorcerer."

"Involved?" he asked mockingly. "All our lives are on the line because of your mother!"

"All of this is because of your father!"

Magic exploded. Raw power from Sky, countered by an almost detached response from Khalid, who snapped a shield in place with a murmured word.

Sky flung her hands out, stepping forward as she tried to sharpen the attack she had instinctively begun.

Khalid laughed, crossing around the couch. I could feel the spell brewing in his other hand. It would cut Sky down.

Grosvenor shouted. Magic was welling from both him and Aiden. But I leaped onto the coffee table, avoiding the contract and grabbing Sky by her ear, then easily breaking through Khalid's shield to grab his ear.

They started to struggle.

I pulled a large chunk of magic from each of them, absorbing it for myself.

Sky screamed. Losing her balance, she momentarily hung from my hold on her ear, before she braced herself against my hip.

Khalid stumbled, then raised his hand to slam the spell he'd been aiming for Sky against me.

"I'll take that too," I whispered, pulling a long draught of power from him, absorbing the spell as well.

Khalid's face paled.

Sky wrapped her hand around my wrist, her confusion and pain and frustration thundering through from the empathic bond made by our skin-to-skin contact.

"Good," I said, holding Khalid's horrified gaze. "Now you know I'm not here to play, sorcerer."

Kader chuckled under his breath. A self-satisfied smile curled his lips as he lounged back on the couch. He hadn't moved at all.

Isa remained as quiet as ever, but his alert gaze was on Cerise, not me. Aiden was at my back. Grosvenor shifted on his feet, gaze flicking from Sky to me as if he was uncertain whether he should intervene.

"Stay where you are," I said to the curse breaker.

He stilled, almost guiltily. As if he hadn't known he'd drawn my attention.

"Oh," Cerise exclaimed. Her blue-eyed gaze was difficult to read. Perhaps shock? Easing into what might have been disapproval?

For the first time since we'd all entered the room, she looked directly at Kader. "She's one of yours."

"That's enough." Aiden's tone was hoarse, edged in magic. "Emma can rescind your invitation easily enough. And we all know where that would leave you, Father."

That wiped the smirk from Kader's face. "I can admire a specialist at work...a piece of art...without nefarious intent."

Aiden snorted derisively.

"Um," Sky ventured. "Can I have my ear back?"

I let go of her. She stumbled a little, then straightened, rubbing her ear while meeting my gaze. "And the magic you took?"

"That's mine." I looked at Khalid. "Consider it a tithe."

The dark-eyed sorcerer sneered at me. But then he raised his hands in surrender.

I let him go. He immediately returned to his post in the far corner by the front windows. I stepped off the coffee table, moving next to Aiden instead of continuing to block the doorway to the hall.

Sky hesitated, rubbing her ear and looking at her mother. Then she shook her head and crossed into the hallway. She stood there for a moment, obviously torn as to where to go.

"Grosvenor," Kader said. "It's almost lunch. Why don't you and Sky pick us up some food?" He shifted his gaze to me. "Is there a place you like in town, Emma?"

"The Home Cafe," I said stiffly, feeling as though I was giving away another piece of myself—but knowing that refusing to answer would make me appear weak.

The curse breaker stepped around the couch, heading toward the hallway and Sky before I'd finished speaking. He glanced at Aiden. "Keys?"

"In the SUV."

"What?" the curse breaker exclaimed. "You leave it unlocked?"

Aiden huffed out a laugh. "Tip generously."

Grosvenor looked affronted as he moved into the hall. "When don't I?" The younger sorcerer stepped around Sky, not looking at or speaking to her, heading for the front door.

The door opened. Slowly, Sky turned and followed the curse breaker out of the house.

"So like you," Cerise spat. Speaking to Kader. "Ordering everyone around."

Kader eyed the witch. "The timing has been bothering me. Not so much the idea that you would strike at me, though that too is out of character. But why now? A bid for power within the Myers coven? Are you planning to usurp your aunt?"

Cerise frowned, smoothing her hand across her skirt. "Of course not."

"We have Aiden," Kader said. "Our powerful, beautiful boy. A blessing to both our lines. To despise our time together is to regret Aiden. And I most certainly don't."

"You just use him," she spat.

Kader raised an eyebrow, then spoke pleasantly. "You just use him."

Cerise reacted as though he'd slapped her. Then she looked at Aiden, her eyes a little wild. "I would never ..."

"Except ..." Ocean whispered, interrupting. "Except what about the hair, and the—"

"Enough," Cerise snapped. "You have no idea what you're talking about."

"What she will soon come to know," Kader said, "when she heads into the study after our chat, or even if she waits until she goes back to the Academy, is that hair and nails aren't used by witches to fortify wards. Not Myers witches."

Cerise's power rippled through the room, as if it might have been tasting each of us. It had been simmering since the negotiations started, but now it licked at my ankles. The third eye on her forehead blinked lazily, then disappeared.

Kader's expression went hard. "Sign the contract, Cerise. I will give you anything to save my life, to stop you from destroying everyone else in this silly, spiteful—"

"You're the one who's threatening everyone!"

"What did you think would happen?" he asked. "That I would let you murder me? Steal what is rightfully mine? And then what? When I'm dead? I should let you dismantle my cabal, everything I've worked for a lifetime to achieve?"

"I would never—"

"Never what? Use Aiden to anchor a spell so dark that even I can't break it? Bespell your daughters toward violence?"

Cerise didn't answer, but her power withdrew, filtering back into her.

"At least tell me you know how to break it," Kader said.

"Of course I do," Cerise said, lying.

Lying.

I didn't even have to be touching her to know. I glanced at Aiden, noting the dawning look of horror in his eyes.

"In principle," Cerise added stiffly. "It will take time and a ritual. That is why I asked Ocean and Sky to join me." Her gaze shifted to Aiden. "I'll need Aiden as well. Possibly all of you."

Then she stood and crossed from the room.

Without signing the contract.

Ocean cast a wide-eyed gaze around at all of us, then specifically at Aiden. He nodded to her, holding out his hand. She practically leaped up from the couch to take it.

She kissed her brother on the cheek, then spoke too brightly. "I'll set the table for lunch."

No one replied as she hustled off into the dining room, then passed through to the kitchen.

"Interesting. First strike from the witches," Isa said. "Again. When we're the dark sorcerers."

"They have more to lose," Kader said. Then he stood and walked out of the room without another word. He crossed into the kitchen to exchange some murmured words with Ocean. Then he left the house through the laundry room.

"Can you see the ties?" Aiden asked Khalid. "The bespellment on the younger witches that Father mentioned?"

Khalid frowned. "I see bonds, as expected. They are blood related."

"And from me to them?"

"Cerise to you. Of course."

Aiden hummed thoughtfully. "So…nothing out of the ordinary. Just the familial ties?"

Khalid sighed. "I haven't examined them closely."

"Maybe you should?"

"Without permission?"

Aiden grimaced. "How close do you need to be?"

Khalid glanced at Isa, sneering, "Shall I help the youngest set the table?"

"Making yourself useful?" Isa said archly. "Why not?"

"Well, she might try to poison me. Again."

His brothers ignored him. But as Khalid crossed by me, I spoke quietly. "If you can see magic, can you manipulate it?"

He smirked. "If you can take magic, can you use it?"

Damn sorcerers and their question-for-a-question games. I gave Aiden a look over his brother's shoulder. He quirked his lips at me with a lift of his shoulders.

"If you feed me a spell, I can cast it," I said, half-lying. Because if I took enough magic, over and over again, I could also gain abilities such as healing, strength, and speed. "But I can't take your magic and then cast another sorcerer spell with it."

Khalid grunted thoughtfully. The similarities between the brothers were so striking that it was becoming impossible to not pick up on them. Between Sky and Ocean as well. But even though we Five had been raised together, trained together, the same didn't hold true—

Khalid was watching me, too closely. Standing in my space.

I held his gaze, asking again. "If you can see a spell, such as the bespellment Kader claimed Cerise holds over Ocean and Sky, can you manipulate it?"

Khalid glanced at Isa, then Aiden. His brothers didn't react. "Maybe," he finally said.

"It's a bluff," Isa said. "Father is fishing, poking holes. Trying to figure Cerise out."

"Her magic is different," Khalid countered. "Stronger, rawer. Its tenor has shifted since she lived at the compound."

I glanced at Aiden for confirmation.

"I wouldn't know," he said.

"Aiden would have been too young," Isa said. "And then you didn't see Cerise for…what? Eight or nine years?"

Aiden nodded grimly.

"It could mean nothing," Isa said. "A witch's power only grows with age, and Cerise has been living in the bosom of her coven for decades."

I thought about bringing up the flowers beside my bed. And the unusual third eye I'd seen on Cerise's forehead, again. But I kept my mouth shut. That was a conversation to have with Aiden, once I was certain it all meant something. And Isa and Khalid's intentions were still unclear. Isa would strike at Aiden in a second if he thought he could gain anything by it. And if Khalid could see magical bonds that the rest of us couldn't, then I had no doubt he could anchor them. Manipulate them.

Khalid raised an eyebrow, silently taking us all in. No one shared anything of what they were thinking. Then the middle brother strolled off toward the kitchen.

Aiden slid his hand along my back, leaning into me. Isa looked pointedly away, reaching for the untouched pile of papers on the coffee table.

"Isa," Aiden said quietly, tugging a black leather notebook from his breast pocket. "I'd like you to look at something."

Isa straightened, leaving the unsigned contract on the table. "You made a breakthrough?" He frowned, presumably displeased that he hadn't been involved in whatever he thought Aiden had figured out about the leeching spell slowly killing Kader.

"No." Aiden held his notebook out, open to a specific page. "I'm worried about something different."

Isa took the notebook, scanning the page. "Is this what your little witch is working on?"

"Yes."

That was surprising. I had no idea that Aiden had shared anything about Opal with Isa.

The older sorcerer smirked at me, as if guessing my thoughts. "We've been discussing appropriate remuneration for…what happened before."

"For kidnapping Opal?" I asked.

"That was Ruwa." Isa spit the words, barely holding on to a sudden spike of temper.

My tone became low and deadly. "You would have used her, sorcerer. In a second, to save your own neck."

"I would have, most assuredly."

"And for that matter," I snarled, "that teleportation spell was ridiculously stupid."

"I thought we were all about to die."

"It could have killed Aiden!"

"Yes, well, he refuses to have his forgiveness bought too."

"It never should have worked. Never should have transported you out of that dimensional pocket at all."

"Ah, but you are wrong there, Emma. It worked—but only because I took Aiden with me."

I glanced at Aiden. Then the final pieces of the puzzle clicked together. "The runes you used to cross into the dimensional pocket in the first place."

"Yes." The dark-haired sorcerer smiled tightly.

"And you put them on Christopher," I murmured, recalling the power I'd taken from the clairvoyant that day. Recalling holding on to Ruwa's magical tie…holding…holding as the dimensional pocket tried to swallow us, keep us.

"Yes." Aiden placed his hand on the small of my back.

I locked my gaze onto Isa again. "You might be able to shift blame to Ruwa for everything else, as well as your own lack of spine—"

"Or a misfiring binding," he interjected smoothly.

"But you left the rest of us there to die."

"How was I supposed to know that you'd save us all, amplifier?"

"Well," I retorted, "you know it now. So how can you possibly believe Opal would ever forgive you, no matter what remuneration you're offering?"

"Oh, it's not the little witch I'm worried about," Isa said blandly. "She has years to gain enough power to seek revenge, if she so wishes. It's you."

I blinked.

"And Aiden," Isa added as an afterthought.

Aiden snorted. "The spell, Isa."

Isa glanced back at the notebook, shaking his head. "It's gibberish."

"Flip the third rune and invert the fifth."

Isa narrowed his eyes, then reached into his pocket and pulled out a tarnished copper pen. He clicked the top. A ballpoint. I'd never seen a sorcerer use ballpoint.

He winked at me. "Less spillage. Makes traveling much smoother."

"He spells the ink while it's in the cartridge," Aiden muttered. With a hint of envy in his words?

"And you can't?"

Aiden twisted his lips. "None of us can. Not even Kader."

Isa waved offishly, pen in hand. "It's a minor talent." Smirking, he returned his attention to Aiden's notebook, writing, working something out. "You've left the arm off the seventh rune and the forward slash from the thirteenth?"

"I'm not an idiot," Aiden said.

Isa continued working. Then he paused, blinking at the page. "A containment spell?"

"I think it might be."

"You had them research the vessel?"

"The inscription suggests it holds the remains of a family member."

"Necromancer?"

"One would assume," Aiden said dryly.

Isa studied the notebook again, his pen hovering just above the page. "Have you cracked it?"

"I've been a little busy." Aiden rubbed his hand over his face. "What are the chances that two witches and a necromancer in their first year at the Academy are going to be able to crack it?"

"Nil. No chance. But …"

"But?" I said.

Isa and Aiden both looked at me as if they'd forgotten I was in the room.

"Trying might have consequences," Aiden said.

Isa nodded, pulling his own notebook out of his breast pocket. "I'll work on it a bit. I'm not sure your witch has transcribed it perfectly."

Aiden shook his head. "Of course you will."

"It's a powerful spell, then?" I asked.

"I've never seen runes used in this combination," Aiden said.

"It's not sorcerer wrought, though." Isa sat down on the couch and placed both notebooks on the coffee table—his on the right, open to a blank page, and Aiden's on the left, opened to the runes he'd gotten from Opal. He started transcribing those runes into his own notebook with painstaking precision. "The use of thirteen symbols points to witch casting. But it's necromancer in origin…is the vessel round? Square?"

"Oval," I said.

Isa grunted in acknowledgement, attention thoroughly fixed on the spell. "Were the runes separated or slightly touching?"

I glanced at Aiden. I hadn't managed to get a good enough look at it.

He pulled out his phone. "I'll send you the picture I have, but it's only one angle."

Isa also pulled out his cell, making sure it was on, then setting it on the coffee table. "You need to warn your witch off."

Aiden grimaced, tapping his phone and sending the picture to Isa. It appeared on the other screen. Isa tapped to accept it, then leaned over to peer at it, zooming in.

"I asked Opal to send more pictures," Aiden said, then he looked at me. "But I couldn't figure out how to ask her to back off in a way that wouldn't actually encourage her."

Isa laughed quietly. "Of course not."

I was wringing my hands. I hadn't even realized I was doing so. And they were cold.

Aiden touched my arm lightly. "Isa's right. This is a complicated, multilayered spell—"

"Or it's possibly nothing," Isa interrupted. "Runes pulled from an old spellbook maybe, but applied by a novice. Aiden had to transpose two just to get a hint that it might be a containment spell. But the fledglings aren't sorcerers, and they certainly aren't training under Kader Azar."

I hadn't heard young Adepts referred to as fledglings before, but I got the gist. "Opal's specialty is dream walking, not runes," I said. "And Jack Fairchild specializes in—"

Isa's head snapped up. "Fairchild?"

"Yes," Aiden said grimly.

"And the family of the necromancer? How many generations do they stretch back?"

Aiden nodded toward the picture on Isa's phone. "Old enough to have possibly contained a chunk of a great-grandmother's soul in that vessel."

"What does it matter?" I asked, feeling exceedingly stupid that I wasn't picking up all the nuances of their discussion.

"The Fairchilds are an old witch family," Aiden said. "Very powerful."

"One of the three founding families of the Convocation," Isa said, going back to transcribing. He appeared to be copying the rows of runes, but slightly differently each time. "Which is ironic."

"Why?" My voice came out reedy. I instantly hated it, hated my reaction. I dropped my hands, clenching them instead of wringing them. "Never mind. I'll contact the school. I'll have them confiscate the artifact." I might not have been able to fix everything, or even anything, with Aiden's family. But taking care of Opal was something that I could do, wanted to do.

Aiden smiled at me gently. "That won't work."

"It will only make the relic more beguiling," Isa added, not looking up.

"They're barely teenagers," I said, feeling myself getting exasperated.

Aiden touched my arm, gently. Again. But it was Isa who spoke.

"And what were you doing at thirteen, Emma?"

I opened my mouth to retort coldly—after which I thought I might just run the sorcerer through with my blades. I'd already delayed doing so for too long.

"What were Aiden or I doing at thirteen?" Isa glanced up at his youngest brother.

Aiden just nodded. "Khalid nearly lost his hand at twelve."

Isa snorted a laugh, closing Aiden's notebook and handing it back to him. "You nearly lost an eye around the same age."

Aiden grimaced ruefully. "Demon summoning gone wrong."

His brother straightened, notebook and phone in hand. "What were you trying to do?"

"Teleport a cake out of the kitchen."

Isa threw his head back and laughed. The warmth of it sounded genuine.

Aiden huffed, glancing at me. "Isa saved my ass on that one. It took the scratches months to heal."

"The pus stank." Isa gave me a glance. "You were lucky Kader wasn't around at the time."

That wiped the smile from Aiden's face, and he looked at me sadly. "Yes, we were lucky to be mostly beneath his attention then. But not everyone was."

Isa looked at me for a moment. Then he nodded, stepping toward the hall. "I'll be in the study."

Ignoring his brother, Aiden turned to me, lightly grasping my shoulders. "Opal's relic is likely nothing. First, necromancers or not, I can't believe that Emily's family would leave anything dangerous within her reach. And second, if it takes Isa more than a minute to work out the spell, then it will take two witches and a junior necromancer…years."

That last exaggeration was accompanied by a smile, solely for my benefit. To soothe me.

"Okay," I said. "But if Isa works it out and it's serious …"

"I'll go to the Academy and take it from them myself." He kissed me to seal the deal. "Meanwhile, I'll drag my feet with helping Opal with the runes. We are a little busy."

I nodded, still feeling unsettled. Then Aiden threaded his fingers through mine and we wandered back into the kitchen to help Ocean and Khalid set the table.

GROSVENOR AND SKY RETURNED WITH LUNCH MORE quickly than I expected—grilled turkey burgers on whole wheat Kaiser buns with perfectly melted Havarti, crispy fries with a garlic mayo dip, and Caesar salad. Kader and Cerise left the rest of us to eat. And as we did, easy chatter filled the dining room instead of malicious magic.

I spent the rest of the day wandering from one task to another, making my presence known throughout the house and property. Playing referee—and feeling somewhat disappointed that no one stepped out of line. Even if I was going to admit that only to myself.

Through it all, as far as I could tell, whatever beguilement had tried to get hold of me the previous day didn't try to reassert itself.

Sky and Ocean spent the bulk of the afternoon brewing tonics in the kitchen, deeply mining Christopher's collection of dried herbs and various wildflowers from around the property. The magic they concocted smelled calming and sweet, rather than nefarious, so I didn't stop them.

Cerise and Kader didn't leave their rooms.

Aiden and Grosvenor spent the bulk of the day fortifying the pentagram in the loft, replacing the obsidian stone with carnelian as Kader had suggested. The carnelian stones had simply appeared in the study overnight, transported onto the property by way of the runed spell Aiden had etched into the desk. Khalid had inspected each one, clearing them for use. Aiden was pissed about accepting a gift of that magnitude from his father, but he wanted the pentagram ready as soon as Cerise signed the contract. So he let it go and used the stones.

We were letting a lot of things go.

I understood my reasoning for doing so, but I wasn't certain how I should feel about it.

It was almost time for tea when I crossed back through the house. Catching a murmur of conversation from the study, I glanced in through the half-open door.

Khalid was bent over the desk where Isa was seated, gesturing toward a series of open notebooks filled with symbols. Runes, by their look.

"… constantly shifting its hold," Khalid was saying. "That's why, even combined, we couldn't break it."

"And now that she's here," Isa said, frustrated, "even with Father fortified in the pentagram, I can't cut off the connection."

"Bone deep." Khalid shook his head, spotting me. He nodded.

Isa looked back over his shoulder. "Emma? Everything okay?"

The question was so genuine, so open, that I just blinked at him for a moment.

"No one is dead," Khalid muttered. "Yet. That's got to be a win." He rubbed his ear, then caught himself doing so.

"Did you make any headway on Opal's spell?" I asked, pushing the door open a little more so I didn't appear to be lurking behind it.

Isa nodded, reaching for a separate piece of paper. "It's intriguing."

"Witch and necromancer working together," Khalid said. "Best guess. Some of the runes have been twisted—"

"Subverted," Isa corrected, holding the paper toward me. The series of thirteen runes had been carefully printed into an oval shape. "Typical for a witch. To take what isn't hers and use it to her own purposes."

I didn't take the paper from him. Not only could I not read it, but I wasn't stupid enough to touch what could possibly be an active sorcerer spell. "And those purposes would be what?"

Khalid smirked at me, giving Isa a look. "Emma is not an idiot."

"No," Isa agreed reasonably, setting the piece of paper back on the desk. "As far as we've figured out without testing it—"

"It's a soul trap," Khalid said.

Isa grimaced ruefully. "Yes."

"It's an actual containment spell?" I said. "And what happens if Opal and her friends break it?"

"They aren't going to be able to break it," Isa said.

"But there is a necromancer in the group …" Khalid said, head tilted thoughtfully.

Isa glared at his brother. "They're not going to be able to break it. Emma doesn't play games well, Khalid. And we need her here right now, not running off to the Academy to rescue the little witch from nothing."

I gave Khalid a look. He'd been deliberately trying to rile me up.

He grinned.

I turned my attention back to Isa. "And if they try to break it?"

Isa shook his head. "Nothing in the runes indicates that there are any repercussions to trying and failing."

"But," Khalid said, "Aiden hasn't gotten more pictures from your little witch yet." His grin sharpened. "So there could be something nasty on the vessel itself."

I looked at him, hard. Then I said casually, "I could have killed you in the front sitting room. And no one, not your father or any of your brothers, would have stood against me."

That wiped the grin from Khalid's face. "Threatening me is—"

"I'm not threatening," I said coolly. "You broke peace in my home."

"I have a right to defend myself."

"The spell I took from you wasn't defensive. It would have torn through Sky. Shredded her."

Isa swore in that arcane language of the Azars, slowly standing but keeping his hands on the desk. "Emma, we are all on edge."

"Exactly. And while I'm on the edge with you, I suggest you refrain from any attempt to push me over." Speaking in metaphor wasn't my strong suit, but I figured the sorcerers would understand. "Ask your brother what it feels like to push me."

"I felt it already," Khalid snarled.

Isa laughed darkly. "You're up and moving, Khalid. I imagine you got the barest hint of what Emma can do."

Bored of trading empty threats, I sighed. "That's all beside the point. Aiden will get a better look at the vessel during our chat with Opal this afternoon. And then he, in consultation with me, will decide what to do."

"Confiscate the vessel," Khalid muttered. "Then threaten those who actually deserve it." He sneered, but didn't make eye contact with me. "The necromancer's family."

"Indeed," Isa said coolly.

"And the spell on Kader?"

They both grimaced, but it was Isa who answered. "We're going to need Cerise to sign the contract."

"We might have to force her," Khalid muttered darkly. "I'm sure Emma could help with that."

I snorted. "Force her to sign a magically binding contract? Oh, that will hold."

I turned and walked away, heading down the hall into the kitchen. The info the sorcerers had provided was churning around in my head, but mixed in with an acute concern for Opal. I felt as though I was suspended in some sort of protective mode, unable to move decisively without hurting someone I loved.

"If you're going to insist on being an idiot," Isa said, still in the study, "at least try to not do it in front of the amplifier. You know that predators can sense blood."

"I am not prey, brother," Khalid snarled. "I've proven that time and time again."

"Not against someone like Emma."

Khalid snorted, but his answering retort was too quiet for even me to hear by the time I crossed through into the kitchen. The witches had cleared out. The cooktop and sink sparkled from the cleaning spells they'd used to tidy up their brewing.

I had come in intending to make tea, but I strode through the empty eating area instead, out the French-paned doors and onto the back patio—following the feel of Aiden's magic.

I spotted the dark-haired sorcerer instantly. He was out of his suit, wearing jeans and a dirty T-shirt, leaning on a shovel just beyond the garden fence, chatting. His sisters were placing a series of Christopher's canning jars on the fence posts and rails. As if they were making sun tea, but with the tonics or tinctures or whatever they'd been mixing and measuring in the kitchen all afternoon.

Ocean placed her hands on her hips indignantly, saying something I didn't quite catch. It sounded sharp, though. Aiden and Sky threw their heads back and laughed.

The light sound made my heart expand so much that I had to struggle to breathe for a moment, leaning against the post at the top of the stairs. Aiden's family dynamic was exceedingly complex—even before I factored in that there might be some sort of magical coercion going on. One minute, they were at each other's throats. The next, they were laughing like nothing was wrong.

Were Kader and Cerise, and how each had raised their children, responsible for that?

The Five hadn't been raised with any laughter or love in our lives. But in getting even a brief sense of what Aiden, his brothers, and his sisters had gone through, I was beginning to understand that except for the circumstances of our birth, the abuse and control we'd experienced wasn't necessarily unique among Adepts.

A whisper of power drew my attention toward the barn. Kader was standing in the shade of the open doorway of the loft, watching Aiden and his sisters. I couldn't quite discern the elder sorcerer's expression, but he seemed contemplative.

Isa moved through the kitchen behind me. Among all three of the brothers, the tenor of his power was the closest to his father. Khalid had left the house through the front door and was crossing toward the barn, where I could feel Grosvenor as well.

Isa passed through the open French-paned doors, stepping just within my line of sight. "It's almost time for tea," he murmured.

"Yes."

"Hot or cold?"

"Hot. With caffeine."

He nodded, watching his brother and the witches, then glancing up at Kader. Just as I was. "I brought you a first flush."

"That was…thoughtful."

He laughed quietly. "Contriving, you mean."

I glanced at him. "I mean what I say, Isa Azar."

He nodded stiffly, shifting his attention back to his father. In the loft doorway, Kader stuffed his hands in his pockets, then retreated into the suite, leaving the door open.

Sky and Ocean had joined Aiden in the garden, moving about as they chatted. Aiden was double-turning compost into the new beds that Christopher had added that spring. I realized they were speaking French. The language was lyrical, pleasant sounding.

"Aiden …" Isa cleared his throat. "I've lost three brothers. One older, and two younger. Has Aiden mentioned it?"

"Did you kill them yourself?"

He grimaced. "No. But I wasn't able to prevent their deaths either. I lost my mother in the same…incursion." He paused as if I was supposed to chime in with some nicety. Condolences, perhaps.

I didn't.

"Three months later," Isa continued. "Cerise Myers showed up at the compound. Sleeping in my mother's bed, running her house, picking herbs from her garden …" He took a slow, quiet breath, shoulders relaxing. "You could end all of this, Emma. Either way."

"I know."

"But you won't."

I didn't answer, mostly because I was still undecided. But it was certainly possible that I could drain Cerise Myers, then take the death spell she'd bound to Kader through Aiden.

It was also possible that doing so would trigger a series of events that I would then be helpless to stop.

If the rest of the Five were in residence? Maybe.

On my own? I wouldn't risk it until I had no other choice.

Isa followed my gaze toward Aiden, who had set the shovel aside and picked up a harvest bin, moving toward the early lettuce. Ocean was combing through the immature pea vines while Sky wandered farther into the empty sections of the garden, seed packets in hand.

"You won't because it would hurt Aiden," Isa murmured, picking up the thread of the conversation. "My father literally bred you in a tube and raised you to be a weapon of mass destruction. I've spent our time apart going through what little I can access of his records, and piecing that together." He paused, giving me space to comment or confirm.

I did neither.

He huffed out a quiet laugh, continuing. "Cerise Myers is Aiden's mother by blood and little else. She left him with Kader at the tender age of seven. Every word out of her mouth since she got here has been a half-truth, and she has us all lined up now like puppets in some play that only she knows the plot of. If there is any plot at all. On top of that, we're all invading your home, your sanctuary from all of…this …"

Isa watched me for a moment longer, his power a whisper deep within his core. He was almost as skilled as his father at hiding it.

It was likely that he had me to thank for that. I'd almost drained him dry, and magic had a way of refilling the spaces within, coming back stronger than before. Similar to how tissue scarred over to protect a vulnerable spot.

"But you …" Isa whispered. "You stay your hand. For Aiden."

I didn't answer the sorcerer. He already had that part of me figured out, so he didn't need it confirmed. But since he also knew what I was capable of, I didn't feel exposed or weak. My attachments made me stronger because they gave me focus. They gave me something to live for, other than just treading the path the Collective had laid out for me. For all the Five.

Or, conversely, those attachments let me hide from what I'd been bred to be.

That was why we'd opened the letter. That was why Kader Azar was napping in the loft of my barn. I wasn't running from my past anymore. And if that past invited itself to stay anyway?

Well then, I'd have my way with it. On my own terms.

The sorcerer bowed his head. "I've never loved someone like that before. It must be…terrifying."

I turned back toward the kitchen. "You had a specific tea you wanted to brew?"

Isa Azar huffed out a laugh, then followed me into the house.

SIX

I WAS FAIRLY CERTAIN THAT THE WITCHES MUST have replicated my stoneware set, because as the sorcerers filtered into the kitchen, more and more mugs kept getting pulled out of the cupboard. Plus the dishwasher was still full with the clean lunch dishes.

Isa started brewing a second pot of the organic Doke Black Fusion first flush when he, Khalid, Grosvenor, and I had been served. After liberally dosing their steaming mugs with milk and sugar, Khalid and the curse breaker wandered off into the front sitting room, each with a couple of ginger snaps in hand. Chatting about the spell work the curse breaker was in the middle of.

Aiden wandered in through the French-paned doors with his sisters, smiling and smelling of earth and sunshine. He set the harvest bin in the sink, then pulled out mugs for himself, Sky, and Ocean.

"Five more minutes," Isa said as his brother reached for the teapot.

Aiden grunted amicably, snatched a ginger snap from the plate next to my elbow, and kissed me soundly before he leaned back against the counter next to the sink. His gaze rested on me warmly.

The time in the garden and with his sisters had clearly eased some of the tension the dark-haired sorcerer had been carrying. Perhaps being out of the suit made him feel more at home as well.

Sky sighed. "I guess I should take a tray up to Mom. She won't come down."

No one answered her as she pulled out the tea tray from the kitchen island cupboard, adding a mug, a plate with two cookies, and one of my blue-lace-trimmed napkins to it.

"Why not?" Aiden finally asked.

Sky shook her head, glancing at Isa.

The sorcerer regarded her calmly, taking a sip of his tea. He'd added only a splash of milk.

Sky grimaced. "She feels outnumbered," she said to Aiden. "Even though I told her that you and Emma were on our side, and Grover is neutral."

"Grover is not neutral," Isa said calmly.

Sky frowned, then took one of the cookies she'd plated for her mother, nibbling on it.

"If anyone is neutral, it's Emma," Isa continued.

Ocean looked at me. "Really?"

Before I could answer, a quiet chiming sound filtered down the hall. I set my mug of tea down, listening. "What is that?"

Grosvenor shouted from the front sitting room. "Aiden, someone is calling on your iPad."

Frowning, Aiden glanced at the clock on the hood fan above the stove. It was too early to be Opal. He pushed away from the counter, crossing swiftly into the study. I followed. A strange sense of doom compressed my chest, and I had to stop myself from shoving past Aiden. It was his iPad. Anyone could have been calling.

Ocean and Sky tucked up behind us.

By the time Aiden stepped into the study and reached for the iPad, which was still trilling away, sorcerers and witches filled the hall.

"It's Opal," Aiden said, settling into the desk chair and pressing the answer icon on the screen of the tablet.

Opal's face filled the screen in profile.

"Opal?" I asked, leaning over Aiden's shoulder.

She turned, looking at me with wide, terrified eyes. Light-blue magic simmered around her irises. "Emma," she gasped.

"Show me, Opal," Aiden demanded, obviously putting together something I hadn't yet.

"Don't be mad," Opal said, panting. Pained. "Don't be mad."

"You know I won't," Aiden said soothingly.

"I mean Emma!" Opal cried.

The witches and the sorcerers clustered together in the doorway and the hall started murmuring. I tuned them out. "I'll be mad when I need to be mad," I said. "Listen to Aiden, please."

Opal nodded, chin quivering. She fumbled with her phone, switching the camera view.

The seam of her blue jeans filled the screen. Then her sneakered feet. And then…and then I wasn't certain what I was seeing.

Opal was situated in what appeared to be the corner of an empty room. The light was low, filtering through filthy windows. Four candles were arrayed around a thickly chalked circle, which I could see only because it was glowing light blue. Witch magic.

Jack Fairchild was down, sprawled across a grimy floor. His arms were spread in a way that suggested he'd been dragged away from the edge of the circle.

Kneeling in the center of that chalked circle, Emily's face and blond curls were streaked with some sort of dark muck—

No.

That wasn't dirt or mud.

"Aiden …" I said.

"I see it, Emma." He grabbed his notebook, paging through to the runes he'd copied from Opal's email.

Because Emily wasn't alone in the glowing witch circle. She was staring toward Opal, panting in pain and terror. She held the oval vessel before her in shaking hands. The vessel—the soul trap, the sorcerers had called it—wasn't open. But some sort of darkly tinted power was seeping from it, flowing over Emily's shoulders and neck, creeping over her hair and face.

Isa pushed through the crowd at the door, shouldering past me to dig through the papers strewn across the desk.

"Opal." Aiden calmly peered at the iPad screen. "Did you try to open it?"

"No!" Opal cried from off-screen. "Okay…yes. But not me. Jack knows a break spell."

Isa found the paper he was looking for, shoving it at Aiden. Aiden pushed it away. "That isn't going to help," he hissed.

"What?!" Opal cried on the other end of the video connection.

"You didn't use the runes?" Aiden asked, more for Isa's sake than his own.

"No," Opal said, sounding a bit calmer. "They're garbage. All together, I mean. They don't mean anything."

Isa swore quietly under his breath.

"They don't, do they?" Opal asked, quavering.

"It doesn't matter right now," Aiden said. "I need to know the sequence of events, Opal. And specifically, why Emily is in the circle with the vessel."

"You don't have time for that," Isa said. "She needs to go get help."

"I can't go for help," Opal cried, obviously hearing Isa. "I'm holding the containment spell. If I drop it, it expands."

"I'll call the Academy," I said. "I need a phone." I gestured blindly toward the cluster of witches and sorcerers behind me.

"No!" Opal cried. "They'll expel us. Please, Emma. Please. Please."

"She's right," Ocean cried from the hall.

"Aiden?" I asked, gripping the edge of the chair.

He swallowed, then nodded. "I can handle it."

Sky pushed into the room, crowding against me. "Does she have salt?"

"No," Grosvenor called from the doorway. "They need to modify the break spell, and—"

"Don't be an idiot," Khalid snarled. "It was the backlash from the break spell that—"

"Sky is right," Ocean interjected. "Salt will neutralize anything. And ask her if there is running water nearby—"

"That would be fine," Khalid said. "If it was a witch spell. It's not."

"Well, it was a witch spell that triggered it!" Sky cried.

The witches and sorcerers kept talking and fighting, getting louder and louder. Magic writhed throughout the study.

The video on the iPad screen froze.

"Aiden?" Opal whispered. The audio glitched. "Aiden?" she asked again, plaintively.

Everyone was shouting suggestions, fighting with each other over the best course of action. I was a heartbeat away from draining them all.

"Enough!" Aiden roared. His power contracted, as if folding in on itself. "Out! All of you." His magic slammed through the study, shoving everyone back but me.

Then, propelled by that push, they tumbled out into the hall and through the front door. Most of them were wide-eyed. Isa looked seriously pissed. The door closed behind them with a loud bang.

I was gripping Aiden's shoulder. I eased my hold. The screen of the iPad was black.

"Aiden," I whispered.

"Give it a second, Emma." His voice was raw. "She'll call back."

I kneeled down beside him, pressing my face against his shoulder while awkwardly holding him and the chair.

The iPad screen flashed.

Aiden shuddered with some suppressed emotion, reaching over to accept the call.

Opal's face filled the screen. She looked livid—which was far, far better than terrified. "Was that them?" she spat, then curled her lip. "Your family?"

"Those were people I'm related to by blood, yes," Aiden said.

Opal narrowed her eyes as if assessing his words. Then she nodded. "Okay. Well, they're a bunch of know-it-alls."

"Yes."

"If I had salt or running water, I would have used it already."

"I know."

She huffed. Then, losing a bit of steam, she whispered, "I know this shouldn't matter, but this is going to get us all kicked out, and Emma ..." She darted her gaze to me, then back to Aiden. "Emma is going to think that she isn't a good guardian, and then I'm going to lose all of you, and Paisley and Christopher, and all because Emily had some stupid idea about some stupid box, and...and ..." She gulped for air.

I leaned forward so that my face filled the smaller screen, the screen that Opal was looking at. I stared into the young witch's tear-filled eyes. "Never," I said. "You will never lose us." It was a ridiculous promise, but I couldn't bring myself to undercut it once I'd voiced it. "Aiden is going to help you get Emily out of the circle, and make sure Jack is okay."

Opal nodded, still not quite believing me.

"I love you," I said, trying not to tear up myself.

"I know."

"Okay." I eased back so that I wasn't blocking Aiden from the screen.

"How did Emily get in the circle?" he asked as soon as Opal's attention flicked to him.

"We set the candles and called up a circle using them as anchors, and tried Jack's break spell first ..." Opal's bottom lip trembled. "I knew chalk wasn't the right thing on the slatted floor ..."

"It's okay. The containment circle looked solid when you showed it to me."

"Yeah, just…I'm feeling tired."

"Did you use blood?"

"No." Her voice cracked, then she firmed it. "You told me not to."

Aiden nodded. Blood-triggered spells were forbidden at the Academy. "Just the chalk?"

"Yes, but it's spelled to me. It was the main project in spellcasting this month."

Aiden hissed slightly.

"What does that mean?" I whispered.

"It's fine," Aiden said steadily. "But it means the circle is perpetually drawing power from Opal." He started sketching a rune on a blank page on his notebook. "So Jack cast the break spell, and it hit the vessel and backlashed?"

"We didn't think it could breach an elemental-called circle."

"Elemental?" I asked quietly.

"The candles," Opal said. "Green for earth, blue for water, you know. And then set at the corresponding points, like east, south."

Aiden flipped a page and drew another rune. "So Jack went down, and Emily stepped into the circle?"

Opal looked away from the phone for a moment. I could hear a quiet whisper, likely Emily. "She's afraid to move at all now. When she moves the spell tightens."

Aiden nodded as if he'd already known that. "It pulled her into the circle?"

Opal nodded. "She says yes."

"It attacked Jack, but only compelled Emily?" I asked.

"No," Aiden said, flipping to another blank page and starting another rune. "It's not that complicated. It was Jack's own spell rebounding that took him out. I'm going to have to ask him what he used, because its sounds ridiculously powerful."

"Jack is ridiculously powerful," Opal said mournfully. "But he has a hard time focusing it."

"It's the secondary spell tied to the vessel that grabbed Emily, because she's the necromancer." Aiden drew a fourth rune, then flipped back through the notebook, making slight additions—mostly thickening lines—to all four sketches. "The secondary spell is designed to stop someone from opening the vessel. So we need to tell it that Emily isn't a threat."

Opal held up a piece of chalk. Even in the low light, it was haloed in light-blue magic. "Runes?"

Aiden grinned. "Yes, runes. One for each of the candles, and—"

"Try not to move them?"

"Right. And don't touch the circle you've already chalked."

He held up the first rune he'd drawn so it filled the smaller camera view. "You remember this one?"

"Grounding," Opal said. "For the earth candle?"

Aiden nodded his head, smiling. Then he whispered to me, "We're in so much trouble."

"She's very smart," I whispered back as neutrally as possible. And clearly failing, given the grin Aiden flashed at me.

"I can hear you whispering," Opal groused.

Aiden laughed. "See the wide section in the center? That's where the candle goes. And leave the line on the bottom corner for last."

"I know," Opal said pissily. The camera moved as she set it down on the floor.

We waited in silence.

"Got it," Opal finally said, picking up her phone again. "Next?"

Aiden flipped a page in his book, holding the second sketched rune up to the camera.

"I don't know this one," Opal said quietly.

"It's a focal. You add the upper right circle last."

"For the…white candle? Air?"

Aiden grinned again. "Yes."

Opal grunted, shifting her position off-screen.

I wanted to pepper her and Aiden with questions. I wanted to know how dangerous this was. I wanted to know how much danger Opal was in. But I knew none of that would be helpful, so I kept my mouth shut. I couldn't even amplify Aiden without risking shorting out the iPad by increasing his magic. But he didn't need amplification to sketch his runes and talk Opal through the spell they were setting together.

MEGHAN CIANA DOIDGE

"Got it," Opal finally said.

Aiden flipped a page in his book and held it to the camera.

"A...sun? Sunlight?" Opal asked, confused.

"Never a bad idea when dealing with a necromancy-based spell," Aiden said. "But see the crosshatching?"

Opal made a thoughtful sound. "The X's? Seven on each side, with space at the top and bottom."

"Yes. And not touching each other." Aiden's tone became strained. He deliberately relaxed his shoulders. "Do you see?"

"Yep. So...like light, but combined with the crosshatch ..."

"Clarity," Aiden said. "Insight. Your dream walker abilities will naturally let you trigger this one."

"Around the blue candle? Water?"

"No. Red. Fire."

"Really?"

"Opal," I said, a warning tone in my voice.

"Okay, okay." I could hear her shifting around, then the quiet scratching of her chalk on the floor.

"Hey, Aiden," Opal whispered quietly as she worked. "You're going to help me clean this all up, right?"

He huffed out a laugh. "I don't know, little witch. I wouldn't mind having you around here full time."

"Aiden," she protested, "I promised Emma."

Aiden reached for me, not taking his eyes from the screen. I twined my fingers through his, aware of my own heart hammering in my chest.

"Done!" she said.

Aiden relaxed further, as if he might have been a bit worried about Opal drawing the clarity rune.

"Okay," he said, flipping to the final sketch and holding it to the camera. "I think you know this one already."

"The eavesdropping rune? How does that help?"

"Well, it's flipped, yes? And see the diamond pinned in the upper-left corner?"

Opal made an agreeable noise.

"And if you pair that with the blue candle?" Aiden asked. "What do you get?"

Opal grunted, stymied.

"Reflection."

"Oh!" she cried, as if she'd just put it all together. "Sneaky!"

"Leave off the diamond for now," Aiden said. "Emily? Can you see Opal at the blue candle without moving?"

"Yes," Emily gasped off-screen, breathless.

"As Opal draws one side of the diamond, you loosen your hold on the vessel, holding it just with the fingers of your dominant hand."

"Okay." Emily's whisper was barely louder than the sound of Opal's chalk.

"The spell should begin to retract, drawn back to its benign state. Then as Opal starts to draw the second half of the final diamond, you will slowly lower the vessel to the floor. You will release it at the exact moment Opal closes the diamond. Okay?"

"Okay," Opal said.

"Okay," Emily whispered.

"Ready?" Opal asked. She'd set the phone down again. The screen pointed up toward darkened rafters.

"Where the hell are they?" I whispered.

"Abandoned building," Aiden whispered back. "Did you see the other spent candles and spell paraphernalia?"

I hadn't. I'd only had eyes for Opal.

"Probably a building just off campus. I bet the Academy actually owns the land, letting the students cast there while thinking they're rebelling." He scoffed. "Witches."

Opal leaned over the camera. "This is going to work, right?"

"You know what to do if it doesn't," Aiden said calmly.

Opal bit her lip.

"Opal," he said firmly. "You shield yourself. You run for help."

She nodded. Then her face disappeared. "Okay," she announced. "Final point."

The iPad screen glitched.

Then it froze.

I sprang to my feet.

Aiden grabbed my wrist. "Give it a moment."

A garbled sound came from the speaker of the iPad. It took me a moment to recognize laughter—peals of on-the-edge-of-hysterical laughter.

"Probably not dead, then," I said, gripping Aiden's hand too hard but unable to relax.

A boy groaned in the background. "What is going on?" Jack had been woken, no doubt by the screaming.

The microphone was muffled for a long moment. Then Opal's voice came through clearly. "Emma?"

"I'm here, but we can't see you."

"Yeah, I think I …" The audio glitched. "…phone…screen…back …"

The audio died.

Aiden grimaced.

We waited a moment longer. The iPad flashed the words *Call Ended*.

I groaned. "The magic fried her phone?"

"Seems like it," Aiden muttered. His tone was suddenly tense, furious. He pushed back his chair as he stood. Then he strode into the hall, heading for the front door, hands clenched at his sides.

Grabbing the iPad just in case Opal found another phone and tried to call back, I followed.

LEAVING THE DOOR OPEN BEHIND HIM, AIDEN MADE it to the front patio before I caught up to him. He strode to the top of the steps, surveying the witches and sorcerers arrayed on the front lawn. The two witches were on the left. Grosvenor stood directly in front of the stairs, with the other two sorcerers on his right. The curse breaker was either playing mediator, or was placing himself in the position of stepping in between the others.

Neither Cerise nor Kader had made an appearance. Aiden's push apparently hadn't included either of them.

Aiden's power churned, boiling around him. I set the iPad just inside the door, hoping to protect it from whatever magic was about to be flung around. I stepped out onto the patio.

The dark-haired sorcerer's siblings and cousin all stared up at him, a range of expressions on their faces. The witches showed concern. Grosvenor was neutral. Khalid was livid. Isa, disdainful.

"This is my home," Aiden growled. "My sanctuary."

"We were just trying to help," Ocean cried, jabbing a finger toward the older sorcerers. "Their advice was—"

"My family!" Aiden shouted.

The wards covering the house flexed—then punched slightly outward.

Sky stumbled a step back, rubbing her arms and gazing at her brother balefully. Khalid hissed.

Isa's lips twisted. "Brother, there is no need—"

"There is a need." Aiden's tone was vicious, on the edge of unhinged. "You've all been bickering like children since you arrived. You interfere where you are not wanted or needed. What if Opal had been the one in that circle, and your arguing had combined to short out the iPad? I've never seen such a malicious suppression spell, and I wasn't even in the goddamn room with it!"

My heart was suddenly thudding in my chest again. I had the terrible urge to run. To run across the yard, climb into the Mustang, and then not stop running until I had Opal safe in my arms. Aiden had been so collected, so calm for Opal, that I hadn't known—

"That child is mine!" Aiden roared. "Mine and Emma's."

Ocean sobbed, burying her face in her hands.

"I will sacrifice every single one of you to ensure the safety of my family." Aiden's tone was low and deadly. He looked at each of them in turn. "I'll let Cerise have Kader. And I'll let Kader have the rest of you."

He stepped down, crossing between them without another word, heading for the barn.

I hesitated to follow, just for a moment.

The wards on the house shifted, flickering outward. Aiden had wordlessly invited everyone back inside.

"Is she okay?" Sky whispered. "Opal? Emma? Is she okay?"

They all looked at me, unmoving.

"Yes," I said, stepping back to grab the iPad, then following Aiden. "I believe so. Aiden talked

Opal through redirecting the suppression spell, but her phone was damaged when she triggered it."

"Redirected," Khalid sneered smugly, his gaze on the witches. "With runes."

"No," I corrected. "He built off the containment spell that Opal had already erected, using her witch magic combined with runes tailored specifically to her."

"Otherwise, she wouldn't have been able to trigger them," Isa said quietly. Khalid's shoulders stiffened at the minor rebuke.

I turned my back on them all, following Aiden toward the barn.

SEVEN

I SLOWED AS I ENTERED THE BARN, WANTING TO GIVE Aiden space if he needed it. I'd thought he might have been heading up into the loft to the pentagram to kill his father himself. Or to kick Kader off the property, damning everyone to his death curse—possibly including himself.

But the dark-haired sorcerer wasn't in the loft. The power of the pentagram thrummed lightly through my teeth and bones, though, so Kader was no doubt utilizing it. And if the elder sorcerer needed to spend so much time suspended in magic that was fortified daily by four other powerful sorcerers, he was in bad shape.

Kader hid his magic well, but perhaps that wasn't all due to skill.

I brushed the thought away, focusing on where I was needed. Where I needed to be.

Aiden was leaning on the workbench situated under the stairs to the loft. Hands spread wide on the plywood top, head bowed over the pepper and basil plants under the grow lights.

Not really knowing what to do or say, I reached around the stair post, grabbing the spare set of keys for the Mustang that hung there. With the keys cupped in my hand, I closed the space between us.

"Emma …" Aiden's voice was raw. His magic still thundered through his veins. "Emma." He turned his bowed head just enough to see me, power blazing brightly in his eyes. "I'm sorry I—"

I held up my hand, letting the keys dangle from my fingers. "What do you say to a drive, sorcerer? Take me anywhere you want." I shrugged. "Maybe they'll all kill each other while we're gone."

He straightened, moving as if every bone in his body ached. My own chest constricted. I knew it was his heart that had just taken the biggest hit. He thought he'd been in the process of watching Opal die—with both of us powerless to stop it. And he'd still tried to shield her—and me—from his terror while calmly fixing the situation.

His gaze flicked from me to the keys in my hand and back again. A smile softened his hard expression, not quite reaching his eyes. "Take you anywhere I want," he murmured. "Am I driving, then?"

Other than occasionally pulling it in or out of the barn if I wasn't around, no one drove the Mustang but me. Though Lani Zachery was slowly setting the groundwork for asking to take it on a road trip in the summer.

"Don't make me regret the offer, sorcerer."

He closed the space between us, hand reaching out to cover my hand and the keys as if he was worried I might withdraw. He brushed his other thumb over my lips. Magic was so bright in his eyes that I couldn't see their natural color.

I bit his thumb.

"Ouch," he grouched playfully. Then he spun me toward the Mustang in some sort of dance move. I managed not to trip, but only because he checked me with a hand on my hip.

Then he took the keys from me and slapped me on the ass. Hard. "In the passenger seat with you, woman," he commanded, stepping around and opening the passenger door for me. "Right where you belong."

His grin and tone informed me that the order was some sort of game. Except I didn't play games. Not well, at least.

But for Aiden, I would try. Using my own set of rules, of course.

Furrowing my brow furiously, I sauntered over. But just before I stepped into the car, I leaned over and whispered, "I'll make you regret that, sorcerer."

He groaned softly into my hair. "God, I hope so."

I laughed and sat down, making certain my dress was clear of the door.

Aiden shut my door, then took a couple of steps back—whereupon he launched himself up and actually slid over the hood of the car. There had to have been magic involved for him to make the move work with so little momentum.

I cinched my seat belt, checking that the data signal on the iPad was active, and confirming that Opal hadn't called back yet. Then I tucked it next to the seat. Aiden jumped into the convertible without opening the door. Still playing. Playing really, really intensely. As if doing so might chase all his conflicting emotions away.

He started the Mustang, put it in drive, and eased it out of the barn. Khalid was on the front patio of the house, smoking. Everyone else had dispersed.

Aiden hit the gas, fishtailing the car on the gravel and shooting us down the driveway.

Straight toward the gate.

"Aiden!" I shouted.

Grinning madly, he barked a command. The gate opened, just in time for us to clear it and make another mad turn onto the road, heading out of town.

I glanced back. My hair was wild, caught in the wind. The gate was slowly closing. Aiden had spun huge ruts into the gravel drive, presumably matching those he'd left by the barn as well.

"Aiden!" I howled above the wind.

He laughed, shouting. "I've been saving that spell to show off." He glanced at me, magic dancing in his eyes. "Did it work?"

"Christopher is going to be pissed about the driveway."

He shrugged. "I'll fix it."

Shaking my head at him, I reached around, stretching against my own seat belt to grab his and buckle him in. As I straightened, he wrapped a hand that should have been on the wheel around the back of my head and pulled me in for a fierce, hard kiss. There was nothing playful in his demeanor now.

I bit his lip.

Grinning, he let me go.

I straightened, then opened the glove box and pulled out a hair elastic. I struggled to smooth my hair back, getting the elastic looped once. Aiden reached over and yanked the tie out of my hair and hand, flinging it from the car.

I stared at him.

He laughed, stepping harder on the gas.

Giving in, I leaned back in my seat, holding the bulk of my hair in my hand and simply watching Aiden drive. His deeply tanned hands gripped the wheel, long legs stretching under him. His face was mostly in profile, though he snuck a few glances at me. His teeth were an occasional flash of white. His bright-blue eyes were his own again, not swamped by his unhinged power.

He was so beautiful.

Aiden had thought he was broken. That he'd been healing, and that he might now be on the edge of breaking again. I felt that complex mix of concern and fear every time I touched him. Since he'd opened his father's letter, then even more so with the knowledge of his mother's betrayal. And now the sharp adrenaline surge from Opal's frantic call.

He thought he was broken. But for me, for what I needed—for what was needed by all the people he himself had declared as family to his blood relatives—he was perfect.

We had to slow to the speed limit while cutting through Youbou. Then we were winding through towering trees, catching glimpses of water, and mostly alone on the road. I checked the iPad again, wanting to make sure we weren't going to lose the signal so that Opal could call.

I leaned against my seat belt again, sliding my hand into Aiden's lap. He flashed a grin at me, shifting forward obligingly as I slid my hand up. I caressed him through his jeans as he rose under my hand, groaning.

He slowed the car further as I tugged at the buttons of his jeans—then sucked in his breath as I worked my way through his underwear, freeing him. I wrapped my hand around his girth, delightfully skin to skin, and started slowly stroking, pausing to tease the tip with my thumb.

I watched his face as I pleasured him. Tension lined his jaw, but for completely different reasons now.

He suddenly pulled off the road, turning sharp onto a logging side road. Gravel and dirt churned under the tires as the forest closed in around us.

I released my seat belt, ducking under his arm to lean over his lap, thankful that the floor-mounted shifter was far enough forward that it didn't impede me. He groaned gutturally as I took him in my mouth, still keeping my hand in play.

I sucked, gently at first, still teasing. But as my own desire ignited, I tightened my grip and took more of him into my mouth.

He panted quietly, murmuring moans of pleasure. More heat flooded through me, loosening all my limbs even as a tension built between my legs.

The car rolled to a stop. My shoulder banged against the steering wheel, but then Aiden was grabbing me, lifting me over him.

"In you," he muttered, moaning. "I want to be in you. Please."

I tried to oblige, settling over him in an awkward tangle of limbs and clothing, and with the steering wheel in the way.

He tore my underwear off with a whisper of magic, slipping his fingers inside me—checking to make sure I was ready. I was. He wrung a groan from me as he withdrew his fingers, gripping my hips.

I slid onto him. Warm and wet, melding with him. My head fell back. His hands tightened on my hips, as if I was his anchor. I set a fast and hard pace, riding up and down his length.

"Look at me," he demanded hoarsely. "I'm not going to last. Look at me, my Emma."

I wrapped my hands around his face, gazing deeply into his eyes. His expression was a mixture of pain and ecstasy. He groaned, fingers digging into my hips, pleasure spasming through him. The orgasm hit him first, practically dislodging me from his lap. Then it flooded through our empathic bond.

I cried out at the suddenness of it, still riding him as he panted underneath me. Reaching my own crescendo just as he pulled my face to him and kissed me hard, darting his tongue in and out of my mouth. I cried out again, my teeth scraping both our lips and tongues.

Shuddering, I braced myself on the seat, allowing the pleasure to linger, then ease.

Aiden reached up to stroke my neck, both our faces curtained in my hair. "I love you," he murmured, kissing me gently.

"Even all sticky?" I said, becoming suddenly aware of our awkward position—and the fact that we were in the middle of nowhere with no running water nearby.

"Especially all sticky," he said quietly. "But don't move just yet? I'd like to be here, in you, for a little while longer."

So I refrained from shifting off him, ignoring the fluids soaking into our clothing. I tucked my face next to his, cheek to cheek. "You were brilliant," I whispered. "With Opal. If it had just been me, or even me and Christopher …" My words got tangled in my throat.

"I'm glad I was there," he said. "I never want to be anywhere else. I just …"

He didn't finish his sentence, and I didn't prompt him. I simply enjoyed the feeling of his chest rising and falling against mine, his stubble on my cheek, and the trickle of emotion from him…lingering desire, contentment …

"I never wanted you to see me like this...among them," he whispered.

"This isn't our life," I said firmly. "It's a momentary blip. An obstacle. And we are both extremely skilled at overcoming...anything."

He smiled thinly, his cheek tightening against my own. "Are we?"

His use of 'we' was laced with so much sarcasm that even I heard it. And that tone somehow sliced across my chest, as sharp as any magically honed blade. Which was absolutely ridiculous.

I shifted back, brushing my lips across his. "Shall I let you inscribe truth-telling runes all over me, sorcerer? Just so you can feel my sincerity?"

He laughed. "How long would they last against the onslaught of your magic, amplifier?"

"For one question, at least. You are highly skilled."

He chuckled. "Well, if I only get one question, it won't be to verify your sincerity. Which I never doubt anyway."

"Oh yes?" I asked. "What question would you ask then, sorcerer of mine?"

He sucked in a breath, staring deep into my eyes. His mouth parted slightly. Hesitantly.

"Would you have me, Emma Johnson? For ever after?"

Back in February, Aiden had teased me about proposing, about making our commitment to each other official. But I hadn't thought the parameters of that through. Hadn't truly thought what it would mean for him.

"Do you really want me?" I asked. "With everything that comes with me? All the danger constantly on my doorstep? Literally?"

"Well," he drawled playfully, "I haven't met Amanda yet. Is she the worst of the bunch?"

I grinned at him. "You're already in love with the worst the Five can offer."

"All right, then." Aiden's tone hushed, turning serious again. "With you, I can weather anything, confront anything. With you I can...believe. With you at my side ..." His eyes welled with tears. They didn't fall, but he didn't try to hide them either.

And suddenly I was crying as well, picking up his emotion but also my own joy. "When the final adoption papers come through for Opal, I want your name on them."

"Yes," he said, wiping a tear from my cheek. "I want that too."

"So then, we'd better get married," I said. "To make it all official."

"Oh yes," he breathed. "To make it all official."

I kissed him gently.

He opened the car door and lifted me from his lap, following me out. Undressing me with reverence, he whispered spells that removed any and all stickiness from our clothing and skin. As he murmured endearments filled with magic, I made quick work of his clothing as well.

When I lay down in the cramped back seat, on a blanket procured from the trunk, and invited him to me just by opening my legs, I did so with whispered promises of my own. Magic traced around us as he climbed over me. With the car doors open and the front seats shoved forward, it gave his legs a little more room—and made for some delightfully utilized leverage.

"I love you," he said again, breath warm in my ear.

"I love you," I said, wrapping my arms and legs and magic around him. "Aiden Azar Myers. All of you. Every broken part."

"No," he whispered, hand cushioning my head while the other hand slipped down between us to tease more slow licks of pleasure from me. "With you, I'm whole."

"Yes," I said.

And I believed it. For both of us. And Opal.

WE DOZED. IT WAS TOO UNCOMFORTABLE CURLED UP together in the back seat to actually sleep. The noise of the forest around us rose again, birds and small animals returning after having been disturbed by the Mustang roaring up the logging road. The iPad was in easy reach, and I'd checked that we still had a signal. But Opal hadn't called yet.

Aiden's heartbeat was steady under my ear, his fingers lazily combing through my hair, gently untangling it from the effects of the windy drive and the sex.

No.

The lovemaking.

And it was completely okay to call it that, even if only in the depths of my mind. To acknowledge that. Because even setting aside all the playfulness, the consideration, and the occasional rune that Aiden usually brought to our bed, our need to be with each other this day—twice in rapid succession—had been completely different.

I raised my head, meeting Aiden's gaze.

A soft smile lifted one corner of his mouth. But before I could speak, before I could express any of what I was feeling, he tugged me into a kiss. And it, too, was different. Gentle but utterly possessive. Lips lingering as if we were trying to breathe for each other, just for that moment.

As if loving, and showing that love physically, was completely different than simply having sex.

"I'm lying here…thinking …" he murmured.

"That you don't want to go back?"

He laughed quietly. "The opposite. Because not going back means giving in, losing. I'd have you, but not everything else I want. Opal, Paisley, even Christopher. The house, the library…the responsibility. I want to be responsible. I want to contribute. Hell, I want to provide for you and Opal, as antiquated as that sounds."

I blinked at him, suddenly fighting back another of those weird washes of tears—from overwhelming joy, I thought. Joy in response to the idea that someone, anyone, wanted to take care of me. For me, not because of some blood bond that had been forced upon them. Upon us.

"I…I don't think I lost sight of that." Aiden thoughtfully furrowed his brow. "I just…I could feel it slipping away."

"It wasn't."

"I know that. Now."

I just smiled at him. He'd already said what I'd been thinking, what I'd been feeling. Even without the empathic connection, I'd be able to sense the contentment rolling off him. The steadiness, the resolve.

"Speaking of Opal …" I said.

"Yes." He kissed me again, then patted my partially covered ass. We'd retrieved the blanket from under us to curl up in, but it wasn't as nice as being snuggled in our bed together.

I propped myself up—reluctantly, though I took the opportunity to check the iPad yet again—as I tried to figure out how to untangle my limbs from his without putting my knee in the wrong place and causing him bodily harm. My hair fell down around my naked shoulders and chest.

Aiden made the low noise he made when we were alone and he thought I was beautiful. Even sexy. Usually right after he exposed my breasts, or when I was on top of him taking my own pleasure.

"Again?" I teased.

He groaned. "My mind says, yes, yes, yes. But alas, I'm most definitely spent. Though there is a rune …" He grinned at me wickedly.

"There's always a rune, sorcerer!"

He laughed as he sat up, shifting so I could find my own footing. He took the opportunity to cup my breast and whisper into my neck, "There is indeed."

I laughed—though I knew I needed to keep moving before I decided we should put his rune to the test.

We climbed out of the back seat. Gently touching each other, we tidied up as best we could, then climbed back into the car.

I drove this time—and quickly discovered that backing down a single-lane dirt road I'd never driven before wasn't much fun. Thankfully, Aiden hadn't gotten far from the main paved road before he'd stopped.

With my head still cranked over my shoulder and the car in reverse, the memory of forcing Aiden to do just that made me smile.

He reached over and ran his thumb across my bottom lip. "What's that smile for?" he murmured.

I smirked, and didn't tell him.

He laughed quietly, lounging back in as much of a twist as his seat belt would allow, watching me with a purely satisfied smile on his face. 'Smoldering,' it would have been called in a book or a movie.

I recognized it as the same look he got when a spell triggered and performed exactly as he'd intended. A mixture of satisfaction and delight, and of intention. A kind of resolve.

We were halfway back to the property when the iPad started trilling. Aiden grabbed it from beside his seat as I pulled over to the side of the road.

It wasn't a video. Just a voice call from an unknown number. Aiden answered it.

"It's me." Opal's voice sounded thin on the iPad speaker—and peeved enough to let me know she was okay.

Some sort of emotion tore out of me. It might have been a sob. And for the first time in my life, I pressed my hand over my mouth and had to fight to keep it at bay.

Aiden grabbed my other hand. "We're here," he said, his voice steady. "Just Emma and me. We're worried about you."

"Yeah." Opal sighed heavily. "I'm in the principal's office. On speaker."

"Good evening, Ms. Johnson." A woman's voice spoke up in the background.

"Principal Whitaker," I said neutrally, wary of anything I wanted to say, needed to say, to Opal. "Aiden Myers, my…fiancé is here as—"

Opal squealed. The high-pitched sound tore through the iPad speakers so viciously that I actually flinched.

The squeal resolved into clearer words. Opal must have taken the phone off speaker. "You're getting married! When! When! Can we have a party?!

Who will we invite? Can I come on the honeymoon? What about Hawaii? Or Greece?" She took a breath.

Aiden was grinning at me, amused and just…happy. Really happy. Not the strange, almost-smothering happiness I'd been feeling since the witches arrived.

I shook the thought away, focusing on the now. The young witch was babbling about dresses and cake, and something about surnames that I wasn't quite following.

"Opal." I spoke her name as sharply as I could while being inundated with so much pure joy.

I could actually hear her settle down on the other side of the conversation. She might have been jumping around. Principal Whitaker was not going to be pleased. The witch was actually a Sherwood by birth, like Opal, but she went by her father's surname to maintain an appearance of neutrality among the witches. She had a low tolerance for nonsense—which had pleased me when I met her, of course.

"Why are you in the principal's office?" I asked.

"A question answered for a question answered," Opal said, bargaining.

I looked at Aiden. He tried to quash the grin that had swamped his face, then gave up and laughed silently.

"That's a sorcerer game," I said. "Witches don't trade information within their coven, because they are …" I realized that I was hanging out really far on this parenting limb.

"Yesssss?" Opal asked, knowing she had me in a bind.

"Nicer," I finished lamely.

Aiden's shoulders were shaking now with silent laughter.

"Well, that's okay then," Opal said cheerfully. "Because my daddy-to-be is a deadly sorcerer!"

Aiden went still. His gaze dropped to the iPad screen as if he could see Opal through it. "Are you all right with that, Opal?" he asked softly.

"Hell yeah!" Then she laughed, slightly manically.

"You know she just declared you deadly in front of Principal Whitaker," I muttered.

Aiden shrugged. "The witch has already met you and Christopher. I have no doubt she's reporting Opal's progress back to the Convocation as well. I'm not going to be a shock."

I could hear another voice in the background. Principal Whitaker, sounding impatient.

"Three questions." I sighed. "Each. And then you will pass the phone to the principal."

"When are you getting married?" Opal asked.

I looked at Aiden. We hadn't discussed anything concrete. He just smiled at me.

"When you're home from school. August," I said. "Why are you calling from the principal's office?"

Opal sighed. "I turned in the vessel. The three of us did, together."

Relief flooded through me. "And?"

"And…are we going to have a party? With cake and everything?"

"Yes," I said. "If you help me."

She squeaked a little, excited. And now I couldn't stop smiling either. The witches and sorcerers might have all slaughtered each other at home. Cerise and Kader might each be poised to murder us all. But I was grinning like a happy idiot on the side of the road.

I focused on being an adult for a moment.

No. A parent.

"Are they kicking you out?"

Opal mumbled something.

I heard it, but I waited for the full confession.

She sighed. "I got a mark on my permanent record. And detention for three weeks."

"What does the mark mean?" I asked.

Opal made a sucking noise. "I don't know. Principal Whitaker is sending you an email. But she needed to hear me tell you in person, because, you know …"

I understood. My own magic didn't affect technology, but as had been amply demonstrated that afternoon during Opal's panicked call, tech wasn't a useful way to communicate with most Adepts.

"Hey, Emma?" the young witch said quietly. "Once you get over being happy I'm alive, are you going to be angry?"

"No," I said. "We'll talk about it. But I won't be angry."

"Okay." She paused, then asked, "What about Aiden? I scared him, hey? I overheard the necromancy professors discussing the vessel and the suppression spell…and, ah, it sounded pretty nasty."

Aiden closed his eyes for a moment, presumably struggling with the vision of the spell that had held Emily in its grip—and with the terror of seeing it spread to Opal if his runes hadn't helped. But when he spoke, his tone was even. "Yes, you scared me."

"I'm so glad you were there," Opal whispered.

Aiden cleared his throat, eyes shining with tears. "Me too, little witch."

"Okay," I said. "Pass me to Professor Whitaker, please."

"Oh, wait!" Opal cried. "Does this mean that I have to change my name to Johnson? Or Myers?"

"No," I said. "You already have a name."

"Okay."

Her tone was odd. I wasn't certain that my 'no' had been the right answer. "You belong to us on paper and in our hearts. But your last name is your own. Your birthright."

"Oh," she said softly, thinking about it. "Okay. I have to go now. Jack and Emily haven't made their calls yet. And then I have to go straight to my room." She sounded exceedingly put out for someone who'd almost died a couple of hours earlier. "Detention comes with extra course work."

"Sleep well," Aiden said.

"Call us tomorrow," I said. "You'll still have phone privileges?"

Opal sighed like someone long suffering. "If you arrange it, yes."

"Pass me to Principal Whitaker, please," I said. Then, reminding myself that sometimes these things had to be said out loud, I added, "I love you. I would have been very, very angry if you died."

"Me too."

Muffled noises came over the speaker, then Principal Whitaker's voice. "Ms. Johnson. Mr. Myers."

"Professor," Aiden responded.

"I've sent you an email, as Opal already mentioned," the older witch said. "It will outline the details of the repercussions she'll be dealing with. But I've been lenient because the children voluntarily turned the object in. I didn't put this in the email, but I did want you to know that the vessel has been confiscated. It will not be returned to Emily's family."

"What does the mark mean?" I asked, not carrying about necromancers or witch politics. "How detrimental will it be?"

"Three marks results in expulsion. No exceptions."

"And?"

"That isn't enough?" she asked, sounding amused. "Would you prefer the punishment be harsher?"

"What I want to know, Professor," I said, my tone icy, "is what Opal needs to do to get the mark expunged. Because presumably, such a system wouldn't exist if that sort of record wouldn't be held against her at some point in her future with the Academy. What will the mark bar her from doing? I won't have her education compromised or her opportunities restricted."

There was a pause at the other end of the line. I looked at Aiden.

He wrinkled his nose, whispering, "Few elder witches are accustomed to being spoken to in that manner."

"What manner?" I didn't bother whispering.

He just grinned at me.

"After a probationary year, Opal can apply to have the mark expunged from her permanent record," Principal Whitaker said slowly. "It's not something we usually do, because life lessons are—"

"All right, good," I said, interrupting her. "One year from today. Please send me the application in another email."

"Ms. Johnson," she said. "The marks, or lack of marks, are a barometer by which—"

"No," I said. "Opal will have every opportunity I can give her. If I had my way, she'd be with me full time, but that isn't what's best for her, for her future. So when I can't have her with me, I trust you to be doing what's right for her. I understand she broke your rules, and the repercussions you've outlined sound fair. But I won't have her dragging around a mark that might be construed as a personal failure. I know how witches work, Principal Whitaker. I know what being deemed deficient means in a witch-dominated society."

"We give all our students the same opportunities."

"We're in agreement, then."

"Yes," she snapped. "Fine. I'll email the extra information you require. Good night."

She hung up.

Aiden was looking at me with his soul-searing, bright-blue eyes. "Sometimes," he whispered, "I love you so much it hurts."

"Yes," I said, unable to articulate the same back to him without the words clogging my throat. "Yes."

The iPad trilled.

Blinking at the display—which showed the same phone number—I answered. "Yes?"

"Yes...ah." It was Principal Whitaker again, firming her tone. "Mr. Myers?"

"Aiden," he drawled, smiling in anticipation.

"Yes, thank you, Aiden. The necromancy professors and I are exceedingly interested in how you aided Opal in quelling the suppression spell on the artifact. And, well...the children claim to not really remember, so ..."

I had to stop myself from laughing. There was absolutely no way that Opal—who seemed to have an acutely sharp recall for spell work—would have forgotten the runes Aiden had sketched for her

"I'd be happy to discuss it," Aiden said. "I'm busy at present, but should be able to call back in a day or two. Video might be better. Shall I email you a time that's convenient for me?"

"Yes, please. Thank you, Mr.... Aiden."

"You are very welcome."

"Good night."

"Good night."

Aiden ended the call, his eyes dancing with amusement. "You work them your way, and I'll work them mine. Opal will graduate with honors, become a specialist, and have her pick of assignments. If that's what she wants."

"Even witches can be charmed?"

"The way in will be through the necromancers. They're insular, but generally less snobby, since they have to breed outside their own bloodlines."

I laughed, though he wasn't joking.

Aiden just grinned at me. Then he sobered. "She's okay."

"Yes."

He nodded. "Let's get the riffraff out of our house. I need to get the peppers and cucumbers planted."

I started the car. Aiden settled his hand on my knee, and I drove us home.

EIGHT

HAND IN HAND WITH AIDEN, I WANDERED DOWN THE hall toward the sound of an animated conversation punctuated by laughter. I glanced into the dining room as we passed. The table was set with stoneware, glasses, and utensils. Large covered platters were placed at its center.

I looked at the dark-haired sorcerer. "So they managed to not kill each other."

"Pity," he drawled. But then he flashed a smile at me. His mood was still relaxed and easy—though I knew that if I could feel his father's magic in the house, then so could he.

Following the scent of fresh bread and rosemary, we stepped onto the white tile of the kitchen floor. My gaze immediately caught on Kader Azar sitting near the French-paned patio doors in an upholstered chair purloined from the front sitting room. The elder sorcerer nodded at me with a twist of a smile. He looked tired, drained. Dangerous.

Paisley was sitting by Kader's right knee, upright, with all her attention trained on the gathering around the kitchen island.

The stools had been set back against the west wall. Sky and Ocean stood on the kitchen side of the island. Isa and Khalid were on the stool side, with Grosvenor at the far end. An intricate web of magic simmered between them. Various groupings of cards were set on the speckled countertop beneath those threads. Most of the cards were face up, revealing a wide array of designs or objects with what appeared to be printing at the bottom. But a short stack sat at the center of the island, face down.

As the witches and sorcerers held their collective breath, Ocean slid her hand into the web, the sleeves of her thin sweater pushed up past her elbows. With a whisper and a touch, she shifted a short section of the web, placing it slightly higher and at a ninety-degree angle. A pulse of power shivered through the entire web, then settled. The section that Ocean had moved turned light blue.

She sighed quietly, then carefully withdrew her hand.

Sky threw her hands up in the air, roaring in victory. Ocean laughed boisterously. Isa and Khalid muttered and shook their heads.

"Too easy," Khalid said.

"Playing it safe never won the game," Isa snorted playfully.

Playfully.

They were playing a game?

Together.

We had expected them to be at each other's throats. But they were enjoying each other's company. If the camaraderie was magically coerced, I couldn't sense it—nor could I trace it back to any likely source. I looked at Aiden.

He was grinning, one hand casually tucked in his jeans pocket, the other loose and relaxed in mine. "Fortress," he said. "Whoever takes the opposing tower wins. But first, you have to build and fortify your own structure. It's usually played one-on-one, though." He raised his voice slightly. "Three sorcerers against two witches? I guess that gives you a chance to win, brothers."

Grosvenor huffed. "I'm partnered with Kader."

"Partnered?" Sky teased. "More like he tells you where to move and you do it."

"So?" The curse breaker shrugged. "We're winning."

"You're currently ahead by a full turn," Isa groused.

Paisley prowled across the kitchen toward us, shoulders rolling, red eyes gleaming. She bumped her broad head into Aiden's thigh, hard enough that he stumbled, presenting herself to be petted. The dark-haired sorcerer obliged.

Paisley turned her head into Aiden's ear scratches, flashing her teeth at me in a playful smile.

"Yes," I said quietly. "Everyone loves you best."

She chuffed agreeably. Then a single long tentacle flicked out from her neck, waving a folded piece of paper before me. I took it, unfolding a note scrawled on hotel letterhead in blue ink.

Check your damn phone. – C

The hotel address put Christopher in Prague. Or at least he'd been there when he wrote the note. So the clairvoyant wasn't on his way back. Yet.

Another tentacle flicked out of the demon dog's otherwise invisible mane, waving my phone before me. I reached for it, but Paisley pulled it away.

I huffed. "So I get the note for free, but I have to negotiate for the phone?"

She wrapped her free tentacle around Aiden's wrist, tugging on him, then looking pointedly at the kitchen island.

The witches and sorcerers, with the woven gossamer threads of magic between them, all suddenly looked elsewhere, pretending they hadn't been watching the demon dog's interaction with us.

"No one invited you to play?" Aiden asked Paisley.

The demon dog huffed indignantly. Then she lowered her head, narrowed her eyes, and peered pointedly toward the dining room.

"I see." Aiden straightened, gazing at his siblings. "Paisley would like to be dealt into the game. And we need one more place at the table."

Ocean's jaw dropped. "She…she eats with …"

Sky threw a look at her younger sister, then said, "Perfect. The table was imbalanced with only nine." She grinned at Paisley. "Did you want to sit near the evil old sorcerer?"

Khalid choked on a laugh.

"I wouldn't make assumptions," Isa muttered. "She's young enough that she could mean any of us."

Sky patted her thighs, ignoring the sorcerers and still speaking playfully to Paisley. "Yes? Did you?"

Paisley opened her massive maw, displaying her double row of sharp teeth, and chortled darkly. The sound shivered up my arms.

"Holy hell," Grosvenor squeaked. Then he glanced over at Sky, looking appalled—presumably in response to his own reaction.

The witch was fighting through her own instinctual fear, stiffly holding on to her smile. Though she'd straightened, holding her hands out as if her palms could ward off the demon dog.

Aiden released my hand, stepping over to the kitchen island. "Whose turn is next?"

Khalid cleared his throat, eyeing Paisley and then glancing over Aiden's shoulder at me. "Mine. If I step back, will Paisley try to rip my throat out?"

"I never really know," I said casually. "Shall I ask her not to eat you, sorcerer?"

"You haven't already?" Ocean cried. Then she blushed fiercely.

I didn't answer.

So apparently, I could play games. For my own pleasure, at least. Though by the look Aiden angled at me, I'd managed to amuse him as well.

Aiden took Khalid's spot at the island. Paisley hooked paws that were too big for her current body on the edge of the speckled quartz counter and pulled herself up. Her nose skimmed the low edge of the magical grid. Sickle claws shot out from her paws.

Across from the demon dog, Sky meeped.

I wasn't certain I'd ever heard a human make that particular sound before.

"Paisley," I said in a warning tone.

The demon dog retracted the claws, laughing at me with her eyes.

I stepped closer.

Aiden drew Paisley's attention back to the game. "Did you see them build their fortresses?" he asked her.

Paisley's forked tongue flicked out, dancing across the nearest line of magic.

"Um, is that a yes?" Grosvenor asked.

"Each player—or in this case, each team," Aiden continued, "is dealt a set of three cards from three decks. With those cards, they build their fortresses. Then, using the defensive and offensive systems they were dealt, they defend their fortress while trying to take or destroy the other players' fortresses." He gestured toward the cards laid out directly before him. "Khalid and Isa were originally dealt a very uneven hand. Heavy on offense, but lacking in supplies and defenses." He pointed to the cards in the middle of the island, underneath the gossamer grid—the small stack of cards facing down, with a few next to it facing up. "They hope to draw cards that help them mitigate that weakness. Otherwise, they will lose in …" He scanned the entire island. "The next two rounds."

"It's not always about digging in, brother," Isa drawled. "A decisive unexpected blow can be very effective."

Aiden grinned at his brother. "We'll see how that works for you, Isa."

I stepped up beside the witches, trying to decipher the card layout now that Aiden had outlined the setup of the game.

"Is Opal okay?" Ocean asked quietly.

"Yes," I said. "She has detention."

The witch waved her hand, relieved. "Oh, totally easy. It's usually exercises to 'improve our focus and dedication.' " She flicked her fingers beside her head while speaking the last few words. "So it's like extra homework, but not a waste of time."

"And you know that how?" Sky asked.

Ocean batted her eyes innocently at her older sister. "Oh, just rumors. You know." Then the younger witch winked at me.

"To start your turn," Aiden said, "you flip a card."

A mane of shortened tentacles sprouted all around Paisley's neck.

Grosvenor muttered under his breath, then appeared to catch himself doing so.

"But …" Aiden raised one finger. "You must not touch any of the active magic in play while doing so. The card you flip will tell you what sort of turn you get to play. Or it might be supplies or treasure. Okay?"

Paisley grunted. All of her attention was seemingly fixed on the small stack of cards in the center of the kitchen island.

"Flip the card," Aiden said.

Paisley's mane snapped forth, crackling with power. She wove her tentacles through the intricate magical grid. Then she tore that grid down, gathering it into a pulsing globe of power. Her maw unhinged, and she swallowed the glowing orb. She flicked her tentacles out a second time, scouring the island of all the cards and eating them too.

The witches and sorcerers all stared at the demon dog, blinking. Including Aiden.

"Those cards don't belong to you," I said mildly.

Paisley chortled. Then she reopened her mouth and spat out all the cards. They landed in a messy but contained pile in the center of the island.

"You might want to count them," I said.

The witches and sorcerers turned and blinked at me now. Except Aiden, who was grinning, amused.

I shrugged. "So did Paisley win?"

Kader Azar threw back his head and laughed. For one heart-stopping moment, his power rumbled through the kitchen, bathing my exposed skin in raw energy. Then, as he quieted to a chuckle, the magic withdrew.

Khalid rolled his shoulders as if shrugging off the residual. Since he was likely the most sensitive among us, I wasn't surprised. "I never did know what was worse," he muttered. "His anger or his mirth."

"Then you haven't ever seen him truly angry," Isa said dryly.

"Well," Kader said quietly, slapping his hands on his thighs. "Dinner?"

The sorcerers, quickly followed by the witches, all roared with laughter.

Grosvenor reached over and gathered the cards. "Paisley wins! Rematch after dessert."

Everyone started hustling around. Isa grabbed a bottle of white wine from the fridge and a bottle of red from the counter. Sky pulled buns from the oven, where they must have been keeping warm.

Khalid grabbed a bowl and started filling it with the buns. "We need an extra place setting."

"Oh, yes," the witch said, ceding the buns to the sorcerer and crossing toward the dining room.

"Cerise?" Aiden asked Sky quietly as she neared.

His sister grimaced. "Still in her room. She was going through the contract, though, when I took her tea up."

Everyone eventually piled into the dining room, where the meal was already laid under stasis spells. The bottles of wine were passed around, and everyone served themselves, standing and reaching across the table, not bothering with the formality of the previous evening.

Cerise's chair remained unoccupied. Paisley perched to Kader's right. Isa was on his left.

The food was simpler. Two roasted chickens, roasted veg, a large salad, and the buns.

"There's pie for dessert," Ocean whispered to me. "Your friend dropped it off…Brian? Said he knew Christopher was away and that we might need it."

"That's nice," I said, though I was slightly disconcerted about Brian wandering up to a house filled with warring witches and sorcerers.

Except that no one appeared to be in the mood to murder each other at the moment.

"Strawberry and rhubarb!" Ocean announced gleefully. "And you had vanilla ice cream in the big freezer in the barn, tucked in with a crazy amount of meat. Like, there must be a whole pig in there!"

"There'd better not be a pig in there," I grumbled, eyeing Paisley. We kept the freezer well stocked with beef for the demon dog, but any pork would have been something she'd picked up—which is to say, hunted down—on her own.

"Are you still going on about the pie?" Grosvenor asked around a mouthful of butter-swathed bun. "You haven't even eaten it yet!"

"I know." She sighed. "I like pie."

I laughed quietly. Aiden pressed his thigh against mine under the table, smiling as he carved a leg from one of the chickens and held it out for Paisley. Sky, on the demon dog's right, grabbed Paisley's plate and held it out to Aiden. He placed the chicken on it, and Sky set it in front of the demon dog.

Paisley licked it. Lasciviously. Her tongue was long, blue, and forked.

"Manners," I said quietly.

Ocean giggled, covering her mouth.

This was a gathering of family, I realized. Not with everyone the best of friends, or even completely comfortable around each other. But still sharing a game and then a meal together.

Cerise appeared in the open doorway to the hall. With all the magic already stuffed into the dining room, I hadn't felt her approach. She gazed at all of us, hands clasped before her.

She looked young. Innocent.

Beautiful.

Poised.

Waiting, watching all of us. There was something behind her bright-blue eyes...something sizing us up. Assessing. Looking through her ...

I blinked.

Casting her gaze down, Cerise smiled. Almost timidly.

That was odd.

Wasn't it?

"I've signed the contract," she said quietly. Then she raised her head, looking directly at Kader. "I'll remove the curse at dawn."

Grosvenor frowned. "It's not a curse."

"I'll need to prepare," Cerise said to no one in particular, ignoring the curse breaker. "And I'll need all of you to participate."

"I see," Kader said, leaning back in his chair. "Why?"

She shrugged prettily. "I'm not powerful enough to cast a multistage spell on my own."

"No," Kader said. His tone was smooth and even, edged in darkness. "Why sign the contract?"

Cerise cast her gaze at Aiden. Her eyes were wide, and clear of whatever I thought I'd seen there just a moment before. "I would never hurt you, my son. Not knowingly. I'll admit I was…I wished ill of your father, but I never intended to kill him."

"You aren't a junior witch, Cerise," Kader snapped. "Playing with a spell you've dug up in your grandmother's library."

His antagonism seemed oddly timed. Why push Cerise now that she'd decided to sign the contract? Khalid and Grosvenor were frowning at the elder sorcerer as well.

Aiden's attention was on his mother, as was Sky's. Ocean was looking at her plate, her fingers curled around the edges as if holding her hands in check. Isa looked at me, then at Ocean, then at Cerise.

Noting what I was noting.

It wasn't just me, or the black-hearted apple blossoms beside my bed. How long had we all been acting oddly? Since the witches arrived? Or even before that? Did I know the sorcerers and witches gathered around my dining room table well enough to even judge their behavior?

Cerise opened her hands to the sides. "I just wanted to draw you out, Kader," she said coolly. "But you didn't come to me, so I had to apply additional pressure."

"To murder me," Kader said. "After draining my power?"

Her lips thinned. "For a conversation."

"A letter would have sufficed."

Cerise looked at Aiden, then smiled sadly. "I sent many, all unanswered."

Kader's eyes narrowed. "Are you certain you got the address right?"

"Since I was held there against my will for so many years, I would think I would remember." Cerise's composure began to crack.

Kader leaned forward, as if he could gaze through those cracks. "About?"

"About what?"

"What did you wish to discuss with me? Your revision of our history?"

"One of us is lying," she snarled.

"Both of us," Kader said, unruffled. "Both of us are lying."

Cerise snapped her mouth shut, glaring at the sorcerer.

Something shifted behind her eyes. Again.

Perhaps it was just a manifestation of her magic. Some Adepts held their power tightly in their hands, so perhaps Cerise did the same with her eyes. Except that didn't line up with how I'd seen her cast.

Kader leaned forward.

He could see it as well.

Cerise smoothed her expression. "I'll need supplies. And help setting up from Aiden, Sky, and Ocean. The moonlight will fuel the spell, and at dawn it will be ready." She reached over, quickly adding chicken and vegetables to her empty plate and wrapping her utensils in her napkin.

We all just watched her, our own food cooling.

She straightened, took the glass of white wine by Ocean, and said, "I'll be in my room. Aiden, Sky, Ocean, please come see me after you've eaten." Then she turned and walked away.

Khalid turned to look at his father. "Why would a curse need a moon-fueled spell to remove it? If Cerise is the original caster?"

"It's not a curse," Grosvenor muttered.

"And dawn triggered?" Isa said. "That's …" He glanced at Aiden. "That's usually reserved for trans-figuration or transformation spells, yes?"

Aiden tore a hunk of chicken from a drumstick, chewing thoughtfully. "As far as I know," he finally said. Then he looked over at Sky. "Has she told you what supplies she needs?"

Sky nodded, her expression solemn. "She's been working on some aspects of the spell since we arrived.

I just didn't mention it because I wasn't certain she was going to sign."

"And if it's a trap?" Isa asked quietly, not really speaking to any one of us in particular.

"To what end?" I asked when no one else answered him.

He shook his head, glancing over at his father. "If she's draining your magic, she's not using it for herself. I can't see any trace of it on her."

"No," Kader said simply. Then he looked at me. "She's not."

"Collecting it?" Grosvenor asked. "Storing it? Can witches do that? I mean, specifically with power that isn't their own?" He looked at Sky.

The witch sat with her head bowed over her plate, copper-and-blond-streaked hair hanging around her face.

"Sky?" he asked softly.

"What do you know about it?" she snarled, standing abruptly and shoving her chair back.

"Not as much as I'd like to know," Grosvenor said, trying to joke.

"I just want this over and done with." Sky tossed her napkin on the table. "I want to be done with all of this shit." She marched out of the dining room, abandoning her dinner.

We all stared at her empty seat. The curse breaker looked resolutely at his plate and started eating again, literally stuffing his face.

"How do you know?" I asked, speaking to Kader. "That Cerise isn't absorbing and harnessing your power?"

He smirked at me. "It's a rare trait."

I leveled a look at him. "Well, you found someone capable, or you couldn't have made me."

Every single person sitting at the table turned and stared at Kader. Including Grosvenor, still in the middle of chewing.

Kader shrugged. "You are unique. Can you cast with the magic you siphon yet, or do you still need to be fed the spell?"

Everyone turned and looked at me then, excepting Aiden. He was glaring at his father.

"The Five gain new abilities," Kader said, looking at me but speaking to Aiden as if benevolently instructing him. "With the other four, it was mostly due to Emma's…ongoing connection to them. Though I imagine distance negates that transference."

"Care to find out for yourself?" I said, grinning at the elder sorcerer.

Grosvenor muttered under his breath. Apparently, my smile was disconcerting.

"Indeed," Kader said easily. "Though I prefer to see you focused elsewhere."

He meant on Cerise. "I'm watching," I said. "I see. All of you."

The elder sorcerer inclined his head, then returned to his meal.

"That's it?" Khalid said. "We have no idea what the witch is planning. The amplifier is another wild card. Not to mention the…Paisley …" The sorcerer jabbed his thumb in the demon dog's direction.

She eyed him as if contemplating eating his hand.

He noticed, withdrawing the offending limb.

That was a smart move. I wasn't sure that Paisley would give him the hand back, not even if I asked nicely.

"Yes," Kader said smoothly. "We will adapt and then respond. Unless you prefer the alternative?"

A moment of silence fell over the table. Apparently, none of us preferred the alternative. But all for different reasons, I was certain.

The elder sorcerer rested his gaze on me. "To answer your question, Emma, I would know if Cerise was holding my power, utilizing it for herself. I'd be able to feel it. As I could feel it lingering on you eight years ago, even though you'd released the spell I fed you."

Everyone was looking at me again. Except Paisley. She took the opportunity to steal all the chicken from Khalid's plate. I shook my head at her. The others could stare at me all they wanted.

"So…maybe she needs to feed the power she's siphoning into the curse?" Isa rubbed his forehead.

Grosvenor stood up, his empty plate and utensils in hand. "I want to make it very clear, for hopefully the very last time, that whatever Cerise Myers is doing to you ..." He looked pointedly at Kader. "It is not a curse."

"No one is blaming you for not being able to break it," Isa said tersely.

"I want you to listen." The curse breaker's English accent thickened. "For one bloody time in your life. It. Is. Not. A. Curse. I knew it before I was even in the same room as Cerise. Whatever spell she's going to have Sky, Aiden, and Ocean help her set up tonight, it will not be to break a curse."

"Thank you, Grosvenor," Kader said quietly.

The dark-skinned sorcerer nodded curtly, then scooped up Sky's half-eaten plate and exited into the kitchen.

Glancing at all of us, Ocean took her own plate and followed him. The sound of water running and the dishwasher being loaded filtered through to us.

Aiden was watching his father. Kader had leaned back in his chair, having barely eaten anything. "You know something," the dark-haired sorcerer finally said.

Kader shook his head, tired. "If I knew anything for certain, I would have acted. Long ago. Ask Emma what she senses."

Aiden looked at me, as did Isa and Khalid.

"My sense for magic isn't as well honed as yours," I said dismissively.

Kader smiled tightly. "I didn't breed modesty into you, amplifier. It isn't becoming."

Aiden stiffened.

"Being self-aware isn't modesty."

"Next you're going to suggest that even you have limits."

"You're certainly getting close to finding out."

Kader sniffed. "Even if the four of us united against you right now—"

"Never going to happen," Aiden growled.

"Ditto," Isa said. "I'm not eager to repeat the experience."

"Exactly." Kader smoothed his fingers along the edges of his napkin. "You're never going to trust me, Emma. But I'm certain you already know that harming you—in any permanent way—would never be a choice I would make lightly. To save myself, or one of my children, perhaps."

"My dinner is getting cold," I said. "Perhaps you'd like to get to your point?"

Khalid's jaw dropped. Isa stifled a smile. Aiden's gaze didn't leave his father.

Kader sighed. "No one converses any more. It's just jotted notes and mad dashes everywhere."

"You didn't breed me for conversation either," I said.

Isa and Khalid slid their chairs back from the table. Paisley took the opportunity to swipe one of the remaining chicken carcasses, setting it politely on her plate and blinking at me.

I nodded at the demon dog.

"No," Kader said musingly. "I suppose we didn't. But you've been out of our employ for over eight years now. And Aiden is…well educated, so I would assume he'd choose a partner who stimulates his mind."

"Is there a point to this, Father?" Aiden asked, barely containing himself.

Kader looked at me. Prompting me. "Emma?"

Backing me into a corner. "I don't like to make suppositions." I glanced at Aiden. "And I only truly know you and myself in this current situation—"

Paisley grumbled.

I gave her a look. "You aren't even supposed to be here."

She tilted her head and blinked at me prettily. She'd been watching TV again. Cartoons, specifically. And learning to mimic the characters' expressions.

Ocean appeared in the doorway to the kitchen, drying her hands on a tea towel. Grosvenor stepped just past her, then leaned against the wall. He had his rune-marked tiles in hand, slowly shuffling through six of them.

"You know I'll take your guesses over anyone else's sureties," Aiden murmured.

I nodded, then tried to piece together what had been bothering me for days. "It's the…if Cerise isn't pulling power from Kader and using it for herself, then where is she getting all the power she is using? The youth spell alone …" I glanced at Aiden. "Witches generally age well, but …" I shrugged.

"It would be dependent on the type of magic that witch is using," Isa said. "But I wouldn't think, given that we can't even begin to untangle whatever Cerise has done to Kader, that whatever power she might gain from it would translate well into magic that could be utilized that way."

I nodded. "Exactly. And then there's the spell she hit me with in the kitchen." I rubbed my chest, then caught myself doing so. "There isn't much magic that I haven't been exposed to …"

"No," Kader said, far too proudly. "There isn't."

"The Myers coven is one of the oldest," Aiden said, after sending a dark look his father's way. "Not a founding member of the Convocation, but they joined soon after, I believe. Their coven archives must be extensive."

"You haven't seen them?"

Aiden shook his head. "Only a few private collections. So Cerise could have tapped into something old, and powerful."

Kader was still looking at me expectantly.

I met his gaze coolly. Then I spoke. "And then there's the mood altering that's going on."

The sorcerers all frowned—excepting Kader, who nodded once.

I settled my hand on Aiden's arm, because I wasn't certain how to articulate the next part without it sounding like some sort of accusation. "If anyone else had tried to hurt Paisley unprovoked, and then attacked me instead, we would never have gone upstairs and had a nap."

Aiden blinked. Then he said slowly, "It was a misunderstanding ..."

I glanced at Ocean, who'd been in the perfect position to see everything in the kitchen. "Was it?" I asked quietly.

Ocean lifted her gaze from the floor, looking at me, and then at Aiden. Then she looked at Kader. "I want to hate you."

"Understandable," the elder sorcerer said benignly.

"You are evil, and you deserve everything coming to you."

Kader set his napkin on the table, spreading his hands wide. "This is not in dispute."

Ocean looked back at Aiden, her eyes swimming with tears. "If we make it through this...I don't want to go back. I want to transfer to the North American Academy." She twisted the tea towel in her hands, waiting.

Aiden frowned. "Students transfer back and forth all the time. I'm sure it can be arranged easily."

Ocean nodded, looking much younger than eighteen. Then she raised her head, looking directly at me. "She...my mother had more than enough time to not cast that spell. Emma was clearly standing there for more than enough time for it to register." She cleared her throat. "It wasn't an accident."

"A test," Kader said, quietly smug.

Aiden exploded out of his chair, hands slamming down on the table as he snarled at his father.

"Only you are a big enough bastard to go around testing people…manipulating magic and fucking with DNA to meet your goals."

"What goals?" Kader asked, unfazed. "Living forever?"

The quiet question hung in the room, Aiden towering over his father.

"Aiden," I said quietly. "It felt different when we were away this afternoon. Off the property."

He straightened, looking down at me.

"It felt content …" I struggled to express any sort of intimacy, given the audience currently facing us. "And not in a forced way. It's been difficult to maintain our equilibrium since Cerise arrived."

"Since I opened the letter," Aiden said, correcting me.

"But it's been worse since Cerise stepped through the wards." I thought about mentioning the third eye I'd seen on Cerise's forehead, about asking if it was normal for a Myers witch. Then, deciding I didn't want to complicate the discussion any further than it already was, I looked at Kader instead. "What's your end game? I assume you want to be amplified?"

He shook his head, looking grim for the first time.

"We would have already asked you," Grosvenor said, still leaning against the wall. "Right away. But anything extra we pump into Kader actually speeds up his…decline. It's his own magic that's sustaining him."

"If it comes to it," Kader said. "If it comes to me against Cerise tomorrow at dawn, I'll ask then, amplifier. To keep the damage contained …" He glanced at each of his sons in turn, then nodded to himself.

"What about the death curse?" Aiden asked, his tone still a low growl.

Kader sighed and stood up slowly. "It might still come to that. Certainly even you can't begrudge me taking my murderer with me."

"You threatened the entire Myers line!" Aiden snarled.

"It's too late for that," Grosvenor said. "The intensity of the leeching spell has doubled, even tripled since Cerise arrived."

"What?" Khalid said. "I've been checking—"

Kader waved his hand. "And I've been compensating. Grover, if you would see me to my room."

The curse breaker stepped closer to the elder sorcerer, but didn't touch him. Kader slowly crossed toward the kitchen.

"Cerise Myers is wielding magic that none of us thinks she should be able to wield," Isa said incredulously. "And we're going to help her?"

"Yes," Kader said.

A one-word order.

The elder sorcerer clamped a hand on Grosvenor's shoulder. Ocean cleared the doorway, hovering by the table. The two sorcerers crossed through the kitchen and then out of the house.

"Why trust Grover?" Khalid snarled, speaking to Isa and Aiden.

"Grover isn't going to try to kill him," Isa said.

Khalid glanced back and forth between his brothers. "I'm not going to try to kill him!"

Neither of them responded.

Shaking his head, Khalid grabbed a roll, then took off through the house and out the front door.

Isa calmly added some salad to his plate and started eating.

Paisley had scoured the chicken carcass of every bit of meat, and was now eyeing the second chicken. Aiden leaned over, grabbed the platter, and slid it across the table to the demon dog. She smiled at him, reaching out with a tentacle and caressing the back of his hand.

"You're welcome," he murmured.

"Aiden," Ocean said quietly. "You know that Mom was appointed keeper of the Myers coven archive about a year and a half ago, right?"

Isa's lettuce-laden fork paused halfway to his mouth. Then he set it down and turned to look at the young witch. "Do you know the spellbook she's using? Have you seen it?"

Ocean shook her head. "I don't. I don't even know if it's connected. I don't know anything else, actually. I'm...I've just been listening to you all ..."

"And putting things together," Aiden murmured.

She nodded. "And after I spoke with Emma last night…I …" She twisted her hands in the tea towel again, so tightly it had to be hurting her. "I still don't know why I brought the poison. I didn't have enough money, so I had to trade my medallion for it."

Aiden frowned. "Your grandmother's protection amulet?"

Ocean nodded, chin quivering.

"Why?" he almost howled. "It was priceless. Irreplaceable. Alchemists are so rare, and …" He caught himself, blowing out a harsh breath instead of whatever else he wanted to say.

"I know." Ocean looked at her brother, setting her shoulders defiantly. "You know I love Mom. But I don't think that…murdering Kader? And, like, maybe really hurting you to do it? That's not right." She whispered the last few words.

Aiden scrubbed his hand across his face. "I'll need the name and location of your dealer. I'll get the medallion back."

"Okay …"

"Right," Isa said, sliding his chair back. "Myers coven archives. Let's see what I can dig up about the collection. It's in Paris, yes?"

Aiden nodded.

"What do you think you can find?" Ocean asked. "Before dawn?"

"Well …" Isa smiled grimly. "It's not as though any of us are going to be sleeping, so you'd be surprised."

Aiden scrubbed a hand across his face. Then, touching me lightly on the shoulder, he followed Isa from the room, heading into the study.

Ocean blinked at me, then at Paisley. "So…pie?"

"Yes," I said. "Help me clear the table."

AS THE THREE-QUARTER MOON ROSE, CERISE WAS pacing out a large circle in the orchard grass, in a kind of clearing alongside the immature apple trees that Christopher had planted in the early spring. She was slightly too close to the chicken coop for my comfort, about halfway between the house and the road.

Though Aiden had sworn that the Myers witches didn't condone blood sacrifice or black magic, Isa was still trying to figure out what might be buried in the coven's archives—and what spellbook Cerise might have excavated from there. But none of us were certain about anything.

Maybe not even Cerise herself, depending on what kind of power she was playing with—or what slowly killing Kader was doing to her, magically.

Normally, not having everything perfectly worked out wouldn't bother me. Except I wasn't the one in the line of fire. Aiden was. I didn't know when I should step in—or even whether I should—if things went sideways. Draining or killing Cerise could lead to Aiden's death, because the spell she was working was anchored through him. And draining or killing Kader could also lead to the same outcome—through

Kader's death curse, if he had enough power left to pull something of that magnitude off.

I didn't exist comfortably in limbo. So as Ocean and Sky joined Cerise and Aiden in the orchard, laden with supplies, I decided to distract myself from pulling out my blades by walking the perimeter of the property with Paisley.

Aiden was on the other side of Cerise's paced-out circle when I left. He didn't look up from whatever his mother was saying, the two of them conversing in French.

The evening was balmy, though I'd thrown on my cashmere cardigan to counter a light breeze that stirred my hair. I made it to the northwest corner of the property, well out of earshot of anyone but Paisley, before I gave in to the impulse to call Christopher. The note he'd given Paisley had directed me to his texts from earlier, all of them an update on the hunt for Bee.

Apparently, Samantha had some contact they were trying to arrange a meeting with to look at the magically fried information she'd stolen from the compound. That sounded completely off mission to me. But again, I wasn't Christopher's keeper. The clairvoyant's messages had also reiterated his warnings—and his frustration that he wasn't seeing more of what was unfolding with Aiden's family.

It made sense that if I couldn't feel any hint of Christopher's magic in the blood tattoo on my spine, then he couldn't feel me either. The distance was clearly muddying his visions.

It was a completely irrational thought, but if it were possible for flesh and bone to feel empty, then that was exactly how my upper spine currently felt.

Paisley passed in and out of the ever-deepening shadows as we turned to cross along the fence, heading east.

The phone rang three times before Christopher answered, his voice a rough growl. "Who's dead?"

"No one," I said.

He swore. "Why else would you be calling?"

I glanced over at the barn in the near distance. A single interior light was on, but otherwise the windows were darkened. Khalid was likely capable of seeing any magic that might be radiating from the pentagram in the loft reflected against the upper windows. But I couldn't see the power that was sustaining Kader Azar in the same way.

"Our maker is dying," I whispered into the phone—and as I did, I made the uncomfortable realization that something about the statement bothered me. "There was a time…a few months after your magic came back in full force, I started to realize how hard it was for you. How difficult it was going to be for you to only have me to anchor you …"

"Socks," Christopher murmured. "I'm okay. I was always okay just with you and Paisley."

"I know. But I…I thought about hunting him down, on the really bad days when I would find you…when I knew that we needed to keep moving. I thought about making him pay …" My voice cracked. "And now …"

"I'm here," Christopher's voice was warm in my ear, edged with emotion. As mine was.

"And now," I said, "he's just a man. And without him, without the Collective as a whole, I wouldn't have you or Paisley ..."

"Or now Aiden."

"Yes."

Silence fell between us, though I could hear that we were still connected. I didn't bother voicing everything else I was feeling or thinking. The clairvoyant knew it already. He'd been with me through it all.

Christopher sighed quietly.

I was achingly aware that the tattoo on my T3 vertebra was dormant. "I miss you," I murmured, turning south at the northeast corner of the property. The grass was shorter in this section, cropped by the cows.

"I'm heading to you tomorrow."

"It will be all over by then. Cerise has signed the contract. She's removing the working at dawn."

"I don't give a shit about the Myers witches or the Azar sorcerers, excepting one," he said. "I'm coming home."

"Bee ..."

"Dead end. Dead." He sighed again. "I'd hoped that if we had a solid connection, the cards or Paisley would lead us to her. But I'm sitting here in a hotel in a foreign country deluged with glimpses of other people's lives, and I just want to be home with you, planting our garden. When does Opal come home for summer break?"

"July."

"That's too far away."

"Yes." I gazed up at the moon, then to the right where the garden sprawled with the house beyond. The main house was fully lit. "Kader did say he would help us find Bee. And if she is in trouble …"

Christopher sighed. "I don't like him playing games with you. You aren't …" He didn't finish the thought, but I understood that he meant I wasn't great at any sort of mental warfare. He was right.

"None of us were trained to negotiate," I said quietly. "To mediate. We just took what we wanted—"

"What he wanted," Christopher snarled.

"They," I corrected.

"Socks …" He hesitated, as he did when working through a glimpse of the future. "Any information from Kader Azar will come with strings attached."

"There are always going to be strings."

"But we're not puppets. Not the Collective's puppets. We never were."

I didn't agree on the 'never' part, but I didn't say so.

Christopher laughed quietly. Without being in the same room with him, I couldn't tell if he was laughing at me or at whatever was unfolding in his mind's eye.

"Are you in the orchard?" he asked in a whisper.

"Not right now. But that's where Cerise is setting up the spell to remove the working on Kader."

"Apple blossom," he murmured, not necessarily speaking to me. "Rebirth. Transition…immortality."

The image, the scent of the bouquet by my bed the previous night came back to me. Apple blossoms with dark centers. I waited for the clairvoyant to elaborate. He didn't.

"So." Christopher's tone sharpened, letting me know he was speaking directly to me again. "Opal tells me that you and Aiden are getting married."

"And did she tell you under what circumstances this was revealed to her? Via a speakerphone conversation with her principal?"

"No …"

I laughed, then quickly sobered. "I love him."

"I know. I see."

"I want everyone to know."

"Okay."

As I turned along the back fence, I decided I was done wandering. So I cut across through the long grass toward the barn. "Come home. You and Zans, if she wants."

"She wants."

"Then we'll all find Bee."

"Text me if you need me," Christopher said. "Don't call again. I thought you were all dead, and I…I hadn't been there to die with you."

"Don't worry, Knox," I said wryly. "None of the Five are dying without you seeing it first. Even with the distance between us."

"Comforting, Socks. So, so comforting." He laughed. "Sleep well."

"See you soon." I hung up the phone.

Paisley appeared out of the deep shadows, nudging her nose under my palm. "Christopher and Samantha are coming home," I said to her. "Which means you don't have to keep leaving."

The demon dog grunted, but didn't seem as pleased as I'd thought she would be.

"It's all right that you couldn't find Bee," I said, pausing to place my hand on her broad head. "We're going to figure out what could be blocking you, and how to sharpen that sense. Okay?"

Paisley peered at me with red-slitted eyes, as if weighing my words. Then she dropped her mouth down in a full-toothed smile.

I tucked the phone in the pocket of my dress and headed toward the barn. Paisley continued patrolling the perimeter. There was one more conversation I needed to have before dawn. In private.

THE BARN DOOR ON THE LEFT WAS OPEN, AND THAT sight was uncomfortable somehow. If Christopher, Aiden, or I opened only one of the doors, we always opened the right. The gaping dark hole where the left door should have been chafed me almost as badly as the kitchen table being modified and moved into the dining room without my permission.

I didn't like stumbling over my own weaknesses. Needing to be in such tight control of my environment was completely exploitable. Though of course, someone else would have to figure out that weakness first.

I was a few meters away when I spotted Khalid leaning back against the barn, next to the open door. Even in the relatively bright moonlight, the sorcerer blended into the shadows with his dark suit, hair, and features.

I had no doubt that he'd seen me crossing through the property from the moment I cut north through the grass. Daniel had once admitted that I glowed to his magic-sensitive eyes, and the same was likely true for Khalid. Fish had told me I looked like a fallen star, but the sorcerer now stepping between me and the open door had a much different perspective.

"No," he said. Power rode the command, though I wasn't sure it was intentional. If it was, it didn't affect me in the least. "You've waited this long, you can wait a little longer."

He thought I was there to kill Kader. I wasn't. But the accusation rankled, so I didn't bother clarifying. "Who are you to tell me what I will and won't do, sorcerer?"

Khalid's shoulders stiffened. "I know you're powerful, amplifier. I've pieced together all the hints of the last few days, and I've felt your touch." He held his hands out slightly to the sides, magic shifting in his palms. "But I've also been working on a side project myself."

I smiled. "A way to bind me? So I can't touch you?"

Disconcertion flickered across his face.

I lowered my voice. "Think about what it was like to be reared by Kader Azar. Now think about being raised and trained without any family. Not a single relative. Just a series of Kader Azars overseeing every moment of every day of your life." I paused, allowing him to process what I was telling him.

Incapacitating Khalid before Cerise triggered her ultimate plan was a bad idea. But that didn't mean I wouldn't do it.

The sorcerer nodded once. The power in his hands continued to fold in on itself, over and over. A characteristic of binding spells. I knew that because of how many had been used against me.

"Now," I continued, "think about how an amplifier like me might be trained by a dozen Adepts like your father, all equal in power and drive."

"You think that you can survive anything I can throw at you," Khalid said calmly. "Because you can keep the magic you steal from others, right? But I wasn't only trained by my father."

A voice filtered down from the loft—but carried by magic, not on the air. "Let her pass."

Kader.

"I won't." Khalid didn't bother raising his voice to address his father. It was obvious that the elder sorcerer was monitoring the conversation by magical means as well. We were too far away to have been heard clearly otherwise.

Out of sight, Kader sighed. "If your concern for me was born out of some affection, I might be moved, Khalid. You always were so transparent."

Khalid's shoulders stiffened. Then the magic snuffed out in his hands. He walked toward the house without another word.

I crossed into the barn, noting that someone had left a light on over the workbench. I'd turn it off before I locked up.

I traversed the wooden interior steps up to the loft. My feet were grass stained. The bright-green nail polish Opal had applied had partially chipped off from all my fingernails now, except for one little finger.

The top of the stairs, then Kader Azar himself, came into view.

The elder sorcerer was situated behind a blazing wall of energy, shot through with five shades of blue varying in both depth and darkness. Sorcerer power from all five Azars, combined into one powerful stasis spell.

His eyes were closed. He had removed his suit jacket, shoes, and socks, as well as partially unbuttoned his white dress shirt. He sat cross-legged, hands on his knees, palms up.

He had easily aged another five years since dinner.

"If you can hold the spell at bay in the pentagram, why come into the house to play cards or eat dinner?" The too-personal question slipped out before I could retract it.

Kader smiled smugly, not bothering to look at me. "Why have you let all of us into your life when you'd rather have ignored us? Or, in some cases, would rather have drained us dry and sent us packing?"

I didn't truly believe that Kader Azar loved his children as much as I loved Aiden. But I didn't answer what felt like a rhetorical question. I sat across from the elder sorcerer, folding my legs between two points of the massively fortified pentagram.

The magic between us felt viscous, vibrating with energy.

"I can't," Kader said, finally opening his eyes. Their whites had yellowed further. "Hold it at bay. Not since Cerise arrived. But I can ease its effects."

"Are you in pain?"

"Do you care?"

"No. I'm just trying to figure out how a witch, reputedly walking the light side of the path—"

Kader snorted.

I had to suppress a smile myself. "How can she foil not just you, but all the others? Including Aiden?"

"You have made him powerful," Kader whispered.

My back stiffened. "He is powerful."

"Yes." Kader shrugged one shoulder. "Will against will. Perhaps Cerise's will to kill me outmatches my will to live."

"Doubtful," I said.

He huffed a quiet laugh. "Indeed."

"And when she tries to kill you tomorrow?" I asked him just as quietly. "Perhaps through another miscommunication? Though hopefully after untangling Aiden from whatever she did to get to you through him. What would you have me do?"

"You aren't looking for orders, are you, Amp5?" There was no malice in his tone. Only darkly tinted amusement.

I just looked at him, not at all ruffled by him using a designation to claim me rather than my name. I had told him to do so. Twice now. And I knew who I was. Emma. Not Amp5.

He sighed quietly. "Protect my sons."

"Protect them? Not you?"

He grimaced. "I've been stuck in this pentagram wondering exactly how I came to this…begging a Myers witch for my life, loathed by my only three living children." He swept his gaze over me. "Onefifth of my life's work seated before me. A glorious achievement. The ultimate testament of my abilities. And you would rather kill me than shelter me."

I had no response to that. It was a fair assessment.

He chuckled darkly, then scrubbed his hand over his face. The gesture made my chest ache. I'd seen Aiden do that far too many times over the last few days as well.

"What has it all been for?" he whispered. "To have every word I speak questioned by those most likely to care for me? To care whether I die? And not just for the power that death might bequeath?"

"That's an excellent speech," I said. "Shall we talk in actual truths now?"

Kader's eyes went hard. The intense expression pulled forth some emotion from me, which I quickly cast aside.

Recognition, perhaps. Not in the sorcerer, but in myself.

I had pushed him to the edge. Which was perfectly fine, because I'd been teetering on that edge myself for days. My footing was firm only when Aiden was anchoring me. Literally.

"Aiden isn't here now," I said, more to myself than Kader.

His eyes narrowed for a moment. Then he reached one hand toward me, slipping through the magic that otherwise sealed the pentagram.

I grasped his wrist rather than his fingers.

"Truth to truth," he murmured.

Dark-blue energy spiraled around our wrists, settling onto my skin but not digging in.

"How long will that last on you?" Kader asked casually.

"A few minutes," I said with complete honesty, though the sorcerer hadn't actually triggered the spell yet. "If I don't fight it."

"And the empathy? Can you control it yet?"

I couldn't, not the way he meant. But I just looked at him, not picking up much emotion at all from the sorcerer. The pentagram was no doubt impeding the innate ability, and I didn't bother trying to penetrate the barrier.

"Ask your questions then, Emma Johnson," Kader intoned, speaking to the truth spell he'd wound around our clasped arms. "I will answer to the best of my knowledge."

"And truthfully?" I said with a knowing sneer. "Because Kader Azar can't sidestep a truth spell of his own casting?"

"Shall I call Aiden to verify the spell?" he asked.

"You won't summon Aiden at all," I said. "Not ever again."

He just looked at me with that same hard flicker in the back of his eyes. A wounded predator.

"Are you going to try to take all of us with you tomorrow?" I asked. "When Cerise finally succeeds in killing you?"

"I've thought about it," he said. "Go out in a blaze of glory, wondering how much of this tiny town I could take with me and what the powers-that-be would do about it in the aftermath."

There it was. The attitude and the belief system that had led to my creation. The creation of the Five.

"And wouldn't those powers-that-be stop you before you could do such damage?" I asked.

"Did they stop you in Peru?"

I smiled nastily. "Why would they have? I was doing their work for them."

Kader snorted. "You have an interesting view of yourself, Emma. Are you above the laws of the guardians? Is your soul untouched because you can lay all the death you've wrought at my feet?"

I had no idea who exactly he was naming as guardians. The mythical powers-that-be, presumably. "I lay nothing at your feet, sorcerer. I'm not your well-trained retriever."

He inhaled, composing himself. "It is impossible to converse with you civilly."

"Impossible for you."

He tilted his head. "I speak only for myself." He paused, sweeping his gaze over me. "Tell me…do the other four still survive?"

I didn't bother trying to lie. It was possible that trying to lie would dissolve the spell between us, and I wanted it in place a little while longer. "They do."

"And do you speak for them as well?"

"I try not to."

He made an agreeable noise in the back of his throat. "Ask me what you need to know to move on with the events that shall unfold tomorrow, Emma. The spell is thinning."

I locked my gaze to the elder sorcerer's. "Aiden. Above all the others. Above yourself. Aiden walks away tomorrow."

Kader's grip tightened on my forearm. "To the best of my ability."

"Beyond your ability," I said steadily.

"Will you sacrifice yourself for him?" Kader asked thoughtfully.

"There will be no need for me to do so."

"But would you?"

I curled my lip, not bothering to answer. Then the spell clamped down on my arm, reminding me of exactly how powerful Kader Azar was. My mouth opened of its own accord. "No. I cannot. I owe too many others my protection. Either Aiden or I must survive tomorrow."

"For the child witch you've adopted."

"Yes."

"It's possible that Cerise has bound Aiden in such a way that I cannot untangle him without killing her," Kader said, carefully measuring his words. "My son would not be pleased if I killed his mother over allowing him to sacrifice himself."

"That's the price you'll have to pay."

Kader smirked at me, as if I'd revealed a great truth to him. "Aiden, above all others. To the best of my ability." He leaned forward slightly. "With your help, of course."

I nodded.

For Aiden, I would deal with any devil or demon. "As long as you understand what my help might entail."

The elder sorcerer threw his head back and laughed. Then he sobered quickly, outwardly tired. "I'm looking forward to it. But I fear it will not measure up to my expectations. I doubt anything could match the glimpse I got of you before you destroyed every recording device, magical or otherwise, in the compound."

I didn't know what to say to that, or how to ignore the revulsion that rose in response to his pride. "Aiden over everyone else," I repeated. Then I peeled my fingers from Kader's arm, effortlessly snapping the truth spell.

Kader withdrew his arm as well, flexing his fingers. "And when Aiden tries to sacrifice himself for one of the others? For you, perhaps? It's up to us to save him from himself?"

"He doesn't deserve to be destroyed in a battle that should be solely between you and Cerise."

"I didn't bring him into it."

"The circumstances of his birth make you a liar."

Kader huffed. "Yes, I used magic to turn Cerise's attention my way. She is a beautiful woman with beguiling, gentle ..." He trailed off thoughtfully.

"Magic?" I finished his sentence for him.

He nodded.

"But there's nothing beguiling about her power now?" I already knew the answer. For myself and my senses, at least.

"No, there isn't."

That was what I'd thought. "Did you just figure that out now? Why wouldn't Aiden have noticed the change?"

"He doesn't know Cerise well."

"Or being in the pentagram eases more than just the spell that's draining you ..." Isa Azar had speculated about Cerise stealing a forbidden spellbook from the Myers archives. But what if something else had been locked away there by her coven? "I've felt something. And I have an adaptive immunity ..."

Kader narrowed his eyes doubtfully. "Cerise Myers is not capable of a mass enchantment. Especially not when so many different Adepts are involved."

"If it was an outright enchantment, it never would have worked on me. Or I would have felt it right away ..." I thought about the moment Cerise had set foot on the property. The recollection felt thin. Dulled, somehow. But I had picked up something from the witch in that moment. "Maybe she isn't controlling it, isn't actively wielding it. You've seen the third eye that appears on her forehead, haven't you?"

Kader waved his fingers offishly. "Of course, a simple manifestation of her witch magic ..." He frowned. "You think she is being directed?"

"You yourself can attest to how susceptible she is to having her 'attention turned' …" I sneered as I repeated his own phrase back to him.

Kader shook his head. "No. It would have to be one of the others currently on the property. No one else could be consistently penetrating Aiden's wards. Plus, both Isa and Khalid conduct daily sweeps. They've all added protections to the property wards."

"You're certain?"

"Yes."

"Then how do you account for the change you feel in Cerise's magic?"

He smirked at me. "How do I account for the change in Aiden's?"

I frowned. "Does the Myers coven contain an amplifier?"

"Two." The elder sorcerer laughed quietly. "None like you, of course. But I meant that Aiden's reach has grown because of those he trains with, learns from, and the situations that he…survives." He smirked at me, as if to imply that I was one of the things Aiden had survived.

I didn't bother to dispute it. It was true.

Kader sighed, closing his eyes.

I watched him for a moment. The power emanating from the pentagram thrummed between us. I knew that if I reached toward the orchard, I would feel the witch magic being ignited there as well.

"Shall I ask your forgiveness?" Kader whispered.

"Would you mean it?"

He laughed sadly. "No. But would you accept?"

"No."

He snorted. "As expected."

"Yes."

Then I stood and walked away. The memory of the words between us was already a dryness in my mouth. Ashy. The deal I'd made with him.

Aiden above all others.

I shoved the idiotic notion away. Words didn't come with their own taste.

I remembered to turn off the light over the workbench before heading back to the orchard, where Aiden and his sisters were still helping Cerise.

PAISLEY WAS PROWLING THROUGH THE IMMATURE apple trees. I could feel the demon dog by her magic more than see her. And although Cerise appeared to be trying to meditate in the center of the circle that had been stamped into my orchard grass, she kept glancing behind herself nervously.

Aiden reached for me, and I took his offered hand. His touch was warm. The energy he was holding tingled across my palm and up my arm. I shivered.

"We're going to be a couple more hours," he murmured. "But you should get some sleep."

I glanced at Cerise. She had her eyes closed, legs crossed. Her hands were on her knees, palms facing up. The pose was strikingly similar to how Kader was currently situated in the pentagram. But instead of rune-etched copper, unlit candles of various colors and sizes were set at intervals around the outer edge of the large circle that surrounded her.

I could feel the slow drip of Cerise's witch magic. But if any foreign magic or power was being activated by her, or directing her, I couldn't sense it. Perhaps Kader was right. The spell was of Cerise's creation alone.

"Moon fueled?" I asked.

Aiden nodded. His attention was trained on his mother, and he didn't offer any clarification. "I'll keep Cerise company. Ocean and Sky are drained, and not just magically." He smiled sadly, his sorrow brushing through the empathic bond that formed effortlessly every time we touched.

Not caring that we were in full view of his mother, I leaned in and brushed a kiss across Aiden's lips. Then I just hovered there, breathing him in.

"Emma." He whispered my name so quietly that I almost didn't hear it. Then he touched his lips to mine, epically gently. "Emma. Get some rest, my love. I'll see you at dawn."

I wanted to drag him into the house with me, curl up on the couch, and just talk. Talk and talk like no one else was listening. I shook off the odd impulse, stepping away. Our still-linked hands stretched between us.

Aiden smiled at me, his teeth a flash of white in the darkness. Then he directed his attention over my right shoulder. "Go with Emma, please."

Paisley stepped from between the nearest two apple trees, the darkness clinging to her in a way that let me know she hadn't been traveling just through our dimension. She was still in her large pit bull aspect, but was now carrying her spellbook and her bovine bone in two of her tentacles.

Out of the corner of my eye, I saw Cerise flinch.

Paisley chuckled darkly. Prowling across the grass toward Aiden, she offered the spellbook and the bone to him.

He tilted his head thoughtfully. "Do I need these?"

She pressed the spellbook into his hand, then tapped it with the thicker end of the bone. She then touched the bone to Aiden's chest, over his heart.

He grinned down at her. "Thank you," he said. "I'll ask you for it if I need it, but I think it's more important that you keep it right now."

Paisley grunted agreeably, tucking the bone and the spellbook away in her invisible mane. It had always been clear that the demon dog's mane hid some sort of access to a storage space in another dimension, but I still had no idea how it worked.

"I need to focus, Aiden," Cerise called out, using that soft, almost childlike tone she kept lapsing into.

"Good night," I murmured, but just to Aiden. I ignored the witch treating my hospitality—our hospitality—as if it was her due. I reluctantly let go of his hand, turning back to the house. "Paisley?"

The demon dog lumbered alongside me without protest.

We crossed the patio, entering the house and catching no sign of Khalid. He wasn't guarding the front door or the barn door. Perhaps, given Kader's rejection, the sorcerer had decided to leave his father to his fate.

Isa had moved into the front sitting room, and was currently sprawled across the couch with his head thrown back, deeply asleep. Reference texts, notebooks, and paper—much of it folded or tucked into envelopes as if Isa had been magically sending and receiving letters for hours—were strewn over the sorcerer's chest and legs, as well as the coffee table.

Paisley started nosing around the spellbooks.

If either Christopher or Aiden had fallen asleep with his neck cranked like Isa's was, I would have woken him. But I was either feeling vindictive or not in the mood to deal with any sorcerers—other than the one who should have been in my bed. So I left Isa alone.

I likewise left Paisley to her rooting around, heading upstairs. I was exceedingly aware that the sorcerers weren't going to be spending the night in their rented rooms at the lodge.

But they'd be gone tomorrow. And if Paisley had her way, Isa's exhausted nap wouldn't end well. I grinned at the thought.

Then I hesitated at the top of the stairs.

A gentle pulse of magic hummed around the edges of the closed door to my upstairs sitting room. I couldn't sense what or who was within the room. Or what they were casting.

Honestly, who had decided to let these sorcerers and witches just run around my property?

Right.

Me.

I grasped the door handle. It resisted my attempt to turn it. Not feeling particularly diplomatic, I thrust my shoulder against the door—along with a pulse of my magic. The door opened. Hopefully, I hadn't torn it from the hinges.

Inside, moonlight spilled in through the windows, gently lighting Grosvenor and Sky where they were tangled together on the couch. The curse breaker was partially on top of the witch, and naked to the waist. A circle of bright-blue symbols was tattooed on the back of his right shoulder. Runes, most likely, but it looked almost like a brand of some sort.

Sky's right hand was deeply buried within the front of Grosvenor's undone pants. The witch was also partly naked, her skin pale in the moonlight, her skirt bunched up around her waist. Grosvenor was cupping one of her breasts, and bent over the other.

The curse breaker spun toward the door, quickly discovering that he couldn't move far without Sky releasing her grip on his genitals. And, before he could have possibly identified the intruder—namely me—he had already muttered a curse. It flew across the room toward me.

I could have sidestepped it. But again, there really were too many people in my house and it really wouldn't hurt for them to understand who they were dealing with when they flung magic around without thinking first.

The curse hit me in the chest, exploding maliciously. It tried to chew on my magic, then withered, curled up on itself, and dissipated.

I kept my expression neutral and my eyes locked to the curse breaker for the time it took the magic to die.

Grosvenor's hand still hovered in the air from flinging the curse. His jaw dropped.

"Immune to that one," I said, smiling. "Good try though."

Fear flickered through the curse breaker's eyes. No doubt, he was trying to figure out how many times someone would need to be hit with the same curse, over and over again, to gain immunity to it. My resistance was mostly due to all the magic I'd stolen from so many different Adepts, over all the years that the Collective had controlled the Five, but Grosvenor didn't need to know that.

"Emma?" Sky whispered, withdrawing her hand from Grosvenor's pants and placing it on his shoulder. As if getting ready to hold him back. It also let me know that she was currently underneath the sorcerer of her own free will—as did the fact that the spell on the door had been cast by a witch.

"The spell sealing the door," I said. It wasn't a question.

They nodded in tandem.

"It only draws attention."

"Okay," Sky whispered. Her eyes were wide.

I stepped back into the hall. "And clean the couch when you're done."

"Of course," Grosvenor said, his voice roughened by adrenaline.

The door scraped against the doorjamb as I closed it. Apparently, I'd loosened at least one of the hinges.

"Did you see her cast a countercurse?" Grosvenor asked in a low mutter.

"No. It just hit and rolled off her."

"Fuck."

"Do you…want to stop?"

"Fuck, no," he growled.

I thought about calling out to tell them I could still hear them, but I continued on to my bedroom instead. I didn't need to frighten the sorcerers and the witches any more than I already had.

Paisley was sprawled across my bed and appeared to be reading a multitude of Isa's papers at the same time.

"You know Isa is trying to help," I said, shutting the bedroom door. "And that cage never would have held you."

Paisley snarled quietly.

I closed the space between us, maintaining eye contact. "I'd like you to return to Christopher before dawn."

She narrowed her eyes at me.

"I know you want to help…but I …" I shook my head. "I don't trust anyone other than Aiden. And I'm worried they'll try to hurt you if you interfere with the casting in any way tomorrow. I need you to make certain that Christopher is okay. Will you do that for me?"

Paisley grumbled, shuffling through the papers disgruntledly.

I sighed, caressing her head. "And please return the papers to Isa when he wakes. Unless you find something that might help us."

The demon dog pressed her nose into my inner elbow, then pointedly ignored me. I didn't want to turn my requests into orders. But I would if she got anywhere near Cerise's casting.

I left Paisley to her investigations, washing my face and changing into a short nightgown. The demon dog had wandered off again, with the papers, by the time I tugged my curtains closed and crawled into bed.

I lay in the darkness, thinking I wasn't going to be able to sleep with all the magic percolating through the house. But I must have dozed off, because the next thing I was aware of was Aiden crawling into bed with me. He was carrying enough residual energy that I could feel it radiating from him, even though he was careful not to touch me.

He set an alarm. The light on his phone winked out as he lay back with a sigh. I shimmied into him, and he curled around me obligingly.

We fell asleep.

NINE

WHEN IT WAS TIME, I BROUGHT MY BLADES. I HAD actually left the house, following Aiden out into the predawn, then turned back for them. I was tired of the games, tired of waiting. Either Cerise would untangle the working on Aiden and Kader, or I would hack through whatever stood in my way.

Experience also told me that whether or not Cerise lifted the spell on him, Kader wasn't going to just walk away. And Isa's and Khalid's motivations were also unclear. Would they try to strike at their father in his weakened state? By that same measure, I didn't completely understand Sky either—especially factoring in the secret relationship with Grosvenor.

It was fairly clear to me, and Kader, that Cerise was responsible for the strangeness I'd been feeling. The mood control. But maybe I was wrong. Isa or Khalid, or even one of Aiden's sisters, could be playing a very long game. Pointing all the evidence toward Cerise for reasons that I couldn't see yet.

As far as I could tell, Paisley wasn't on the property. The demon dog rarely missed a chance to study magic, but I was hopeful that she'd stay away as I'd requested.

Cerise was waiting for us all, dressed head to toe in white lace. She stood, feet bare, in the orchard grass of the broad clearing, along the western curve of the large circle, facing east toward the rising sun. Her dress glowed softly—as did the eight smaller secondary rings set outside the main circle. As I drew nearer, the second-last to arrive, I realized that the smaller rings were actually large lace doilies, each one a different design. All of them pulsing with light.

Moon-fueled?

There was no way that Cerise had knit or knotted—or however lace was made—eight doilies big enough for an adult to stand on overnight. She'd been building the elements of this removal spell since she'd arrived. Perhaps even before that.

Except she couldn't have known that eight Adepts, plus Kader, would be at the house before she'd arrived herself.

We'd each been assigned a doily—directed to our proper places with a nod from the elder witch—just as we'd been assigned seats at the first dinner. Mine was directly opposite Cerise's. An empty spot sat to my right, then there was Aiden, then Sky. Grosvenor was on my left, then Isa, and then Ocean. Each of us just close enough that we could have touched fingertips, but too far to link hands.

Kader was standing within the main circle, but close enough to my assigned spot that I could have reached out to take his hand. He was wearing his tan-colored suit, but his feet were bare in the grass. I would have expected Cerise to have placed him in the center of the circle, not closer to one side, since he was the focus of the spell. But I had never seen a moon-fueled, dawn-triggered spell before, so I had no frame of reference.

Khalid was the last to arrive. Like the rest of us, he paused a step away from the lace doily that had been assigned to him. Its design was simple, with just two thick lines of lace slashed through it. My own doily was intricate—lace flowers and leaves adhered to a spiderweb of tiny stitches.

The flowers looked like apple blossoms. Though it was possible that my overactive brain was trying to sort through all the puzzle pieces that had led up to this point, and I was now reading into everything I saw and heard.

But if I was admitting that—even if just to my-self—I could also admit that all the lace patterning reminded me of the game the witches and sorcerers had been playing in the kitchen.

"Join me, please," Cerise said, opening her hands outward and then sweeping them in cupped toward her chest. Her voice was heavy with magic, nothing remotely childlike about it now. "It is time to end the discord between our families. Kader is right." She nodded her chin toward the elder sorcerer benevolently. "The union between us resulted in Aiden, and he…is…cherished."

I glanced at Aiden. He was watching his mother closely, but didn't appear thrown by her abrupt change of heart. Presumably they had talked while setting up the spell. Perhaps he'd helped his mother sort through the situation?

Or whatever power Cerise was channeling prevented him from seeing the change, even as my immunity was deflecting it.

Though the tension in Kader's shoulders informed me that I wasn't the only wary one. Both Sky and Ocean looked even more serene than Aiden. Grosvenor was listening intently, scanning the layout and structure of the spell circles as if committing them to memory. Isa was expressionless, stone faced.

Beside me, Khalid's eyes were narrowed on Cerise.

"Your place, please, Emma," Cerise said. "Before the dawn breaks. And Khalid …" She gestured with her right hand, as if guiding us into place. Then she cried out, "No! Not the blades! Emma!"

My bare foot was hovering over the lace doily. I paused, just looking at the witch. She was going to have to explain herself if she wanted me to put down my weapons.

"The…spell …" She stumbled over the word. That was telling. "It is far too delicate to bring a sharp edge to it. Set them within reach if it gives you comfort …"

That was some sort of dig. Thankfully, I was also immune to stupidity.

Mostly.

"Aiden?" I asked.

The dark-haired sorcerer looked thoughtful. "All blades?" Aiden asked his mother. "Or just the ones that Emma is carrying?"

Frustration flashed across Cerise's face before she smoothed her expression. "Emma is going to need her hands. If she raises the blades to the sides, she might compromise the spell. Hurry, please."

I crouched to set the blades on either side of the lace doily when Cerise spoke up again.

"Behind you would be better, dear."

I set the blades behind my feet, hilts toward the circle. I could pivot and grab them just as easily as dropping into a crouch.

I glanced over at Khalid, the two of us the last to step into our individual circles. "Anything you'd like to share with the rest of us?" I asked him, since he was the most sensitive to magic among us. I didn't bother to be quiet about it.

He opened his mouth as if it took effort to do so. "The spell looks fine to me. I would have thought it to be overkill for a simple reversal."

"If it were simple," Sky snapped, "you'd have figured it out months ago."

"Please," Cerise murmured. "Breathe. Release the negativity. Just breathe. Breathe love in and breathe love out."

I stepped onto my doily, feeling the dawn slowly creeping up behind me. Khalid took his place to my right. Grosvenor was already standing in place to my left. Now that I was a step closer to Kader in the main circle, my view of Cerise directly across from both of us was partially impeded.

"Feel the ground beneath your feet," she intoned. "The strength of your physical body, rooted, solid. Breathe from deep within."

Cerise's directions were starting to sound like a few of the yoga classes I'd tried. Witch spells were generally more arcane. Or at least more poetically bent.

The sunrise was right behind me now. I wasn't certain why I was feeling it so acutely.

Magic rustled around us, as if the trees and the earth were waking from a long slumber. All the hair rose on the back of my neck and across my arms. Something was coming. Stalking forward.

Something that had been stalking…me.

For days.

I'd been trying to figure out which one of Cerise or Aiden's other family members had been trying to control me, to gently beguile us all. But this…feeling…this flare of pure instinct was something else. I looked to Aiden to see if he was sensing what I was, but his gaze was on his mother as he took deep, full breaths.

Ocean, Sky, and Grosvenor were doing the same. Isa and Khalid were watching Cerise, though the wariness had drained from their expressions.

The sunrise was creeping across the yard, hitting the back of my heels. Triggering the moon-fueled spell on which I stood. It flared across the intricate lacy webbing of the doily under my bare feet. Energy hummed up my legs. Then, as the dawn continued to slip forward, it ignited Grosvenor's and Khalid's circles, then the large central circle.

Bright-white magic, slightly tinged with blue, began to spiral around me as the spell gained power. It rose to my ankles, then my knees, then my thighs. Encasing me, but not touching.

The lace doilies under Isa and Aiden flared. Nearer to me, magic spiraled around Grosvenor's and Khalid's ankles and began to slowly rise.

The circles around Ocean and Sky flared.

Kader glanced around, turning just enough that I caught sight of Cerise's lace doily flaring under her as well. The power in the doily appeared slightly dingy in contrast to Cerise's pure-white dress.

Wait. A white lace dress.

Was Cerise dressed as a bride?

And white power, white magic. Was moon-fueled witch magic white? Shouldn't it still be a shade of blue?

I turned to Khalid. "White? Does the spell look white to you? Khalid!"

The dark-eyed sorcerer blinked, shaking his head, then looking at me.

"Does it look white to you?" I asked again.

He nodded, then frowned.

The central circle flared, energy streaking upward into the ever-brightening sky. I had to blink to regain focus. When I did, I found myself staring at Kader. He was examining the circle that now contained him.

Except he didn't appear to be tied to it in any way. Not yet.

The energy churning around me settled slightly, intensifying into a spiral around my knees.

"Now," Cerise intoned, not sounding at all like herself. "Now." She began muttering quiet and lilted words that didn't sound like French to me. Witches often spoke their spells out loud, though usually not—

My arms rose of their own accord, reaching out to the sides. The arms of the others all did the same. My fingertips brushed Khalid's fingers on my right and Grosvenor's on my left. They in turn touched Aiden and Isa. Then Ocean and Sky. And finally Cerise.

Power shot out from each of the individual circles—thick strands of lace linking the eight of us. Then with another push of power from Cerise—a power I could now feel—more thin panels of lace connected each of the eight circles to the main circle.

I withdrew my arms, opening and closing my hands into fists. Had my limbs actually moved on their own? Was Cerise manipulating us all that effectively? Except I couldn't feel anyone in my head—and I knew that feeling intimately.

Another push of power from Cerise radiated through both sides of the main circle. It touched the individual circles, feeding off each of us, then returned back to Cerise. She gathered the power siphoned from us and thrust her hands forward.

Dingy white magic slashed through the main circle, calling forth a web of diamond-patterned lace that hovered around ankle height. As the linking lace had spiraled out toward him, Kader shifted slightly to the side, standing between Khalid and me now. He was situated within one of the pattern's large lace diamonds.

I had a clear view of Cerise. Her eyes were blazing blue, head thrown back, arms spread wide. I ran my gaze around the circle. Every single other person, including Aiden, matched Cerise's posture.

Except me. And Kader.

All their blazing blue eyes were peering skyward.

White magic webbed all around us.

"Kader," I whispered.

"I see it." He glanced at me, then at each of the others. Then he looked down at himself, at his hands.

"It's not connected to you," I said.

"No." But even as he said it, the web around him expanded, then contracted. Then another slow expansion and contraction.

As if it were …

Breathing.

Cerise started muttering again. As before, I didn't recognize the language.

Magic shivered through the lace doily under my feet. My mind began to drift. Everything was so…pretty.

The power…the people…the dawn-lit sky above …

I smiled, feeling warm, blissful.

"Amp5!" Kader barked.

I flinched. I hated that name. That designation. I raised my head, not realizing that it had fallen back, already snarling at the sorcerer.

My maker.

The Collective incarnate.

He deserved everything coming to him. He deserved to die a slow, painful death, to feed—

"Emma!" the elder sorcerer shouted.

I blinked.

To feed…what?

Kader Azar came into focus before me. He was reaching toward me, offering me his hand.

Another pulse of energy rode Cerise's muttered words. The desire to kneel flooded through me.

I didn't.

Everyone else sank down onto their knees. Their hands were placed palm up on their thighs, their heads fallen back. Including Aiden.

But not Kader.

"Emma," the elder sorcerer said urgently. He was gesturing toward the center of the circle.

A crystal vase filled with flowers had appeared on the grass, set within the diamond lace pattern. The flowers looked…familiar.

I blinked.

The vase turned into a mason jar, similar to the one Paisley had eaten.

I blinked again.

No. Not a vase.

It was…a statue of some sort? A shapely figure holding an urn above its head. Cast in a bronze-colored metal.

I blinked again and the crystal vase with familiar blossoms reappeared—the apple blossoms with the dark centers that had been set beside my bed. The flowers were a magical construct of some sort.

"Do you see it?" Kader hissed.

I nodded, though I wasn't completely certain.

A whisper ran through the lace spell, then another, and another. Until it emanated from seven different throats. Cerise's spell, picked up by the others.

Except they were all speaking in one voice now.

"What are they saying?" I asked.

"I'm not catching all of it," Kader said. "But the chant is…'The Hallowed. The Hallowed.' It could be an ancient Celtic dialect?"

My heart started racing, fear shivering down my spine. Which was good, because it washed away the last lingering traces of the compulsion.

Compulsion that Cerise had tried on me multiple times over the last two days.

No.

Not Cerise.

At least not just Cerise.

I looked at the vase that wasn't a vase, at the center of the main circle. It was an idol of some sort. The kind that might have been worshiped by some cult hundreds or thousands of years ago.

My gaze snapped to Kader. "I think we're about to find out what Cerise Myers dug up in the coven archives."

"Yes," he said grimly. "And it's been feeding off me, through Aiden, for well over a year now ..." Magic shifted through the diamond lace of the main circle, calling Kader's attention. But his point was clear.

Whatever being was contained in that idol wanted out. And it needed way more than just sips of Kader's magic to get free. Would it take all of our deaths? Or just Kader's? Was that why Cerise—or whatever was controlling Cerise—had put him in the main circle with the idol?

The chanting rose in intensity. The same foreign phrase that Kader had translated for me repeated over and over again. The Hallowed. The Hallowed.

Power pulsed through the spell again, highlighting the outer circles one at a time. Beginning with Cerise, then jumping between Sky and Ocean, then Aiden and Isa, then Khalid and Grosvenor.

The spell welled up under my feet, trying to draw magic from me. Not trying to drain me, though. More like it was sharing all the magic it had gathered, then adding mine to the mix.

I could feel the spell well enough that I knew I could attempt to thwart it at any time. But I understood that what was happening might well be what was necessary to remove the spell from Kader—

A cracking sound erupted from within the circle. The noise was so sharp and brutal that I thought it might have been Kader's neck breaking. I might have missed the sudden death of the sorcerer while staring at my feet.

I raised my gaze to see that he was still standing before me, though. The elder sorcerer was staring at the vessel—which now had a lengthwise crack running through its widest section.

I'd been compromised. Again. Not completely incapacitated, but definitely slowed down. Except it wasn't Cerise who'd been influencing our moods, making us more amenable. It was the Hallowed, manifesting through Cerise. It absolutely explained the shift in the witch's power.

And it also made clear my own vulnerability, and the way the magic had initially been able to sway even me.

I had never faced…whatever I was about to face.

Kader shook his head as if trying to clear it. Then he turned and thrust his hand toward me again. Darkly tinted sorcerer magic had gathered around his other hand. Whatever was happening in Cerise's circle, it didn't appear to stop the sorcerer from casting. An oversight. Or Cerise didn't think the spell could be torn down from within.

But then, Cerise really didn't know me at all.

Which meant she'd have no idea why the only sorcerer still standing, still holding himself outside the enchantment of the spell, was offering his hand to me.

I glanced over Kader's shoulder at Aiden. He was completely enthralled, kneeling, head thrown back. A dark-blue globe of power pooled in each of his hands, that same power gleaming from his eyes.

The others were all in identical positions, though Aiden's magic glowed the brightest.

Emanating from Cerise's connection point to the main circle, energy started licking down the diamond-patterned lacework that stretched from edge to edge. The chanting picked up in speed and power, becoming unnaturally loud now.

The Hallowed. The Hallowed.

"Stop thinking, Emma," Kader shouted over the sound. "You know what needs to be done." The sorcerer's eyes were blazing with power. His face had thinned, appearing almost skeletal. Whatever was contained in Cerise's idol was consuming him. Quickly.

"Amplifier!" he shouted again, demanding. Then he softened his tone. "Emma."

"You have no right to my magic," I snarled. "Or that name." I had no idea why I was taking the time to protest. Except that…except that it might have been nice to stay in place, to greet the Hallowed…to open myself to the Hallowed …

Kader bared his teeth in a smile. "I'd like to save my sons. How would you prefer to go about it? Pick up your blades, then slaughter everyone between yourself and Cerise? If you wait long enough, that might be your only option. If she…if it…can turn them against you, that is exactly what's going to happen."

I curled my fingers into fists, looking at Aiden again. If I tore through Cerise's spell on my own, and if she sent Aiden at me in response, I knew I would be able to quell him without harming him.

But if they all attacked me at once? I couldn't guarantee anything.

"Can you turn the spell against her?" I shouted at Kader, straining to be heard over the chanting.

He shook his head. "It's still witch magic, which I cannot wield. But I might be able to sever the connections. One at a time."

"Without killing Cerise?"

The power seeping through the lace diamonds in the main circle was closing in on Kader, creeping forward from the sides as well now.

"I doubt it," he said.

"What about…what about destroying the idol?"

He grinned at me. "Risky, amplifier," he shouted back.

"Contain it, then? While I hold Cerise?"

The lace diamond that Kader was standing within brightened at its tip, energy slipping down its sides. As my own natural resistance became full immunity, I could feel the compulsion finally. A beguiling tendril of dirty white energy licked Kader's cheek, drawing his attention away from me.

The grin slid from the elder sorcerer's face.

He took a hesitant step forward.

The lace started to shift around him, the pattern blurring. The top section of the diamond opened, creating a passageway to the vessel, the idol.

Damn it.

I slammed my palm against the power that sealed the main circle between Kader and me, finding little resistance. I was tied to the spell, because my lace doily was tied to the spell, however lightly. And since I was part of it, I could pass through it.

I grabbed Kader's hand before he could turn fully away, slamming my power through him. He stumbled to the side, then whirled back toward me. The fingers of his free hand clawed, crackling with the dark pulse of the spell he'd been calling forth. He was reacting as if I'd attacked him, not amplified him. As if he was about to wrench my heart from my chest.

Still standing in my individual circle, I pulled him closer, hitting him with another flood of power. His pupils dilated, spreading wide enough that only a hint of yellowed white edged his blackened eyes. A terrible grin stretched across his too-thin face—filled with pain.

Then his hand dropped to his side. His expression softened, and he laughed. A deep throaty laugh, head back, throat exposed.

For a moment, I thought he might have been fully taken by Cerise's leeching spell. That by amplifying him, I had somehow increased the connection of the spell.

The chanting stopped. So abruptly that my ears continued to ring with its din.

Kader tugged me toward him, pulling me from my individual circle into the main circle. The spell allowed me to pass through with minimal resistance.

The diamond lace pattern shuddered, quivering. Then it started narrowing, as if to squeeze us.

Kader thrust his free hand toward the ground. A blackened pentagram seared itself across the grass, just big enough to encompass our feet without slicing through the main circle. Another spark of power from the elder sorcerer sealed it—and sealed us within it—the moment after it encompassed our feet.

He did it all without a word of power, nary a murmur of a spell.

Then he spun me. Placing his hand on my hip, he guided me back a step. The pentagram shifted with us.

No.

An echo of the pentagram hovered around our ankles. I could still see the seared lines across the grass a step behind us.

Kader shifted into me again, moving me through a more and more complicated series of steps. I stumbled, trying to keep my footing while still amplifying him.

He was dancing. Or trying to dance.

With me.

Trust was most definitely a missing component, though. Hence the stumbling.

More power exploded around us, filling the pentagram. The magic was dense but not suffocating.

We spiraled through the main circle, keeping to the outer edge but never breaking the seal. Somehow, we were collecting the diamond lace as we twirled around and around the idol.

Cerise and the others remained silent. The sounds of the still-cooped chickens started filtering in. Then a lone car on the main road. Though we should have been mostly concealed from the road, I seriously hoped Cerise had added a layer of obfuscation to her main circle.

Kader shifted his hands, switching which of my hands he clasped and which hip he held. Then he switched the direction of the dance, of our slow spin. Our bodies were close but not touching. When we'd met, eight years ago, he was taller than me. But the rapid aging of Cerise's spell meant he stood slightly shorter now.

Magic gleamed in the elder sorcerer's blackened eyes. And for the first time since he'd arrived, I felt the full depth of Kader Azar's power, his magic. He couldn't hide it while I was amplifying him.

He was beyond formidable.

If it came to it, I might not actually be able to kill him. Not on my own. Not even with Cerise's hallowed spell eating him from within.

It was a good thing I didn't believe in impossibilities.

Kader laughed, pulling me against him and murmuring, "My darling daughter ..." His arms snapped out, spinning me. My hair was dancing in the ever-thickening magic of the pentagram—the unleashed and amplified sorcerer power. "Look at you. True beauty. Such power."

We stopped, magic still churning around us. The echo of the pentagram sealed over the edges of the one burned into the grass. We'd completed three circuits—two counterclockwise and one clockwise—before returning to our origin point.

The lace of the main spell was twined around the pentagram, as if it had been gathered along its points and spokes.

Kader released my hand, only to touch my cheek. His blackened eyes blazed with power—his and mine combined.

He would have been unstoppable with me at his side.

His smile sharpened, as if he were reading my mind.

And maybe he was.

Then I realized I couldn't read his emotions through our skin-to-skin contact. That was utterly disconcerting.

I gave him one last blast of amplification. His eyes narrowed into self-satisfied slits as he greedily absorbed the energy without flinching.

I leaned into him, whispering against his ear, "I might still kill you tomorrow."

He laughed huskily. "Always a possibility with you…and everyone in your life. Emma." His use of my name was pointed, claiming.

I stepped back.

Still smirking, and now radiating power, Kader turned to face the idol and Cerise. As he raised his hands to the sides, dark-blue tendrils of magic started slipping into and twining through the reams and reams of white lace he'd somehow coiled around the pentagram during our dance.

"Claiming the spell?" I whispered, standing tightly behind him.

"Testing the response …" He trailed off, fingers spreading as if feeling for something I couldn't see.

I glanced back at my blades lying in the grass. "I could just take Cerise out of play."

Kader hummed thoughtfully, still easing the threads of his magic through the white lace. "Might be too late for that. The entity might have taken too much control. We'd still need to bottle it."

"And I'd be responsible for killing Aiden's mother."

"I gather that's what has saved my neck for the last few days."

I changed the subject. I didn't go around simply murdering people, for a variety of reasons. I didn't need to list them all for the sorcerer who had been largely responsible for the death toll I'd racked up prior to my twenty-second birthday.

If I thought about it too much, I might forget that Aiden still held some feelings for his father.

"And if you can't claim it?" I said. "Can you at least block it?"

"Yes," Kader murmured. "But only gradually. The key is to replace the anchor points without—"

Cerise raised her hands. The light-blue witch magic blazing in her eyes also welled in her palms. The third eye on her forehead winked open. Power shuddered through the main circle, as if the lace was trying to untangle itself from the spokes of Kader's pentagram.

The elder sorcerer increased his own output, energy flowing out of him freely now as he outright attempted to claim the main circle.

Cerise reached to her sides, palms facing Ocean on her right and Sky on her left. The younger witches were still kneeling in their individual circles, heads thrown back.

Tendrils from the lace doily—I couldn't tell whether it was the actual fabric or the yarn or rope from which Cerise had constructed them—lashed around Sky's and Ocean's wrists. They cinched so tightly that I could see them cutting into flesh, even through the magic churning and clashing within the main circle.

"Kader," I whispered. "We're going to have to switch to plan B."

Power pulsed under Sky and Ocean.

They screamed.

Their eyes snapped open, faces etched in agony. Both of them were suddenly and completely aware of what was happening—as if Cerise had severed the connection to the primary spell that had held them in thrall. Now she was pulling power directly from them. Blood seeped from their wrists as they struggled to free themselves.

Another pulse of energy ran through their individual circles, and the younger witches screamed again. And again.

Kader grunted, then reestablished his footing as if he'd felt a push of power that I hadn't.

"Plan B!" I shouted, pressing my hand against the magic that held me in the pentagram with the sorcerer.

"No," he snarled. "Bringing the blades in would be too volatile. The point is to avoid releasing the entity."

Ocean screamed again, then slumped to one side. I hoped she'd simply passed out—as opposed to suffering a stroke.

Sky was sobbing. She had gotten one of her hands free and was actively trying to tear through the lace that still bound her other wrist. She met my eyes through the maelstrom of power that the elder witch and the sorcerer were throwing at each other, sobbing. "Emma!"

Another strand of the lace beneath her unraveled. She noticed it a second before it struck, lashing around her neck. She got her hand under it, but was already struggling to breathe.

The lace doily under Isa started to pulse. With Ocean knocked out—or dead—Cerise was going to pull Isa into the act of repulsing Kader's attempt to claim the circle. To contain whatever was in the cracked idol.

Aiden was next to Sky. The younger witch was still fighting, but her eyes were fluttering as she also fought to hold on to consciousness. When she went down, Aiden would be next.

"Let me out of here," I snarled. "Or I'll tear my way through."

"Not advisable," Kader said coolly, but I could hear the strain in his voice from the level of power he was wielding.

Isa's eyes snapped open. He snarled. Power exploded around him, contained by his individual circle, as he fought the strands of lace that had latched onto his wrists.

Kader flinched.

"Can you hold against them all?" I asked, trying to be rational, not reactionary. We were dealing with magic I knew nothing about. That was how Cerise had played me so badly. "If she gets Isa and…Aiden…even with me amplifying you, can you hold?"

"I can."

"And if she's killing them?" I asked softly, my gaze on Aiden now. On the glowing lace doily under his knees, pulsing with power. "If she sacrifices each of them to the spell? Maybe even to the entity?"

Kader snarled something in that arcane language that belonged to the Azars. Dark-blue power exploded around us, scouring the last of the delicate lace pattern from the main circle.

Across from us, Cerise mewed in pain.

Then she shook her head, settled her shoulders, and tore more energy from the circle.

Sky slumped.

Isa screamed.

The lace doily under Aiden's knees unfurled and latched on to him viciously, immediately cutting into his hands, wrists, and forearms. He grunted in pain, brow furrowing.

Cerise brought her hands together at her chest, her fervent, blazing, blue-eyed gaze locked to Kader.

And to me.

I caught the moment the elder witch saw me in the pentagram with the sorcerer. She frowned and tilted her head. But not as if she was thinking. More as if she was listening to someone.

Aiden started hissing in pain, twisting against the bindings that held him.

"Get me to Cerise," I whispered to Kader. "Just get me to Cerise."

"This is too much, amplifier. Even for you. If Cerise gains you, she will be too powerful for the rest of us. We need to step back—"

I grabbed the back of Kader's neck.

He went rigid, presumably thinking I was about to snap it.

Instead, I turned his head toward Isa, who'd broken the first tendrils holding him but was now fighting at least a dozen others. And flagging.

Then I rotated Kader's head toward Aiden.

The dark-haired sorcerer was also fighting. Tearing through the lace doily under his knees, chest heaving in pain, blood seeping from slashes across his arms, neck, and face.

My struggle to breathe was purely psychological, but knowing so didn't reduce the terror at seeing Aiden hurting. A terror that threatened to overwhelm my senses, my rational mind.

Power thundered through the main circle, held at bay by Kader's pentagram. A sharp sound drew my attention away from Aiden. The crack on the idol had widened.

And for just a breath, I swore I could see a shadow moving within it—an iridescent blackness.

A cool flood of adrenaline slid through me—hairline to neck to chest to stomach—then filtered down to my bare toes. "Get me to Cerise," I said coolly. "I'll contain her. Not kill her. While you get the idol secured."

Completely without consent, I started pumping more power into the sorcerer. And as I did, I felt the first flicker of his emotions—a flood of willfulness, underpinned by a thread of uncertainty.

Kader reached up, wrapping his fingers around my wrist as he'd done eight years ago. I felt the shift in his emotions—resolution and pride.

"Listen to me carefully, amplifier," he whispered, turning his head back as far as it would go. "If I'm putting this together well enough, I assume that Cerise needed the power of the others to break the containment spell on the idol. But for that entity to manifest fully into our dimension, our reality …" He trailed off.

Trying to be patient, even as Isa gave in and started screaming in earnest, I gave the elder sorcerer more and more of my power. Blood now speckled the grass around Aiden. "You think it needs a body," I said, putting together the rest. "I thought she was going to sacrifice you to release it."

"You can't let it have me, Emma." Kader squeezed my wrist almost painfully. "It's one thing for it to control a witch such as Cerise. But if it could fully manifest through her, then it already would have. Cerise's ties to the Myers coven most likely kept it in check. Otherwise, the coven would have sensed its intrusion and cleaned things up, as witches like to do."

Even while watching his sons being magically consumed, Kader still managed to sneeringly maintain his ingrained sorcerer prejudices.

"I won't let it have you, Kader. Let's go." I removed my hand from the back of his neck.

He held on to my wrist. "No. You'll have to kill me. I'm dead already if it gets me, because those who will come then will slaughter me without mercy."

"Those who will come?" I said mockingly, twisting out of his hold.

He let me go with a pained wince. I had probably been rougher than necessary.

Kader met my gaze. "The Collective made you powerful for a reason." He jabbed a finger toward the idol. "Entities such as whatever is contained in that urn do not walk the earth unchecked."

Behind the idol, Cerise was amassing more and more power. Whatever she hit us with next was going to hurt.

"Even the Five united—"

"We don't have time for a lesson," I snarled. "I'll kill you if it gets hold of you."

"Instantly," he said. "You can't hesitate."

Isa slumped.

Aiden screamed, over and over.

The magic beneath Grosvenor started pulsing.

I spun, unleashing my power, fingers clawed toward the edge of the pentagram.

But before I could dig in and try to tear through it, Kader placed his hand on my back, pushing me forward.

I took a step.

The pentagram shifted with me.

Another step and I was beside Khalid. His head was still thrown back in an expression of ecstasy.

Two more quick steps and I was beside Aiden.

He'd been watching our progress, half-slumped to the ground. Ribbons of his blue sorcerer power still twined around him, as if he'd tried to shield himself and had only been partially successful.

He slammed his free hand to the magic between us as I stepped by him.

I met his pained gaze, brushing my fingertips across his palm, even though I couldn't actually touch him. "I'll be right back."

He smiled, a fierce flash of teeth. "I'm right behind you."

I turned and ran, pulling the pentagram and Kader with me.

I made it three steps before Cerise unleashed her spell. It slammed into Kader's pentagram, shredding it so thoroughly that my momentum actually carried me through, tumbling into the onslaught of power.

I lost all sense of time and space, of up or down.

Then, my shoulders crashing into something metal, I hit the ground.

I pressed my palms into the grass, making it to my knees, blinking Kader into focus. He was still on his feet, nearer to Cerise than me. I must have taken the brunt of whatever the elder witch had hit us with. Power emanated from him, burning in a wide beam directed at Cerise.

The metal object behind me was warm. It hummed with its own power. There was something soothing about the warm vibration, something inviting—

I rolled away, coming up facing the idol. The center section of the urn was cracked completely in half now, yet somehow the top section remained still suspended above it.

Because more than just metal bound the entity inside.

The Hallowed.

I instinctively brushed away the whisper that crossed my mind—and then was suddenly uncertain as to whether it had simply been my own voice, my own thought.

"Emma!" Aiden shouted from somewhere far, far away. "Emma!"

I turned my head, tearing my eyes away from the urn with far more effort than was reasonable. I saw the dark-haired sorcerer as he drew a fistful of power, then punched it against the magic containing him, keeping him away from me.

He screamed, fighting his mother's spell as it attempted to latch onto him even more viciously.

The Hallowed.

I was moving before the words finished echoing through my mind.

Not just words—a title.

A benediction. A belief.

I charged past Kader. He pulled back on his spell an instant before I would have hit it. He spun to the side, ducking. I lunged for Cerise, even as she turned the torrent of power that she'd been holding against Kader on me.

The torrent just…died.

Or rather, it opened up.

For me.

My hands slid through the edge of the main circle, crossing through the power that pulsed in the individual circle in which the elder witch stood. I latched onto Cerise's wrists. I was already pulling power from her before her eyes widened in shock. I had moved faster than she could react.

That was fast.

Even for me.

My momentum slammed the witch back against the edge of her circle, which held her firmly enough that she didn't fall.

Witch magic hammered against me as Cerise rallied to fight back. I drained her, pulling energy that felt oddly unfocused and feeble—especially for someone who had just been holding Kader Azar at bay, one-on-one.

Cerise slumped against me, her power diminishing under my hands rapidly. Too quickly. As if she were somehow already drained. Another trick perhaps? I kept pulling and pulling, pivoting with the witch in my arms as I turned to check on Kader.

The elder sorcerer was weaving his tattered mobile pentagram back together with the idol at its center.

Cerise mewed in pain against my chest. I turned my focus to the witch's power, not wanting to take too much, too fast. I had promised that I wouldn't kill her.

I could feel the magical bindings the witch held to the main circle. I slowly lowered Cerise to the ground as I gathered those ties for myself. There were more than I'd expected.

That was odd.

I tugged on the shortest tie, and suddenly I could feel Ocean on the other side of it. Acting on instinct, I let the tie go instead of claiming it. It snapped back to Ocean, and the younger witch simply vanished from my mind, my senses.

I glanced to my right. Ocean was still slumped in her circle, deathly pale. As I watched, her chest rose, then fell.

Cerise's power sputtered under my palm. I turned my attention back to the other ties I'd collected from her. Would letting all of them go at once inadvertently release the entity at the same time?

Damn it.

I hated screwing around with magic I had no actual ability to cast.

I tugged the thickest tie, finding Sky on the other end. I released the binding.

I found Isa, releasing him.

I found Aiden—

Cerise started convulsing under my hand. There was a chance I was now killing her.

I met Aiden's gaze. Everyone else was still down, excepting Kader. Even Khalid. But my sorcerer was watching me.

Looking at me as if he loved me.

Even as his mother died by my hand.

I released the tie binding Aiden to the main spell. Then Grosvenor and Khalid.

I still held three ties, and I could feel at least one more bound to Cerise that I hadn't claimed.

The first tie bound Cerise to the individual circle in which we both stood.

The second stretched away from me without end. At a guess, it was bound to the individual circle that was supposed to be holding me.

The third tie led to the main circle.

The binding I hadn't claimed yet was attached to the idol.

And I had no idea which of the four ties to release first.

If I released the connection to Cerise, I might collapse the entire spell. Thereby releasing the entity.

If I disengaged my own connection, I might not be able to hold on to the rest of the ties, which would then revert to Cerise. Or, worse, they might dissolve to release the entity, which would grab Kader in turn.

If I released the binding to the main circle, it was likely to dissolve all the others at the same time.

A conundrum.

Maybe even the first conundrum ever that I couldn't just hack my way through, knowing I'd make it to the other side.

The wrong move, the wrong choice, and Aiden might lose his entire immediate family.

Release the wrong tie and I might lose Aiden.

So…I hesitated.

Cerise stilled, but I kept my hold on her wrist.

"Hurry up, boy," Kader snapped, shooting a glance at his youngest son.

Aiden snarled something—some kind of arcane command that tore through the remnants of the spell binding him in place. Power quaked through the main circle, shuddering through the ties I still held.

Cerise gasped, her eyes snapping open.

Aiden stepped into the main circle, passing through the boundary as easily as I had. It was tuned to his magic, after all. It had to be in order to leech power from him.

Cerise grabbed at my arm—I was already holding her wrist—pulling me to her even as she rose up. She bit down, hard enough to actually pierce my skin.

I shook her off without effort, tossing her head back and forth a few times before she lost consciousness again.

Blood rose in tiny spots on my forearm.

"Emma?" Aiden asked.

I glanced up at him. He had joined his father, working to fortify what I assumed was a containment spell for the idol. Whatever they were doing had succeeded in thinning the connection that hovered just under my palm. The final tie, which I hadn't taken from Cerise yet.

"I'm fine," I said. "I'm holding the ties to the main circle, and—"

Something warm slid over my hand, twining up my wrist and licking the spots of blood on my arm.

"Emma?" Aiden asked again.

"Keep focused!" Kader snapped.

The fourth tie. The tie that bound the idol to Cerise. Somehow, without my actually claiming it, that tie burrowed into my skin, pulsing through the bite marks even though they were barely scratches.

I took the tie for myself, dropping the three others at the same time. The power of the main circle flickered, then died. The individual circles sputtered, then faded away.

Ocean and Sky collapsed fully onto the grass.

Isa moaned.

Aiden and Kader both barked words of power, fighting back against the entity.

Because they didn't know.

It already had hold of me.

I rose, calling up my magic as if I could actually manipulate it, wield it. I visualized a barrier between myself and the binding cinched around my forearm.

Except …

It was already inside me. It had gained access by piercing my skin, sipping at the power in my blood.

It was in my bloodstream, flooding through me.

The Hallowed.

Magic exploded around me as I unleashed one last wild attempt to hold the threat at bay. The wave thundered through the orchard and across the grass.

Someone cried out. Sky, I thought.

Aiden pivoted toward me. Kader's eyes grew wide as he followed his son's gaze.

Warmth curled through my mind. "Yes," I whispered. "The Hallowed."

The Hallowed.

The Hallowed.

And it was …

We were …

Yes.

We.

We were …

So …

Powerful …

TEN

WE STRETCHED OUR ... ARMS ...

Yes. We had arms.

And legs.

A strong body.

The Hallowed.

We stepped toward those who would keep us in check. Sorcerers.

They stared.

Their fear was...delicious. We could still taste their power. It had sustained us through the transition. It would continue to feed us.

No. That was...wrong. I didn't feed off—

The elder sorcerer laid hands on us, grabbing our forearm.

No one touched us without permission.

We flung him off. He tumbled away through the green carpet, coming to a stop at another sorcerer's feet.

Grass. Not carpet. Isa. Isa's feet.

We turned to the barrier impeding our forward progression.

"Emma?" the sorcerer standing to our left whispered, reaching out to us.

We raised our hand to shove him away—

No! I yanked my hand back, stumbling slightly.

"Emma?" Aiden asked again, though he didn't try to touch me.

"I'm…I'm …" The Hallowed slithered through my mind in a slow, soothing caress. "We…we are so…powerful."

Ignoring the sorcerer, we stepped toward the barrier sealing the idol within.

Pentagram.

The sorcerer didn't think like a witch, so his spell wasn't anchored deep enough to prevent…leakage.

We slammed our hands forward, clawing and tearing at the power that dared stand against us. Our skin seared. Pain streaked through our senses, but we shoved it away.

We.

Were.

Just.

That.

Powerful.

Shouting erupted behind us. Multiple voices. Other magic welled. We could smell it, taste it.

It was divine.

As we were divine.

The barrier crumbled at our assault. We stepped within, reaching for the idol. Our hands…our fingers…our beautiful limbs were…reddened and stiff.

Bleeding.

Badly hurt.

We picked up the idol.

Power pummeled against us. Exploding against our strong body, causing us to stumble. Different tenors of energy. Multiple assaults from multiple directions.

Trying to stop you.

Us.

Trying to stop…us.

But we would be unstoppable.

We raised the idol over us, over our…head. Then we turned toward the sorcerers and witches who dared keep us from our truth, from ourselves.

They had collected behind us in a half circle as we'd retrieved the idol. The elder in the center, black lightning erupting from his hands. Two others …

Aiden and Isa.

… stood on either side. One of the baby witches on the ground behind them. Awake, her hand stretched before her, but not yet on her feet.

Ocean.

Ocean was alive.

Soon, all would be kneeling.

More energy bloomed behind us. We didn't have to turn to look, because our body, our mind, could sense magic—sorcerer and witch.

Khalid and Sky. What about Grosvenor? And…Cerise?

The elder sorcerer unleashed his spell. It streaked across the carpet—*grass*—toward us. But we pulled power to us at the same time. All the essence still remaining in the idol, all the power still buried in the earth around us from the witch's spell.

We dropped our hand, palm out. The spell hit us.

We absorbed it.

Absorbed it?

Claimed it.

Lightning ran through our veins, chasing pain throughout our system. The power was ours.

All the power was ours.

Because we were the Hallowed.

We tossed the useless idol to the side.

We flung out our arms.

And we smiled.

We smiled and smiled, and unleashed our power. We latched onto every single magical being in the clearing with us, and we pulled their magic from them.

Without touching them?

They screamed, falling to their knees.

Pain. Pain. Pain.

We felt their pain. Their terror. Their fear. Some of them fought. Some were already too weak to fight.

And we felt it all.

It was …

… terrible.

The empathy? I laughed. You can't have me without the empathy. The Hallowed snarled in my mind, raking mental claws through my thoughts, through my defiant laughter.

The empathy.

We would adjust.

We pulled back our energy, gathered our power.

We …

Were …

So …

Powerful.

Unstoppable.

We smiled at the people panting and moaning in the clearing. The three sorcerers slowly gained their feet.

Kader. Isa. And Aiden.

We smiled.

We could be…benevolent. We could care for our people. Because we were the Hallowed. We were worshipped. Exalted.

We unhinged our mouth, pushing breath through our throat, remembering what it was to talk.

"We are the Hallowed. You will bow before our might. Our strength. Our beauty. You will love us."

No. No. No.

We took the power embedded in our bones, in our every cell, and we reached out with it…gently. We harnessed the empathy. We used it.

We caressed and cajoled.

We promised comfort and warmth.

We radiated our power. It flooded the clearing, then the orchard, in undulating waves that licked against the property boundary before receding.

We were breathtaking. Overwhelming. We were all. "We are the Hallowed."

The sorcerers and witches bowed, though the coven witch remained inert. A husk of her former self. Before we were whole, when we were still trapped, we had beguiled the Myers witch into doing our bidding. Whispering tantalizing bits of our power through pathways already rendered susceptible by the sorcerer many decades before.

Him, we knew the moment she fed the first taste of his power to us. Him, we craved.

And through him, we thought to once again walk the earth.

But then we saw our other half. Felt her, tasted her. So we watched. Waiting. Testing. Then hatching a plan in the witch's mind. More difficult prey needed more tantalizing. More difficult prey needed more power to entice. So we planned. We used the witch as bait. Finally, our second half took the witch's magic, and …

We …

Were …

So …

Powerful.

Bait? The entire spell? All the…family drama?

Bait. But look how perfect we were together.

We swept our arms forward, encompassing our worshippers. From them, we drew sustenance. With all our power combined, we would claim this part of the world. We would feed and feed ourselves. And when finally satiated, we would feed the others. This body made that possible. This strength. This power.

We had been so hungry, compressed into such a tiny fraction of ourselves. But once well fed, we would rise up.

The nine would regret restricting us. The nine would regret making us small, breaking us. The nine would tremble at what we would become. With this body. This strength. This power.

The nine? The nine…who?

Let them come. Soon…soon…we would drain the nine, one by one. But first, look at how our worshipers loved us.

We smiled.

The witches and the sorcerers had gathered before us. Their stilted steps had smoothed out as we laced power around them, embracing them. The youngest kneeled first, then most of the others. Peaceful, loving gazes fixed to us.

They adored us. Idolized us.

They would give us everything we asked for, everything we needed, even if it cost them their own lives. They knew, held suspended within our power, that we were benevolent. Loving. They understood that our power must be unleashed to bring that same love to everyone, everywhere.

The elder sorcerer resisted our call the longest. We reached out to him specifically, sending a murmured promise to him along a tendril of power, caressing his cheek, connecting us.

He settled onto his knees, face up, and turned to us. Ours.

All of them.

Ours.

We reached for their power again, for their magic, and they gave it to us willingly. We pulled and pulled, harvesting it for ourselves, feeding our body, fortifying our strength.

We knew… we knew we had only so much time before the nine arrived. We needed all the magic before then. We needed to solidify our hold on these vessels and ourselves.

The more magic we held, the more we were bound together. Never to be pulled asunder again.

Except …

One of the dark-haired sorcerers straightened

…

His feet were bare in the grass. He strode toward us, head bowed reverently. He'd been hurt earlier. Half-healed slashes marred his face, neck, and arms.

His magic had been delicious. But the Myers witch had refused to let us drink as deeply as we had wanted.

You. Not me. I would never—

The sorcerer walked through our glorious net unimpeded. He brushed away our beguiling limbs of power as he bent to pick up the cracked idol.

What need did he have of the idol?

To contain us?

Hurt us?

We lashed out with—

No! I curled my fingers into fists. Unable to pull my arms back, I could at least stop myself—

Us.

We.

We were the Hallowed.

The sorcerer looked at us then, meeting our gaze when he should have been on his knees like the others. His eyes blazed with a fierceness that was breathtaking. He was…we could feel him, his emotions…so clearly. As if they were our own.

Aiden.

Aiden.

Aiden was terrified and…sad. Aiden was resisting…resistant, immune to…me…us.

Aiden was immune to the Hallowed.

A heady pride swept through me. All this time he'd thought…he'd been concerned about being addicted to my power. He had worked on the refraction rune for months, yet here he was. No runes, standing before me, standing in the maelstrom of my power personified, and—

We realized he was beautiful. Almost as beautiful as we were. We realized that we loved him.

Differently from how we felt about the others, who were devoted to us but unworthy.

He was ours.

Our match.

"Emma," Aiden whispered, still walking through the flood of our power. "Emma. Love."

We allowed him to approach. We invited him closer and closer, gently allowing our hands to settle on his shoulders, caressing him with our power, our majesty.

The unplundered depths of his power beckoned to us, teasing from within his eyes. We blinked and leaned a little closer.

He pressed the idol against our chest.

It was cold.

Nasty.

We raised our hand to shove it away. To push him. To make him—

No!

No.

Not Aiden.

Never Aiden.

We paused.

We…struggled…drawing in some of our power to fortify our connection, to cement ourselves within. To quell ourselves.

To placate ourselves.

Then we…capitulated.

We agreed to not hurt the sorcerer—

Aiden.

We looked into the sorcerer's eyes again. We would not hurt Aiden. His magic was divine, delectable. We were more—much, much more—than he, but we wouldn't hurt him—

Aiden.

We wouldn't hurt him to get to his power. It was ours already.

He already belongs to us, I whispered. So we don't need to make him kneel or push him away.

We stepped closer instead. The cracked metal of the idol dug into our skin as we wrapped our hand around his head, slipping our fingers through his thick, silky hair. A sensation both familiar and utterly new at once.

We laughed.

We liked feeling.

We liked feeling with this body especially.

Aiden.

His lips brushed ours. Magic undulated between us. We breathed him in, sipping the power that he had offered us freely.

He bit our lower lip.

Playfully?

We drew away, watching him.

Biting could mean many things. We might have misjudged his intentions …

He smiled, wickedly. So deliciously wicked.

We laughed, touching his face. Feeling the tiny spikes on his cheeks and jaw, rough against our skin.

Stubble. Aiden hadn't shaved that morning, hadn't put on his suit. And that meant something… indicated something. But I… I …

The sorcerer ran his fingers down our other arm, capturing our hand and then raising it to his lips. He kissed our palm, sending delightful shivers across our skin. We liked that feeling. We wanted more. So we watched, waiting to see what else he would do, what other gifts he would give us.

He pressed our hand on the side of the urn, keeping his hand over ours. His fingers wove between our fingers, so we were both touching the metal.

We frowned.

We didn't understand the game.

We didn't like to play. We didn't like being played with, especially when we didn't know the rules.

Holding the urn pressed between our chests, the sorcerer tugged our fingers from his hair, kissed our palm, then placed our hand on the other side of the urn.

We… growled. But the sound was odd to our ears. Not the right response in our new body. We needed to speak more words. But we couldn't find the—

The sorcerer placed his other hand over ours, pressing our flesh into the rounded sides of the idol. All of our fingers touching the cold metal now, the urn still digging against our upper ribcage.

"Emma," he said again.

Our name.

My name.

Ours.

No. You are the Hallowed. I'm Emma.

"We are the Hallowed!" we cried. We clamped onto the power inside us. We tried to burrow in deeper. "We are powerful. Beautiful. The world will tremble at our step. They will bend. Kneel."

Power lashed out from us as we fought ourselves again. That wild energy buffeted Aiden, flooding the clearing, then the property in another wide wave. Splashing against the boundary line, then rolling back to us.

We gnashed our teeth. We howled again. Lashing out, again and again, but never gaining hold.

The kneeling witches and sorcerers started chanting again. Over and over.

"The Hallowed. The Hallowed."

I could understand the language now.

Calling us. Worshiping us. But their emotions flooded back to us, that fear and pain writhing over us.

We did not like that.

We didn't like to feel pain, discomfort.

We didn't like being made to feel…scared.

We withdrew into our body, into our strength. We tried to burrow deeper. But there was a wall there, an impassible wall of smooth, impenetrable stone.

Why fight us at all? Together, we were magnificent. Why not open the barrier? Allow all of us passage? A home, a nesting place.

We snarled at the sorcerer still standing before us, still holding our hands to the urn though we didn't want to touch it at all. "Why do you not bow?" we asked. "Why do you not love us? Worship us?"

Aiden laughed, low and dark. The fresh onslaught of his emotions overrode the lingering residual of the others, transmitted to our skin and somehow into our minds.

We did not like that connection. We did not understand it. How it was even possible.

No. You don't understand it.

Aiden pressed his hands over ours with such force that our bones ached, and his worry and concern gave way to adoration and pure happiness. "I already worship you, Emma. Every time I catch sight of you unexpectedly, my heart…hitches. Every time you smile at me, or laugh, I feel like I could be lost with you forever and never notice. Every time I'm inside you, I only want to be deeper, embedded into your soul."

"Aiden …" I whispered.

"Don't leave me, love." He kissed me gently. "Put the Hallowed back in the urn."

No! We will not go back.

"All the power?" I asked Aiden.

"Yes," he said. "You don't need it. You don't really want it, do you?"

But we…we together… "We could rule the world."

He nodded. "Yes, we could. But we don't want to. We want our home, our family."

We.

We.

Aiden.

Opal.

Christopher.

Paisley.

And me.

That was my 'we.'

"Yes," I said.

I reached for all the foreign energy still seeping into me from the idol, not all of it anchored yet. I traced that magic—the Hallowed—until I found it all, spread through my system, weaving through my veins, drilling into my bones.

I wasn't so easily beguiled.

I wasn't so easily broken.

I grabbed hold of that energy, as I would have if I were draining another Adept.

And I pulled.

The Hallowed fought back.

A fierce tide of anger—of betrayal—surged through me. Claws slashed at me, rending my very soul when they couldn't hook into flesh and bone.

But my soul was already in tatters.

And my heart …

I bit down on the pain, refusing to give it voice. I held Aiden's gaze, even as my own eyes burned.

My heart was already impenetrable.

"Emma?"

"I'm…holding…it …" I gasped. "I can hold."

Aiden nodded, then he began chanting, "The Hallowed. The Hallowed."

I trembled as the entity trying to take root in me writhed and howled.

He calls us, it whispered. He wants us. We. We together …

"Aiden," I cried. "That's not…don't feed it."

"Listen, Emma," Aiden murmured. "Listen to the magic."

I shook my head, dismayed. I wasn't going to be able to hold the Hallowed much longer. I didn't know how to put it back in the urn. "I can't fucking hear magic, sorcerer!" I snapped.

He laughed, deep and earnest. But he kept chanting.

"The Hallowed. The Hallowed."

The entity…shifted, peering through my eyes for a moment, watching Aiden. Looking to strike. Through me.

He calls me, it whispered.

Then Kader was beside us. And Isa. And Sky. Cerise, Ocean, Khalid, and Grosvenor were all still down, their magic muted, drained. Kader, Isa, and Sky pressed their hands over Aiden's and mine. They took up Aiden's chant.

Their voices were rough, gazes sharp, words deliberate.

It was a spell.

A casting of pure intent.

All of them were focused on one thing—retrieving the Hallowed.

Their magic was in my reach, dancing over the back of my hands and arms.

They were feeding me a spell, and cloaking it in the same words that had fed the Hallowed, released the Hallowed, and been demanded by the Hallowed.

I grabbed the magic dancing on my skin. From Aiden. From Kader. From Isa, and Sky. I tangled their power, their intent, around the entity.

It fought.

It clawed.

It screamed.

I could feel how it had woven itself through me, mimicking the tendons and fasciae that held muscle to bone. I shuddered, tears of pain streaking my cheeks unchecked. But I threaded the spell through the entity. I wrapped it up tightly.

And then I shoved it back in the urn.

Power exploded around us.

Sky screamed.

Isa stumbled back, losing hold of the urn.

A torrent of power churned around Aiden, Kader, Sky, and me, our hands all pressed to the idol.

And I could move. My limbs were my own again, under my control. Every cell in my body ached. But I could move.

"In the pentagram!" Aiden shouted. "All together!"

Isa reached back into the energy lashing at our hands and arms. Biting, clawing, trying to grab hold. Of any of us.

We shuffled back a couple of steps, clearing the edges of the pentagram Kader had initially seared into the grass. That felt like...eons ago.

My breath hitched. My heart started pounding.

A belated reaction, I realized, striving to be rational.

I shook off the thought, the residual echo of being trapped in my own body. I bent my knees, slowly bringing them to the ground, and the others did the same.

"We have to seal the urn," Aiden said, his voice pained, heavy with magic.

"Just get it sealed in the pentagram first," Kader said.

"That isn't enough," I said. "It moved through the earth to get me, through the bonds of Cerise's spell."

We set the urn on the grass, our hands still pressed to metal that was showing no signs of warming under our touch.

"One step at a time, amplifier," Kader growled. "We have to get it away from you. Then we'll worry about sealing the breach."

"Or rehousing it," Isa said grimly. "I imagine if the Myers coven could have vanquished it, they would have."

"Yes," his father said agreeably. "But we are not Myers witches."

"Hey," Sky snapped. "Right here with you all, buddy."

Kader chuckled.

Aiden sighed. "Emma removes herself first."

"What? No," I said. "I'm the primary contact."

"Exactly, love," Aiden said. "You pull your hands, then Isa, Sky, and Kader."

"That leaves you last," I growled, narrowing my eyes at him. "No."

"Aiden initiated the recall spell," Kader said. "Brilliantly done." He gave his youngest son a proud look.

Aiden grimaced, meeting my eye, not his father's. But I knew that somewhere, buried deep inside him, he felt lavished by the praise. So I smiled at him.

He flashed his teeth at me. "It isn't going to grab for me, because it's going to go straight for you. And then Cerise."

"Agreed," Isa said. "It's already carved those pathways. And even if Emma is inhospitable, she holds too much power for it not to try again."

I wasn't certain if I should be insulted or flattered. I settled on ignoring the know-it-all sorcerer.

"We move as quickly as we can—Emma, Isa, Sky, Kader," Aiden repeated. "Then me. We clear the edges of the pentagram. Kader seals it within."

His father nodded. "I can deepen the pentagram at the same time. Layer it into the ground."

Aiden glanced at everyone else. "And then we'll add consecutive layers to the containment spell."

Sky nodded, her face drawn.

All of their magic was drained. Not only from casting the recall spell, as Kader had called it, but also by me. More specifically, the Hallowed through me.

The entity wearing me like a skin suit.

I shuddered.

"Emma?" Aiden asked quietly. "Are you with us?"

"Yes. I'm here. I can't...I don't know any containment spells, but I can boost all of you, replace what's been taken from you."

"Lovely," Kader said brightly. "Shall we? The skin feels as though it's being chewed from my hands."

Isa and Sky groaned simultaneously in agreement, then they looked at each other and burst out laughing.

I glanced at Aiden, confused.

He just grinned at me.

I really didn't understand people at all.

I tugged my hands free, flipping backward out of the pentagram before my fingertips had even left the urn.

Isa flung himself back. Then Sky.

Kader straightened, taking a much more dignified step back.

Then it was only Aiden holding the idol. The churning energy that was the Hallowed swirled around his hands. He looked up, meeting my gaze.

I couldn't read his expression. And for a moment, my heart stopped. Thinking…thinking he'd lied to me. To get me to release my hold.

To save me.

Over himself.

But then, still crouched, he slowly peeled his hands back from the urn, slipping one foot behind him over the edge of the pentagram. Then he pulled his hands away and stepped back with the second foot.

Kader barked a word of power. The edges of the pentagram snapped into place. The elder sorcerer swayed on his feet as Isa settled a hand under his father's elbow. Kader didn't brush him away.

"Running water," Sky said to Aiden, her tone stressed. "I'll need a trench."

Aiden jabbed his finger toward the edge of the orchard nearest the house. "There's a watering system."

Sky took off running, glancing back with concern at her sister, then at Grosvenor. The curse breaker was still sprawled on the grass, gazing skyward. Ocean was propped up on one hand next to Cerise, who was curled up in the grass. The elder witch's chest slowly rose, then fell. Ocean's expression was conflicted.

"Grover," Aiden said, pacing the exterior of the pentagram. His expression was strained. "We're going to need you."

The curse breaker groaned, perhaps meaning to be playful. But he sounded drained.

I offered one hand to Kader. The other, to Isa. Kader folded my hand into his warm grip without hesitation. I fed him a gentle flood of power while looking at the other sorcerer with a tight smile.

Isa wasn't so eager for my touch.

"Don't be an idiot," Kader snapped.

"Have you ever considered the bond it must form?" Isa asked his father coolly.

"It wears off. With time and distance," I said. "One amplification doesn't tie you to me forever."

"Why would you care?" Kader said, still taking all the power I was feeding him. "Do you think Emma can somehow influence you? Into doing what? What could she possibly ask of you that you wouldn't already be willing to do?"

Isa glanced at Aiden. His youngest brother was pacing the pentagram, pausing every few steps to utter a word that cut through the grass at his feet, taking out a swath a half-meter in length and fifteen centimeters deep. He was forming the trench Sky needed.

Without looking back at me, Isa stuffed his hands in his pockets and walked over to check on Khalid, still sprawled in the grass, gazing up at the blue sky.

"Fool," Kader muttered. Then he patted the back of my hand and released me.

I thought about what it must have looked like, felt like, for everyone else when the Hallowed was radiating through me. Utilizing my abilities to siphon their power, then screwing with their heads with some sort of projection of my latent empathy. An ability that had always been passive for me, but which had been weaponized by the Hallowed.

Which might mean that I was perfectly capable of doing everything the Hallowed had used me to do.

As I watched Isa bend over Khalid and murmur something to him, I found I couldn't blame him at all for not wanting to be amplified by me. For not wanting to be influenced by me.

A pain rippled through my chest. Logically, I knew it must have been anxiety or guilt.

But illogically, it felt as though another large chunk of my soul had just been shredded even further.

Sky ran into the clearing, dragging the hose with her from the orchard, spraying water everywhere. She splashed her mother and her sister, seemingly without remorse.

Ocean gasped, then glowered.

Grosvenor rolled to his feet, unsteady for a moment. I offered him my hand. He took it with a grim smile, his gaze on Sky as she approached the pentagram.

I fed the curse breaker a touch of my power as gently as possible. His fingers tightened on mine, light-brown eyes widening. I offered him a slight smile, then upped the wattage of the amplification. He inhaled deeply, rolling his neck and shoulders.

Kader grunted in satisfaction, then stepped over to the pentagram. He crouched, placing his fingers into the trench Aiden had dug. Magic flooded through the churned dirt, sealing it.

Sky set the hose in the trench.

It would have to stay running.

Kader straightened. He and Aiden stood shoulder to shoulder, peering through the boundary of the pentagram. Waiting.

"Salt?" Sky asked.

Aiden nodded. "In the barn. I'll help you."

"No." Sky turned to look at her sister. "Ocean. On your feet."

Ocean glanced at her mother. None of the rest of us had bothered to check on Cerise yet. Not even Sky. "But…Mom …"

"Now," Sky demanded. "She's alive. Which is more than she deserves."

Ocean frowned. "You saw what that thing did to Emma! It must have manipulated Mom—"

Sky jabbed her finger at their mother. "She took that…that…idol from the coven archives! Archives she was supposed to be protecting, overseeing! You know she did! She used us. She would have killed us in order to release it, in order to get revenge on Kader!"

Ocean's chin trembled, her large light-blue eyes falling on her mother. Then she nodded, whispering, "Salt. We'll imbue it with a barrier spell."

"We'll imbue it with everything we've got." Sky stepped over to her sister and held her hand out. Ocean grabbed it, then Sky helped her to her feet.

Arms wrapped around each other, they walked away without looking at their mother again. As they stepped by me, I offered them my hands.

"Let us get the salt first," Sky said with a glance at the pentagram. "You might need all your reserves."

I didn't mention that my reserves were fairly vast. I just nodded. Then, as the two younger witches ran for the barn, I finally stepped over to check on Cerise.

The trench had filled with water. Aiden stirred his finger through it, murmuring arcane commands. The water began to run, flowing clockwise.

"The entity is going to breach the pentagram," Grosvenor said.

No one answered him. But even as he started laying out his rune-marked wooden tiles, the energy sealing the pentagram started flickering.

I stepped around Cerise, putting her between myself and the pentagram, so I could keep an eye on what was happening with the Hallowed.

On the other side of the clearing, Khalid had gained his feet and was pacing with Isa. Way in the background, Sky and Ocean entered the barn.

I crouched over Cerise—and found myself wishing that Christopher was home. Then I was wishing that the other four had been at both our sides. The Hallowed would never have gotten hold of me if the Five had stood against it.

But that was because we never would have gotten into the circle in the first place.

Cerise Myers would never have been able to get the Hallowed onto the property. Bee would have plucked her intentions right out of her head—possibly literally if she were feeling vindictive. Or protective.

I pushed thoughts of Bee and the others aside, placing my fingertips at the base of Cerise's neck.

Aiden had helped me with the Hallowed. We hadn't needed the other four.

I had completely drained Cerise Myers. I'd known it already, but I touched her to make certain. It had never been confirmed whether or not I could actually permanently take another Adept's power.

I glanced over to the pentagram, looking at Kader. The elder sorcerer might know. Assuming the Collective had ever bothered to keep the victims I hadn't killed while draining them alive. I doubted whether the lives of those victims, or whether or not their magic would ever return, had been important to the project. His life's work, the elder sorcerer had called it.

So Cerise's magic might come back.

Or I might have just ruined the rest of her life for her.

No.

She'd definitely done that herself.

Cerise's eyelashes fluttered, as if she was dreaming.

Khalid had crossed the clearing, crouching on the other side of Cerise and checking her pulse. His gaze was on me.

The boundary of the pentagram fell. Aiden, Kader, and Isa, standing at roughly equidistant points from each other, clapped their hands together and barked the same sharp command.

Fire ignited along the edges of the pentagram.

Khalid glanced over his shoulder, then back at Cerise. His expression was guarded.

Grosvenor continued setting out his wooden tiles on the far side of the moat. He was building some sort of spell adjacent to each point of the pentagram. He moved on to the fourth point as the fire raged.

It was clear that the sorcerers didn't think the fire barrier was going to hold the Hallowed. Even though I'd amplified Kader, and Aiden wasn't as badly drained as the others.

"You stripped every last iota of magic from her," Khalid said. His head was bowed, not looking at me.

"Yes."

"And a few of the others, nearly so." He flicked his gaze to my face, then looked away toward the trees.

"Yes."

He nodded, then straightened up, brushing off his pants. His attention was on the magical fortifications being erected around the pentagram. Sky and Ocean were on their way back from the barn, each struggling to carry a large bag of the road salt Aiden always kept on hand.

"Would you like me to return what I took?" I asked.

Khalid glanced at me. "Can you…do so specifically?"

I couldn't. All the magic I currently held was a combination of everything I'd drawn from them all. But I would end up just absorbing it myself if I didn't transfer it. "Does it matter?"

He shrugged. "Maybe not." He looked back at the pentagram. "I'm not needed at this stage…and I don't mind the dampening. It hurt a hell of a lot more, but you're better than anything I've smoked in the last few years." He laughed joylessly, then nodded toward the others.

Ocean and Sky had joined the group around the pentagram. The fire was half the height it had been a moment before.

"It …" Ocean stammered. "It's eating the fire."

"It would appear so," Grosvenor said cheerfully. He reached to take the bag of salt from Sky, but the witch gave him a withering look.

He backed away, hands raised as the witches stepped back, tearing open the bags.

"I'm not needed at this stage," Khalid repeated quietly. "But I'll take you up on the offer if the entity gets by everyone else."

"You think you can fight it?"

Khalid was quiet for a moment. Then he said, "I'll try." He wandered off to stand near his father.

Sky and Ocean had linked arms in an impromptu circle with the bags of salt between them. A wash of power rose at their murmured bidding, pulled from the earth, twining around the bags of salt. Apparently, the witches didn't need my amplification if they could access the power that lay in my property.

My property. Property that Khalid had characterized as having been walked on by divine beings. I presumed that was my power and Christopher's he referred to, plus Samantha more recently. Perhaps Aiden, Paisley, and Opal as well. But why my magic would feed the land when I couldn't amplify spells or other objects, I had no idea.

The fire edging the pentagram snuffed out. I could see the idol clearly now. It was still set in the middle of the pentagram seared into the grass, surrounded by the moat of running water, and with Grosvenor's wooden tiles beyond. The metal urn was still cracked. And the energy I'd poured back into it had poured back out—that glittering darkness. It surged forward in a slithering motion, a long tail still anchoring it to the urn. It started moving around the inner circumference of the moat.

Aiden hissed. "We're going to need to move it."

"Too dangerous," Isa said.

"I have a permanent pentagram for this exact reason," Aiden argued.

Grosvenor laughed. "For this exact reason? Emma seriously keeps you on your toes, cousin."

Isa ignored the curse breaker. "If we can move it, we can contain it."

Sky and Ocean dropped their hands, each grabbing a bag of salt. The sorcerers stepped back as the witches stood across from each other, each just outside a set of the curse breaker's tiles.

I stepped up beside Aiden. He threaded his fingers through mine without looking away from the witches.

Magic flowed around Sky's and Ocean's hands as they each tipped their bags of salt, sprinkling a thick line of it in the grass. Murmuring in conjunction with each other, they moved in opposite directions, quickly crossing paths on the far side of the pentagram.

"Witches don't usually speak quite so…quietly," I whispered to Aiden. "When casting in front of an audience."

"Really?" Aiden smiled. "In my experience, witches don't appreciate an audience of sorcerers when casting."

"Ah. Just in case those sorcerers are taking notes?"

"Sorcerers are always taking notes."

I laughed quietly. "Very true."

Sky and Ocean lapped each other a second time, then paused. The bags of salt looked half empty. Switching directions, they laid a wavy pattern over the thick straight line of salt they'd already sketched, lapping each other again and returning to their starting points with empty bags.

Light-blue energy ran around the salted circle. It started humming.

Sky tied her empty salt bag in a knot, slapping it against her thigh. "I'd like to see the asshole cross that!"

"I'd rather not," Isa replied coolly. "Since that's pretty much all that we have to throw at it."

Ocean squinted at the moat, then crouched, her toes almost brushing the humming salt line. The glittering amorphous shape that was the Hallowed was pressed against the water's edge, right across from the younger witch.

"Stay back," Sky hissed.

Licks of what looked like fire shot through the entity's collected energy. It had absorbed the sorcerers' spell.

My jaw dropped as the implications of that hit me.

Ocean ignored her older sister, pointing a shaking hand toward the water barrier. "Is it…is it building a…bridge?"

Isa and Khalid swiftly crouched on either side of the witch. Isa grimaced, then swore. Khalid clenched his fists, baring his teeth for a moment. Though what exact emotion he was fighting, I didn't know. Then he glanced at Isa.

His elder brother met his gaze. Some sort of silent communication passed between them, and finally, Isa nodded.

Khalid looked over at Aiden, his gaze momentarily dropping to our still-entwined hands. "I'm going to need access to your armory."

"The safe's open," Aiden said. "I expect to see both of Ocean's poisons in it when I lock it back up."

The middle Azar brother rose without another word, striding off toward the house.

"You think he'd try to steal the poison?" I asked. "Now?"

"No," Aiden said. "I think he might try to use it, if necessary. And I don't want a drop of it on your...our land."

The energy that was the Hallowed thinned to cross over the water at one specific point, rapidly amassing on the other side of the trench.

Isa hissed.

Grosvenor clenched his hands to fists, leaning forward slightly as the Hallowed came up against the first of his contributions to the containment spells—a cluster of wooden tiles. The curse breaker's spell held it at bay.

"If the Hallowed breeches the salt line ..." I began.

"No," Aiden said. Bluntly, harshly. He dropped my hand and tugged his notebook out of his back pocket, flipping it open to a blank page.

"You don't even know what I was going to suggest," I said quietly.

He shook his head. "I'm not having this conversation."

"Aiden ..." I was getting annoyed.

"No." He pulled a pen out of his pocket and started drawing a rune in his notebook. No doubt something that would explode, given his tone.

"You can see that it appears to be absorbing the magic." I crossed my arms—then dropped them when I realized what I was doing. "Like I can."

Aiden shook his head, still not looking at me.

Kader stepped closer. The elder sorcerer's gaze was riveted to the Hallowed as it amassed itself up against one of the curse breaker's piles of wooden tiles. "It's learning."

"You aren't part of this conversation," Aiden snapped.

"Well, apparently neither is Emma." Kader smirked at his son. Though only briefly.

One of the wooden tiles started to shift out of alignment. I actually stepped forward in disbelief, thinking I was seeing things. The Hallowed had turned the water against Grosvenor's spell. It had somehow formed the liquid into a long finger and was slowly inching it forward, pushing the tile.

"It used the fire against the water," I whispered. I had seen the flames licking through its iridescent body.

"Yes." Aiden's hands had dropped to his sides. He shook his head. "It broke the pentagram with power taken from you. From all of us, perhaps." He spoke as if not realizing he was talking out loud.

"Smothering the fire with the remnants of the barrier spell," Kader said. "Then harnessing the fire to bridge the water ..."

Something snapped as the Hallowed flipped the tile completely out of alignment. It tumbled across the grass and came to rest against the salt line.

"Grosvenor's magic is complicated," I said, already anticipating the Hallowed's next move. "It will take it time to learn a pattern to break the witches' final containment spell." I turned to Aiden. "You can't fight it. Not even if I amplified all of you."

"Emma …" he growled.

"It's going to grab one of us," I said, surprised to hear my voice sharpening with fear. I shoved the useless emotion away. "We secure Ocean, Sky, Grover, and Khalid in the house, behind the wards."

"No," Aiden repeated, actual anger laced through his frustration now. "Absolutely not."

"The entity won't be able to get through the wards."

"If you let it have you, it will be able to do whatever the hell it wants," Aiden snarled.

My heart rate ratcheted up. I didn't want to suggest what I was about to suggest, but I really didn't see any other way. I pressed my hand to Aiden's chest. "You can do this," I whispered. "You knock me out—"

"No, Emma—"

"Yes. You get me in the pentagram."

"I can't hold you there!"

"You can for long enough. Just…keep me knocked out. Long enough to get the other four."

Aiden closed the space between us. Anger was etched across his face, his voice a low growl.

"Apparently, you've forgotten that one of you is missing right now!"

"I can do this," I insisted—hearing the lie in my voice even as I said the words. I pushed past it. "I'm already resistant to it. And that'll become immunity. It can only grow."

"I can't," Aiden said. "End of discussion."

Kader cleared his throat. "I disagree."

Aiden turned a vicious look on his father.

Kader held up a placating hand. "It can't be Emma, I agree. Even if the rest of the Five were on site, it would still be utterly foolish to sacrifice her."

Aiden snarled something nasty under his breath. It carried magic that shivered across my collarbone and neck, though likely not intentionally.

"But …" Kader trailed off as all of us turned to watch the Hallowed dismantle the rest of Grosvenor's spells, gathering them all at the edge of the salt line. "We do need to move it. So we need a new vessel. One that we can, as Emma put it, knock out and drop into the pentagram."

"Who would you suggest, Father?" Aiden said sarcastically.

Kader turned and glanced over his shoulder, looking at Cerise prone in the grass. "It's a Myers' coven problem. The idol was in their care. Their guardianship. We let the one responsible deal with it."

ELEVEN

I REMOVED MYSELF ALMOST IMMEDIATELY FROM THE argument that started between Kader, Aiden, Isa, Ocean, and Sky over Kader's pronouncement. None of them had any apparent interest in listening to anyone but themselves, and I was tired of being ignored. Instead, I stood at the edge of the final boundary line, watching as the Hallowed remained stymied by the witches' magically imbued salt.

The entity was now an amorphous blob of energy, shot through with various shades of blue magic. It was shifting Grosvenor's wooden tiles around and around, as if trying to find a sequence to break through the barrier. The curse breaker crouched beside me, gaze riveted to the shifting tiles.

Khalid was slightly behind me and farther to my left. When he'd returned from raiding Aiden's safe in the study, I had amplified him on request. Now, between that amplification and the amount of magic the sorcerer was carrying, he practically hummed with power. His hands hung at his sides, his long, scarred fingers flicking and gesturing. No doubt running through the arsenal of spells he planned to use against the Hallowed if it came to that.

All three of us were actively tuning out the still-ongoing argument. Sky was doing most of the talking for the witches, Ocean tucked behind her sister, arms protectively crossed over her chest.

Cerise was still prone in the grass, still unconscious.

"Could you break the salt circle?" Khalid asked in a low murmur. He was speaking to Grosvenor.

The curse breaker glanced toward the group clumped aggressively together to our far right. Sky and Isa stood practically nose to nose now, the witch's expression fierce. Her light-blue eyes were glowing, the sorcerer's expression filled with disdain.

"Yes," Grosvenor finally said. "But I'd need another tile."

That got my attention. "One you didn't use to fortify the containment spell?"

"Well, I wasn't trying to break anything then, was I?" he muttered peevishly.

I ignored him, returning my attention to the entity as it shifted the rune-marked tiles again. "So it might not break through?"

"It's going to break through," Khalid snarled quietly.

Grosvenor nodded. "Just not the same way I would. But Sky and Ocean put everything they had left into …" His voice trailed off as his shoulders shifted, his gaze riveted on the collection of tiles that the Hallowed had just arranged at the inner edge of the salt circle.

Khalid leaned closer. He blinked and swore, then pulled a short blade out of his suit jacket pocket—courtesy of an expansion spell, presumably. The wide platinum blade was single edged and inlaid with gold runes. The sorcerer stepped away, then began moving the blade through a series of complicated swoops, twists, and jabs. As he did so, the runes on the knife began to glow, and the hum of energy surrounding the sorcerer expanded.

"We've got less than five minutes." Grosvenor directed the statement to the group still arguing toe to toe, raising his voice to be heard.

They all paused, taking a collective breath. Aiden's gaze settled on me, anger etched across the beautiful planes of his face. Fiercely sexy.

I grinned at him, then winked.

He blinked.

I was pretty sure that was the first time I'd ever winked at anyone. My grin widened. Apparently, standing on the precipice of letting an unknown entity possess me for the second time, I was feeling playful.

Aiden narrowed his eyes at me. Then he shook his head, emphatically. 'No.'

I laughed quietly. It was adorable that he thought he could order me around.

The dark-haired sorcerer smiled then, but it was a tense, terribly pained expression. As if looking at me hurt him.

And suddenly I wasn't feeling so playful.

Isa tried to step around Sky. She jumped in front of him, fingers outstretched before her. Protecting her mother from the sorcerer.

I looked away from Aiden, back to the salted circle—into which the entity had managed to dig a long notch. It was breaking through.

"No, you make me move." Sky's voice caught my attention. She was firmly in Isa's face.

"I will," Isa said. "If you leave me no other choice."

"The Hallowed won't take Cerise," I said. Again. I'd tried getting that point across to them at least three times before I'd given up. I loathed repeating myself, and the Azar sorcerers were seriously testing my patience.

But it didn't really matter.

When I had positioned myself by the final barrier, the Hallowed had immediately keyed in on me, building its spell less than a hand's width away. So when it finally broke through the salt line, it would come for me before any of the others. I would fight it—but only as much as I had to in order to stop it from using me to kill everyone else.

And then Aiden wouldn't have any argument left.

I realized no one else was speaking. They were listening to me, finally. I kept my attention on the entity as it further hollowed out the niche it was digging into the salt. "Not only have I drained the witch …."

"Rather thoroughly," Khalid interrupted, stepping up to take his place beside Grosvenor again.

I ignored the disgruntled sorcerer. "But it had already decided Cerise wasn't powerful enough for it to fully manifest through. That's why it focused on Kader." I'd pieced together the Hallowed's desires, from when it was trying to merge with me. And not just desires. A simple knowing. An understanding.

Those thoughts, those intentions, had been in my own head. I could still feel what I'd felt when it—

"How do you know?" Aiden asked quietly, his voice cutting through my own thoughts. "Can you communicate with it, Emma?"

I shook my head. "Not now. But…before, yes. It wanted Kader. It must have gleaned your father's existence through Cerise, along with her sense of the power of the sorcerer Azar." I'd intended that title to be sarcastic as I said it, but I didn't pull it off at all.

Kader actually was that powerful.

"And then it homed in on you," Aiden said. "Emma—"

"It has to be me," Ocean whispered, interrupting her brother. Speaking to the ground rather than any of us.

Sky flinched, then clenched her hands into fists and whirled on her sister.

"You all already know it," Ocean said, firming her voice and her stance, speaking over Sky's unvoiced protest. "I'm the least dangerous among all of you. I'm the…the…easiest to kill, if it becomes necessary."

Ocean's terrible offer to sacrifice herself hung between all of us, none of us wanting to acknowledge the truth of it. Or how ridiculously idiotic it was.

"Yes," Kader said, nodding.

Right. The elder sorcerer wasn't one to conceal anything that advanced his objective. Not that I knew what his current plan was. Or if he had one at all.

"What?!" Aiden roared.

Isa opened his mouth, responding in a torrent of that Arabic language the Azars spoke. Aiden and Kader responded in kind, power churning around the three of them. Such similar tenors of magic, but Aiden's power sang the brightest for me.

I had to get him out of the clearing before the Hallowed broke through the salt line. He would be too much of a temptation. For both of us.

"Amplifier," Khalid said, quietly enough that it was doubtful that anyone but myself and Grosvenor could hear him. "Please step back."

"I'm not going anywhere," I snapped at the sorcerer without looking at him, my gaze still on the witches. Sky had her hands on Ocean's shoulders, presumably trying to hug her, but the younger sister was standing her ground and attempting to argue—in French now.

Aiden would retreat from the Hallowed only if he had someone to protect while doing so. His sisters.

"We need to do this," Grosvenor growled. "Now."

The curse breaker started placing tiles between my feet and the salt line. The extent of the salt holding the Hallowed back was the width of my thumb now, thinning more as I watched.

"You can't leave," Khalid said. "It has obviously keyed on you. And it's obvious that you can take multiple hard hits and not go down, so you'll be bait."

I'd never been bait in my entire life. I wasn't even the trap. I was the killing blow. The final—

I shook off the inappropriate flush of arrogant indignation and took a single step backward in the grass, silently agreeing to their as yet unarticulated plan. Grosvenor instantly started placing rune-marked tiles in the space I'd vacated. "The entity got through the curse breaker's last boundary spell."

"This isn't a boundary," Khalid said quietly. "It's a snare." The width of the curse breaker's tiled spell stretched slightly wider than the doorway the Hallowed was in the process of carving into the salt line. "You draw it to you. Grosvenor holds it."

"And you try to hack it into pieces?" I eyed the blade he held at his side. "If it could be killed, why would the witches tuck it away in the idol?"

Khalid smirked. "Objects of great power get stored for later use and then are lost, amplifier."

"We're not going to kill it," Grosvenor said. "We're going to hold it just long enough to get it into the permanent pentagram. Same plan, just with a slight twist. Less risk."

"Is this Aiden's plan?" I asked. I hadn't noticed the three of them talking, but I had obviously missed something.

Grosvenor began on a third line of tiles, adding only three this time. Then two more. At first glance, his spell work was constructed in a similar fashion to a game of dominos. Except he connected symbols according to what he was building, rather than simply going by visual matches.

The salt line set between his haphazard rectangle of tiles and the Hallowed was the width of a pencil now.

"No. Isa's plan," Khalid said. "With Cerise as the backup."

Isa and Kader were still in intense discussion, though they had lowered their voices. But Aiden was watching us. Watching me.

Then he looked at the circle, checking the Hallowed's progress. His eyes widened. He clamped a hand on Isa's shoulder.

I turned toward Khalid fully, so that Aiden couldn't read my lips. "What have you got on you that will take me down?"

He gazed at me for a moment, then grimaced. "Nothing that won't hurt. Something of my own design, so it won't just bounce off you."

I nodded. Then I pressed the side of my foot against Grosvenor's hip. The curse breaker was still fiddling with his spell. "Move now."

Grosvenor danced his fingers over the tiles in a complicated sequence, activating their magic. He hesitated, glancing between the spell and the Hallowed. The entire bulk of the entity was pressed against the whisper-thin wall of magic still holding it in the salt circle.

Isa whirled around in response to whatever Aiden had said to him, stepping our way. Aiden was right behind him. Kader reached for Ocean. Sky shoved herself between her sister and the elder sorcerer.

We had seconds.

"Get Sky and Ocean to the house," I said, shoving the curse breaker to the side with my foot.

"And if they won't go?" he asked, scrambling to his feet.

"Make them," I snarled, squaring off along the tiled spells simmering at my feet. Khalid stepped tightly to my left. His hand ghosted up my back as whatever spell he thought could bring me down built in his palm. Energy shivered up my spine.

I turned to look at Aiden as Khalid settled his hand on the back of my neck. An electrical charge warmed my skin.

I was ready. I'd do what I needed to do, as always. Except this time, I was protecting someone I truly and utterly loved, not just following orders.

"Khalid!" Aiden snarled.

The Hallowed breached the salt circle, its entire bulk surging for me. Khalid's blade was already swinging, left handed. Grosvenor's snare triggered.

Mind-bending, knee-trembling power exploded behind me, wiping out sight and sound in a blaze of golden light.

Behind me?

I dropped into a crouch as Khalid stumbled under the unexpected assault. I whirled, trying to see whatever was approaching us without losing sight of the Hallowed. Blinking into the golden, pulsating light, my eyes burned with tears from staring into the onslaught of magic. Pure power.

A shadow appeared, walking toward us as if walking through a gilded tunnel. Two legs...body...two arms...shoulders...neck...head ...

Above me, the Hallowed shrieked, tearing free from the curse breaker's snare.

The entity's voice raked through my mind, scrambling my brain. I fell to the ground, convulsing. Unable to stop myself.

The Hallowed would come for me. I had to be...I had to ...

I couldn't let it get Aiden.

Struggling, I gathered my power, preparing to be taken, to be invaded body and soul.

I'd broken free from it once. I could do so again.

The golden light faded.

Blue sky appeared overhead.

The Hallowed didn't strike.

I stopped convulsing. I slowly turned my head.

A petite blond in a teal silk dress was standing in the clearing. Her hands were on her hips, lip curled in displeasure.

Behind her, a whirling circle of energy twisted in midair—the source of the golden-tinted onslaught of power.

A portal.

I had never seen one before, but I wasn't an idiot.

Beside me, Khalid forced himself up and onto his knees. Aiden was a couple of steps away on my right. I managed to prop myself up on one hand.

Only seconds had passed.

The newcomer turned and shouted over her shoulder, "Found it!" Then she strode forward, scanning the orchard. I took her in at a glance, my mind reeling. Clear blue eyes, lightly tanned skin, pinked cheeks and lips. She moved as though she owned every molecule of the earth and the air surrounding her.

I couldn't feel a drop of power coming from her.

She was epically dangerous.

'The nine ...' I remembered the Hallowed whispering the name in my mind. She was one of the nine.

The nine what?

The blond took Aiden in with a grin as he crouched beside me, placing himself between me and the dangerous being strolling toward us. Everyone else simply watched, their reactions seemingly all just slightly delayed versions of my own.

If she was here to kill us all, we were already dead.

But the blond just winked at me as she stepped right past me, over Grosvenor's tiled spell and through the doorway the Hallowed had carved into the salt circle.

The Hallowed.

I scrambled back, my reactions all delayed. I gained my feet even as I dragged Aiden with me.

Inside the spent layers of the barrier spells we'd raised against the Hallowed, the blond reached down and picked up the idol.

Isa stood in front of Kader and Ocean. Sky and Grosvenor were off to one side. Between them and the entrance to the circle, I tried to tuck Aiden behind me. Unsuccessfully, as he tried to push in front of me in turn.

Across from us, on his own, Khalid stepped away, hands raised before him. But his face was…his expression was filled with awe as the newcomer stepped through the opening in the salted circle. She was carrying the cracked idol. And the Hallowed was somehow being held within it. I could feel its energy.

The air around the idol rippled, as if the Hallowed had tried to attack or make a break for it, and the blond had effortlessly quelled the attempt.

If she had, she'd moved so quickly that even I couldn't see it.

The blond took two more steps, pivoting to scan all of us again. Then she smirked at me. "Thanks for the assist," she said. Her accent was American. West coast, I thought.

Before I could respond, she tossed the idol over her shoulder. Her movement was casual, seemingly effortless, yet somehow the idol flew in a long arc all the way to the portal. The golden magic swallowed it.

"You're going to need a bigger box," the blond shouted, chortling.

If that was some sort of joke, I didn't get the reference.

"And you're welcome," she called in a singsong voice.

As if in response, the portal imploded, then disappeared.

The blond blinked, then grimaced. "You are such an asshole, old man," she muttered.

I doubted she knew I could hear her.

She looked at all of us again, brushing her hands together. We stared back.

"I am Haoxin," she said, chin raised, shoulders back. "The guardian of North America. One of the nine. We apologize that we momentarily ..." She tilted her head thoughtfully. "That we lost track of the Hallowed. Nasty bit of work. Goes around calling itself 'the mother of the dawn' every few centuries." She brushed her hands together a second time, as if perhaps remembering the touch of the Hallowed—though she'd made collecting it appear effortless.

Haoxin looked at me.

Expectantly.

I opened my mouth. And for a moment, I thought I might have forgotten how to speak. I was terrified. Yet at the same time, some part of me wanted to kneel before her and kiss the hem of her silk dress.

Across from me, I could see the same conflict reflected in Khalid's expression.

"I am…Emma—"

Cerise sat up with a groan.

Haoxin's gaze locked on her. Faster than I could track, the blond stepped to the witch, crossing the width of the clearing seemingly in that one step.

My stomach bottomed out. If she turned against us, I wasn't sure I could drain her before she snapped my neck. I wasn't sure I'd see her before she snapped my neck.

That she could kill me so easily, I had no doubt.

Ocean cried out. The same shocked gasp came from the others, though Aiden and Kader had already followed my gaze.

"Myers witch," Haoxin snapped, peering down at Cerise.

The elder witch blinked up at her, confused.

"Your coven has been the guardian of this evil for over three centuries! But you …" Haoxin sneered. "You decided you could control it. I've punished idiots for far less."

Haoxin reached for Cerise, who was cowering at her feet.

Then she paused, hand hovering just over the witch's shoulder. She tilted her head thoughtfully. Again.

Haoxin's hand dropped to her side as she straightened, scanning each of us arrayed around the charred and trampled grass.

Cerise was mumbling something, her palms up, pleading. Or perhaps worshiping.

Haoxin's sky-blue eyes settled on me. "I see someone has already punished you accordingly, witch."

I blinked.

The self-proclaimed guardian of North America was suddenly standing before me. Just out of my reach.

I quashed the impulse to reach for my blades lying in the grass a few feet away. And at the same time, I forced myself to again ignore the need to bow before her.

It wasn't magic. Or charisma. I would have been able to feel her in my head if she were a telepath.

A slow smile curled over the guardian's pinked lips. "What a treat you are, amplifier. You're the one who drew my attention in San Francisco the other day."

Her apparent misunderstanding of how much time had passed since I'd caused any sort of incident in San Francisco should have seemed like a weakness. Instead, it only confirmed what I already suspected.

Haoxin was …

Staring at me with one eyebrow raised, she had paused as if expecting me to answer her. But my heart was beating so madly I wasn't certain I could speak over it.

Haoxin frowned thoughtfully, glancing around her again. This time, her gaze swept higher, as if taking in her entire surroundings.

"Where am I, anyway?"

No. She was looking for landmarks.

"Lake Cowichan," I said. My tone was steady, normal. "Vancouver Island, British Columbia." I paused, then added, "Canada."

"Ah! Good," she said. "It felt like the northwest coast. But the season threw me. I'm always pleased to have an excuse to stop by the bakery." She leaned toward me, grinning. "Though Jade hates it when I drop by unannounced."

If I was supposed to know who Jade was, I couldn't remember. This close, I could actually see power twinkling in Haoxin's eyes—like barely contained mischief that could wipe us all from the face of the earth with a single uttered command. A simple flick of her wrist.

I felt numb, yet completely alive at the same time.

"I'll give your best wishes to the Godfreys. And will let them know you have everything under control. Otherwise, you'll have all of them all over you." She flicked her gaze across all of us again, lingering on Kader. She furrowed her brow thoughtfully. "You do have it under control, yes? Emma?"

I nodded. "Yes, thank you…guardian."

Haoxin took a step around me, then leaned forward on her toes, aiming a wicked grin at the elder sorcerer. "You're in my territory now, sorcerer. I am not so…lenient as some of the others."

"I am happily retired," Kader said smoothly.

Haoxin sniffed. "See that it remains that way."

Then she turned and walked away.

I watched—we all watched—in silence as the golden spiral of the portal yawned open before her. She stepped into its maw, then disappeared.

As one, we all turned and looked at Kader.

He grimaced, settling his hand on Isa's shoulder as if his son might have been the only thing holding him upright. I didn't believe it for a second.

Sky stepped toward Cerise. The elder witch was frowning, gazing down at her limp hands in her lap. Then her head snapped up.

She met my gaze, knowing what I'd done to her.

She deserved worse.

Not that I was her judge. Because apparently, that task fell to a demigod who had claimed all of North America as her territory.

I turned away, reaching for Aiden and pulling him with me toward the house.

TWELVE

FINDING MYSELF WITH NOTHING TO DO WHILE THE sorcerers and the witches sorted themselves out, I pulled Christopher's notebook out of the pantry and flipped through it in search of his granola recipe. I'd found the Tupperware container that usually contained the granola empty—washed and on the drying rack—when Aiden and I had come in. So I'd boiled eggs instead, forcing him to eat two with toast before he and the other sorcerers holed up in the barn. They wanted to be absolutely sure that Kader was no longer connected to the Hallowed. Or to Cerise.

As I was stirring cinnamon into the ingredients I'd carefully measured into a large metal bowl, Paisley, wearing her regular pit bull aspect, wandered in through the open French-paned doors. Ocean was only a few steps behind her. The witch looked tired. Her magic was just a low simmer.

Paisley crossed around the kitchen island, bumping her head into my thigh hard enough that

I had to shift my footing to compensate. Ocean perched on one of the stools, setting her elbows on the island and her chin in her hands.

Sky was still upstairs with Cerise. Both Aiden and she had confirmed that the elder witch was completely drained of magic. Not that any of us were thinking of questioning a so-called guardian, who walked through portals and plucked up ancient magical entities with her bare hands, all seemingly without effort.

I touched Paisley on her broad head. "I'm glad you're back. I'd like you to stay on the property now, please. Christopher is coming home."

The demon dog looked at me, blinking. I grabbed a whole almond and carefully balanced it on her nose, as I'd seen Opal do the last time she was home. Paisley chuckled darkly. Then she flipped her head back, sending the almond shooting upward. She widened her jaw and caught it in her mouth as it descended.

"Impressive," Ocean said, clapping her hands together softly.

Paisley flashed a sharp-toothed smile at the witch. Then she trundled off into the still-empty space where the kitchen table should have been. Without any preamble, the demon dog sprawled on the white tile floor, aligning her body with a sunbeam that was slowly creeping into the house.

I noted that she hadn't agreed to stay on the property. I would have to enforce the rules. When there were fewer guests in the house.

"What did you put in that?" Ocean asked, eyeing the clump of ingredients in the metal bowl.

"Just what's in the recipe," I said, dumping the contents of the bowl onto the parchment paper lined cookie sheet.

Ocean tugged the open notebook toward her, scanning the handwritten recipe as I chopped and pressed the big lump with the edge of the spatula, trying to flatten it. I'd seen Christopher make granola at least a half-dozen times, but it had never looked so clumped before going into the oven.

Ocean glanced at the unbaked granola, then at me, grinning. Widely. "You're supposed to melt the coconut oil first."

I narrowed my eyes at her, then looked down at the lumpy mess of rolled oats, honey, sunflower seeds, and chopped almonds. "It doesn't say that!"

Ocean smirked. "It's nice to know you aren't perfect at everything."

I snorted, then just stared at the granola. The ingredients were too expensive to throw out.

"Just bake it," Ocean said. "But, like, stir it every six minutes, instead of just at twelve minutes when you add the coconut."

I'd already added the coconut.

Ocean blinked at me. "Did you already add the coconut?"

I grimaced.

She laughed, the sound light and pleasant. "Just be careful not to overbrown it."

"I did reserve the cranberries," I said stiffly, turning to shove the granola into the preheated oven. Though I had remembered to do that only because I'd seen Christopher sprinkle the dried fruit on last before allowing the granola to cool. Taking the witch's advice, I set the timer for six minutes.

"Emma …" Ocean started to say. Then she trailed off, glancing toward the hallway.

I'd heard and felt Sky traversing the stairs only a moment earlier myself.

"Yes?" I prompted, tidying up my prep area and pulling out a cooling rack.

Ocean shook her head, grimacing.

Sky appeared in the doorway to the hall. "Mom wants to leave," she said, her gaze drifting over Ocean—then homing in on me.

"Leave, then," Ocean snapped.

"You're really not coming with us?"

"I'm really not."

Sky stepped into the kitchen. Magic shimmered around her clenched hands. "I can't believe you blame Mom." She pointed a finger at me. "Emma got influenced by it too!"

Only an hour alone with her mother and Sky had completely reversed her position. So Cerise Myers's influence on her daughters wasn't all magically induced.

I took a slight step to the side, so as to avoid any unintentionally thrown magic. I didn't want to get any more tangled in the Myers/Azar family squabble than I already was.

Ocean glared at her sister. "You're the one who was pissed at her before! If Mom hadn't released it, hadn't brought it here, Emma wouldn't have been involved at all. Mom set it on us all. She could have killed Aiden! And I know you know that she would have killed us in that…that…stupid spell, if that was what it had wanted. I think she might…I think she was killing us, before Emma stopped her."

"It infected her!"

Ocean shoved her stool back, going toe to toe with her shorter older sister. "You're not stupid, Sky. You've taken the same classes as I have. It couldn't have gotten hold of Mom without her inviting it in."

I wasn't so certain about that. The Hallowed was far, far more powerful than an average demonic possession. But again, I wasn't going to get further involved.

Sky shifted her attention to me. "Emma, please—"

"Emma already said no," Ocean growled, stepping into Sky's space.

I hadn't actually outright said so, but—

"She stole all of Mom's power! All her magic!" Sky cried. "Mom won't…if she's not a witch, she won't have any value to the coven—"

"Well, it's a good thing she extorted all that extra cash out of Kader." Ocean folded her arms huffily, then set her hip against the island counter, firmly placing herself between me and her sister.

Sky's face crumpled. "You know what he did to her."

Ocean nodded. "I know what she says he did. And I know bits of what he pretends happened. But I didn't know that our house, our...lives had been funded by him already. What did she need more money for?"

"The Hallowed," I said. All right, apparently I wasn't going to keep out of it. "It's expensive to fund the lifestyle of a self-declared goddess."

"Mother of the dawn," Ocean mumbled. "That's what the...guardian called it."

"No," I said. "That was what the Hallowed called itself."

Sky stepped around her sister, still carefully keeping the length of the kitchen island between her and me. Her eyes were wide, pleading. "Emma, please. You could just give Mom back some of what you took."

"Sky!" Ocean snapped. "Aiden and I said no already. It's punishment, like the...like Haoxin said. The magic will come back."

I wasn't so certain about that either. Those I drained rarely survived the process. And of those who did, it was possible that only the Five had ever come back from a complete draining. Assuming it was even possible to drain one of the Five completely.

"You aren't her judge," Sky snarled. "You aren't a jury of her peers."

"No," I said, keeping my tone calm. "But her coven is. What happens when she returns without the Hallowed?"

Sky inhaled deeply, smiling slightly, as if encouraged by what I'd said.

I obviously hadn't articulated my point.

"We keep it to ourselves," Sky said. "No one needs to know what happened—"

Ocean scoffed. "You think the sorcerers are going to keep their mouths shut?"

"I think," Sky spat, "that it doesn't matter to witches what sorcerers say."

"The guardian knows too. She might have even spoken to Aunt Marron before coming here. You have no idea what might be waiting for Mom in Paris."

"At least I'm not abandoning her!" Sky cried. "I'm not a selfish bitch—"

"You are so blind!" Ocean shouted.

I slammed my hand down on the speckled counter of the kitchen island. Power exploded, swamping the room, then snapping back to me.

Both witches froze, staring at me wordlessly.

I kept my tone low and even. "Ocean is an adult. If she wishes to finish her schooling elsewhere that is her choice."

Sky lifted her chin defiantly, opening her mouth to speak.

I looked at her.

She snapped her mouth shut, averting her gaze.

"Cerise's magic is fully drained," I said. "I don't know if it will come back. I also have no idea what the guardian would have done if she'd been the one to punish your mother. But I do know what her coven would have done. Trying to unleash an entity that the coven was tasked with guarding? Almost killing two other coven witches in the process? Her own daughters? Drawing the attention of the guardian nine?"

"One guardian," Sky grumbled.

"Who do you think was on the other side of that portal?" I asked coolly.

Sky grimaced.

The front door opened, then clicked closed quietly. The low hum of Grosvenor's magic preceded him down the hall.

"It might have been a death sentence," Ocean whispered.

"The Myers coven doesn't believe in capital punishment," Sky snapped.

"But they would have magically bound her," I said. "In some fashion."

The timer went off. I started to turn around, but Ocean jogged around the kitchen island. Apparently the younger witch needed something to do. I stepped to the side and let her pull the granola out, then stir it on the cookie sheet.

Sky's shoulders slumped. She didn't appear to notice as Grosvenor strode into the kitchen. His step faltered, and he stuffed his hands in his pockets, rucking up his suit jacket. His gaze riveted to Sky's back.

Ocean shoved the granola back in the oven, setting the timer. Then she crossed to sit on the floor by Paisley, lifting her face into the sun and deliberately turning her back on her sister and the sorcerer.

I plugged the sink, turning on the hot water and adding soap.

Grosvenor stepped closer to Sky, lowering his voice. "Ocean will be okay. Just give her—"

"Of course she'll be okay," Sky snapped defensively. "She gets to walk away."

"I'll help you get Cerise back to—"

"No," Sky growled. "I want nothing to do with you Azars."

I caught Grosvenor's flinch out of the corner of my eye. Sky saw it too. Her furious demeanor cracked. Then she sobbed. Just once, loudly.

Grosvenor reached for her, but she shoved him away and took off down the hall. I heard and felt her heading up the stairs.

I turned off the hot water and started washing the measuring cups I'd just used.

Grosvenor cleared his throat. "The…ah…the Azars …" He sneered at that, but I knew the derision wasn't directed at me. "The sorcerers are leaving. Aiden wanted you to know."

Nodding, I dried my hands on a tea towel, crossing through the kitchen and into the hall, heading to the front door.

Behind me, Ocean asked the curse breaker quietly, "Are you okay?"

I didn't hear his response as I opened the front door and stepped out. Aiden was standing at the top of the stairs, looking down at Isa, Khalid, and his father.

Kader Azar laid his dark-eyed gaze on me and smiled. He looked younger, more refreshed. Not completely back to health, though.

Aiden turned to me. "No bindings. On either of us."

"Thank you for your hospitality, Emma," Kader said. His tone was smooth and cultured. Unruffled. "For your protection, and the gift of your magic."

I waited, not bothering to answer because it was obvious he was winding up to something.

His grin widened. "I owe you a lead on your missing team member. I will contact you with anything I hear of interest, to repay you as swiftly as possible."

I nodded—even as Aiden shouted, "No!"

"No?" I echoed, confused.

Kader laughed quietly.

Aiden snarled at his father, then sighed heavily.

Khalid, grinning broadly, muttered to Isa. "So that's how it's done."

"For him." The eldest Azar brother shook his head. "Only for him."

"I'm not following," I said, thinking about my blades only steps away in the study.

"I made everyone sign a blood-bound nondisclosure agreement." Aiden ran his hand through his hair.

"It contained a 'no contact' clause," Khalid said, still grinning. "No contacting you, Emma, specifically. Which you just voided. For Kader, at least."

"You haven't gotten your mother's signature yet, Aiden," the elder sorcerer said.

"I'm aware." Aiden wrapped his hand around the post at the top of the stairs. I got the distinct impression he was doing that instead of attacking his father.

"It didn't take you long to get back to playing games," I said.

Kader shrugged. "I'm simply pointing out the irony."

"Which is?" Aiden snapped.

His father smirked. "It wasn't I who put you and your loved ones in danger." And with that final observation, Kader turned away, heading toward Aiden's SUV. Apparently, the sorcerers were borrowing it.

Khalid followed his father, but Isa lingered.

"It's just a matter of time with you," Aiden called after the elder sorcerer.

Kader turned back, deliberately sweeping his gaze over the property and me, then lingering on Aiden. "No," he finally said. "I will never bring you any harm that I can control."

Aiden snorted. "There's a lot of leeway in that statement."

Kader hummed quietly. Then he said, "I look forward to speaking with you soon."

The elder sorcerer nodded to me, then turned away.

Grosvenor wandered down the hall behind us, leaning against the doorjamb with his arms crossed.

"You're not going with them?" I asked.

He shrugged. "Different flights."

I was fairly certain the Azar cabal could afford to own at least one private jet. But I didn't feel like speculating on why the curse breaker couldn't be dropped somewhere along the way.

"So that's it?" Isa gazed up at us, hands shoved in the pockets of his suit pants.

"What more do you want, sorcerer?" I asked coolly.

"You're lucky you're walking away, Isa," Aiden said. "Don't push it."

Isa looked at his younger brother for a moment. Then he spoke with utter sincerity. "I don't want to be at odds, brother. I was serious about building a relationship with you, before Ruwa took it all too far." He shook his head. "You think that all I want is a connection to Emma…and your housemate …" He waved his hand, not voicing Christopher's name out loud.

Interesting. Isa was still trying to keep secrets from his father.

Sorcerers and their games.

"But I'd be happy to limit my contact. We could meet elsewhere." Isa glanced toward the SUV.

Khalid had started the engine and pulled forward from the side of the barn and into the driveway. Waiting on Isa, but not patiently.

"I'm not going anywhere else, Isa," Aiden said.

His brother huffed. "Aiden, I …" Then he shook his head, flinging his hands out to the sides. "You know you're the one who tried to kill me, right?"

Aiden threw his head back and laughed.

Either the attempted murder of a sibling was hilarious on a level I didn't understand, or the dark-haired sorcerer was seriously sleep deprived.

Isa chuckled quietly. Then he shoved his hands back into his pockets, turning away.

Aiden sobered, watching his brother go. Then he called out, "Thank you, Isa. For the help with the containment spell on Opal's vessel. I wouldn't have been able to quell the suppression spell so efficiently without working it through with you."

Isa simply waved over his shoulder, climbing into the front passenger seat. In the back, Kader was mostly hidden behind the tinted windows.

Khalid pulled the SUV up the driveway. Aiden and I watched them go. Grosvenor stepped forward and held his hand up, waving goodbye.

The gate at the top of the drive opened as the SUV approached, drove through, and turned onto the main road. The gate closed.

I glanced at Aiden. "Was that you?"

"No," he growled, though there wasn't much heat in it.

"He has to get in his final power play," Grosvenor said. Then he glanced back toward the front door.

Inside, Cerise was standing at the base of the stairs.

I hadn't felt her approach. And as a creeping sensation that had nothing to do with magic writhed up my spine, I realized there was something utterly disconcerting about not being able to feel someone in my own home.

Magic shifted behind Cerise as Sky descended the stairs. She stood behind her mother.

Cerise was once again outfitted in cream from head to toe, wearing a silk blouse, linen skirt, and high heels. Her eyes were covered with overly large sunglasses.

"I'm so glad he's gone," she whispered, biting her lip. "The last days have been unbearable."

Grosvenor frowned.

Aiden's expression was placid. As if he'd come to some conclusion, specifically about his mother, and was now utterly at peace with his decision.

I closed the space between us in a single step, brushing my fingers across the back of his hand. He shook his head, then twined his fingers through mine, squeezing.

"I have some papers for you to sign, Mother," he said, releasing my hand and stepping toward the house. "You, Sky, and Ocean."

"*Pardon?*" Cerise said, slipping into French. "*Moi? Et pourquoi?*"

Aiden stepped past his mother, heading for the study. Sky followed him wordlessly.

Cerise stared at me.

For a long time.

I held her gaze, even through the sunglasses.

Finally, she smirked. "Blood always runs true. Aiden will remember that in time." She turned, following her son down the hall, her heels clicking on the fir flooring.

"Piece of fucking work," Grosvenor muttered. Then he jogged down the patio stairs, heading for the barn.

I stayed where I was, letting the comforting sense of the property settle around me. Waiting. Though I knew I wouldn't have to wait for long.

An argument sparked in the study. Then a door slammed. Magic snapped into place—most likely sealing all sound within the study—and Sky barreled down the hall and out onto the patio. She stood beside me, chest heaving, hands clenching and unclenching.

"Kader did something really shitty to you," she finally said. "When you were a kid. Right?"

I just looked at her.

"I signed," she snapped. "I can't talk about you or anything that's happened, excepting my own mother's deeds since I might have to testify against her at tribunal. I've been gagged. By my own brother!" Sky breathed in deeply.

Ocean slowly wandered down the hall and out onto the patio to join us. She perched on the side rail.

"I'm just …" Sky shook her head. Then she whispered to me, "How could you have possibly forgiven him?"

"I didn't," I said smoothly.

"But…why then? Why help?"

"Because I love Aiden."

Sky snorted. "Aiden hates Kader."

I didn't bother answering her.

She sighed. "I'm not sure I'm going to be able to forgive her."

"Sometimes…you don't." I looked at Ocean. "The granola?"

She nodded. "Cooling. I added the cranberries."

"Thank you." I stepped back into the house. Sky took off toward the barn while Ocean followed me inside.

Thirty minutes later, partway through making a batch of ginger snaps that Ocean had persuaded me to use raw ginger for, Cerise left the house. And then the property. Without saying goodbye to her youngest daughter. I didn't bother watching the elder witch and Sky pull away in a taxi, though Aiden and Grosvenor did.

Ocean just kept hand rolling the ginger snap dough with me.

I'D LEFT AIDEN, GROSVENOR, AND OCEAN BURIED IN books in the front sitting room to pull the last batch of ginger snaps from the oven. And as I did, energy shifted along my spine, coalescing on my T3 and T4 vertebrae.

I dropped the still-hot cookie sheet on top of the stove and was running for the front door before I'd even made the decision to do so.

Shouts erupted from the sitting room as I passed by, yanked open the door, and barreled out onto the front patio.

A hulking black SUV pulled into the driveway. Samantha's vehicle. Christopher stepped out of the SUV and opened the gate. Samantha pulled through and paused, waiting for Christopher to climb back in.

"They're friends," I heard Aiden say from behind me. The sorcerer and witch magic that had been gathering around Ocean and Grosvenor abated.

The clairvoyant looked toward the house. His eyes were whited out with his magic. I started down the steps, racing across the yard.

Christopher met me halfway.

He swept me into a fierce hug. Power shifted up and down my spine as I pressed my face into his neck—and tried to ignore a pressing urge to cry.

"I know," he murmured. "I know."

Samantha parked the SUV beside the barn—and was out of it and heading for the house almost before the engine had shut off. Her power boiled around her. "Where is he?" she howled.

"Gone," Aiden said. He sounded far too amused for someone facing down a riled telekinetic who wasn't known for her ability to control herself.

"What?" she shrieked.

I pulled away from Christopher. My T3 vertebra thrummed with magic, as if making up for the days we'd been disconnected. The clairvoyant's eyes were blazing with so much power that I wouldn't have been surprised to discover he was currently navigating multiple futures in his mind's eye. My continuing to touch him wouldn't help him find stability.

"I missed you," I said.

"I know," he repeated. Then he cupped my face, kissing me lightly on the forehead. "Now, tell me…does the new sorcerer swing both ways? I can't get a read on him from here."

He meant Grosvenor.

I laughed involuntarily.

Grinning, Christopher dropped his hands to his sides, taking a step back from me. A twisted smile let me know he needed the space.

"You are a shock to the system," he murmured. "But I don't feel so empty now." He glanced over to the house.

Samantha was engaged in a hissed argument with Aiden. Or at least she was trying to argue with him, but the dark-haired sorcerer was simply smiling. Looking more relaxed than he had for days.

Ocean and Grosvenor were just staring at the telekinetic.

"It's not the same," Christopher said as we slowly walked toward the house. "With just Zans. The connection isn't the same. Even with the cards …"

"Yes," I said, when he didn't complete the thought out loud.

Paisley appeared in the open front doorway. She settled her gaze on Samantha, head lowered, upper lip curled, revealing sharp teeth.

That couldn't be good.

The demon dog gathered herself to spring.

"Left!" Christopher shouted, grimacing.

Paisley leaped.

Samantha stepped left.

Knocking Ocean and Grosvenor to the side, Paisley sailed past Aiden, trying to compensate for the telekinetic's move in midair. She managed to clip Samantha's shoulder.

Apparently, the demon dog could attack one of the Five. Or she was somehow managing to ignore her programming.

Samantha stumbled off the front path, hitting Paisley with a pulse of her power and shoving her away.

The demon dog hit the grass, rolled, then swung around to snarl at Samantha.

Christopher exhaled. "That was going to be…bloodier."

"I already apologized!" Samantha shouted, even as she produced a trio of metal objects from her pocket. The ball bearings spun around one hand while she held the other hand out to ward Paisley away.

"Another apology?" I asked.

"Yes," Christopher said. "Samantha can't seem to get over treating Paisley like a dog. She refused to book extra beds, or a third meal. And I wasn't…focused…all the time …"

"That's why she was sleeping here."

"Yes. And now we know just how far Paisley can walk through dimensions."

"Shall we intervene?"

He sighed. "It will be less violent that way."

I stepped away from the clairvoyant, somewhat reluctantly. He wasn't the only one who'd been feeling unfettered over the last few days.

I crossed to Paisley, brushing my fingertips across her broad head. She spat and snarled, but she didn't knock my hand away.

"How have you had her for eight years and not trained her better?" Samantha snapped at me. "I couldn't get her to listen to me at all. For all I know, she's been leading us nowhere!"

Paisley flattened her ears and growled. The skin of my arms prickled.

"That's enough," Christopher said quietly, speaking to Samantha as he stepped by her and onto the front stairs. "We trust Paisley. We believe in her."

Aiden reached for the clairvoyant and the two men hugged, pounding each other on the back.

"Missed you, brother," Aiden said gruffly.

Christopher grinned, tilting his head in the way he did when he was looking at someone with his magic more than his eyes. "I hear we have a wedding to plan."

"What?" Ocean cried, grinning madly. "Are you and Emma getting married? Why isn't she wearing a ring?! You haven't bought her a ring yet!?"

"Ugh, really?" Samantha eyed me. "Married?"

Paisley snapped her teeth in the telekinetic's direction. I held Samantha's gaze as I stepped closer, the demon dog keeping pace at my side.

I paused, slightly too close for comfort. Watching Samantha's eyes widen as she tried to decide if I was going to attack her.

"Next time you drag Christopher and Paisley with you," I said coolly, "make sure your intel is solid."

She opened her mouth to protest.

"No," I said. "I want you to have eyes on your target before you even think of calling any of us in."

Samantha grimaced. "I needed …" But then she didn't finish the thought. Instead she just nodded, then said, " 'Us'? You'll come with me next time?"

I nodded, already turning away and climbing the stairs to the patio. "Aiden and I will come if you need us, as long as it doesn't interfere with Opal's schooling or her breaks."

"I can't believe you didn't kill him," Samantha said, setting one foot on the bottom stair but not stepping up.

I glanced at Aiden and smiled. "It's barely time for tea. Who knows what could happen between now and dinner."

Aiden laughed huskily.

"Um, hi!" Ocean said brightly, speaking to Christopher. "I'm Ocean. Aiden's youngest sister."

"Yes," the clairvoyant said with a teasing grin. "I know. I'm Christopher. Emma's youngest older brother."

"The gardener?" she asked. "Because it's really obvious that it isn't Emma."

Christopher chuckled. The white of his power had settled in his eyes, forming a thick ring around his light-gray irises.

"Grosvenor Azar." The curse breaker offered his hand to the clairvoyant.

Christopher reciprocated, staring at Grosvenor for a few moments, then shrugging in disappointment. "I see."

Not breaking their grasp, the curse breaker grinned amicably. "You see? What do you see, oh clairvoyant?"

Samantha snorted loudly. "Rude. Though I guess that goes without saying for anyone with that last name."

"Does that include me?" Aiden asked, still amused.

"Hell yeah," the telekinetic groused. But she was grinning now. "You're the worst of them. All up in our business. Pushy. Well, the worst next to your father."

"He's the only other Azar you know," Christopher said mildly, crossing into the house. "I smell ginger snaps."

"Emma just finished baking," Ocean said, obviously torn between following the clairvoyant and casting furtive looks at the telekinetic.

Samantha finally acknowledged the witch with a put-out sigh. "Yeah, yeah, I know. I'm gorgeous."

Ocean flushed. But she didn't look away.

The telekinetic shook her head. "Way too old for you, sweetheart. I don't play with baby witches."

"How old?" Ocean jutted out her chin. "You can't be even ten years older than me."

I laughed. I couldn't help it. Even for my life, the day was verging on absurd.

Aiden twined his fingers through mine. "Let's get tea."

"Can I tear you away from your books long enough?"

He looked concerned. "I can eat cookies and read at the same time. I haven't found a single mention of the guardian Haoxin—"

"What?" Samantha cried. "A guardian?" Without waiting for an answer, she barreled up the stairs, shoved her way by us, and marched into the house. "You are such an asshole, Knox! I asked you what was going on! Multiple times!" Her voice faded as she approached the kitchen. "We could have chartered a plane …"

Christopher mumbled something in response that I didn't catch.

I looked up at Aiden. "I'd wait until she's calmed down to ask her, but apparently Samantha knows something about guardians."

"Does she ever calm down?" Grosvenor asked.

I just looked at him.

He grimaced. "Apologies, amplifier."

"So …" Ocean said quietly. "Does Samantha like girls?"

"You're heading to the Academy," Aiden said. "There will be plenty of girls to romance there."

Ocean frowned. "Boring witches and sorcerers and necromancers." She smiled slyly. "I want to walk on the wild side." And with that pronouncement, she did a little spin and strode into the house.

"Right," Grosvenor smirked. "Good luck with that." Then clearing his throat, he said, "I'm heading out. I just wanted to give…everyone else a little lead time."

He meant Sky, I presumed.

"Stay for the night," Aiden said. "I'll drive you to the float plane tomorrow morning. I've got to pick up my SUV anyway. Then you can fly into Victoria and catch an international flight from there."

Grosvenor glanced at me, then away. "I have a sense that I'm courting death every moment I'm here. And…it keeps getting worse."

Aiden clapped him on the shoulder. "Perfectly understandable. A couple of ginger snaps will ease the feeling."

Pulling me with him, Aiden stepped into the house, leaving the sorcerer to follow us. Or not.

AIDEN, CHRISTOPHER, AND I WERE GATHERED around the kitchen island eating breakfast. The granola had turned out surprisingly good—thanks to Ocean. Then we heard Aiden's iPad start to trill in the study.

Grinning, Christopher took off down the hall.

I raised an eyebrow at Aiden. "What if it's your father?"

"Then he's about to get a delightful surprise."

Laughing, I rinsed my bowl in the sink, catching the clairvoyant's exuberant greeting all the way down the hall.

"Hello, my little witch."

Opal.

Aiden took my bowl from me, waving me away as he cleaned up. I took off for the study, finding Christopher seated at the desk, chatting with Opal on the iPad.

"I'm glad you're back," the young witch was saying as I entered the room. "Emma missed you. Is Aiden's family gone?"

"Ocean is still here, sleeping. But the last sorcerer took off this morning," the clairvoyant replied.

"Grosvenor. Gorgeous boy. Not even remotely interested in me."

Opal pouted playfully. "He must be blind."

Christopher nodded sagely. "Indeed. When are you coming home?"

"Yeah, about that …" Opal held up a thick parchment envelope and a card. It looked like some kind of formal invitation. "I've been invited to the Godfrey coven summer retreat. At the end of June."

"Witches!" Christopher grinned. "Yes!"

"But it's just for Emma and me," Opal said sadly.

Christopher huffed. Then he shoved the chair back. "I'll let you talk, then. Don't hang up without saying goodbye."

"Okay!"

I exchanged places with Christopher, peering at Opal more closely. The lighting on her end was bad, though it was late morning in her time zone. As if she was in a closet.

"Hey, Emma," she said. "So…you'll take me?" She looked at the invitation. "It's in somewhere called Tofino. And Juniper says there will be surfing and maybe we'll even see some whales."

I had no idea who Juniper was, other than a witch from or related to the Godfrey coven. "We'll discuss it."

Aiden stepped in behind me, leaning forward so Opal could see him. "Good morning."

"Good morning." She grinned at him. "We found a sorcerer!"

"Sorry?"

"For our group. You said we needed a sorcerer."

"Right. Wonderful."

"Yep, it took a couple of days but I tracked down an Azar."

"Excuse me?"

"Melanie Azar. As best as we've figured out, she's, like, your second cousin or something."

"An Azar," Aiden repeated, sounding disconcerted.

"Yep." Opal grinned even more. "Anyone else would have been too boring."

Aiden huffed out a laugh. "Is that why you're in a closet?"

"Nope." Opal glanced around and pulled the phone closer. I got a better look at the young witch. There was something different about her hair. "So," she whispered. "You'll never guess what happened …"

"Why are you whispering?" I asked suspiciously. "And what did you do to your hair?"

"It's called streaks, Emma," she said, already exasperated.

"Are they permanent?"

She shrugged and then held the vessel that had caused all the trouble up to the camera. The vessel that she'd supposedly turned into the principal of the Academy.

I sighed. "Opal …"

She flipped it, so the lid hung open on its hinge.

It was empty.

"You'll never guess who we met," she crowed excitedly. "A soul seer!"

I blinked.

"You know. A necromancer who can, like, manipulate soul magic. She opened the case and released the soul trapped within it. Or, like, the sliver of the soul that was in it. I didn't totally follow all of what she did. She was just…so…cool."

"And she had streaks in her hair," Aiden said, mildly amused.

"Yep! And she said she'd knit me some rainbow heart arm warmers, just like the ones she was wearing."

I wasn't completely certain what arm warmers were, but Opal seemed delighted at the prospect.

"So …" Opal blinked at me. "You'll go surfing with me, Emma?"

"Yes," I said. Aiden settled his hand on my shoulder, and I covered it with my own. For a moment, I thought my chest might explode.

Joy, I reminded myself. This was what extreme joy felt like.

"Yes," I said again. "Surfing. And then you can help me plan the wedding."

"Yay! Okay, got to go before I completely miss breakfast." She pressed her screen and the video winked out, completely forgetting her promise to Christopher not to hang up.

I pivoted the chair to face Aiden.

476

He knelt before me, gazing up at me. "You're sure? About getting married? I don't want…I mean, the Hallowed was doing some pretty heavy influencing of us all, and—"

I kissed him. Deeply. Lingering with my lips on his, tongues caressing. Then I whispered, "What kind of spells are you planning to embed into my ring, sorcerer?"

He laughed, pulling me out of the chair until I was kneeling against him. "Anything you want, Emma. Anything you want."

"That will do, my sorcerer. That will do perfectly."

POWER BOILED OUT OF ME, FLOODING THE ROOM. I stretched into it, fingers splayed, head falling back.

I was …

So …

Powerful.

Adored.

Loved.

Worshiped.

"Emma."

Warm hands cupped my face, lips gently brushing my own.

"Emma. It's just a dream."

Aiden.

I became aware that I was standing, sheets tangled around my feet. A torrent of power still raged around me. My power, my magic.

I gasped, drawing in a long breath of air. Almost as if I hadn't been breathing a moment before.

"It's okay," Aiden murmured, still caressing my face gently. "You're here. You're still here with us."

Us.

I blinked.

I was standing at the end of my bed. The room was dark, but I could clearly make out Aiden. He was naked, as if he'd leaped out of bed.

I blinked again.

"Pull it back, Emma," Aiden murmured.

The power, he meant. I must have been flooding the entire house. I reined in the energy boiling from me—and only then realized that I'd been picking up emotions. And not just from Aiden.

Tamping down on my magic, I stepped slightly to the side, so I could see past the dark-haired sorcerer.

Christopher, Samantha, and Paisley were kneeling before me. Their heads were thrown back, magic blazing in their eyes. Ocean was clinging to the doorframe, her chest heaving.

They were all in various states of undress.

I had pulled them from their beds. I'd been manipulating their emotions without even touching them.

I looked at Aiden, suddenly terrified. "The Hallowed …"

"No," he said. "Just you, Emma. Just a…bad dream."

Samantha and Christopher straightened, sharing a glance. Then the telekinetic crossed to Ocean. "Show's over, witch."

"But …"

"Out."

Samantha closed the door in Ocean's face. The wards carved into the frame were still active.

My heart was pounding. I was still coated in my power, still feeling the echo of the others' feelings. Love. Adoration. Worship.

"What the hell was that?" Samantha snarled quietly, leaning back against the door with her arms crossed.

"That was Emma," Christopher said. "Unleashed. Without needing to touch us."

"Did I…was I draining you?" I asked in a whisper, hearing the fear in my voice but unable to do anything about it.

"No," Samantha said bluntly. "You just…enticed us in here."

"Could it just be the tattoos?" Christopher said. "Ocean didn't seem to be affected the same way. And Aiden, you were right beside Emma. So why didn't …" He trailed off thoughtfully. "You're immune?"

"Apparently," Aiden said, watching me.

Samantha and Christopher shared another glance. Paisley sidled up to me and pressed her broad head under my hand, offering comfort. I breathed in deeply. My heart rate settled.

"Well," Samantha drawled, "it's never a surprise when one of the Five gains a new ability. But, honestly, you were already fucking scary, Socks." She stared at me for a few moments, her expression inscrutable. Then she shrugged. "At least you're on our side."

She opened the door and exited.

"Is Emma okay?" Ocean asked. Apparently she'd been waiting in the hall.

"Always," Samantha snapped, pulling the door with her. "What the hell time is it? Too early for coffee?" The door latched behind the telekinetic.

Christopher slipped his hand over my shoulder, pressing his fingers to my T3 vertebra, over the magic tattooed there that bound us. His eyes flooded with the white of his power.

"Did I hurt you?" I asked again.

He shook his head. "No. The opposite, actually. But…it bothers me that I'm not immune, like Aiden. For the same reasons."

"The blood bond," Aiden said simply.

The clairvoyant nodded but didn't look happy. He dropped his hand, stepping away without telling me what, if anything, he was seeing of my near future. He left, shutting the door behind him.

I turned to Aiden. Whatever he saw on my face made him gather me into his arms.

"It's just another skill, Emma," he murmured into my hair. "You'll hone it, as you've done over and over again."

"A latent ability," I said with a sigh. "Triggered by the contact with the Hallowed."

"Tapped into by the Hallowed, more likely."

I groaned, enjoying the strength of his body pressed against mine. Letting him hold me aloft, if only for a moment.

Paisley crawled up onto the bed, sighing dramatically as she took up one half of it. Aiden chuckled. We climbed into bed with the demon dog, tangling our limbs together in the tight space she allowed us.

"Can you adapt the wards on the bedroom?" I asked, shimmying back into Aiden. Trying to get as close to him as possible, skin to skin. Allowing his steady resolve to anchor me in the moment. "So that if this happens again, no one else is affected?"

"I'll start tomorrow."

"Thank you."

I knew who I was. To Aiden, to Opal. Even to myself.

I wasn't going to forget that or run scared from what I was able to do. I would conquer these new abilities.

Because I didn't have any other choice.

Aiden pressed his face into the back of my neck, and I rested my hand on Paisley's chest. Allowing the both of them to pull me back to sleep.

THE MUSIC BOX

A KNOCK AT MY DORM ROOM DOOR DREW ME FROM the pile of first-year spellbooks strewn across my rumpled bed. For the next three weeks, I wasn't supposed to be talking to anyone. Except in class or at meals. I glanced at the time on my busted phone. Technically I'd only been serving detention for three hours. Ugh.

Confining myself to my room was extra punishment. Self-imposed, really. For disappointing Emma. For scaring Emma.

I might have been only thirteen, and I might have been hundreds of miles away from home. But I knew that my guardian didn't like being scared, feeling helpless. Mostly because I was pretty sure that the only time she'd ever really been scared was when I was in trouble, and she couldn't help me.

And that made her do…things.

Deadly, bloody things she didn't want to do, but would do…for me.

Whoever was waiting for me in the hall knocked again. A sharp rap of knuckles. I tossed off my cocoon of worn, layered quilts, grabbing the comfy dark-red sweater I'd stolen from my adoptive uncle's closet the last time I was home, and headed for the door. Christopher—Emma's brother who wasn't really a brother. It was complicated—wouldn't miss the sweater. He was always warm.

It wasn't a long walk from the end of my bed. Three steps at most.

I opened the door to see an elder witch blinking down at me over the rim of her glasses. Principal Whitaker. The head witch of the Academy. Her eyes were light blue. Intelligent, sharp. Streaks of gray ran through light-brown hair partially pulled back from her temples. The chain hanging from her glasses was strung with purple pearls.

"Opal." She scanned me up and down, lips twisted disapprovingly.

Probably because I was wearing jeans and a T-shirt, not my school uniform.

"Principal Whitaker." I pulled the sweater on, shoving my arms through sleeves that hung way past my hands, all the way down to just above my knees. Perfect.

Two other first-year students were standing behind the head witch.

Jack Fairchild and Emily Hawes.

Witch and necromancer.

Fledglings, like me.

My "cohorts," according to the principal, who had obviously collected them on the way to my room. Necromancers were housed on the ground floor, grouped by year. Jack's room was just down the long hall from mine. Sorcerers and shapeshifters occupied the middle floors of the residential wing, mostly.

Emily's blond curls were shoved back by a pink headband, making her green eyes appear even wider than normal. The necromancer was clothed in ripped dark-blue jeans, black sneakers, and an overly large black hoodie. The hoodie was emblazoned with a dark-fuchsia bejeweled skull-and-crossbones on the back. A fourteenth birthday gift from her much-older brother last month. She smiled tentatively, but her fingers were locked in a twist that looked almost painful.

Standing slightly taller than Principal Whitaker—and still growing—Jack was wearing his navy-blue school uniform, but his shirt collar was open. His expression was blank, but his blue eyes were filled with a sullen willfulness. As usual.

I knew that look, and that description. Because the same had been said about me on more than one occasion. Before now. Before finding my family, and understanding how I fit. Dealing with still being a kid. Talented. But not on my own anymore, not abandoned. I had multiple people who wanted to take care of me, and not at all because of my magic.

Still, even more so than me, Jack didn't like being told what to do by anyone.

Jack's skin was almost the exact same brown as mine. But he kept his hair clipped close to his head. I liked to feel the wind in mine.

"Come with me," Principal Whitaker said, turning on her heel without another word.

I tugged on my black boots, leaving them unlaced. They'd been magically shined to a high gloss.

I'd been really bored during my three hours of self-confinement.

Stumbling, I pulled the door to my room shut. The head witch was already halfway down the hall. Emily and Jack were waiting for me. I hadn't expected to see either of them for days, so this felt awkward.

"What's going on?" I hissed. "Are we in trouble? Again?" I racked my brain, trying to figure out what rules we'd broken. Aside from the most recent ones. Or at least which rules we'd broken that someone had now found out about.

Emily shook her head, sending her curls bouncing.

Jack curled his lip, shoulders stiff as he shoved his hands in the pockets of his pants and strolled after Principal Whitaker. His long legs ate up the distance, though his pace was slow.

Jack Fairchild was seriously pissed. It would have been an easy guess that the phone call with his adoptive parents four or so hours ago hadn't gone well. Except I'd seen him right after, and he'd looked pretty pleased with himself. By contrast, Principal Whitaker had looked like she'd eaten something really sour.

Emily crowded next to me, her shoulder brushing mine as we took off after Jack. The phone call with her family had left the necromancer in tears. Her eyes still looked a little red and puffy. Though we were all in equal amounts of trouble for having triggered a potentially deadly suppression spell on an artifact after sneaking off campus, Emily was the one who'd stolen the artifact from her family vault in the first place.

The Academy had subsequently confiscated the heavily spelled music box, which supposedly held a piece of Emily's great-grandmother's soul. The Hawes family would not be getting it back.

My phone call with Emma and Aiden had been perfect. I accepted my punishment, and my guardians cared more about my happiness than any stupid school rules I might have broken. Though I'd been worried I was going to get kicked out of the Academy. That wouldn't have been good, because it would have made Emma feel as though she'd failed me.

Thankfully, even though Emily, Jack, and I had all been given three weeks of detention and a mark on our records, we hadn't been suspended. Even if the Hawes necromancers were pissed about losing the artifact, convincing Jack and Emily to fess up had been the right strategic move. After almost getting Emily killed.

"What's up with Jack?" I asked in a whisper.

Emily shook her head, then spoke so quietly that I could barely pick up the words. Her accent was different from Jack's and mine. East-coast Canadian. "Don't know. Haven't seen him since earlier."

Jack threw a look back over his shoulder at us, rolling his eyes in the direction of Principal Whitaker. Then he smirked.

Okay. He wasn't pissed at us, then.

Probably just annoyed at the head witch ordering us to follow her without any explanation. Jack liked everything laid out clearly. Not that he wasn't willing to break rules. He just wanted to be in control when he did.

Despite our similar backgrounds, I was way more adaptable. More resilient. At least that was what I'd heard various foster parents mutter behind my back to various social workers. My last foster parent, Capri Pine, had been both those things in one. But my chosen family never expected me to be anything other than what I was.

But both the Hawes and the Fairchild families were old and powerful bloodlines. For completely different reasons. Mired in tradition, as my soon-to-be adoptive dad, Aiden, would say. So were the Sherwoods, my own familial line. But I hadn't been raised a witch. Jack was adopted like me, so the blood that ran in his veins wasn't technically of Fairchild origin either.

His attitude came from the same place as mine—from losing our birth parents and living on the streets, then surviving more than one magical assault. And kidnapping. Not that Jack was chatty about any of that.

Emily had told me the Fairchild coven had a dark reputation. But I figured if you had the power to back it up, it didn't really matter what other people thought of you.

None of that stopped Jack from thinking that just about everyone was beneath him, though. Or maybe it was more that he didn't bother fitting in. Conforming. That was pretty ironic, because he was in the top five in our year, like me.

Principal Whitaker led us down the northeast stairs, exiting into a long hall I hadn't been in before. We walked in silence down the corridor for what seemed like forever, passing door after door. Which presumably meant we were on the ground floor of some wing of the main Academy building.

The hallway ended at a set of steel doors surrounded by a thick frame of rune-carved dark wood. The doors looked heavy.

I resisted the urge to take a picture of the runes for Aiden. My spell-burned phone was barely functional—so my deadly sorcerer-daddy-to-be was shipping me a replacement. But last I'd checked, I could still take a photo and send email. Usually.

Principal Whitaker turned to look at all of us. Then she nodded. "The vessel that Emily stole from her family vault has provided a rare learning opportunity." Emily shifted her feet, looking at the ground. "Don't make me regret including you."

With that weird warning, the head witch wrapped her hand around one of the steel door handles. Energy shifted, and without the witch even pulling on it, the door clicked, then swung open as she stepped back.

Jack grunted quietly.

It took a lot more than that to impress me. The Fairchilds might have had a dark reputation, but my chosen family was off-the-charts powerful. The kind of power that cowed the darkness. Harnessed it and transformed it. With secret identities and everything.

Still, Aiden might like a look at the runes.

Principal Whitaker strode through the doorway. Whatever lay beyond appeared to be cloaked in pure blackness.

I tugged my phone out of my pocket, snapping an in-motion photo as I followed Jack. Emily was at my side. Even if I'd stood still and framed it up, the photo might not turn out. Magic was weird that way. And everything in the Academy, except for the shielded media rooms, emanated a lot of power.

UTTER BLACKNESS ENGULFED ME. A PRICKLING SENsation slid over my chest, shoulders, and neck, intensifying across my eyes and forehead and tingling in my ears. Gasping, Emily grabbed me. Her hand was cold.

I tried blinking away the weird energy and clearing my sight. It didn't work.

Then I slammed into Jack, my nose crunching into his upper spine. Emily stumbled into me. We both teetered on the edge of collapse, but Jack reached back, holding my shoulder to steady me. Sending more energy shivering across my skin, even through my thick sweater.

I blinked rapidly, forcing my eyes to adjust to what I thought might be some sort of magical shielding as I found my footing, still gripping Emily's hand.

A black-painted room took shape before us. Principal Whitaker was standing just ahead to one side, her eyes and brow furrowed in concern.

She beckoned to us. "Children …" She shook her head. "Students, watch your footing. Stay behind the line. I'd forgotten how disconcerting the null room can be the first time you enter."

The line?

I glanced down. The floor was also a flat black, and hard like rock. But seamless, not tiled. And I had stepped on a thin copper line that looked like it was etched all around the room. Jack was standing fully on the other side of that line, flexing his hands as if they hurt.

"Now!" Principal Whitaker snapped.

I pulled my foot back, moving with Emily to the edge of the wall. At some point, the door had closed behind us. All the matte-black paint—or whatever was coating the walls—made it difficult to see the space.

Magic. That was what was coating the walls and floor and ceiling.

Or maybe it was a lack of magic?

That was what 'null' meant, right?

Jack stepped back over the copper line, which was somehow easier to feel than see. He inhaled, shuddering. Then he threw a nasty look at the principal.

Her lips pulled down disapprovingly, but she didn't rebuke him.

Taking in the rest of the null room, I crossed to join Principal Whitaker. Emily trailed behind me. My vision seemed to clear in layers, as if I was adapting with every blink. The murky shadows retreated until I could see all four walls and another steel door on the far side of the room. A half-dozen professors with notepads or notebooks in hand were grouped behind the copper line along the opposite wall.

In the center of the room, surrounded by a glimmering shield of power, the Hawes family artifact sat on a pedestal that appeared to have been carved from a tree trunk. I wondered if the dead tree was still rooted in the earth, with the null room built around and over it. If it was, I wondered whether that was supposed to ground magic or allow witches to access it.

As she followed my gaze, Emily bumped into me again. Just a few hours ago, the tiny blue-and-gold music box had tried to kill her. Actually, it had been the suppression spell we'd disturbed that had tried to kill her—to stop her from unleashing whatever else the artifact held.

Emily's great-grandmother's name and date of death were etched across the gold bottom of the hinged oval container—only readable with a complex reveal spell that had taken us hours to figure out. And after emailing her cousin to poke around in their family archives a bit more, Emily was left with the impression that her great-grandmother might not have been actually dead when the piece of her soul was harvested and contained in the music box. More like it had been done by the rest of the family combined to weaken her. Because she'd gone all dark and crazy.

We hadn't mentioned that rumor to Principal Whitaker. Or to our parental figures. As far as I knew, Emily's elder brother—who had answered the phone call from Principal Whitaker—hadn't offered any extra info either.

The necromancy professors had collectively lost their shit when they saw the artifact. Or at least 'collectively lost their shit' had been Jack's interpretation of them racing to and from the principal's office after we'd turned the artifact in. We'd been ordered to stay put in the exterior seating area. Jack had said it with a weird accent and a wide grin, like maybe he was quoting someone.

"Your being here is a privilege," Principal Whitaker said stiffly—but looking over at the other professors, not us. "But I…and your guardians…believe it is important for you to understand what you were attempting to meddle with. The artifact is an exceedingly dangerous necromancy working." She glanced at Emily.

She shifted her feet, avoiding the elder witch's gaze.

Principal Whitaker sniffed. "The Hawes family should have destroyed it long ago. And they will answer to the Convocation for that oversight."

That was new information.

Except Emily grimaced. So she'd known that already.

Principal Whitaker settled her gaze on the professors across the room again. More necromancers, I guessed. As a first-year witch, I didn't have classes with any of them. "Unfortunately, the knowledge of the artifact's creation, and therefore the knowledge of how it might be destroyed, has been…lost to the generations. So the family locked the artifact away."

Emily was the youngest Hawes necromancer. Necromancy normally only fully manifested in those who were female-born. There wasn't a single male necromancer currently attending the Academy, and the generation of her family before Emily was born had been mostly male. That presumably meant that certain spells or hereditary talents hadn't been passed along.

I looked over at the necromancy professors—none of them seemed to know what to do with the artifact currently being stored behind multiple wards in a so-called null room either.

"We happen to have an apprentice currently in residence who is well suited to the task of …" Principal Whitaker trailed off as she flicked her fingers. "Of dealing with the artifact." Three fingers on each of the elder witch's hands bore rings. Jeweled bands of gold, probably filled with magic.

I wondered if that power would be stripped away if she stepped across the copper line. Or if the null room just suppressed the use of magic, causing that prickling sensation I'd felt when I entered.

Principal Whitaker fell silent. Waiting, I thought.

The other necromancy professors chatted among themselves, quietly enough that I couldn't pick up any actual words. I hunkered down and finally tied the laces on my boots, drawing the principal's attention.

I grinned at her widely, already knowing that it would piss her off. Not because she was scared of me. Just that she'd become colder since she'd met Emma and Christopher. Wary, maybe. And I was totally cool with that.

She sighed quietly.

It was also possible that every time she looked at me Principal Whitaker remembered releasing me into the custody of a dark sorcerer. Ruwa had walked into the Academy wearing my dead mother's face and kidnapped me right out of the principal's office. There was nothing the elder witch could have done about it—the shapeshifting abilities Ruwa had gained by binding herself to a demon fooled everyone—but I wondered if she was still waiting for some sort of fallout.

I straightened. Emily had tucked herself up next to Jack. He stood with his arms crossed, glowering at the artifact on its pedestal like it was his sworn enemy.

Jack carried a lot of power. And it had a habit of getting away on him. He had taken a huge hit when his break spell backfired, knocking him out. He'd also been pissed afterward. Annoyed that I had thwarted the suppression spell he'd triggered, possibly saving Emily's life, before he could wake up.

Not that I'd done it on my own.

Jack turned his glower on me. His dark-blue eyes were flashing. Literally. I could actually see his magic flickering.

"Let it go," I muttered.

He curled his lip.

Emily angled her shoulders so she was partly between us. It was a position she took often, whenever it seemed like Jack and I might fight. "Opal's right," she said, not actually looking at either of us.

If Emily weren't part of our group, Jack and I probably wouldn't have been friends. Just because we were both adopted—or, in my case, about to be adopted—didn't mean we had much else in common.

"I'm always right," I said, grinning.

Jack snorted, but he couldn't outright deny it. We'd known each other for months now, and he'd never proved me wrong once.

For example, I had thought using a break spell on a delicate artifact had been a terrible idea. And, after some deliberation, I'd thought we should add a sorcerer to our group and figure out the runes sealing the music box first. I'd been right on both counts.

I was now actively recruiting a sorcerer. Yesterday, I'd posted a listing on the school's Exchange—both online and on the first year's notice board—with very specific requirements. The first three applicants had been duds. Not powerful enough and really boring. I had another applicant lined up to interview at dinner.

"What are we waiting for?" Jack grumbled under his breath.

Principal Whitaker gave him a look, but didn't answer.

I shrugged, pulling out my phone to see if it worked any better in the null room. Or at least in this part of the null room.

The cracked screen was dead.

So that was a no.

The far door opened, and a person swamped in a red poncho stepped into the room. She strode over the copper line, not even shuddering or faltering as she did so. Her hair was a riot of color. Wisps of blues, pinks, and purples mixed with light brown, dancing around her pale face and shoulders. She waved at the necromancy professors, grinning at Principal Whittaker. "Sorry I'm late! Slept in."

It was late afternoon.

On a Sunday.

The large satchel slung over her shoulder bounced on her hip as she crossed toward us. The fringe of her poncho was beaded. It clacked and tinkled as she walked. The noise was weirdly swallowed, smothered by the null room, as if some part of it was magic.

As she stretched a hand toward the principal, I could see that she wasn't much taller than Emily. Her wrist and part of her hand was covered in heart-shaped rainbows. A knitted rainbow. "Principal Whitaker."

The elder witch blinked, then shook the newcomer's hand stiffly. "Morana. Thank you for joining us."

"Well, you did say I could use it as one of my work-study credits."

Principal Whitaker nodded.

The stranger—Morana, apparently—shifted her gaze to Jack, Emily, and me. "Are these the delinquents?"

Principal Whitaker cleared her throat disapprovingly, then appeared to hesitate. Though why she wouldn't rebuke an apprentice in her early twenties, I had no idea.

Or maybe I did. She needed the apprentice to take care of the artifact. And doing so was dangerous. The suppression spell had already tried to kill us once.

"Morana Novak," the elder witch said, introducing her. "Necromancer of the Godfrey coven. Soul seer."

Emily stiffened beside me.

So 'soul seer' meant something. Or maybe Emily was reacting to Morana's coven affiliation. The Godfrey witches oversaw the Pacific Northwest, so I'd heard of them already. Though I'd missed out on cupcakes at the Godfrey bakery when Ember and Capri had taken me into Vancouver. Ember Pine, my lawyer, was Capri's cousin. I'd been too busy escaping back to where I belonged.

"Mory," the soul seer said, cheerfully blunt.

Principal Whitaker nodded at the correction, then gestured to Emily. "Emily of the Hawes necromancers. A first year."

"Oh, hey," Mory said. "I think we share a great-uncle and a cousin or two. You know necromancers."

Emily nodded, blushing.

I didn't know what the soul seer meant, but I would ask Emily later.

"Jack Fairchild." Principal Whittaker nodded toward Jack on my right. "First-year witch."

Jack nodded stiffly, most likely pissed that the elder witch hadn't introduced him properly. He was a bit rabid about that sort of thing.

Mory's grin widened. "Jack! I know your auntie!" She bared her teeth, hooking her fingers into claws.

Weird.

"Total badass," the soul seer continued. "Great tech. I can use my phone anywhere in the Academy, mostly thanks to Jasmine. Not to mention that she seriously helped save our collective asses last year."

Jack's shoulders stiffened. He cast a furtive gaze at Principal Whitaker, whose expression remained neutral.

Was Mory mimicking fangs and claws? Jack's aunt was a werewolf? That was really weird. Especially because the Fairchilds were a super-old witch family. And witches like that were really prejudiced. That was one of the reasons Ember had wanted me to join the Godfrey coven. They were different, apparently. They held more power than the Sherwoods, and so were less likely to be intimidated by my unusual family.

Jack shifted uncomfortably. "You're from Vancouver?"

"Yep." Mory was already looking at me, reaching out her hand to shake, though she hadn't offered it to anyone else. "Opal, right?"

I took her hand, even though most Adepts didn't touch and it was weird that she already knew my name. Her skin was as pale as Emma's, but a slightly different tone. A huge contrast to mine. I gazed at the knitted rainbows on both her wrists. They were some sort of fingerless mittens.

"Opal Sherwood," Principal Whitaker said. "Witch. Dream walker."

"Soon to be inducted into the Godfrey coven," Mory said.

That was new information. To me. And probably also why the soul seer had known my name ahead of time. Principal Whitaker didn't seem surprised.

"You and Olive's niece, Juniper." Mory squeezed and then released my hand. "I just ran into Juniper in the hall. She's second year. She has your invitation. I won't be there this year. Plus, the necromancers usually clear off before all the witchy events take over." She shrugged, the beads on her poncho clacking together. "I'll tell my friend Burgundy to say hi. She's training to be a healer."

"Burgundy?" Principal Whitaker asked, frowning. "A healer of the Godfrey coven?"

"Yep," Mory said.

I had absolutely no idea what the soul seer was talking about, but I wasn't going to admit it. "I like your mittens," I said instead.

Mory blinked. Then she laughed huskily. "Arm warmers! I'll knit you some. It's always cold at the Academy."

I nodded. "It is."

The necromancer threw a look at Principal Whitaker.

She grimaced. "We've had this conversation."

"And it's still cold, especially in the dorms."

The elder witch sighed. "The artifact, soul seer?"

"Right." Mory brushed her hands together. "Let's see this bad boy."

She wandered over to the tree trunk pedestal, tugging something out of her satchel. Crossing the copper line didn't seem to affect her. Again. She crouched, placing something on the floor.

It was...a turtle?

I blinked, pretty sure I was seeing things. Maybe an illusion masking something else? But blinking didn't change the view. A small green turtle was trundling around on the black floor.

Mory dumped her satchel to one side, circling the tree trunk and peering at the artifact. "The ward?" she asked, her tone remote and blunt.

Principal Whitaker pressed her hand against the wall behind us, murmuring a phrase in a language I didn't know.

Smart. You really didn't want to give access to a room as powerful as this one to first years. Or to any students, really.

The glimmering shield around the tree trunk disappeared.

Mory leaned forward, eyes narrowed on the tiny music box. "Well, this is a nasty piece of work." She glanced over at the grouping of necromancy professors.

An older woman with short, wavy silver hair spoke up. "The suppression spell is still in place. It's witch magic, but we can try to—"

Mory shook her head. "Not a problem, Professor. But I'd shield the kids if I were you."

Principal Whitaker murmured another phrase, and magic sprang up all around the room along the copper line—a secondary ward. The other professors muttered in protest, but quieted quickly in response to a glance from the elder witch.

Smirking, Mory pulled off her poncho, dropping it at her feet. She was wearing a plain black T-shirt underneath. The turtle—if that's what it actually was—made for the red pile, burrowing into it. The soul seer cupped her hands on either side of the artifact. A necklace strung with gold coins swung slightly forward of her collarbone.

Another mutter ran through the professors. The youngest of the group appeared to be sketching the scene in her notebook.

"You see that?" Jack whispered, angling his head and shoulders to speak to me because I was way shorter than him. "The necklace?"

"And the turtle," I said just as quietly.

He nodded.

Objects of power, based on the reaction from the professors. If not for the copper ward line, I might have been able to feel energy pouring off both.

Mory flipped the lid on the music box.

No muttered spell.

No working out the runes. Or anything.

She just flicked the latch and the artifact opened.

As far as I could see. Or feel.

A dark coil of power spiraled from the tiny music box, rapidly expanding. The same suppression spell that had hit Emily and tried to stop her from accessing the power stored in the artifact. The power that came from the part of her great-grandmother's soul trapped within it.

Okay. I had just put the whole 'soul seer' thing together.

The dark shadow stretched up over the necromancer. Then it reached around Mory's head and shoulders, as if it was planning to smother her.

Principal Whitaker stiffened.

Emily moaned, grabbing my and Jack's hands. Mine was covered by the overlong sleeve of my sweater.

"Yeah, yeah," Mory said sarcastically. "Oh no! I'm so, so scared."

The suppression spell lunged for the necromancer. And then it just …

Disappeared?

Jack muttered under his breath, "Did you see that?"

I started to shake my head—but then my brain caught up to what my eyes had already seen. I was pretty sure that Mory's coin necklace had just eaten the suppression spell. I was also pretty sure that wasn't necromancy magic. "The necklace?"

Jack nodded, staring at the soul seer.

Across the room, the necromancy professors were collectively losing their shit again. Though quietly. Professor Whitaker was smiling. A pleased expression that I'd never seen on the elder witch's face before.

Mory didn't seem at all thrown or hurt. She reached out, appearing to tickle her fingers on the front of the blue-and-gold music box. "Come out, come out. Time to cross over."

Reacting to something I couldn't see at all, Mory stepped back, gazing forward and slightly up as if someone taller than her was standing before her.

The necromancy professors went quiet.

Dead quiet.

Emily shoved herself in front of Jack and me, then tried to shield us with her body.

"What do you see?" Jack hissed.

Emily shook her head, swallowing. "Shade? Ghost? She looks like...looks like a picture, a painting, in the study at home."

"I'm Mory," the soul seer said. Then she frowned and snapped her fingers. "Nope. Pay attention to me." She tilted her head, listening. Then she launched into a rapid, one-sided conversation with the invisible ghost. "A Novak...I have every right. Because it's time for you to rest." Another pause. "There is a Hawes necromancer right there ..." She pointed at Emily.

My friend stretched up to her full height, lifting her chin defiantly.

"Emily. Tell your granny it's time to rest," Mory said patiently. "To cross over. She's been held on this plane for far too long already."

"It's time to rest, Grandmother," Emily said. Her words were steady and sure. Confident. "Thank you for...protecting us. But you deserve a rest. Now."

Mory nodded. "Yes." She reached out her hands, hovering them over the artifact, palms up.

An indistinct grayed-out form appeared in front of the soul seer, holding her hands. A woman, standing at least a foot taller than Mory and clothed in a flowing dress. Her hair was a cascade of curls down her back. She was looking at Emily, not the soul seer.

She looked like Emily but older.

And more...evil.

A wicked grin spread across the ghost's face. She tried to step away from Mory.

But the soul seer didn't let her go. She murmured, "Rest now. Rest now. Your great-granddaughter carries your name, your power into the future. You can cross over now."

The ghost looked back at Mory, leaning in closer and closer. The soul seer didn't seem worried or scared.

The turtle had abandoned the poncho and was now perched on Mory's booted foot. Its long neck stretched up, gazing at the soul seer.

Slowly, the ghost just...faded.

The soul seer didn't move, didn't react.

Something was happening that I couldn't see, but Emily and the necromancy professors were enraptured.

Jack glanced at me questioningly.

I shook my head.

Then Mory abruptly scooped the turtle up in one hand, grabbing the artifact in the other. She crossed toward us, toward Emily, who still partially shielded Jack and me with her body.

A murmured command from Principal Whitaker dissipated the ward along the copper line, and Mory offered the music box to Emily. The soul seer was definitely holding a green turtle with white-orbed eyes in her other hand. It wiggled the long claws of its front legs, looking at Emily.

The head witch opened her mouth to protest.

Mory interrupted her, speaking to Emily. "This belongs to your family."

Emily took the music box. The lid was still raised.

"Slicing into someone's soul is wrong," Mory said firmly. "Just plain wrong. No matter how powerful having that artifact made the Hawes necromancers."

Emily nodded. Her shoulders curled forward as she cupped the music box. "I understand."

Mory stared at her a moment longer, then said quietly, "I'd hate to have to remind you, Emily. Me or…someone like me."

Principal Whitaker clamped her mouth shut.

Emily bobbed her head, then looked at the music box in her hands instead of holding Mory's hard gaze.

Mory glanced at Principal Whitaker, and they exchanged a nod. Then the soul seer collected her satchel and poncho, exiting the null room without another word.

I didn't like that Mory had threatened Emily—though I also thought it was creepy that a piece of her great-grandmother's soul had been harvested like that.

But I also secretly hoped Mory would still knit me the arm warmers she'd promised.

The Academy was often cold.

"You are dismissed," Principal Whitaker said, striding across the room to speak with the professors who'd grouped around the tree trunk pedestal.

I glanced at Emily. Her hands were shaking. Jack was watching her with narrowed eyes.

"Can I show the artifact to Aiden?" I asked. "Because he helped us? I'll give it back."

Emily handed me the music box so quickly that I almost dropped it. As if it hurt her to touch it. "You can keep it for as long as you like."

Even pushing up the sleeves of my sweater to fully expose my hands, I couldn't feel any of the magic the artifact had once held.

Emily took off toward the door, her head still bowed, shoulders curled. Even though she'd stood straight and tall when talking to the ghost, when placing herself in front of Jack and me.

Jack took the music box from me. He looked at it all over, grunted, then handed it back.

"Impressive," I said.

"More than impressive." He watched Emily as she opened the door, shoving his hands in his pockets.

"Let's get something to eat."

Jack glanced over at the gathering of professors. "We're not supposed to fraternize while we've got detention."

"Think they'll notice?" I didn't.

Jack grunted, as agreeable as he ever was. He kept pace with me as I headed for the doors.

EMILY WAS LEANING AGAINST THE WALL A FEW FEET beyond the door, which had opened with a brush of my fingers despite seeming to be made out of thick steel. Her hands were stuffed deeply in the pockets of her bejeweled hoodie. The hood was pulled up, but not quite covering all her curls.

I didn't have any pockets big enough to carry the music box, so I just held it loose in my hand.

Emily looked up at us as we approached, her eyes reddened again. She sniffed, then looked down at her feet. "You hate me now," she muttered miserably. "Because all necromancers turn evil…eventually."

"So?" I shrugged.

Jack grunted, agreeing.

Emily blinked at us, confused. A wide grin spread over her face, and she pushed herself off the wall. "So…we're okay?"

"Yep," I said.

Still grinning, she linked her arm through mine, then grabbed Jack the same way.

We headed up the hall like that. Awkwardly, because Emily was practically bouncing between us.

"We've got a sorcerer to interview at dinner," I said.

Jack groaned. "You're still on that?"

"I think it's a good idea, Jack," Emily said, still smiling.

He snorted.

"I've got the perfect person lined up," I said. "She's top of her class in runes and methodology."

"Fine."

I flashed Jack a grin over Emily's head. "Fine."

With a sorcerer in our group, we wouldn't have had so much trouble with the artifact. Wouldn't have had to turn to family for help. Wouldn't have then had to give up the artifact so we didn't get suspended.

A shapeshifter would be a good idea as well. Just not a wolf. They traveled in packs.

It wasn't that I wasn't cool with the rules and all. I was just perfectly happy breaking them when anything else was too boring to contemplate.

Also, I wondered how hard it would be to learn a spell to streak my hair, like Mory's had been, except maybe in gold and silver …

Acknowledgements

With thanks to:

MY STORY & LINE EDITOR
Scott Fitzgerald Gray

MY PROOFREADER
Pauline Nolet

MY BETA READERS
Anteia Consorto, Terry Daigle, Gael Fleming,
Beth Patterson, and Megan Gayeski Pirajno

**FOR THEIR CONTINUAL ENCOURAGEMENT,
FEEDBACK, & GENERAL ADVICE**
Sara Jo Foley – for spotting that I'd totally spelled
Kader's name wrong throughout Amplifier 2!
SFWA
The Office
The Retreat

About the Author

MEGHAN CIANA DOIDGE IS AN AWARD-WINNING WRITER based out of Salt Spring Island, British Columbia, Canada. She has a penchant for bloody love stories, superheroes, and the supernatural. She also has a thing for chocolate, potatoes, and cashmere.

For recipes, giveaways, news, and glimpses of upcoming stories, please connect with Meghan on her:

New release mailing list, http://eepurl.com/AfFzz
Personal blog, www.madebymeghan.ca
Twitter, @mcdoidge
Facebook, Meghan Ciana Doidge
Email, info@madebymeghan.ca

Please also consider leaving an honest review at your point of sale outlet.

ALSO BY MEGHAN CIANA DOIDGE

Please also consider leaving an honest
review at your point of sale outlet.

DOWSER SERIES ✦ BOOK 1

CUPCAKES, TRINKETS, and other DEADLY MAGIC

MEGHAN CIANA DOIDGE

DOWSER SERIES ✦ BOOK 2

TRINKETS, TREASURES, and other BLOODY MAGIC

MEGHAN CIANA DOIDGE

DOWSER SERIES ✦ BOOK 3

TREASURES, DEMONS, and other BLACK MAGIC

MEGHAN CIANA DOIDGE

DOWSER SERIES ✦ BOOK 4

SHADOWS, MAPS, and other ANCIENT MAGIC

MEGHAN CIANA DOIDGE

DOWSER SERIES ✦ BOOK 5

MAPS, ARTIFACTS, and other ARCANE MAGIC

MEGHAN CIANA DOIDGE

DOWSER SERIES ✦ BOOK 6

ARTIFACTS, DRAGONS, and other LETHAL MAGIC

MEGHAN CIANA DOIDGE

ORACLE SERIES ✦ BOOK 1

I SEE ME

MEGHAN CIANA DOIDGE

ORACLE SERIES ✦ BOOK 2

I SEE YOU

MEGHAN CIANA DOIDGE

ORACLE SERIES ✦ BOOK 3

I SEE US

MEGHAN CIANA DOIDGE

RECONSTRUCTIONIST SERIES ✦ BOOK 1

Catching Echoes

MEGHAN CIANA DOIDGE

RECONSTRUCTIONIST SERIES ✦ BOOK 2

Tangled Echoes

MEGHAN CIANA DOIDGE

RECONSTRUCTIONIST SERIES ✦ BOOK 3

Unleashing Echoes

MEGHAN CIANA DOIDGE